# Dixon Hawke's Casebook II

## The Case Of The Missing American

and other stories

First published in Great Britain in 2017
by DC Thomson & Co., Ltd.
Meadowside,
Dundee,
Scotland
DD1 9QJ

www.dcthomsonshop.co.uk
To purchase this book in paperback form.
Or Freephone 0800 318 846
Overseas customers call +44 1382 575580

Edited by Derek Uchman and Steve Finan
Typeset by Steve Finan.
Cover design by Kurt Uchman.

ISBN 978-1-84535-699-6

Printed in Great Britain by Clays Ltd, St Ives plc

# This is Dixon Hawke

The famous detective Dixon Hawke returns as the scourge of crooks, murderers, smugglers, swindlers and kidnappers.

There are 27 stories here, but they stand as testament to a literary giant. The great criminologist Dixon Hawke is the most-written-about fictional character in the English language. He starred in more than 5,500 stories, almost always written in short story form – a mystery "quick hit" to devour in one sitting.

And Hawke is a mystery in his own right. He reveals his history and background sparingly, but the more you read the more his character can be pieced together. His talents are prodigious. He is an expert in many fields, an unflappable man under pressure, a dangerous man to threaten and possessed of a formidable analytical mind. The reader gets no insight into his thoughts, fears or suspicions – everything is revealed in what he says and does.

His assistant, the inimitable Tommy, is eager, tenacious, and quick to raise his fists if the situation calls for it. And it often does. Like Hawke, he is a character of his times in stories of his times.

No excuses will be made for our investigative duo. They appear here in all their 1940s authenticity. In putting this book together, we took the firm decision to not alter or delete the story elements and language as they were published. They are an intrinsic part of the stories and we wanted to present them complete and unaltered. They give an insight into an era which is slipping from living memory.

We hope you enjoy this second selection of classic tales.

Derek Uchman and Steve Finan.

# Thanks

To:
Barry Sullivan, David Powell, Richard Prest, Craig Houston, Gillian Martin, Sylwia Jackowska, John Wilkie, Nikki Fleming, Fraser T. Ogilvie, and all the talented writers over the decades who brought Dixon Hawke, the greatest detective of them all, to life.

# Contents

# THE CASE OF *The Missing American*

**"Milligan's the name, Hubert P. Milligan." Dixon Hawke looked at his caller closely. Hubert P. Milligan was tall and inclined to stoutness, while his face was florid and a double chin was evident. Hawke judged him to be in his early fifties.**

"And what can I do for you, Mr Milligan?"

"Well, I guess I'd better give you the lay-out first. My sister was married to Thompson Keyes. Keyes was in the leather business at Galveston in Texas, and he made quite a bit out of it, around five million dollars. He died a few years back and left the business to his son, Bruce, my nephew.

"Bruce didn't get any money until he became twenty-five — that was four months back. Six months ago Bruce came to this country on a trip, on the family yacht. As far as I know he spent a month or two in London, and after that — well, he's disappeared."

"Disappeared?"

"It looks that way to me. He should have shown up to claim that five million bucks right after his birthday, but he didn't. We thought that he might be enjoying himself too much over here and let it pass. But Reynolds — he' s our lawyer — got kinda worried seeing as there were a lot of papers for Bruce to sign, so we wired the yacht. Holman — he's the captain — wired back to say that he hadn't seen Bruce for almost four months, so I came over here to find out what it's all about. As soon as I'd heard what happened I went along to the police, but it seems they can't do much about it. One of them advised me to try you, so here I am. Do you think you could find my nephew for me, Mr Hawke?"

"Have you any reason to suspect he might have got into trouble?"

"No, but Bruce was good at getting into scrapes when he was a youngster, and he's kinda high- spirited at the best of times." Hawke lit his pipe before replying.

"As it happens, Mr Milligan, I'm not doing much just now, and I'll look into the matter for you."

"That's wonderful!" exclaimed Milligan heartily.

"Now, I'll want a few details. You can give me a description of your nephew?"

"There's a picture of him on the yacht. It'll tell you more than I could. If you'll come down, Holman will tell you all that happened there."

The yacht Navajo lay at Westminster Pier. Her white paint and luxurious fittings were a little dulled by the grime of the city, but Hawke appraised her trim lines with a true yachtman's eye.

Milligan escorted Hawke and Tommy on board, and sent a deck-hand hastening to summon the captain to his luxurious cabin.

Captain Holman was a short, stocky man with tiny eyes set close together in his head.

"This is Dixon Hawke, the detective," said Milligan, making the introductions. "He's going to try and find Bruce for us."

"Glad to know you," said Holman, touching his cap.

"Captain Holman," said Hawke, "can you tell me all that has happened since the Navajo docked here?"

"Sure I can. We docked here around six months ago. I can't remember the date, but I'll get that from the log. The day after, Mr Keyes went ashore and put up at one of these big hotels, the Aster — "

"Astoria?"

"Yep, that's it, the Astoria. He said he'd be ashore some time, so I took the ship down the river for an overhaul. When we got hack I phoned Mr Keyes and asked for orders. He said he didn't want the ship yet, but he'd let me know. A couple of weeks later he arrives one night with a pile o' baggage and brings it on board. He told me he was going into the country to stay with some friends he'd made, then he was going north. I was to take the ship to Granton and wait for him there.

"Well, I took the ship up to Granton and waited around, maybe a month, but Mr Keyes didn't show up. I didn't know what to do, but after a bit I rang all the hotels in Edinburgh, and asked if he'd checked in or made a reservation. None of them had heard of him, so I decided to come back here after leaving a message for Mr Keyes with the harbourmaster.

"I waited around some more, and was beginning to get worried when I got a wire from his lawyer back in the States to ask what had happened to him. I wired right back saying I hadn't seen Mr Keyes for a few months, then Mr Milligan comes over. That's all I know."

"Keyes didn't mention where he was going to stay in the country or who his friends were?"

"Naw, he didn't. He just stayed aboard long enough to tell me to go north, then left. He seemed in a mighty hurry to get ashore again."

"You mentioned baggage. Did Mr Keyes bring all his luggage on board?"

"Yes, but he left it all here. He did mention that he was taking a grip with him."

"Then it appears that he didn't intend to stay long with those friends of his. That's about all I can learn here."

"What do you think now?" asked Milligan, when they came out on deck.

"Can't say yet," replied Hawke. "I'll go along to the Astoria and see what I can find out there."

The Astoria was one of London's newest and most palatial hotels, well patronised by visiting Americans. After much patient explaining, and showing the photograph which Milligan had given him, Hawke finally stirred the manager's memory enough to recall Bruce Keyes.

"Ah, yes, Mr Keyes. He was with us for about two months."

"When he left here did he give you any idea where he was going?"

"That I can't say, but, if he left a forwarding address, it should be at the desk."

Inquiries at the desk, however, revealed that Keyes had left no forwarding address.

"Well, since I seem to be barking up the wrong tree, there is no reason to detain you further," Hawke said to the manager, "and thank you very much for the help you have given me."

The manager coughed. "Perhaps, Mr Hawke, if you were to question the young lady — "

"Young lady? What young lady?"

"I remember now. It has just come to me that Mr Keyes often brought a Miss Clare to dinner here. Miss Clare is a theatrical person, and is appearing at the Apollo."

Ten minutes later Hawke was at the Apollo, just in time to have a few words with Rosemary Clare before the afternoon performance of the revue in which she starred.

"I believe," said Hawke, "that you were friendly with a Mr Keyes, an American."

"Bruce! Oh, how is he?"

"I was hoping that you could tell me that. You see, Miss Clare, nothing has been heard of Bruce Keyes since he left his hotel."

"What! I always wondered why he didn't write after he had promised. But where is he?"

"That's what I am trying to find out. He told you he was leaving London?"

"Oh, yes, he had to make a trip north, then go back to the States. Apparently his father had relatives somewhere in Scotland, and he was going to look them up. Then he had to get back to Texas. He said he'd have to hustle — it's his expression — as he hadn't left much time for his trip to Scotland."

"He didn't mention that he was going to spend a few days in the country before he went north?"

"No. I told you he hadn't much time. Nothing has — has happened to him, has it?"

"No, I don't think so. It's just that he's gone off and left no address. His uncle was rather worried about his silence and asked me to find him."

"His uncle? That would be Uncle Hubert?"

"Yes, that's right. You have heard about him?"

"Yes, and I wondered — "

"You wondered what?"

"Nothing, only Bruce gave me the impression that he and his uncle were none too friendly, but it isn't really important."

"It is of the utmost importance," declared Hawke. "What did Bruce Keyes say about his uncle?"

"He called him a dirty double-crosser. I don't know why. That was all."

It was enough, however, to set Hawke's agile brain working at top speed. Miss Clare's insistence that Keyes had had to hustle to complete his programme differed from the story Holman had told. Hubert Milligan's solicitude for his nephew also took on a new significance.

"Tommy," said Hawke, "Keyes must have got his luggage to the yacht in some means of transport, and I'm hoping it was a taxi. Take this photograph and go along to the rank outside the Astoria. Ask the drivers if any of them drove Keyes to Westminster Pier. If you find one who did, get all the information you can from him."

Hawke walked slowly back to Dover Street, turning the problem over in his mind. In Shaftesbury Avenue he heard himself called by name, and turned to see his old friend Chief Detective-Inspector Duncan McPhinney of Scotland Yard.

"Hello!" greeted the inspector. "I'm glad I ran into you, Hawke. I sent someone along to see you this morning, an American — Milligan, was it?"

"Milligan, Mac?"

"Yes, Milligan. I wanted to know how you got on with him. He came to see us about a missing nephew, and seemed to think we could find the chap at once. I explained the routine to him, but he wasn't a bit pleased, so I sent him along to you. I had quite a job convincing him that you were the man for the job, though."

"You had, Mac? I didn't get that impression when he came to see me. Tell me more of what he said."

"Well, when he came to me he was all for finding his nephew at once. I told him we'd do all we could, but that it might take weeks, months, even years, before we got wind of the young chap, providing he didn't break the law. Milligan seemed a bit put out at this, so I thought I'd send him along to you. He turned right about at this, and said he'd prefer to leave things in the hands of the police. I was amazed at this, but I thought he might not like to call in a private detective. I kept on at him, however, and at last he said he'd see you, rather sulkily though."

"Mac, this is most interesting. I've accepted the case, but I'm beginning to wonder what it's all about." He gave McPhinney a brief description of the case so far.

"If I were you, I wouldn't trust this Milligan," commented McPhinney at the end of Hawke's story. "Well, I'll have to be getting along now. If you need any help, I'll be at the Yard."

Hawke had barely reached Dover Street when Tommy arrived at the flat, and reported that he had found the driver hailed by Bruce Keyes.

The driver had taken Keyes and a large pile of luggage from the Astoria to Westminster Pier. Keyes went aboard the yacht and the taxi-driver followed with the luggage. When the taxi-driver had all the luggage aboard, Keyes did not ask him to wait, but paid him off with a substantial tip.

After Hawke had heard this report of Tommy's, he decided to return to the Navajo, and give an account of his progress to Milligan.

They went aboard and found Milligan in his cabin, and, at the sight of him, Hawke was momentarily amazed. The man's face was redder than ever, beads of perspiration stood out on his forehead, and his double chin quivered like a jelly. He was seated at a table and at his elbow was a half-empty bottle of whisky. At the appearance of the detectives he gulped a liberal dose of the liquor, and his hand shook as he held the glass to his lips. To Hawke it was obvious that the man had received a tremendous shock.

Milligan gave a smile at Hawke's greeting, though it was obviously forced.

"I've made a few inquiries, Mr Milligan, and so far I've discovered about as much as you told me — that your nephew came aboard the Navajo. I haven't found any trace of where he went after that, but I can still make a few more inquiries."

"Well, Mr Hawke, I've been thinking things over, and maybe I acted a little hastily in asking you to find Bruce. Maybe if we leave matters alone he'll turn up of his own accord."

"You mean you want me to drop the case?"

"Well, just leave it for a time. If Bruce doesn't show up in a week or two, I'll call on you again. About your fee — "

He dived into a pocket and produced a wallet bulging with notes.

Hawke had been slightly suspicious since his talk with Rosemary Clare, but this latest development made him even surer of his suspicions.

"Mr Milligan," he said tersely, "this morning you were anxious for me to find your nephew. Now you ask me not to find him. I am most dissatisfied with your conduct, but I have no option but to do as you ask. Should you require my services further, they will not be available. As to the fee, I never charge for cases which I cannot bring to a satisfactory conclusion."

"Well now, Mr Hawke, I didn't want you to take it that way. You see, I've got an attack of fever coming on, and I want to get back to the States where it's warm. I'm sure Bruce will be all right — he can look after himself."

Milligan stopped to pour himself another drink.

Hawke rose to go. "You're leaving then?" he asked.

"On the morning tide. The weather's fine. We should have a better trip back than I had coming over."

"Then I'll wish you good-bye," said Hawke, making to leave.

"Good-bye, Mr Hawke."

Hawke and Tommy had just finished dinner in Dover Street that evening. They were about to start their coffee when the telephone bell rang. It was McPhinney and he was strangely excited.

"Hawke, I've just heard something that you should know. Captain Holman of the Navajo was fished out of the river half an hour ago. He's at the Seamen's Hospital and appears to be pretty badly hurt. I'd get down and see him if I were you."

Hawke thanked McPhinney for the information, and lost no time in getting the car out of the garage. When they reached the hospital, however, it was to hear that Holman had died a few minutes previously.

"He had been in the water about an hour when the patrol boat picked him up," said the doctor, whom Hawke had asked for details. "He was unconscious and that probably kept him alive so long. There was a large wound on the back of his head causing a fracture of the skull."

"He didn't regain consciousness?"

"Only for a minute or two towards the end."

"Did he speak?"

"He tried to — muttered a few words. As far as I could make out what he was trying to say was, 'Put it on ice'. That's all I heard."

Hawke was disappointed, but decided to risk another visit to the Navajo to watch Milligan's reaction when he heard that Holman was dead.

There was considerable activity on board the Navajo when Hawke, McPhinney and Tommy reached the pier. Where before only one or two of the crew had been visible there were a dozen or more busy about the hundred and one tasks necessary before the yacht could put to sea.

Hawke asked for Milligan and was told he was in his cabin.

Without knocking, the detectives entered the cabin and saw Milligan, seated as before at the table, with the whisky bottle well within reach. The man's eyes were red-rimmed and bloodshot, and it was obvious that he was drunk.

"I've just come from the Seamen's Hospital," said Hawke, without apologising for his intrusion. "Captain Holman died about twenty minutes ago. I thought you'd like to know."

"Yes — sure," replied Milligan, a little hazily. "Sorry, an accident, must've fallen overboard. Didn't miss him until it was too late."

"Too bad he was unconscious," went on Hawke, and watching Milligan narrowly, "though the doctor did say he said something before he died."

Hawke deliberately paused for a moment. "Yes. We thought at the time he was wandering. Then I began to wonder if it might mean something to you. He said, 'Put it on ice'. What do you think he would mean, Mr Milligan? "

Milligan's face changed from a dark red to a deathly white. Sweat ran down his face and his eyes bulged in their sockets. His lips moved, but no sound came. Hawke knew he had tumbled upon Milligan's secret.

There was a sharp knock on the cabin door and a steward entered, bearing a bowl of cracked ice in his hands. "Here's the ice, Mister Milligan," he said. "I'm sorry I've been so long, but the darned fridge stuck."

A horrible suspicion flashed across Hawke's mind.

"Tommy, keep Milligan here! Steward, take me to the refrigerator!"

Hawke followed the steward to the galley. The refrigerator was a large one, capable of containing a large quantity of fresh meat. In one corner was stacked a pile of boxes containing goods which had to be kept at a low temperature. Hawke took a swift glance, then began searching amongst the stacked boxes. Underneath them he discovered a decent-sized packing-case. He called for a chisel and prised away the lid of the case. As the lid came away, Hawke saw it contained the body of a young man bent double in a stiff, unnatural posture. Hawke recognised the face as Bruce Keyes.

Hubert Milligan's nerve went entirely to pieces when he was confronted with the body of his nephew. He was ready to tell everything, if there was a chance of saving his own precious skin.

Even the detectives, hardened as they were to tales of villainy, felt a thrill of disgust, as Milligan unfolded his tale of callous treachery to McPhinney.

"It was all planned a long time ago," said Milligan. "For years I had sponged on my brother-in-law, but when he died I realised that I couldn't sponge any more, for Bruce and I hated each other. I wanted that five million bucks, even if it meant killing the young pup. When he said he was taking a trip in the yacht, I thought it would be a good chance of getting rid of him, so I got at Holman. I promised him a quarter of a million dollars if Keyes were to disappear on the voyage.

"Holman waited for an opportunity, and, when Keyes came on board that night, he signed his own death-warrant. The crew had been sent ashore for a bit of leave, and only Holman and a watchman were aboard. Keyes hadn't the least suspicion and he fell right into the trap.

"Holman knifed Keyes and put his body in an empty packing-case, and hid it in the fridge. He intended to get rid of the body on the way to Scotland, but didn't — he kept it so he could blackmail me for more money.

"Back in the States they began to get anxious, so I came over. There I made my first big mistake. I knew that it would look queer if I didn't report that Keyes was missing, and I guess I overdid the anxiety to find him. Then you told me to see that chap Hawke.

"I had to see Hawke then, as it would seem mighty funny if I didn't after causing such a rumpus at Scotland Yard. I didn't reckon he was so smart, this Hawke.

"Well, after Hawke had left the Navajo, Holman cursed me for a fool for bringing him in, then told me that the body was still in the fridge. I was frightened all right then, for I had thought Keyes was lying somewhere in the ocean. I didn't know what to do, but I had to get rid of Hawke somehow, in case he found out about the body in the fridge.

"Holman promised to get rid of the body on condition I promised him half a million bucks when the Keyes money should finally come to me. I told him he was a double-crossing rat and he came at me with a knife. I took the knife away from him and tossed him overboard."

Instead of five million dollars, Hubert Milligan received a sentence of fifteen years in an English prison.

"What Milligan forgot," said Hawke later, "is that if you're going to be an accessory to murder, what you need is lots of nerve. Milligan went to pieces at the first sign of things going wrong, and he couldn't have shown me his guilt any more than if he'd sent a signed confession."

—o0o—

# THE CASE OF The Leading Lady

**The door-bell of Dixon Hawke's flat rang sharply, and the detective and Tommy Burke, who were going through some records, looked up at each other.**

They heard the bustling footsteps of their housekeeper, Mrs Benvie, and then a deep, cultured voice: "I must see Dixon Hawke at once."

Tommy made a face.

"That's a gentleman I'm not going to like," he said. "He'll expect all the world for sixpence, and be annoyed if he doesn't get it!"

Hawke chuckled, while a mutter of conversation ensued downstairs. As the housekeeper came up to announce the caller, Hawke said: "I've often told you not to judge by appearances, old son. Now you're going one better and judging before you've had a chance even to see the visitor."

"I'll bet you he's dressed to kill, and got wavy hair," said Tommy promptly.

He had some cause for being pleased with his guess a few minutes later, for the man who was ushered into the study was certainly dressed to perfection. But his hair was smooth, straight and well-groomed, all in keeping with a dark, handsome face with a rather long nose, and a pair of flashing brown eyes. Tommy knew him the moment he set eyes on him.

"Ah, Mr Hawke." The man stepped across the room and offered a lean, brown-tanned hand. He was tall and well-built — a man fit to be a screen idol. And, in fact, he was next door to one, for Hawke, as well as Tommy, recognised Julius C. Barber, one of the most popular serious stage actors of the day. His manner just then was nervous and jumpy. His voice seemed to be controlled by a great effort.

Tommy told himself that Barber was suffering under the strain of considerable emotion, and the dislike he had conceived for the man's abrupt manner with the housekeeper disappeared.

"I suppose you've recognised me," went on Barber. "I — "

"Of course we have," said Hawke with a smile. "Sit down, please. We were just going to have tea. Will you join us?"

He did not wait for an answer, but rang the bell.

Tea for three was ordered, although Barber looked impatient at the delay. As soon as the door had closed behind Mrs Benvie, he burst out: "I don't like to be abrupt, Hawke, but I really haven't time for talking over tea. I have to be at the theatre for a special scene rehearsal — we're putting on a new show tonight. One of the first in London for a long time. It's — it's absolutely essential that I should be there, as well as Miss Drayton — my leading lady. I — "

Again Hawke interrupted him.

"I won't keep you long enough to make you late, believe me! And you'll forgive me for saying that you look in need of a little refreshment! First-night nerves, I suppose?"

"I wish to heaven that was all," snapped Barber. "I hardly know where to begin, but — well, Miss Drayton's missing."

He flung the words out as if they were a challenge. "She hasn't been seen since the rehearsal yesterday afternoon. Another was called for this morning, and an understudy had to take her part. But without Miss Drayton the show will flop — I know it!"

Hawke leaned forward, gravely.

"When you say 'disappeared ' do you mean voluntarily, or against her will?"

"I don't know — that's the devil of it! I — curse it, Hawke, of course it's against her will!"

Barber glared, and Hawke rubbed his chin thoughtfully. He passed the obvious contradiction and inquired: "What makes you think so?"

"She's never missed a rehearsal before — she's absolutely dead keen on this play. And we haven't heard a word from her for twenty-four hours!"

He paused as the housekeeper brought in tea. Barber accepted a cup and some biscuits. The tea seemed to do him good and he was more collected as he went on.

"I'm afraid I'm rather woolly-headed this afternoon — it's my own play, and I'm particularly anxious for a big send-off. You will hardly need telling why I've come — I want you to find her."

"So I gathered," said Hawke somewhat drily. "But what help can you give me?"

"None — none at all. I lunched with her yesterday, and we went straight to rehearsal afterwards. Later, she said she had an appointment with a hairdresser, and went off in a cab straight from the theatre. She hasn't been seen or heard of since. If a rumour leaks out that anything's the matter with her, it will ruin the first night. People won't go to see an understudy, I tell you! The circumstances are difficult enough as it is — we have to start at six o'clock to let the audience get home before dark, and — "

"Six o'clock tonight! And it's now four!" Hawke exclaimed. "Why on earth did you leave it so long in coming to me?"

"I tried everything I could," declared Barber. "I've been waiting desperately hour by hour in the hope that she would turn up. If I go to the police, the Press will get to hear of it. You're my one hope, Hawke. Will you try to find her?"

Hawke pushed his tea to one side.

"I'll do what I can," he promised. "Well go to her flat immediately, and we can talk on the way."

"Good. I've a taxi waiting outside," said Barber.

On the journey to Alice Drayton's Westminster flat, Barber went into rather more detail. The actress had been very keen on the play, but something had been worrying her.

She would tell no one what it was, but several people knew it existed. But, he claimed, he would not believe that she would let him and the rest of the cast down. Wherever she was, she was being detained against her will.

"Who might do that?" demanded Hawke.

"I haven't the faintest idea. On the surface of it, it's absurd. But there can be no other explanation, Hawke!"

It was clear, nevertheless, that Barber was afraid there was. He had contradicted himself more than once, and to Tommy it seemed as if the man was close to an emotional breakdown.

They reached the flat at last, and went up to it in the lift of the block where it was situated. As they neared the door, it opened.

Barber drew up sharply.

A short, thin-faced man came from the flat, and looked coldly at the actor. Hawke and Tommy drew back a little, while Barber said: "What the devil are you doing here, Penson?"

"The same as you, I expect — trying to find Alice," snapped the man named Penson. "What have you done with her?"

"What have I done! What have you done with her, you mean! "

"I've a good mind to break your fool neck for that," rapped Penson. "By the fates, all you think about is keeping the centre of the stage yourself. You know only too well she'll act you into a corner, and you've staged this disappearance to prevent it."

It looked as if Barber would lose what was left of his self-control. He took a lunge forward, with his fist clenched, and but for Hawke's re-straining grip would have struck the other man. Hawke spoke at the same time as he moved.

"Easy, Mr Barber! Talking like this won't help us."

"Who the deuce are you?" demanded Penson.

"My name's Dixon Hawke," returned the criminologist quietly, "and Mr Barber has called me in to try to find Miss Drayton."

"That's a fine story," Penson sneered. "He might have done that to pull the wool over my eyes — and other people's — but if you want to know where she is, make him talk."

"Supposing we discuss this in the flat and not in the passage?" asked Hawke.

"There's nothing to discuss — "

"Oh, yes, there is," said Hawke sharply. "You've made a serious and obviously considered accusation against my client. I want it explained at once."

Penson's eyes narrowed. Tommy thought he would try to get away, but he did not, and the party went into the flat, which was being looked after by a middle-aged servant.

Penson, it appeared, was Alice Drayton's business manager. It soon grew clear that if she failed to appear, he would lose his commission on her salary — and that possibility was frightening him. He sobered down a little, although it was apparent that he and the actor were bitterly antagonistic.

Hawke questioned the servant, but she was unable to give him any information. That finished, he sent Tommy Burke to the taxi-rank outside the Wells Theatre, where the new show was to appear. Tommy inquired of the drivers there who had driven Miss Drayton on the previous afternoon.

The driver, a man named Gloster, was out with a fare, but might be back at any time. Tommy, who was well-known, spent half an hour in the cab-men's shelter, until the door opened and Gloster appeared. He was a big, middle-aged man, friendly of countenance and very quick with his tongue.

He heard Tommy out, and then rubbed his chin.

"Well, me young cock-o-lorum, I took the lady, that's a fact. Pretty piece, I ses to meself, me having an eye for a nice pair o' ankles, that's a fact. 'My flat,' she says, as if I knew where she lived, which is also a fact, young feller-me-lad ! Then on the way she taps on the glass. 'Drive me to Waterloo Station instead,' she ses, an' blow me, that's what I did. Off she went, and gave me a shilling tip, so there you are."

Tommy telephoned the gist of Gloster's statement to Hawke, who by then had reached the Dover Street flat again. Hawke said: "Go over to Waterloo, old son. Make inquiries among the porters and others regularly on the station. I can tell you that Miss Drayton wore a grey costume and a scarlet hat, with scarlet gloves. Add that she's exceptionally pretty, and you might get some results. When you've finished, come back here."

"Right-ho, guv'nor," Tommy rang off, thanked the cabbies for their assistance, and tipped Gloster a shilling. Then he had an idea and said to the cabby: "Can you take me to the place where you put Miss Drayton down at the station?"

"Why sure I can, me old son-of-a-gun," declared Gloster. "Hop in the old chariot, and I'll drive you there in state."

He treated the rest of the cabbies to a blatant wink, and then started off with his fare. He put Tommy down at the main line entrance, and then started back to his rank.

Tommy made several inquiries without any result. Then he found an old, thin-faced porter, Ben by name.

Ben, according to his fellow-porters, never forgot a face, and he had been at the cab-arrival platform all the previous afternoon, except when he was carrying someone's luggage. Tommy had already checked up the time Miss Drayton arrived — it had been just after five o'clock.

Ben looked at him suspiciously, but grew communicative when he was tipped.

"I was 'ere from ar' past four to a quarter past five, sir, never 'ad a job. All the time I was 'ere. An' I don't remember seein' your young lady."

Tommy pressed the elderly porter further with questions, but Ben was adamant, and others supported him in saying that he would have remembered the lady in question had she arrived. Puzzled, Tommy telephoned Dixon Hawke, and the criminologist said: "So Gloster the cabman says she was taken there, and Ben the porter says she didn't arrive. One or the other is probably lying, old son."

"If one of them is, it's Gloster," said Tommy decisively. "He's one of those hail-fellow-well-met kind, and I don't trust him. But why on earth should he lie?"

"We'll find that out," said Hawke quietly. "There's a change of orders, my lad. Go to Barber's flat —it's in Chelsea. Number 31, Dring Court. Have you got that?"

Tommy felt a thrill of excitement. Something in Hawke's voice suggested that there was a development of which he knew nothing.

"Right-ho, guv'nor! Will we find her there?"

Hawke chuckled. "You're too optimistic! Get there and wait for me."

Tommy took another taxi. There was no time to be lost, for Hawke's manner made it clear that the matter was urgent. In any case it was nearly five past five. In less than an hour they had to find the actress, or the first night would be a failure.

Was that wholly true?

In his scurrying from one place to another, Tommy had not been able to give much thought to the other issues — the enmity between Barber and Benson.

Had one man or the other lied? Had the accusations which had come so freely from each of them any foundation in fact?

Barber might well want to take the centre of the stage, and it would not be the first time a criminal had asked Hawke for help, thus planning to escape suspicion.

Habitually, Tommy looked through the small window of the cab as they went along the road; Hawke was always careful when he was on a case, and had taught Tommy to be as cautious.

With a start, Tommy realised that he was being followed by another cab; and Gloster, in ordinary togs, was at the wheel.

He leaned forward and slid open the glass partition.

"Make it faster, cabby, can you?" But it happened that immediately afterwards another cab cut in in front of them, forcing them to slow down. Gloster drew within a few feet of the first cab. Tommy felt his heart beating fast, and then he saw Gloster pull out to pass him.

He shouted through the open partition: "Slow down! Slow down!" Instinctively the cabby obeyed — and then Gloster cut across his front wheels! Had they been going at speed a serious crash would have been inevitable. As it was, the shouted order had slowed them down by ten miles an hour.

Nevertheless the cabby had been compelled to wrench at his wheel to avoid crashing into the back of Gloster's vehicle. The cab struck heavily against the kerb, and heeled over. For a moment Tommy thought that a crash was unavoidable, and the driver could do nothing to prevent it.

It was a sickening moment.

Then, slowly, the cab righted itself. Tommy, thrown into one corner, slithered to the centre of the seat. It was soon apparent that the cabby was more scared than hurt, but a policeman came hurrying up to take particulars.

The delay made Tommy fume, particularly since Gloster had gone on ahead. He did not doubt that the driver was going to Barber's place.

Another taxi — the day seemed full of taxis — took Tommy at speed to Barber's flat, and when he got there he saw Gloster coming away.

The man was walking hurriedly — doubtless he had parked his car some distance away — with his back towards Tommy. The latter's cab drew up alongside, and Tommy swung open the door, and stood for a moment on the running-board. Then he flung himself bodily at Gloster.

Taken completely by surprise, the big cabby went crashing. Tommy fell on top of him, but Gloster's size and weight made the odds considerably against the youngster. Gloster was swearing viciously, using every foul trick. Tommy felt powerful hands tightening on his throat.

And then someone came to his assistance. Gloster was dragged off and Tommy struggled to his feet. He saw Hawke and Penson together, and several other people nearby.

Hawke was smiling somewhat grimly. "Thanks be that you're all right, old son! Can you get along on your own?"

"I — I can have a good try," gasped Tommy.

He followed Hawke and Penson into Dring Court, and stopped outside Barber's flat. Hawke knocked sharply. There was a pause and then the door opened.

Hawke pushed his way past the startled Barber, who had opened it — and there on a couch, with her hands and feet tied, was one of the loveliest girls Tommy had seen in his life!

"There you are, Hawke! She's in his flat — it's Barber's foul game! That cabby came here to warn him, but there wasn't time to get the girl away!" said Penson.

Barber drew back, white to the lips.

"That's a lie, Penson! I came in here a few minutes ago, and had the shock of my life when I saw her. I've been trying to get those knots undone."

"How many people do you expect to believe that?" sneered Penson.

Barber looked desperately from one man to another. He drew himself up — and then he turned to the couch, and began to unfasten the girl's cords. Penson went forward also, but Hawke stopped him.

"Just a moment, Penson. There is a question you can answer. How did you know it was a taxi-driver fighting with my assistant?"

Penson drew back. "I didn't say — "

"You certainly did!" snapped Hawke. "Now for the whole truth. You arranged with Gloster yesterday to take Miss Drayton away, for some reason only you know. Then Gloster phoned you about Tommy's inquiries at the station. You knew things were dangerous, and so you told Gloster to bring Miss Drayton here. She is probably lightly drugged — probably, too, she was able to walk up the stairs although not aware of where she was. Then Gloster bound her, to make the case look black against Barber. That's why Gloster was here so long."

" It — it isn't true!" gasped Penson.

"It Is! Gloster saw Tommy coming here and tried to stop him. Isn't that so, Tommy?"

Tommy nodded, while Penson swung round on his heel. But Tommy was standing grimly in the doorway, and the man realised that there was no escape. Hawke thought he would try to make a fight, but instead Penson lost his self-control completely.

"All right, blast you, it's true! I used to manage Barber. He left me and made a fortune — I've never forgiven him for that. Then he took Alice away from me — no one knows how I loved her, how I planned to marry her! He robbed me of her and I planned to ruin them both!"

"Why both of them?" asked Hawke quietly.

"Barber because he needed a packed house and an enthusiastic audience tonight. I knew he would be lost without Alice. And Alice because if she was doing badly she would be more likely to turn to me. I didn't mean to harm her, Hawke, you must believe that!"

"I think I do," said Hawke grimly, " but you and Gloster will face a charge of abduction, if not worse."

Then from the couch Barber turned round.

"She's recovering, Hawke! She'll be all right for tonight, she must be!"

"Let her have every second of rest she can, and I think probably she will be," said Hawke after a brief examination of the actress. "Her pulse is steady enough, and she's running no temperature. Penson, you're coming with me to the police."

The police were already outside with Gloster. Hawke made his report and then hurried with Tommy to the Wells Theatre, where they thoroughly enjoyed a show in which both actor and actress put up a superb performance.

"What made you suspect Penson, guv'nor?" asked Tommy later.

"Because it was clear that he was only pretending to be worried. Barber was really frantic. If either man was guilty, Penson was the one. I believed my presence would frighten him — that, or your good work at the station certainly did! And the likely place for him to send her was to the flat — in the hope of incriminating Barber.

"A precious scoundrel, one way and another — but there'll be a happy ending between Barber and Miss Drayton, or I'm no student of human nature!"

—o0o—

# THE CASE OF

## The Burnt Loaves

"Stop thief!" The cry echoed above the rumble of London traffic, while along the crowded Marylebone Road a little man ran like a deer.

He had an agility far above the average, for he dodged cleverly in and out of the crowd, evading all hands thrust out to stop him.

His thin, furtive face was set and tense, as if he realised the chances were against him.

A policeman's whistle shrilled.

Three or four men in blue were running full pelt after the fugitive, who had reached a clearer patch of road, and then dived into a side street. As he did so a youthful, well-knit figure joined in the chase. Tommy Burke, who had heard the shouts of alarm, had started from a good position and was soon yards ahead of all the others.

By the kerb were two or three tradesmen's vans.

The fugitive took a desperate glance behind him, saw Tommy's nearness, and leapt into one of the vans. Luckily for him the engine started first shot, and he eased off the brake as he let in the clutch.

The van jumped for a moment, seemed about to stop, but as Tommy reached the running-board it gathered speed.

The driver thrust out his hand, catching Tommy on the chin. The force of the blow was not great, but Tommy was off his balance. He went flying off the running-board, and only the stalwart figure of a policeman just behind him saved him from a nasty fall.

But it did not help the situation.

The policeman also lost his balance, and they fell together, not heavily enough to do either of them any harm, but enough to wind them.

When Tommy picked himself up, a small crowd, including several policemen, had gathered.

The van was out of sight.

"Hang it!" exclaimed Tommy. "I thought I had him."

"You didn't do so badly," said one of the policemen. "You didn't have time to notice the number of the van, I suppose?"

"No," said Tommy. "But the driver will be back, won't he?"

But the driver wasn't coming back. This was made clear when another constable came along. "It's just one of those times when everything goes wrong," he said.

"The van driver was delivering bread to one of the blocks of flats and slipped down some stairs. He's been taken to hospital, and it will be some time before we can question him. Until then we can't find out who he's driving for."

Tommy looked rueful.

"I read the name and address automatically as I ran," he said, "but I can't remember it now. If it comes to mind I'll let you know at the station." "Better come round with me," said a sergeant, who had recognised Dixon Hawke's assistant, "and give us a report. That van should not have been left unattended."

Thus it was that Tommy kept Hawke waiting for more than an hour for some tobacco which he had gone out to buy, and when he reached their Dover Street flat, Hawke was chewing the end of an empty pipe.

Tommy apologised, and went into a rush of explanations.

"Steady!" exclaimed Hawke. "If you made a report as mixed as that to the police, they'll think I've got a dud for an assistant."

Tommy chuckled, and explained more concisely and in greater detail.

"Apparently it was a really barefaced robbery," he concluded. "The thief made an appointment to see some small, unset diamonds, grabbed them off the glass counter, and ran.

"There was about five thousand pounds' worth."

"Quite a haul for a snatch-and-run thief," said Hawke, and Tommy knew that something about the case intrigued him. "And there are several other interesting features. It's a pity you can't remember the baker's name — you're sure it was a baker's van?"

"Oh, yes," said Tommy. "I saw the gold lettering — Baker and Confectioner."

"That's progress of a sort. What colour was the van?"

"Green," said Tommy promptly.

"Good! A green van with gold lettering. Was the name in the middle or at one side?"

"In the middle," said Tommy, and he frowned in concentrated effort. "Just a moment, guv'nor ! It was a short name, not very common — got it! Rudge — B. Rudge, of Brake

Street!"

Hawke smiled. "You hadn't forgotten, you see — you just went about remembering it the wrong way. What are you going to do?" he demanded as Tommy reached for the telephone.

"Tell the police," said Tommy.

"Let's go round and see this baker ourselves," said Hawke. "We haven't anything of special importance to do this morning."

"What is there in it that interests you?" asked Tommy, as they stepped into the hallway for their hats and coats.

"I'm not going to do your thinking for you," said Hawke. "Everything is there for you to see. Get your mind busy, old son!"

Tommy did, but rather unsuccessfully.

To him it looked like an ordinary enough robbery, with only one note out of the usual run — the brazen nature of the thief.

It was quite usual for a thief who was cornered to take a parked car or van — although not so easy since the Government's car-locking order had come into force.

Brake Street was on the other side of Marylebone, but in Hawke's big car they reached the baker's premises in a few minutes. There was an attractive shop window, with several girl assistants inside.

A middle-aged woman, with a badge stating she was manageress, approached them.

"I would like a word with the manager about the deliveries in the Dover Street area," said Hawke.

"You will want to see Mr Rudge, the proprietor," he was told, "and he is busy in the bake-house, I'm afraid." "We'll see him there," said Hawke promptly.

"Well, it isn't usual, but I will find out if he will see you."

The woman disappeared, to return after a few seconds.

"Come this way, please."

Past sacks of flour, boxes of dried fruit, and stores of all kinds, they were led into the bake-house.

It was a machine bakery with a big revolving oven. Tommy felt the heat stifling him, but looked around with interest at two white-smocked men and half a dozen girls also in white.

The bigger of the bakers, burly, red-faced, and sweating freely, looked at Hawke with annoyance. "Don't you think I'm busy enough as it is, with a small staff because of the war, without being worried by complaints?" he demanded.

"You misunderstand me," smiled Hawke, and he explained briefly, but comprehensively. The other assistants stopped work to listen.

Rudge's annoyance quickly changed to concern.

"This is really worrying," he said. "And I can't thank you enough for informing me so quickly. Bert Adams — the man driving that van — is a valuable roundsman. I'll have to find out how he is at once. And" — Rudge frowned "there is this delivery to finish, and the afternoon's round, not to mention a van-load of bread missing!"

"Bad luck," sympathised Hawke. "But if you give me the number of the van I'll have the police locate it — the thief won't have driven it far."

Rudge obliged, and Hawke used a phone in a small office near the bake-house. Tommy remained in the big room, intrigued by the conveyor system of cutting and weighing bread and making cakes.

The girls worked deftly, and he was too fascinated to notice Hawke return. Rudge looked up as Hawke said, "but now I'm going to be a nuisance again. Bert Adams is the roundsman, you say. Has he been with you long?"

Rudge frowned.

"No — only six months. Er — you are Hawke, the detective, aren't you?"

"That's right."

"Well, I can tell you, then," said Rudge in a low-pitched voice. "If it weren't for the war I wouldn't have employed Adams. He's a really good worker, but dishonest. He's been sentenced for stealing several times, but with men so hard to get I gave him another chance."

Hawke looked thoughtful, as he said: "His accident may prove genuine, in which case he can't be implicated in this," he said. "But it's as well to know the facts. I — "

He stopped abruptly, for the other man had just opened a door of a small independent oven — and thick smoke poured into the bake-house. Rudge threw up his hands in despair.

"More trouble! That's a special bake of bread for a small restaurant — burned to nothing!" He stepped to the oven and his assistant muttered an apology.

Rudge said nothing, and the two of them brought out the ruined batch of loaves.

Hawke called Tommy aside, and they were not sorry to reach the cooler and cleaner air of the shop.

Once outside Tommy said, "Did you suspect the van-driver, guv'nor?"

"Suspect is hardly the word," said Hawke. "We'll go and see the jeweller now, I think. I — " he stopped suddenly, and pulled up short beside the big car.

"There's just a chance that the accident wasn't serious, but was genuine. Stay by the bake-house, Tommy, and keep your eyes open. The van-driver might return — and it's even possible that the thief you saw will call to see him."

"I don't follow that," said Tommy, "but I'll keep my eyes open, guv'nor."

He watched Hawke drive off, and then approached the rear door of the bake-house.

The yard had two empty vans in it, and before he had been there five minutes someone began to load one of them.

"Put that burnt load in," said Rudge's voice, "and if you can't get rid of them, bring 'em back."

" Right-ho," said the man loading.

Tommy kept on watching.

Some miles away Hawke entered the shop of Abel Kohn, jeweller and watchmaker.

It was a small shop, but obviously a prospering one. A little, plump man with furtive brown eyes was talking to a burly man Hawke recognised as Chief Inspector Blair, of New Scotland Yard. The little man was Kohn himself.

"I don't like your manner, Inspector," he was saying. He talked with a faint lisp. "I prepared the stones as requested by a customer, that is all."

"You ought to have taken more pre-cautions," said Blair. "You don't usually neglect them, Kohn."

"What are you suggesting?" demanded the jewel-merchant, bristling.

"I'm just telling you that it looks like wilful negligence," said Blair. "If I was representing the insurance company I wouldn't pay out, believe me."
"That is insolence!" flared Kohn. He might have gone on at some length, but saw Hawke enter and stopped immediately. He smiled blandly, rubbing his hands.

"Good-morning, sir. What can I do for you? I — oh, it's Dixon Hawke." He looked nonplussed and in no way pleased, which was not surprising. Kohn had long been suspected of working as a "fence," and he was as wary of Hawke as of the police.

"What do you want?"

"I'm on the same errand as the inspector, I expect," said Hawke mildly. "Did you know the baker has been located, Blair?"

"Yes." Blair was none too gracious; like many of the officers at Scotland Yard, he was inclined to resent Hawke's interest, although there were times when he was glad enough of the private detective's help.

"And I can tell you more — the van was stranded in a side street no more than half a mile from where it was taken."

"That will please Rudge," smiled Hawke. "He wants to get it out on the round again. Has it been searched?"

"Of course — and tested for finger-prints. But the thief wore gloves and there's nothing to help us."

"It would be an idea," said Kohn sharply, "if you two gentlemen discussed your troubles elsewhere. As for you, Inspector, I shall expect an unqualified apology for your quite unjustifiable accusations."

"I haven't accused you of anything — yet," said Blair grimly, and he pushed his way past Hawke to the street. Hawke showed no inclination to go, and Kohn peered up at him, unable to hide his nervousness.

"What is it, Hawke?"

"I'm going to be frank," said the criminologist. "The police evidently think this is a frame-up for the insurance companies. They think you staged the robbery in order to claim insurance.

"Are they right?"

Kohn stopped rubbing his hands. There was something impressive about him then.

"No, Hawke. I am not going to get indignant, because I know you're right, and they do suspect me. But I had no idea it was a trap."

"Right!" Hawke spoke briskly. "I'm going to believe you, and assume that you are anxious to get the diamonds back."

Kohn nodded. "I am. They are insured, of course, but only at their peace-time value. I shall lose over a thousand pounds if I have to rely on insurance."

"All the more reason you should help me to find the thief. Now — how was the appointment made?"

"For viewing the stones, you mean? By telephone."

"In whose name?"

"The name given was Frazer, and normally I might have asked questions, but in London these days, business is so bad that chances must be taken."

"You hadn't seen the thief before?"

"No. He was a complete stranger."

"Did you have the diamonds loose on the counter?"

"On a velvet cloth," said Kohn. "There were eleven stones in all, and he got away with eight of them."

"Did he come by foot or by car?"

"By foot — I was watching for him. There were no cars in sight when he arrived."

"I see," said Hawke quietly. "All right, Kohn, I'll do all I can to get your stones back for you."

"I'm sure you will," said the jeweller, and as Hawke left the shop Kohn was rubbing his hands together.

Hawke drove to the bakery. Tommy was looking bored, but brightened up at the sight of the big car.

He stepped on to the running-board.

"Well, what's happened?" asked Hawke.

"Nothing much," said Tommy. "One van has gone out and another one has come in — presumably the one the thief pinched — there was a policeman at the wheel."

"How soon after I had gone did the first van go?"

"It was loaded about a quarter of an hour later, I suppose. Rudge told his man to try and get rid of the burnt loaves. I think that was about the only thing of interest!

"No one else has entered or left."

"All right," said Hawke. "But you're going to stay here, old son!" He laughed at Tommy's obvious dis-appointment, and added, "Ring me at the flat the moment the van comes back."

Tommy looked nonplussed, but Hawke was away before the youngster could ask questions.

Hawke drove to the police station near Dover Street, and Inspector Blair greeted him in no very good temper.

"I don't know what you're so interested in," he grunted.

"It's obvious to me that Kohn staged the robbery, but it isn't going to be easy to prove it."

"I doubt even if it can be proved," said Hawke, "because I don't think it happened. No, don't start going off the deep end," he added sharply. "Have you checked up about the accident to the baker's roundsman?"

"Yes. He's been sent home — it wasn't much, but it was genuine enough."

"Did you know that he has been sacked from several jobs because of dishonesty?"

"No. I didn't. But — hang it, Hawke, he had the accident all right! He dislocated his shoulder and they had to put it back at the hospital."

"Do you know his address?"

"Yes." Blair pulled a notebook from his pocket. "97, Edgeware Road. Are you thinking of going to see him?"

"It might be an idea," said Hawke "Coming?"

Blair nodded and they hurried to the address.

It was a small flat at the top of an old house, and a middle-aged woman answered the door.

"Is Mr Adams in?" asked Hawke.

"No, 'e ain't! 'E 'as to work for a living."

"We don't want impertinence," snapped Blair. "Has he been here since he left for work this morning?"

"No, he ain't! "

"I think I'll have a look round," said Blair.

But the flat was empty, although they could not be sure whether the woman told the truth. When they were once more in the street, Blair looked keenly at Hawke and demanded: "Well, what do you make of it now, Hawke?"

"One thing answers itself," said Hawke quietly.

"Bert Adams is supposed to be at home because of a dislocated shoulder, but isn't there. The woman, presumably his wife, is afraid of something — and the something is obviously the possibility that we suspect Adams of some kind of crooked business. So the quicker you find Adams the better."

"But I can't see what he has to do with it," said Blair.

"We'll find that fast enough," said Hawke cryptically. "I'm going to my flat — can I drop you anywhere?"

"No — I'll take a cab to the Yard and get a call out for Adams," said Blair

Hawke was at his flat a few minutes later, and he had hardly sat down before the telephone rang.

"Guv'nor — the little crook has — "

Tommy's voice sounded excited — but on the word "has" he stopped abruptly. There was a strangled cry, and then the telephone went dead.

Hawke was on his feet in a trice, and he rushed down to the car, parked outside. His face was set and grim as he started for the bakery.

Tommy Burke had suddenly seen the runaway enter the bake-house yard, followed by a second, older man. Almost on their heels the van which he had seen go out earlier had returned. Its driver and the others went inside the bake-house.

Tommy went forward to look through a window, but could see nothing. He glanced into the delivery van, and saw that it was empty but for a dozen burned loaves.

Opposite the yard was a telephone kiosk.

He hurried to it, so intent on getting word through to Hawke that he did not keep a look-out, and he didn't see the two men come from the bakery. The first he knew of trouble was when the kiosk door opened, and a strong hand closed over his mouth.

A "cosh" descended on his head, and he lost consciousness, unaware that he was carried across the by-road and taken into the yard. He was bundled into a delivery van and the door was locked on him.

The thief and Adams, the supposedly injured driver — it was they who had caught Tommy phoning — now hurried into the bakery. It was empty, work being finished for the day. They crossed towards the office, there to warn their boss, Rudge.

Hawke, meanwhile, made short work of the run. He reached the bake-house yard and parked the car alongside the van in which Tommy was imprisoned. Unaware of that, he entered the bake-house and stepped across to the office.

Rudge and the two others looked round in surprise.

Adams cursed, and with the little thief leapt towards Hawke, but the detective slipped an automatic from his pocket. They stopped and Hawke said quietly: "So I've caught the three of you together?"

Rudge drew a deep breath.

"What are you talking about? I don't know what these two have been doing, but I've had no part in it!"

"Haven't you?" demanded Hawke.

"I'll make you change your mind. A conveniently-placed van into which your crook employee has slipped with stolen jewels — Adams at the wheel, a man who can put his shoulder out without difficulty, and always pretend to have had an accident.

"I was pretty sure about how it was worked."

"Adams is a thief, as I told you, and the other man's a stranger. I know nothing about it," snapped Rudge.

"Oh, yes, you do," said Hawke.

"The diamonds were brought here. The thief drove the van here — no one would notice that, it's so usual — left the jewels and then stranded the van half a mile away."

"It's a lie," sneered Rudge. "If you think it's true, where are the diamonds?"

"In the burnt loaves!" said Hawke with calm assertion.

"No modern electrically-controlled oven would burn bread like that unless it was deliberately set at too high a temperature. Where are the loaves?"

Rudge turned pale.

He might have started a fight, but for Hawke's gun. Instead, he led the way to the van.

Hawke saw the loaves and Tommy was sitting up, conscious, and with a loaf cut in two. In the middle of the dough — which was hardly cooked inside the crust — something glittered like fire!

"I had this idea when I came round!" exclaimed Tommy. "The diamonds are here, guv'nor!"

"And so are the three crooks," said Hawke.

"All ready for Blair when he arrives.

"Rudge, you made a vital mistake. Vans have to be locked if left for more than five minutes. This wasn't and that made me very curious.

"The rest came automatically.

"It looks," he added whimsically, "as if your bake-house is going to be much more short-handed in future!"

—oOo—

# THE CASE OF
## *The Doped Footballers*

Dixon Hawke and Tommy Burke enjoyed watching a game of football as well as anybody. Having successfully completed a case in the North of England, they could not resist stopping over the Saturday at Pelton to see the annual meeting of those two historical rivals, the Pelton Rovers and the Roundhampton Athletic (or Robins, as they were called on account of their bright-coloured jerseys).

And now, during the brief half-time interval, they had to admit they were watching a hard-fought game, the home team leading by one goal to nil.

A big contingent of the Robins' supporters had come over for the game, and they were noisily assuring themselves that their champions were going to equalise and turn the tables in the second half.

Tommy could not help grinning at the assurance of one red-faced veteran, who stood quite close to them in the crowd.

"One goal against means nothing to us, I'm tollin' ye," he angrily told one of the home crowd.

"We're goin' to win in this half, an' I'm willin' to bet five to one on it. So there."

Five to one was long odds to offer between two such equally-matched teams as these.

Hawke was not surprised when half-a-dozen of the Pelton supporters took up the man's offer. He booked their bets in a business-like manner, and then stared anxiously towards the field, where the teams were just running out from beneath the stand.

A murmur went round the crowd, a murmur that expressed horror so far as the home supporters were concerned.

What had happened to Ralph Watson, their star centre? And where was Hal Towler, their incomparable goalie?

Both had played a splendid game during the first half, but now they were missing.

Just for a few minutes the crowd thought they had been delayed for some reason, but when Thackeray, the skipper of the team, put Charlie Bates back in goal, and arranged his depleted team minus two forwards, there arose roars of inquiry on all sides.

"What's the idea? Where's the rest of 'em?"

"Where's Watson and Towler?"

The uproar was so tremendous that the referee held up the game while fat old Tom Bowling, the veteran secretary of the home side, explained through a megaphone: "Watson and Towler have been taken ill. Both are unable to play."

Amid a chorus of booing and yelling voices, the whistle for the second half shrilled out.

Tommy Burke had picked the Pelton team as the winners. He was as concerned as anyone about the disaster that had occurred during the interval.

As the depleted home side stemmed a dashing attack, he turned to the detective.

"Rummy business this, guv'nor. What could have happened to 'em? They were the two best men on the field."

The game went on, and within ten minutes the visitors had scored, thus equalising.

The boos of the home side almost drowned the cheering.

They felt that their weakness was being taken advantage of, and all kinds of wild rumours began to go round the ground.

Watson and Towler had quarrelled and knocked each other out, said one astonishing whisper. They had got drunk, said another. They had quarrelled with the referee and been suspended, said a third. Tongues buzzed busily. Never had there been quite such a sensation on the Pelton field.

The weakened Rovers put up a great fight, but Charlie Bates, in goal, was nowhere near as good as Towler, and, half an hour before the end, the Robins got another magnificent shot past, putting them one up. After that, all the efforts of the Rovers failed to pull down this lead before the final whistle blew.

The disgusted crowd hung round the ground, waiting to hear further explanations.

The red-faced man, who had bet five to one against Pelton, went round collecting his bets, and was in one or two cases accused of having had inside knowledge.

"Yes, I had a pal doping their lemons at the interval," he grinned.

"It's a regular habit o' mine. Pay up and look pleasant. It'd have been all the same if you'd played at full strength second half. We was meant to win today."

Hawke and Tommy were nearly at the turnstiles when they were hailed from the left. Turning, they saw Dr Ward, a police surgeon, who had been engaged on more than one case with them in the past.

He greeted them warmly, for it was some months since they had met.

"Aren't you coming over to the pavilion to sniff at this funny business?" he demanded.

"Should have thought it might have interested you."

"Funny business? Do you mean Towler and Watson being dropped?"

"Yes. I've just been across to see them. They're sleeping like logs. I've never seen a cleaner case of doping in all my life. They dropped asleep during the interval."

Hawke's eyes glistened angrily.

Crime and criminals were part of his everyday life, but it was not often he came across crookedness in sport. That sort of crime angered him more than anything else ever did.

"I'd like to see them," he admitted.

Five minutes later he had been introduced to the group in the dressing-room. The two footballers were stretched out on a table, snoring lustily. All efforts to shake them out of that sleep had failed, and cold water and ammonia bottles had no effect.

Dr Ward had advised leaving them to sleep it off.

Meantime, the officials and the rest of the team were holding an inquiry.

If their comrades had indeed been doped, then how and when had it been done?

They had played fully up to form during the first half, and there were a great many witnesses who knew for a fact that neither of the sleepers had taken more than a small drink of water and a suck at a lemon during the interval.

Yet a few minutes before the second half began they had complained of sleepiness, and fallen into their drugged slumber.

At Hawke's suggestion the doctor examined them for scratches that might have been made by hypodermic needles. Ward found none, although Watson had been marked in several places on both legs by kicks, and Towler had been kicked high on the hip. But, as that could happen to anyone in a strenuous game such as they had played in, not much could be gathered from that.

From head to foot the two sleepers were examined, and Hawke had particular attention paid to their feet, searching their boots for projecting nails himself.

He had heard of doped nails before this, but to-day there was no suspicion of that. Their boots had not been tampered with.

He pursued his investigations for more than an hour, and then the two sleepers awakened, complained of a headache, and seemed little the worse for their adventure, although their disgust was acute when they heard the result of the match.

As a matter of fact, I felt a bit sleepy when I came off after the first half," admitted Watson.

"So did I," added Towler, "But I thought nothing of it. Thought it might have been the hot pavilion.

"Do you mean to say we were doped?"

Unwilling to bring the police into the matter, the manager of the Rovers privately asked Dixon Hawke to take over the case, and as the Dover Street detective was more or less on holiday just then, he accepted.

The Rovers were playing on Wednesday at Burford Cross, and although Hawke did not attend the match, his assistant did. Tommy came back in the early evening with the astonishing news that a similar thing had happened again.

Thackeray himself, who played out-side right, had fallen asleep in the same extraordinary manner during the interval, and Towler, in goal, had been treated to a second period of enforced sleep.

Again the Rovers had tried to battle on with two of their best men short, and again they had lost. The evening papers were full of pars about the strange coincidence.

Hawke was at the station to meet the team when it returned.

He had not been idle that afternoon, but kept the results of his work to himself.

Thackeray and Towler looked a bit pale but were quite fit enough to talk about their experiences. It was Towler whom Hawke mostly questioned.

"I want you to think back over the first half and try to remember if anything out of the ordinary happened to you. Try to think over every minute of the time. Did anyone bump you extra hard? Did you feel any pricking sensation, or anything of that kind?"

"Not a bloomin' thing," growled Towler, limping rather badly.

"They hardly got near my goal to test me. All I remember is getting cold waiting for something to do."

"You're limping. How's that — a kick?" The goalie nodded.

"Which of the other side did that? Can you remember?"

Towler grinned.

"You won't get much of a clue out of that. It wasn't one of the others who did that at all, but one of our own men, Hoskins, over there. He tried to beat Simes, their centre, who jumped for the ball as I ran out and punched it clear, and landed on me instead of the ball."

He scowled. "I forgot to tell him about it after the other business happened. He's a bit too wild with his feet. Did the same thing to me once before."

Thackeray had nothing more interesting to impart. The affair looked like being an unsolved mystery.

The disheartened Rovers wondered if they were going to win a game at all this season, or whether this mysterious sleeping sickness was going to follow them throughout.

"Beats me why anyone wanted to do it," grumbled the manager to Hawke later on.

"It isn't as though there's heavy betting on these games."

"All the same, I heard that someone was laying odds of five to one against you here in Pelton before the match came off," remarked Hawke.

"By Jove! There was? Who the deuce was that?"

"I'm not sure yet, but after your next match I hope to know more about it. Meantime, can you give me the addresses and histories of all your own men?"

"Our own men? Why, yes, of course, but — " Hawke did not explain, but spent some time that evening studying the particulars that had been sent him.

Two of the team appeared to be comparative newcomers, new that season, Hoskins, the centre-half, and Gunner, the left-back. Tommy was rather surprised when he was put on to the job of shadowing each of these for the rest of the week.

He did not see much of Hawke during those days, and the detective seemed to spend most of his time dressed like an out-of-work tough in some of the downtown saloons.

Each night he read Tommy's reports, but the two men under observation seemed to lead blameless lives, spending their time either at the training centre or at their homes.

Gunner lived with his wife on the north side of the town, and Sid Hoskins had lodgings down by the river.

On Friday night, Hawke did not get back to their hotel until after midnight. Tommy was waiting for him.

"Thought you were never coming, guv'nor."

"I've been laying bets," confessed the detective with a grin. "I've bet a hundred pounds that Pelton will not do the 'hat-trick' by losing this Saturday, and I've got odds of seven to one. Pretty good going, eh?"

Tommy goggled.

"Gosh, who laid those odds?"

"Calls himself Smith, but, as a matter of fact, it's the same red-faced, jolly-looking man we saw taking bets that first Saturday afternoon."

Tommy's jaw dropped more than ever.

"Crumbs, that's funny! I had something to tell you about him. Soon after dark this evening he visited Hoskins at his digs. I was on watch at the time. He stopped in there for more than an hour, and when he came out he left by the backyard instead of coming out in the street. What do you think of that, sir?"

"We'll think more about it tomorrow," said the detective, "but just now I'm going to sleep."

Which he duly did, leaving Tommy awake trying to puzzle things out.

The following afternoon was wet, but a tremendous crowd turned out to see the match, for everyone was wondering whether the disasters of the last two matches were to be repeated.

The Rovers had not got their strongest team out, Towler being replaced by one of the reserves, and Thackeray being still off colour since his mysterious attack of sleepiness.

But, all the same, the Pelton Rovers were eager to avenge their two recent losses, and in the first half they ran their opponents off their feet.

Their idea seemed to be to score as many goals as possible in the first half, in case the "hoodoo" was put on them again during the interval.

The interval came at last, with the score at three to one in their favour.

Directly the half-time whistle blew, Hawke made a bee-line for the pavilion.

He had not missed a single move of the first half, and now there was an ominous light in his eyes as he marched up to the manager.

"Now there's going to be fireworks," thought Tommy. "The chief's got something up his sleeve."

Hawke had.

"You'll be playing one man short again next half," he announced to the bewildered manager. "They've done it on Watson. He will be feeling sleepy by now.

"He'll be off in a few minutes."

Over in a corner, Watson was sitting on top of a box, stifling a yawn.

"What's that?" he demanded. "You say they've done it on me? Who? When?"

"Do you feel sleepy?" queried the detective.

"Rottenly so. I believe you're right, but I'm blessed — "

"How did you get that kick on the knee?" rapped out Hawke. "Who gave it you?"

Watson looked down carelessly at the broken bruise, which he had not even troubled to sponge.

"Oh, that? Blessed if I remember. Got it in some scrimmage or other, I suppose."

"Well, I can tell you how it happened," went on Hawke.

"You were actually kicked by one of your own side, by Hoskins. I saw it happen."

He looked at Hoskins severely, and the tall, angular half-back nodded.

"Believe I remember," he said. "It was an accident. Sorry!"

"A lot of those accidents happen to you," went on Hawke. "In the match with the Robins you kicked Watson and Towler. Last Wednesday you landed on Towler again, and Thackeray as well."

The man slid from the table.

"Look here, what are you getting at?"

"Your boots," snapped Hawke, stepping forward. "Let me see the studs."

The half-back darted a frightened look at the detective, then turned to run, but a dozen willing hands seized him, dragged him back, and held him while Hawke examined the studs on his boots, and looked ready to pull him to pieces when the Dover Street sleuth pointed out that two distinct pin points nestled among the leather grip studs.

"Those were doped before you kicked Watson. Now he's also asleep. You understand?"

"I didn't! I tell you — "

"It's no good, Hoskins, we've got it on you. I can have these pins examined by competent experts, and they will be able to tell me just what dope you used. Of course, you were never suspected, as you were on the home side. It was a dirty trick, but clever.

"Who put you up to it?"

Hoskins looked round savagely at his glowering colleagues, the men he had betrayed. Perhaps it was their fierce looks that scared him.

"A chap called Holloway," he moaned.

"I — he did everything. It was his idea. He paid me ten quid every time I brought it off."

"Is he fat, with a red face?" questioned Dixon Hawke. The other nodded. "Very well, I have to pay him a hundred pounds if your team loses.

"I'm afraid I'll also take a policeman along with me as witness that I pay my debts."

Which he did. There being two policemen in plain clothes, as well as Tommy; and although the Rovers did not lose that day, but succeeded in fighting out a draw without Watson, Holloway was there to argue about splitting the odds.

Five minutes later he was being driven to the police station between stalwart constables, and, within an hour, confronted by Hoskins, he had admitted the whole miserable plot.

It was a South American arrow poison he had used to doctor the pins in the studs of Hoskins' boots, and he admitted that, if the season had proved profitable because of the Rovers' losses, he had intended trying the stunt on a more important team the next year.

But when the footer season opened next year both he and the treacherous half-back were spending their time in a place where no football results were read, and the Pelton Rovers soon climbed back near the top of the league again.

—o0o—

# THE CASE OF *The Ready-Made Clue*

**"Ho, ho!" said the expression on P.C. Hobson's face. "What's all this 'ere?"**

A dusty and unshaven tramp, who had just come in from the main highway, had had the effrontery to nod a greeting as he clattered in his hobnailed boots across Hatherton's sun-drenched market square.

The officer did not respond in the genial manner in which, for instance, he had just welcomed a similar greeting from Mr John Straker, chief clerk to Mr Arthur Pick, solicitor.

Mr Straker had just gone to Mr Pick's office, towards which the tramp was also headed.

The constable pivoted slowly round, his face offensively blank as he studied the tramp's every movement.

His eyebrows went up and he took a pace forward as he watched the tramp cup his hands around his eyes in order to peer in at Mr Pick's window.

But shooting a swift glance over his shoulder, the tramp abandoned his scrutiny and set off briskly down the street, turning left at the end of the block.

P.C. Hobson followed him as far as the corner, where, for about twenty minutes after the itinerant's disappearance round the bend at the top of the hill, where Mr Pick's private house was situated. He remained there, taking a rest.

But suddenly the drowsy peace was shattered by a hoarse shout from the top of the hill, and Hobson turned to behold Mr Arthur Pick's swarthy, thick-set male servant, Dawkins.

"Hurry. It's murder," gasped Dawkins, as Hobson puffed up the slope to the house.

"Mr Pick's been stabbed."

Hobson had a look at the still figure which lay on the thick carpet of a drawing-room furnished like a museum, and he noted the wavy-bladed Malayan kris which protruded from between the shoulder-blades, when, happening to glance out of the window across the fields, he saw the tramp once more.

Hobson ran across the newly-dug garden, following a trail of footprints, and broke through a gap in the wooden fence.

As he set off across the field beyond, the tramp turned and observed him, then broke into a run.

Stricken to a standstill by the sudden horrifying thought that the stabbed man might still have life in him, P.C. Hobson hesitated for a moment in an agony of uncertainty, and then decided it was his duty to go back and instruct Dawkins to summon a doctor.

When he got back to the house he discovered that the valet had already done so.

The tramp had by this time got too good a start, and so Hobson phoned his station, from where a district call was put out.

A ride on the tail-board of a lorry took the fugitive tramp into the heart of a great Midland city forty miles away, before he was captured, and it was in the Central Police Station of that city that Dixon Hawke and his assistant, Tommy Burke, first saw him.

For them, as for Detective-Inspector Gray of Scotland Yard, who had been working with them on a Government inquiry, the tramp was not at first a particularly interesting figure.

No individual, amidst all that bustling life, could be of outstanding interest.

"It'll be another hour or two before they get that bomb crater on the main line filled in," declared Inspector Davis, a local C.I.D. man. "If you don't relish the idea of hanging about you can come down as far as Hatherton with me. There's a main line junction there.

"The only drawback is," he went on, on discovering their ready assent, "you'll have to put up with a tramp as a travelling companion. He's fairly wholesome, though, as tramps go. They've given him a bit of a rinse and dusted him over."

"What's he wanted for?" asked Tommy.

Davis shrugged his shoulders slightly. "Dunno exactly. I fancy I heard the warrant officer say something about murder. Stabbing charge. He's quite tame, though. Won't give us any trouble.

As I was saying," he went on, turning to Gray, "About the confounded muddle over that bally traveller's cheque book ..."

The journey was made in a large saloon car, the tramp sitting on the back seat with Gray and a constable, to whom he was handcuffed.

Tommy sat on a folding seat facing them, and Hawke sat by the side of Davis, who drove.

"And is wandering about without visible means your main occupation?" Gray asked the tramp when hedge tops and trees were streaking past the windows of the limousine.

"Me? Certainly not! I'm an artist," said the tramp, who had given the name of Michael Grogan.

"Pavement artist?"

"Huh! That muck in the Tate Gallery and the Royal Academy isn't to be compared with my pictures!"

"When d'you paint them? What do you do with 'em?"

Grogan's expression changed in a subtle manner, and it became clear to Tommy and to Hawke, who had turned in his seat, that he was a distinctive personality.

"I paint them as I roam the countryside, mister. And I keep 'em in my head."

"Hm? Then what?"

"I don't use brushes and canvas. I think my pictures, right down to the last dab of colour. Then I lose interest and start to work thinking another. I've never actually painted one."

"Are you trying to be funny?"

"What's your own opinion?"

"I should have thought you'd hardly be in the mood for providing amusement," put in Hawke, studying him with interest.

Grogan looked suddenly furtive and hunted.

His bronzed, bristly face had unusual expressive power, and his every change of thought seemed to register there.

46

"Those bally intellectual tramps are the worst," asseverated Davis. "They devote all their thoughts to the ennobling subject of work. But they never actually do any."

"I know," agreed Gray. "Ask one to chop firewood, and the axe isn't sharp. Give him the axe to sharpen, and the grindstone wants fixing. Ask him to fix the grindstone and he wants a man to help him. Give him a man to help him, and then the man gets all the work to do, and the 'hardworking' tramp goes on a sit-down strike."

"Or turns rough," suggested Davis.

"I never turn rough, mister," said Grogan.

"This is all a mistake. I don't know anything about any murder. I aroused suspicion because I ran when I saw the slop running towards me. It was instinct. That slop had followed me through the town. I sat on a stile just outside for a while, and then started across a footpath. Then I happened to look round, and I saw him running towards me. So, naturally, I ran. That's all I know."

A burly, apple-cheeked superintendent with a gingery, toothbrush moustache was criticising P. C. Hobson when the party arrived at Hatherton Police Station.

Superintendent Bennett was a plain-thinking, country police-officer who used doubtful language in a brisk and cheerful manner.

"So you didn't think about the foot-prints in the garden when you planted your great plates o' meat on 'em, did you. Why, you great long slab!"

He gave the visitors only the most perfunctory greeting, turning his attention, almost immediately, to Grogan's feet.

"Hobnails?" he queried. "Yes. And the footprints in the garden — what's left of 'em — are hobnailed."

"It don't follow they were mine," said Grogan.

"It don't follow they were old Pick's. He had too much money to go in for hobnails. Unless they were diamond ones. Your face is familiar. Haven't I seen you round this district before?"

Grogan shook his head.

"You seen him before, Hobson?"

"No, sir."

A few moments later, Bennett was telling the visitors, in the heartiest manner, just what had happened, and how he proposed to go about procuring the necessary evidence.

The visitors chuckled as, with the greatest good humour — in the manner of one who has just accepted a challenge to deliver a lecture — Bennett put his foot on a stool and rested his elbow on his knee.

"I shall go down to the chemist's and get some plaster of paris, see? And I shall make casts of a couple of the clearest of those footprints.

"And then I shall send 'em, along with Grogan's boots, to the county C.I.D. They'll have gutta percha replicas made, if necessary, and there won't be any possibility of mistake."

"What about the question of motive?" put in Hawke, with the slight display of shyness becoming a layman in such heavy official company.

"Motive! H'm. H-rr-umph ! Robbery. Footprints lead right up to the French windows of Mr Pick's study, and back the same way. Garden mud on the carpet. Grogan was wandering about thinking the place had been left unattended. Bit of luck if it had. Lot of stuff in it. Antiques, old brasses, miniatures, and so on.

"And while he was wandering about," added Bennett, "Pick came on him suddenly, and he snatched that old dagger off the wall. There are lots of those things stuck up on walls, all over the place."

Events moved with dramatic swiftness during the next few minutes.

A tall man, with a ruddy complexion not acquired in the open air, and a flabby body that, at first glance, gave the appearance of being well muscled, came in response to a phone call from Bennett.

This was Mr John Straker, Mr Pick's chief clerk.

"It's just who I thought it would be," said Mr Straker to the surprised company, after taking one look at Grogan. "It's no use trying to hide your identity, Grogan."

Grogan's lower lip was trembling, and his fingers wound and unwound in convulsive movements as he turned appealingly towards Hawke.

"I didn't kill him," he declared. "I knew something had happened when I heard Dawkins enter the drawing-room and call out Mr Pick's name, and then rush out shouting for the police. I thought I'd better make myself scarce."

"He's Mr Pick's half-brother," explained Straker, "and he seems to have a lot of gipsy blood in him, or something. Anyway, he's always lived that roaming life, and he's been coming back periodically to sponge on Mr Pick for funds."

Grogan's lips curled and he looked increasingly scornful, as Straker, determinedly antagonistic, went on.

"In fact, I think he must have been blackmailing Mr Pick. He's squeezed large sums out of him …"

"Hey! Where d'you get that? Large sums!"

"I have access to all Mr Pick's accounts. I've been acting as his private secretary, as well as his chief clerk."

"Twenty pounds," declared Grogan. "That was as much as I ever touched him for. And I'd make that last me a year. Sometimes two. I've tramped from Spain to Sweden on less."

Straker shrugged his shoulders.

"The accounts tell a different story," he said, and glanced significantly at the superintendent.

"You've already made a couple of statements which have proved false, Grogan," said that official.

Grogan, who had now learned Hawke's identity, grasped him by the coat lapel.

"Find out the truth of this for me," he pleaded. "Either somebody's trying to plant the blame on me, or the fates are working against me. All I know is —I didn't do it.

"I was a fool to tell all those lies," he went on, "but it was for my daughter's sake. I didn't know what to do.

"You see, Arthur's brought her up, and she doesn't know her old man's a hobo by choice. She'd lose caste, and social standing always did mean a wonderful lot to all my family."

"Would that be the young lady from London that stops with Mr Pick sometimes?" queried Bennett.

Straker nodded in affirmation.

"Her mother died when she was an infant, and Grogan went off and left her on Mr Pick's hands. She thinks her father's dead, too."

"The principal reason why I went off," put in Grogan, "was that I couldn't stick the life of a family of middle-class snobs. It's my only vice: insisting on living like a human being instead of like a stuffed shirt."

"What happened when you arrived at Mr Pick's house?" asked Hawke.

"You ought to get legal advice before you talk," said Straker, meticulously adjusting his soiled yellow gloves, which he wore unbuttoned, and rolled about his wrists.

"I'll talk," said Grogan. "I've nothing but the plain, unvarnished truth to tell, and you don't need lawyers for that.

"I'd looked in through the window of his office in the town," he went on, "and when I saw he wasn't there, I went straight up to the house. He was a man who never moved out of his one groove, and I knew I'd find him in his study. It's always been the same, every time I've returned here throughout the past twenty-odd years.

"I went in by the back way, so's to be unobserved, and stepped in through the French windows of his study, and sat down and waited for him.

"I'd been sitting for about a quarter of an hour when I heard Dawkins moving through the front hall from the direction of the kitchen. I heard him entering the drawing-room and call out: 'Mr Pick. My God! What's happened? Murder, murder!' He opened the front door, and I heard him calling out to the slo — the constable there.

"I thought: 'Hullo, something's wrong. Maybe I'd better get out of this,' and so I promptly hopped it."

"I must say," murmured Hawke to Bennett, after Grogan had been removed to the cells, "I feel an urge to believe his story. Would you have any objection to my looking over the material evidence with you?"

The superintendent agreed.

After Davis and the constable had left, Hawke, Gray, and Tommy visited Pick's home, The Firs, a large detached house in spacious grounds.

Dawkins, whose deferential tones were quite out of keeping with the sinister appearance imparted by a broken nose resulting from an accident, showed them round the house and grounds, and stated that he had been taking a quiet "snooze" in the kitchen immediately prior to the discovery. He was not aware of Grogan's presence, and had not heard anyone approach or leave. He was, as the visitors noticed, a trifle hard of hearing.

Hawke got down on his knees and examined the carpets in the study, the drawing-room, and the hall, near the spot from which the kris had been taken.

He also picked up a copy of a magazine from the study floor and put it under his arm.

"I'd like to have a run-through this. I'll bring it back," he promised.

Then he went right round the house and made a careful examination of the well-scrubbed steps at each of the three entrances, and also of the door knobs.

Gray expressed his determination to get back to London.

"I'll stay here for the night," said Hawke. "This affair gets interesting."

Tommy had the impression that his employer was in the process of brilliantly uncovering a startling truth.

"There's a wicket gate at the end of the garden path, opposite that side entrance," remarked Hawke, after Gray and Bennett had left them. "Slip around and find where it leads. I'll go and book rooms down at the hotel which the 'super' mentioned. Hatherton Arms, wasn't it?"

Tommy nodded and turned back towards The Firs.

Darkness was closing in rapidly when he found his way round to a back lane on the other side of the wicket gate.

A narrow, gravelled path, walled in on each side, wound a tortuous course downhill.

Opposite the backs of a terrace of tall houses, it turned sharply left.

Tommy directed the beam of his torch on each side of the back steps of these houses, and found that each one had a quantity of the crushed red gravel on it that covered the lane.

"Most of the inhabitants use that back way," he later reported to Hawke. "If you're thinking that the murderer used that way, and that you might trace his footprints, I'm afraid you'll be disappointed."

Hawke nodded appreciatively.

"Hatherton is full of these convenient back ways," he said.

Next morning, shortly after breakfast, Tommy found Hawke looking decidedly pleased.

"I've found something that I expected to find," he said, "and that's usually a sign of progress."

Bennett came. He was looking even more pleased, and his pleasure reversed Hawke's.

"That dagger thing," he said. "What d'you think? Got Grogan's fingerprints on it. Clear as you could wish."

"Really! Was that fellow just filling me up with lies? I can't believe it. I'd have made a bet he was telling me the truth."

"Our fingerprint expert's still up at the station. You can come and see for yourself."

The fingerprints on the handle of the kris, which they inspected ten minutes later, provided a damning piece of evidence against Grogan, who, however, still fervently protested his innocence.

Hawke was preoccupied, and, at times a little irritable, for the rest of the morning. Then, just before lunch, he seemed to have a sudden inspiration.

He returned to the police station, and when Tommy saw him next, he was wearing a faint, triumphant smile.

After lunch, Hawke and Tommy adjourned to the billiard room, a converted loft, approached by way of an outside staircase, leading to a wooden platform, on to which the billiard room door opened.

Straker, as Hawke had learned by inquiry, was there practising billiard shots, waiting for the arrival of a friend.

In the role of spectators, they sat on the leather upholstered seat, and Hawke, casually toying with Straker's lemon-coloured gloves which had been left there, opened a conversation about murder.

"Funny business over those fingerprints on the handle of that dagger," he said.

"Quite remarkable in fact!

"It suddenly dawned on me how strongly imprinted they were, and that was the whole point. They were difficult to rub off, and d'you know why? They were several years old! There were other prints besides Grogan's, but his were quite unmistakable. He must have handled it last time he was here. Or perhaps it was even longer ago. Goodness knows.

"The thing had been there for years.

"The faint film of grease from the skin must have acted as a protection against oxidation which affected the metal in between the ridges."

Straker picked up his whisky glass, took a sip, and seemed to become possessed of a dreamy fascination as he regarded Hawke.

"And talking about fingerprints," said the detective. "I learned that your offices have just been redecorated. I notice you got some of that green paint off the back door bolt on your fingers.

"It's inside your gloves, look. Apparently you didn't put them on until you got back inside Pick's house, for you left a green fingerprint on the knob of the side door of The Firs."

"What're you getting at?" snapped Straker.

"That painting was only done yesterday morning. You've been to The Firs since then by way of that back lane. I noticed the red gravel on the carpets in the hall and the drawing-room. It's quite different from that left by Grogan in the study.

"Grogan really did sit there reading a magazine," Hawke went on, "and he'd hardly have done that if he had committed a murder, would he? You see, there are other sets of Grogan's fingerprints in this case. On the glossy pages of that magazine."

Both Hawke and Straker showed an increasing tenseness as the detective became more accusing.

"Are you trying to make out that I killed Pick, relying on years-old fingerprints to turn suspicion elsewhere? It's ridiculous. How should I even know about those fingerprints?"

"It has often struck me," said Hawke, "that, occasionally, everything in nature conspires to bring about one particular end.

"This was such an occasion.

"Just think how circumstances dovetailed in. You had had a row with Pick, possibly connected with some defalcations, from the consequences of which you'd been hoping to save yourself by marrying Pick's niece, who is, of course, Grogan's daughter.

"I found all that out this morning from one of your colleagues, who knows a little about you, and hears more than you would imagine.

"Anyhow, to proceed with my theme. Circumstances built themselves up to that inevitable culmination.

"A row with Pick. You got some drink inside you, returned to your office, and saw Grogan look in the window. You knew he'd go straight up to Pick's house, and, on a sudden impulse, you slipped out the back way. From that moment fate seemed to adapt itself to your design.

"Or perhaps you were just the instrument of fate. "

Whatever else he had been, Straker was certainly not a willing victim of fate. Sudden chagrin overcame him and, with murderous force, he threw a billiard ball at the detective.

Hawke ducked and it shattered the glass behind him.

Tommy bounded round the table and dived at the fuming man and together they crashed through the doorway, coming down heavily on the edge of the platform.

Straker was not as powerful as he looked, and the pair quickly overcame him and handed him over to the police.

"The amazing thing is," said Hawke subsequently, "that he didn't know Grogan's fingerprints were on that dagger.

"He just put his gloves on to conceal his own, but had no notion how well everything was working out for him. Fate, fickle old fate, was on his side all right."

"Only up to a point," chuckled Tommy.

—o0o—

# THE CASE OF *The Crusted Snow*

"Look out, there!" "Mind your backs!" An excited roar followed shouts from a dozen people, every voice merging into one great shout. Dragged to the crest of the snow-covered hill a toboggan carrying five people was pushed on the downward slope.

Fast gathering speed, it flashed past the spectators, and shining eyes and red, glistening faces showed in the light of a half moon. Frost had bound the snow to the bare branches of giant trees, to the shrubs and the hedges, to the roof of Willingdon Hall.

"Hi there, guv'nor!"

Dixon Hawke heard the shout as Tommy Burke flashed past him on a smaller toboggan, behind a pretty girl muffled to the neck.

Hawke smiled, and then turned as footsteps crunched in the snow behind him. A tall, handsome man in a heavy Ulster greeted him.

"Hallo, Hawke! What do you think of the party?"

"You deserve everyone's thanks, Willingdon," said Hawke promptly.

"Oh, nonsense," said Mark Willingdon gruffly. "These people deserve a break if anyone does."

Week after week Mark Willingdon threw open the doors and grounds of his country house, entertaining as many as twenty war-workers at a time. Food was plentiful, the bedrooms were comfortable, and rarely was there any disturbance from the skies.

Dixon Hawke and Tommy Burke had been on a case in a nearby town. Willingdon had seen them, and had immediately invited them for the weekend. And Tommy was certainly getting every ounce of enjoyment out of it.

"Hallo, Daddy! Coming for a slide?" A tall, smiling girl approached, with two men escorting her. Hawke saw two things immediately. First, that she was lovely; second, that she only smiled with her lips. Her eyes, he thought, were worried and anxious. Nor did he think there was need to look far for an explanation of that, when he saw her two companions.

One man was also forcing a smile, although his eyes looked angry. The second man made no pretence at being in a good humour. He was shorter but broader than the other, and his hair was dark. The first man was fair.

"I'll leave that to you youngsters," said Willingdon. "Peggy, I don't think you've met Mr Hawke. Hawke, this is my daughter. And —" he looked at the fair man, who made a show of affability, "this is Mr Deane, a friend."

"How do you do?" said Peggy and Deane almost at the same time.

"And another friend, Mr Mordaunt," said Willingdon.

Mordaunt did no more than grunt, and the trio walked to the top of the hill. Half-a-dozen people were dragging a sledge to the top.

Deane kept a hand on Peggy Willingdon's arm. Mordaunt walked a yard away from her on the other side.

When they were beyond earshot, Willingdon murmured to Hawke: "I wish I knew which of these two men Peggy really cares for. Deane's a much better tempered fellow — in the Army and a decent sort. Mordaunt has some kind of Government job, and it hasn't improved his manners. However, let's get back to the house for a drink."

Before they had gone ten yards, however, something whizzed past Hawke's face. He turned — and a snowball struck his hat, sending it flying. Laughing, he stooped and picked up a handful of snow, crushed it, and hurled it at the youngsters who had started pelting him.

It was a signal for a general battle!

In a few minutes toboggans and sledges were quite forgotten, and the air was thick with flying snowballs. Hawke and Willingdon beat a hasty retreat, but as they drew beyond reach of the missiles, Willingdon exclaimed: "Would you believe that! The surly brute!"

"That" was Mordaunt, who had hurried away from the crowd, but met a stray holidaymaker who promptly tossed a snowball at him. Mordaunt's voice echoed clearly across the snow as he shook his fist and shouted: "Don't act the fool! Haven't you grown up yet?"

Then he strode on to the house.

Hawke smiled.

"His temper certainly isn't at its best."

"This will probably finish him with Peggy," said Willingdon.

"Probably she has already made that clear," said Hawke. "It could explain his general manner."

"By George, yes! I hadn't thought of that," said Willingdon.

They went in by the side door. Despite the efforts of several servants, the stone-paved hall was wet, and here and there lay fragments of crusted and melting snow. Rows of Wellington boots were lined up by one wall, but traces of snow continued along the back quarters to the front hall.

In a few minutes they were in the study, and Willingdon took out a decanter of whisky and two glasses. Hawke was looking at the carpet in one corner of the room, and his expression made Willingdon say: "You look as if you're trying to compete with Mordaunt!"

"That's a frown of concentration, not bad temper," said Hawke quietly. "How many people come into this room?"

Willingdon stopped pouring whisky. "No one should, unless I send them. Why?"

Hawke stepped to the corner and picked something up. Willingdon saw that it was a piece of crusted snow, melting a little.

"Great Scott! No one has been to that corner — not you or I, I mean."

"That's what aroused my interest," said Hawke.

He watched Willingdon closely. The latter put down the decanter, and stepped to the corner, where stood a small safe. His tall figure was tense.

"Don't touch that!" rapped Hawke, and Willingdon drew his hand back quickly from the door of the safe. "There might be prints."

Hawke stepped to Willingdon's side as the other said in a sharp, angry, voice: "Nonsense, Hawke! I don't believe anything has been touched!"

"It's as well to be on the safe side," said Hawke, taking a handkerchief from his pocket. "Is there much of value in there?"

"Ye-es,"said Willingdon in a strained voice. "There are several hundred pounds — I went to the bank today and drew enough for the month. And — there are the family jewels, Hawke. I've kept them here since the bombing started in London. I thought they would be safer with me. Hurry man, don't keep me in suspense!"

Hawke pulled gently at the door. It opened without any trouble, and Willingdon uttered an exclamation.

"It's unlocked!"

"I'm afraid so," said Hawke grimly. Not only was the outer door unlocked, but the door of the inner compartment was ajar. Hawke pulled it wider open, to find that the safe was empty.

"I—I can't believe it," gasped Willingdon. "I put a small jewel-case in there just before I came out, and everything else was there then!"

"What time was that?" asked Hawke.

"It couldn't have been a quarter of an hour before I met you outside." Hawke glanced at his watch.

"That means the safe was untouched quarter to ten, and we've been together for half an hour. But we may be able to establish the time of the theft more accurately than that."

"How?" asked Willingdon.

"Is there always an even temperature in this room?"

"Yes—it doesn't vary when the windows are shut. It is centrally heated, of course."

"Good," said Hawke briskly. "I'm going to my room to get my kit. Will you send for Tommy, and tell him to come up here without taking his boots off?"

"I'll do that," said Willingdon. "But why with his boots on?"

"You'll see," said Hawke quietly.

Hawke moved towards the door as Willingdon pressed a bell, but before he reached it the latter said in a low voice: "Hawke, those jewels were family heirlooms. I must get them back! I'm not so worried about the money as about them. I — I don't want a scandal. Thank heavens you happened to be here! I would have hated to go to the police."

As the last word was uttered, the door opened from the outside. Peggy Willingdon stood on the threshold for a moment, her lovely face animated but clearly anxious.

"Did I hear the word 'police '?" she demanded.

"I'm afraid you did," said Hawke gravely. "Your father will explain, Miss Willingdon, but I earnestly request you both to keep the facts to yourselves, at least for the time being." Leaving the girl mystified and worried he went up to his bedroom. He had a full set of equipment with him, but after taking it from his case he rested in an easy-chair for some minutes. Not only did he want to give Willingdon a chance to talk to his daughter, but he needed a respite for concentrated thinking.

He had no opportunity to do that on his own, however, for Tommy came clumping into the room in his heavy boots to which snow still clung. There was snow on his Mackintosh and even in his hair. His face was a bright red, glowing with health.

"Someone said you wanted me, guv'nor."

"Yes," said Hawke. "Have a seat now, old son, and let me give you a memory test. How many people did you notice going to or coming from the house for half an hour before the snow-fight started?"

Tommy looked puzzled, but answered promptly.

"There were three different lots, that's all. A man and a girl who had been sky-larking in the house — he girl was on a small sledge with me. Three older men, auxiliary firemen, I think. And then that stunning Willingdon girl, Peggy."

"Can you be sure there were no more?"

"Yes — except that Miss Willingdon had her two boy-friends with her. I was watching the house most of the time, looking for you," Tommy added with a grin. "But what's the matter, guv'nor?"

"Robbery," said Hawke, briefly. He picked up a frozen piece of crusted snow from one of Tommy's boots, and laid it on the floor. "Hop out again, and if any of the people you saw are missing, try to find them. Don't count Miss Willingdon. I know where she is."

"Right!" Tommy was, as always, eager to get busy on anything mysterious. "What's missing, guv'nor?"

"Five hundred pounds, mostly in notes, and some family jewels."

"By Jingo! A haul for someone!"

Tommy hurried out and Hawke went quickly to the study. Willingdon and his daughter were sitting there, grave-faced. As Hawke entered he glanced at his watch, and then placed the lump of crusted snow on the carpet near the safe. He had carried it on a piece of cardboard so that the heat of his hands did not melt it.

"What on earth is that for?" demanded Peggy.

"A little experiment," smiled Hawke.

"Have you made any progress?" asked Willingdon.

"There hasn't been a lot of chance yet," said Hawke, "but I've narrowed the list of suspects somewhat. It's a great loss to you, Miss Willingdon, I know. The jewels would have been yours one day, I understand."

"On my marriage, yes," said Peggy. "But it is going to be extremely difficult for you to find them, isn't it? There are so many strangers here, and you can never be sure of the type of people who come for these weekends."

"That's so," said Willingdon.

"I had never realised before how risky it might be to give such people the run of the house."

Hawke frowned.

"I wouldn't jump to conclusions," he said. "Poor — or so-called lower-class — people are just as honest as the so-called upper-class. In fact, as far as honesty is concerned, there isn't a pin to choose between them. However, I am not going to jump to conclusions either."

"Aren't you going to start a search of the rooms?" asked the girl.

"Later, if necessary," said Hawke quietly.

Meantime Tommy Burke was watching the holiday-makers in that carnival of snow. They seemed so happy that it was beastly to know that some of them were suspected of stealing from their benefactor. But he had no time for loose thinking, and he was quick to see two things.

The fair-haired Deane was laughing and joking with the civil-defence workers, and in no way proclaiming the fact that he was an Army officer. He had told Hawke, Willingdon and Tommy that he preferred to be in civvies because his uniform might otherwise cause some awkwardness.

Tommy had formed a good impression of Deane then, and the impression was confirmed. But he was more interested in Mordaunt, who was missing.

It was not difficult to see about the grounds, for dark-clad figures were shown up vividly. The noise of laughter and high spirits faded, and then he saw Mordaunt who was walking by himself.

Tommy saw the man stop. He looked down at something in his hand. It was paper of some kind, and he bent down, looked about him, and then began to move snow away from a small bank. He pushed whatever he was holding into the hole, and then straightened up, and glanced round.

Tommy tried to dodge out of sight behind some trees, but was too late. Mordaunt saw him and snapped: "Who the devil is that?"

Tommy moved quickly to one side. He slipped, however, and then Mordaunt was on him. By then he was on his feet, and dodged a heavy blow from Mordaunt. He countered, but Mordaunt was no fool with his fists, and a much stronger man. He struck again, and the blow sent Tommy sprawling to the ground.

"You confounded, interfering, little fool!" snapped Mordaunt. "I've a good mind to break your neck!" "Tommy scrambled to his feet, pale-faced.

"I'm ready if you want to try," he answered, and for a moment he thought that Mordaunt would come for him again. But instead the man swung round and walked away.

Tommy shrugged and went to the hole. After some trouble he found it, and brought out what Mordaunt had hidden. He stared down, excited and yet not wholly surprised. A wad of notes, probably five hundred pounds worth, was in his hand.

He used his torch to make a more thorough inspection of the hiding-place, but found no trace of jewels. Then he retraced his steps, hurrying to the house.

Half-way up the stairs he met Mordaunt. The man had a suitcase in his hand, and was obviously planning to leave. Tommy stood square in front of him, grim and determined. He saw the fight of recognition in the other's eyes, and was prepared for a rush. But before it came, a door opened and Hawke appeared.

Tommy said sharply: "I've got the man, guv'nor! Mordaunt had the notes in his pocket."

"Oh," said Hawke quietly. "Have you anything to say, Mr Mordaunt?"

"Nothing that is any concern of yours," flashed Mordaunt.

"But it is of Mr Willingdon's," said Hawke.

Mordaunt's eyes blazed, but he swung round on his heel. "Oh, all right, confound you! Let's get it over."

They crowded into Willingdon's study. Deane and Peggy were there. Willingdon was saying:

"I am really delighted, Deane, and I only wish that I was less troubled by the robbery, so that I could be more single-minded with my congratulations." He looked up with surprise as the others entered and said quietly: "This is a full day, gentlemen. Peggy has just told me that she has become engaged."

"Congratulations," said Hawke. And then deliberately: "Aren't you going to extend your good wishes, Mr Mordaunt?"

Mordaunt glared at him.

"You know what I've come for. I knew all about the engagement earlier in the evening. Now let's get this over. Hawke's snooping young friend caught me with your money."

"Good — good heavens!" gasped Willingdon.

"You!" exclaimed Peggy.

"Where are the jewels?" demanded Willingdon, and then with an effort. "Just a moment, Hawke. I know you will respect my wishes. This comes as a considerable blow, but provided the money and jewels are returned I shall make no charge."

"Before we settle that," said Hawke, "I have one or two observations to make. We are assuming that the same man had the jewels and notes, and also that he stole them in the first place. Now I have carried out an experiment with a piece of ice from a boot. I know, because of the way in which a piece melted in this room, that the thief was at the safe some twenty-five minutes before the discovery of the theft. A careful checking of the time proves that none of the A.R.P. people were here then. In fact, only Mr Mordaunt or Mr Deane were here."

"Great Scott!" exclaimed Willingdon. "What an ingenious idea! But I don't see how it affects the issue."

Mordaunt's face was set and stern as he said, "Nor do I. I'll confess that I took all the stuff. I knew where the keys were kept, and thought I could get away with it by blaming someone, since so many people were here. But — well, it's all over. Are you sure you're not going to give me in, Willingdon?"

"Before that, another thing," said Hawke. "Where are the jewels, Mordaunt?"

"When I realised the game was up I threw them away in the snow," said Mordaunt. "I tried to hide the money."

"Did you?" asked Hawke. "I don't think so. Moreover, I think your confession and your behaviour is nothing more than a strange, quixotic gesture! You didn't take the jewels, but you know who did. The thief, you learned, had won the hand of the woman you love. For her sake, because you think only the thief can make her happy, you have done this."

Mordaunt looked flabbergasted. Deane had lost all vestige of colour and said thickly: "That's a vicious lie, Hawke!"

"No, it isn't," flashed Hawke, "And I'll tell you what made me first suspect you. You dressed in civilian clothes on the pretext of making it pleasanter for the civil defence workers. I thought you the last man to be so considerate for others and looked for another reason. Your uniform was too conspicuous and you needed to change it, but I will guarantee the jewels are in your pockets."

Deane was edging towards the door, but Tommy reached it first. Peggy stepped slowly to Mordaunt's side.

"Did you really do that for me, Jim?"

Mordaunt spoke awkwardly.

"All — all I wanted was to make you happy, Peggy. I saw Deane with the jewels. He put the notes in the pocket of his army greatcoat in the hall. He is still carrying the jewels on him. I got the notes and proposed to hide them, and later make him put the jewels with them, so that all of it would be found."

Willingdon said quietly: "Return the jewels, Deane, and then leave my house. Hawke, I really can't thank you enough."

"Nor can I," said Peggy Willingdon. "You've helped me to see how nearly I made a tragic mistake."

And her hand clasped Mordaunt's.

—oOo—

# THE CASE OF
## The Laughing Jackdaw

**Dixon Hawke, the famous Dover Street detective, laughed as he passed a letter across the breakfast table to his assistant, Tommy Burke.**

it read: "Dear Mr Dixon Hawke, I am making a collection to feather my nest, and have put you down for a subscription of £1000. Please have the cash ready in pound notes, as I shall call for it in the course of the next few days.

Yours ever,

JACKDAW.

P.S.—If you don't recognise my name, I must refer you to the poem about my famous ancestor, the Jackdaw of Rheims."

Tommy was outraged.

"Well, of all the cheek!" exclaimed Tommy as he handed back the letter. "Let's see, in the poem, didn't the Jackdaw of Rheims pinch the cardinal's ring?"

"He did, but this new jackdaw seems to prefer cash," chuckled Hawke.

"But he must be mad, coolly asking you to shell out a thousand quid! We get some crazy letters here, but this beats the lot," decided Tommy.

"Do you think it's a joke?"

"Either that or an advertising stunt," agreed Hawke, and, with a busy day before him, he put the letter out of his mind.

A tricky case had just drawn to a close, and his task that morning was to call on his client's solicitors to make a final report on a matter dealing with a forged will.

"You needn't come along to Gresham, Gresham & Wallace with me," he told Tommy. "It's going to be a thoroughly dull conference, and you'll be better employed filing all the data on this case. When I get back we'll add the final report to the file, and then go off for a few days' well-earned holiday."

Tommy set to work, his mind filled with the prospect of lazing on the beach and forgetting, for a few days, that crime and criminals existed. Time went by swiftly, and he was surprised to discover that Hawke had been away over an hour when the phone rang.

"Perkins here — clerk to Gresham, Gresham & Wallace," announced a voice from the other end. "Can I speak to Mr Dixon Hawke?"

"He's at your office!" exclaimed Tommy.

"He most certainly is not," came the quick reply. "My employers have been waiting for him for more than an hour. The appointment was for ten o'clock, and it is now a quarter-past eleven."

"But he left here at twenty to ten, giving himself plenty of time to get to Tavistock Square for the appointment," protested Tommy.

"Perhaps he called in somewhere else first and has been delayed."

"I don't think so. He had no other appointments this morning," declared Tommy.

Nevertheless, he rang Chief Detective-Inspector McPhinney at Scotland Yard, only to learn that Hawke had not been seen there. Calls to various other possible places produced the same result, for nobody had seen the detective. He seemed to have disappeared from the moment he left Dover Street.

Tommy was growing anxious and considered ringing police stations and hospitals, in case his guv'nor had met with an accident, when the phone rang again.

"Is that young Tommy Burke?" queried a gay voice. "Jackdaw speaking — you know, the descendant of the little black bird that collected the cardinal's ring! Well, I've added a gem to my collection. I've got Dixon Hawke!"

"What do you mean?" demanded Tommy.

"What I say. You needn't look for Hawke any more. I've grabbed him, and I've got him sitting in my nest! Now, now, don't be rude, young fellow! I'm a peace-loving bird. I don't like violence."

The cheerful voice rattled on in a talkative manner, but Tommy was no longer listening. He had reached for the second telephone which stood on Hawke's desk and was whispering to the exchange. Keeping Jackdaw talking by interjecting a few remarks, he learned from the exchange that the crook was speaking from the public telephone at the bottom of Dover Street.

Putting the phone down quietly without ringing off, Tommy turned and ran. He scarcely expected the man to be still at the phone, no matter how quickly he moved, but when he got there the booth was occupied. A tall man, with a khaki trench-coat, collar turned up, and hat brim turned down, so that most of his face was hidden, was clattering the receiver rest up and down.

Tommy ventured into the adjoining call-box, keeping his face averted.

"But look here, exchange, the phone has suddenly gone dead," he heard the man shouting. "It's no good you telling me that they haven't rung off, or that I am still connected — the fact remains that I am getting no reply. I am a patient man, but — "

Abruptly he slammed down the receiver and swung out of the call-box. Tommy watched him hurry to where a large black saloon waited and slip in behind the wheel.

Luck certainly seemed to be with the young detective, for only a few paces away a taxi was standing with its flag up. He ran to it.

"Follow that car in front," he ordered, showing his card to the driver.

"Right-ho, Mr Burke. I'll stick to him like glue," replied the driver, and the taxi spurted forward after the Jackdaw's car.

Even as he moved, Tommy began to feel strange. A queer muzziness came over him, and it was as though the back of the taxi was full of mist. He looked vaguely about him. Somewhere he could hear a faint hissing, which he traced to a thin rubber pipe.

This protruded through the open crack of the glass partition separating him from the driver.

As he reached for it, the driver turned his head for a quick look, and Tommy heard him laugh harshly. A sneering voice reached the young detective.

"Smart, ain't you? But not as smart as Jackdaw. You did just what he figured you would!"

Then as Tommy tried to grab the pipe, his dizziness increased. He could smell sickly, sweet fumes, and the interior of the cab seemed to spin round him. He tried to shout, to bang on the window — anything to attract the attention of the people outside — but instead he crumpled up in an insensible heap on the floor.

Dixon Hawke returned to Dover Street to find McPhinney there.

"What on earth — " began the private detective, for Duncan McPhinney was staring at him as though he had seen a ghost.

"Is this a joke of Tommy's?" demanded the Scotland Yard detective crossly.

"He phoned me and said you'd gone missing. Then the phone exchange got in touch with me to say that he had rung them to trace a call made to this number from the public booth at the end of the road. He also wanted them to tell me that Jackdaw — that was the name — had collared you, and that he was after Jackdaw! Then you come strolling in as though nothing had happened! Where have you been?"

"At the office of Messrs Gresham, Gresham & Wallace, solicitors," replied Hawke. "I arrived there at five to ten, and left about fifteen minutes ago."

"B-but — " McPhinney had a look of utter surprise on his face.

"Tommy told me that their clerk phoned him saying that you hadn't arrived there, and that they'd waited more than an hour for you!"

Hawke wasted no time on argument. He phoned the solicitors, and the clerk promptly denied having made any call to the detective's flat that morning. The exchange then confirmed the call which had been received from Tommy. McPhinney and Hawke went to the public booth at the end of Dover Street, where they were lucky enough to find a loiterer who had seen Tommy enter a taxi shortly before 11.30. There the trail petered out.

"Jackdaw?" Hawke repeated the name on return to Dover Street.

He was showing McPhinney the impudent letter he had received that morning, when the phone rang again.

"A little black bird whispering in your ear, Hawke — a Jackdaw," announced a laughing voice. "Don't bother to get the exchange to tell you where I'm speaking from. It is a call-box at King's Cross, and I shall be away long before you can get over here. I am ready for your subscription, and I am afraid I find that the cost of feathering a nest has risen. I find I shall want five thousand pounds from you! All in pound notes, Hawke."

"And what makes you think I'll give you five thousand pounds?" demanded the detective.

"The fact that I am sure your assistant — the inimitable Tommy Burke — is worth all that to you," came the retort. "Tommy is in my nest, Hawke. He is not very comfortable, I am afraid, for he is tied to a bedstead and gagged. Also, if you don't do what I want, Hawke, he will be even less comfortable, for, although I hate violence, I need funds.

"My partner, a delightful gentleman known as Killer, also needs funds, and he doesn't share my dislike of violence. If I don't get that five thousand tonight, Killer proposes to chop off the right hand of your right-hand man, Hawke, and deliver it to you in a parcel.

"If we don't get the money tomorrow, you'll get his left hand; and so on, ad infinitum — or rather, until there is no Tommy left to post to you."

"You wouldn't dare!" snapped Hawke.

"My dear old sleuth, there's nothing I wouldn't dare, and there's nothing Killer wouldn't do, to collect funds, so you'd better listen hard to what I have to say."

Very curt now, the smooth voice instructed the detective to put the notes into a case and take them to the Wystbourne-Wellsea cross-roads on Wystbourne Common — about 20 miles south-east of London — at a quarter to twelve that night.

"Wait at the cross-roads until a car stops there. I shall switch my lights off and then on again," explained Jackdaw. "Incidentally, the car will be a London one, which Killer collected for our use this morning. You will come across to the car alone, Hawke, and hand the case with the notes in through the window.

"Just remember, Hawke, don't try any funny business!" Jackdaw's voice became grim. "Tommy will be in the back of the car, and Killer will be with him. If you have tipped off the police and tried to set a trap, or if you are not alone — in fact, if you try any trick — Tommy will be dead when you pick him up.

"On the other hand," added Jackdaw, laughing gaily again, "if you carry out instructions, and I find the notes in order, Tommy will be handed to you unharmed. We can both go our ways — you to work out how to trap me in the end, and me to collect the next subscription on my list."

"How do I know that you will hand Tommy over when you have the money?" demanded Hawke. "You have my promise."

"And what is that worth?"

"As much as yours! Look here, Hawke, be sensible and treat this as a business deal," urged Jackdaw, now serious again. "I have put over a fast one on you by grabbing Tommy. To get him back, you have to pay five thousand pounds. Why not pay up and make sure he is safe, then bother about catching me later?" Hawke actually laughed.

"You've got a cheek, Jackdaw!" he declared. Then to McPhinney's amazement, he added: "All right, I agree that we treat this as a business deal. I shall be at the rendezvous tonight, and I shall bring you five thousand pounds in one-pound notes.

"If you promise me that you will hand over Tommy safe and sound, I promise you that I will come alone, that I will not surround the area with police, or anything like that. I realise that it would be futile, for you will obviously have scouts out, and not show up if you see any unusual activity in such a lonely spot.

"Also, Jackdaw," went on the detective calmly, "I will come unarmed, and not try to make any attack to capture you single-handed when handing over the money. In fact, I propose to carry out your instructions to the letter, so mind you keep your part of the bargain."

"I will — I promise," replied Jackdaw, and laughed again.

"Have you gone quite mad?" demanded McPhinney, when Hawke turned from the phone. "I was listening in on the other receiver, and I heard it all. Look here, Hawke, you can't give in so tamely to such a demand.

"I know what Tommy means to you, but this chap is crazy. We can easily trap him."

"Not so easily," retorted Hawke. "You can be sure that the car will be covered, and any tricks we try to put over, although they might catch the crooks in the end, are likely to give the man called Killer time to finish Tommy off.

"No, Mac, I'm not crazy. I have been thinking hard during that conversation, and there is only one way of handling this matter."

"And that is by paying over five thousand pounds!"

"Exactly. I'd better get on to the bank and arrange to collect the money," replied Hawke.

"You'll mark the notes, of course."

"Quite unnecessary," was Hawke's astonishing reply.

Shortly after half-past eleven that night, Hawke was at the cross-roads on Wystbourne Common. It was a wild and lonely spot, with straight roads meeting miles from anywhere.

Hawke drew his car up at the roadside and sat waiting, a neat brown attache case on his lap. He had not long to wait before lights showed far in the distance down one of the roads and grew into the unmistakable shape of an ordinary car. It slithered to a stop in a dark patch of shadow. The lights were switched off; for a moment all was dark and still, then side and tail lights shone again.

Hawke quietly stepped from his car and walked across to the waiting car.

"Any dirty work afoot, Hawke?" queried Jackdaw's voice out of the darkness.

"No police hidden behind hedges, no weapons on me — I keep my promise," retorted the detective.

"I think you're telling the truth," came the reply. "We've kept a sharp watch around here. You haven't a bomb in that case, have you, so that it will blow up when I open it?"

"Do you want me to open it?" queried Hawke, peering into the car, where he could just make out the hunched figure of Jackdaw.

"Yes," decided the crook.

"Show me first that you've kept your part of the bargain!" ordered Hawke. "Where is Tommy?"

With a light laugh, Jackdaw reached over and turned a switch, and for an instant a faint light lit up the interior of the car.

Hawke saw that Tommy Burke was there, stretched out on the back seat. He was very pale, bound and gagged, and, crouching over him, was an enormous figure.

Before the light was extinguished, Hawke saw that the muzzle of a pistol was pressed against the side of his assistant's head.

"Are you going to open that case?" demanded Jackdaw.

For answer, Hawke opened up the case and handed over a packet of one-pound notes.

"Good! That's the stuff I want," decided Jackdaw, reaching out greedily and ruffling the notes, eyeing them carefully as he did so. Then he took the case with the rest of the money.

When he drew back, Hawke saw that he held a small automatic in his hand.

"You're a queer fish, Hawke," Jackdaw muttered. "I expected you to attack me then. That's why I was prepared."

"1 have kept my promise— I always do," snapped the detective. "Now, you keep yours."

"Certainly!" Jackdaw uttered a quick order, the door of the car opened, and Tommy Burke was rolled out into the road.

At the same moment the car leapt forward, accelerated and sped away.

"But, Guv'nor, you shouldn't have done it! " protested Tommy Burke. "1 mean, it's not just the five thousand quid, but letting a thug like that get away with it! I'd have found a way of escaping."

To the young detective's amazement, Hawke only chuckled drily, as he helped his assistant into the car.

"Aren't we going after them?" asked Tommy, when the car turned in the opposite direction to that taken by the crooks.

"We are going to Wystbourne Police Station, where I have an appointment," was Hawke's surprising reply.

Hawke's first question on arrival at Wystbourne Police Station only added to Tommy's bewilderment.

"Well, any peculiar motorists picked up yet, Sergeant?" queried the detective.

"Yes, sir," replied the local sergeant, looking as though he, too, was not quite sure if he was on his head or his heels. "Call just come from Wellsea. Two men picked up there in a car — neither in a fit state to drive. Both of 'em were rolling about, shrieking with laughter and waving handfuls of pound-notes."

"Got them!" exclaimed Hawke jubilantly.

Before he hurried to Wellsea Police Station, he put a call through to Chief Detective-Inspector McPhinney at Scotland Yard, with the result that that bewildered officer was soon on the scene.

McPhinney arrived to find two men under arrest. One was a smart, keen-faced young fellow, who frankly confessed that he called himself Jackdaw.

"His real name is Heaton-Smith, an ex-Commando, who has made the mistake of thinking he can make money more easily by crime than honest work," explained Hawke.

"A few years in jail for abduction and demanding money with menaces will show him the error of his ways. His real trouble is a perverted sense of humour."

Hawke turned to the other prisoner, whom McPhinney recognised instantly.

"Calls himself Killer," said Hawke "but records at the Yard have him down as Butch Horton, who has already done many stretches for robbery with violence. A thoroughly bad type. It will be good to have him out of circulation for a long time."

"It will," agreed McPhinney, "but look here, Hawke, this isn't good enough! How on earth did you catch them?"

For answer, Hawke pointed to the strange collection of one-pound notes which littered the table at the police station.

"I kept my promise — no police traps, no guns, not even marked money," he chuckled. "All I did was to impregnate those notes with a compound formed from nitrous oxide — the laughing gas used by dentists — intoxicating stuff, which makes those who inhale it quite light-headed.

"That's why I kept my head turned away when opening the case, although I knew it would take several minutes for the fumes from the notes to do their work," he told the crestfallen Jackdaw.

"It struck me that you like a laugh," concluded Hawke, "so I thought I'd give you one.

"But the last laugh is mine!"

—oOo—

# THE CASE OF The HUMAN TARGET

**At the far end of a strip of grass, between two lanes of trees, stood a large round target, raised off the ground. Two arrows were lodged in it, both close together, but not quite on the bull. At the other end of the long, narrow clearing, Sir Fenton Jowitt took aim and loosed off another arrow. The bow twanged, and the arrow sped through the air, to lodge right between the two already on the target.**

Sir Fenton dropped his bow.

"Tcha!" he exclaimed to himself. "I need more practice, lots of it, if I'm to beat Leslie."

He took out a cigarette. Before he lit it, he walked across to the tree nearest him and sat down at the base, where the roots formed a natural seat. Striking a match, he inhaled deeply on his cigarette. Then he glanced up at the sky and at his watch.

70

"Hmm ! It's getting too late now for any more."

He leaned back and gazed up into the sky, lazily blowing out a cloud of smoke. He was completely unaware of his danger. The noise made by countless birds covered up the twang of the bow amongst the trees halfway down the opposite side.

The well-aimed arrow flashed through the still air. Sir Fenton never saw it. He uttered a smothered sound as it tore right through his throat and bit into the tree behind. He was pinned upright when his heart stopped beating.

As Dixon Hawke and Tommy Burke entered Inspector Tindale's office in Witchford, the young country police officer looked up.

"Good-morning, Mr Hawke, and you, too, Tommy. I have just finished sorting out all the information you asked for that case of yours."

The telephone bell rang.

"Excuse me." Inspector Tindale took up the receiver. "Hello. Yes. Who? Where? Oh, yes, Severn Manor. Good gracious — dead? Yes, yes, I'll be right there."

Tindale turned his startled features upon his two visitors.

"That was Leslie Jowitt, Sir Fenton's nephew. He says they've just found the baronet dead — murdered, by the look of things." Hawke looked up.

"Sir Fenton? Why I knew him — irritable person, but very decent. Murdered, you say?"

"Would you care to come up?

You knew him — "

The door of the Georgian manor was opened by a white-faced butler. He took them at once into a pleasant room where a young man of medium height, but powerful build, sat writing at a desk.

"Inspector Tindale," announced the butler.

The young man rose, his face set and grave.

The policeman shook hands.

"I'm terribly sorry, Mr Jowitt. Where did this happen?"

"Down in the archery alley — that's what Uncle called it. It's a quiet spot down in the south-east corner of the estate."

He looked inquiringly at Hawke and Tommy, causing the inspector to apologise.

"I say, I beg your pardon. Mr Hawke — Dixon Hawke — and Tommy Burke."

Leslie Jowitt did not reply immediately. Instead, he swung round to a small table behind him and picked up a box which he had difficulty in opening. He turned back with a forced smile on his face as he held out the box of cigarettes.

"Smoke? This matter has turned me upside down. I've smoked half a dozen in the last half-hour. How d'you do?"

He shook hands.

"Was your uncle shot?" inquired Tindale.

"No," the nephew replied. "No, it's pretty horrible — he was stabbed through the throat with one of his own arrows."

"What?"

"An arrow, yes! It's — it's ghastly. You will want to go there straightaway. I've got a couple of gardeners down there. D'you mind if I stay here? I'm feeling pretty sick. James, our butler, will take you there."

"Before I go — when was he found?" asked Tindale.

"Just shortly before I phoned you. James and I found him — he must have lain there all night. It's terrible to think of it."

"Since last night! Why wasn't he missed before?"

"Well, you see, Uncle was a trifle eccentric, I suppose. He wandered in and out without warning. We just assumed last night that he had gone quietly up to bed. James, taking up his cup of tea this morning, found that my uncle's bed had not been slept in. I knew he'd gone out for a bit of archery practice about nine last night. I thought maybe he had taken ill. James and I went to the archery alley straight-away."

Inspector Tindale looked at Hawke.

"Sir Fenton was a keen member of the archery club. Mr Leslie is a member, too, and if I may say so, a very good shot. Well, if you will excuse us."

Inspector Tindale moved to the door, Hawke and Tommy following.

They were led by the butler for about a quarter of a mile until they came upon the long, narrow clearing. They entered it at the archer's end and could see at the other end the raised target holding the three arrows. All eyes, however, focussed upon the figure stretched out in the middle of the clearing at the shooting end. Two yards away his bow lay against a tree. All round the dead man lay trampled arrows, one or two were broken, and the quiver, which had held them, was crushed as if stamped upon.

Tindale, Hawke and Tommy strode towards the body.

"Crikey!" exclaimed the police officer, as he gazed down in horror.

From the baronet's throat protruded the shaft of an arrow.

"There's been some fight!" exclaimed Tindale.

"It has been quite a vicious fight, judging by the signs," Hawke agreed.

The three of them studied the evidence of the struggle which had apparently taken place.

There was a long scratch across the dead man's forehead and down one cheek. The man's clothing was dishevelled, and the collar and tie torn away from the neck.

Hawke went forward to make an examination. He lifted the man's head and looked at the back of the neck. He saw that the arrow had gone right through, although only less than a quarter-inch of its tip was showing. Tommy, watching his guv'nor, saw Hawke's brows knit together in a frown.

The inspector was walking round the body, his eyes studying the ground.

"Hullo, what's this?"

He bent down, then straightened up, holding the two pieces of a broken pipe which he had found by Sir Fenton's side. The pieces had been partially hidden by the arm. Tindale put them in his pocket.

"Well," he said with a sigh, "there's not much more we can do here. I think we'd better go back to the house and do some questioning. My photographer and two men should be there now, waiting instructions,"

Back in the manor house they found Leslie Jowitt more composed.

"Have you any idea as to who might have killed your uncle?" asked Tindale.

The nephew shook his head wearily.

"None at all. Uncle was not an easy man — irritable, you know. He wasn't exactly popular, but I really cannot think of anyone who would go as far as do this awful thing."

Tindale produced the broken pipe. He laid the two bits on the desk.

"Your uncle's. I found it." Jowitt stared at the pieces.

"But — but Uncle did not smoke a pipe."

The nephew's voice was raised in surprise.

"What — not your uncle's?" Tindale exclaimed. "Then it must be the killer's. I say — a clue. D'you know it — have you seen it before?"

Leslie Jowitt shook his head. "No, I can't help you there. Wait! Maybe James would know — he's quite a connoisseur of pipes."

In answer to a ring, the butler appeared, and Tindale pointed to the broken pipe.

"Any idea as to whom that belonged?"

The man looked quite startled for a moment, but, after studying the pieces for a while, he said slowly: "I think it is Mr Latimer's. At least, I've seen him with a pipe of that particular shape."

"D'you mean Lionel Latimer, the owner of the adjoining estate?" was Tindale's question.

The butler nodded.

"Who is this man Latimer?" asked Hawke.

"My uncle and Latimer have been enemies for years," explained Jowitt. "Many years ago, Uncle was in business, and on several occasions he outsmarted Latimer, and ever since then they have kept up a feud. Latimer bought the adjoining estate three years ago. Since then, he has given endless trouble over trumped-up disputes about boundary lines. Only two months ago I was just in time to stop a fight between them."

"It looks, then," broke in Inspector Tindale, "as if he came on the estate last night while your uncle was practising and quarrelled with him, resulting in the murder. Well, we must see Latimer straightaway."

Leslie Jowitt came along with the police and the detectives. It was a mile drive in Hawke's car, and Jowitt explained that Latimer stayed in the lodge, with one woman as a daily help.

As the car drew up, the door opened and a small, wizened woman looked out.

"Is Mr Latimer in?" asked the inspector.

The woman's eyes showed her surprise.

"Who? You lookin' for 'im, too? Dunno where 'e is."

"D'you mean to say you haven't seen him this morning?" asked Inspector Tindale.

" 'Is bed ain't bin slept in either," added the woman.

" 'Is gun's gorn, too, the one wot 'e shoots rabbits with."

"That means he's probably shooting down at the quarry," declared Leslie Jowitt.

"Out shooting rabbits — rather strange, is it not, considering he does not seem to have slept here last night?" Hawke pointed out.

Tindale was frowning.

"Fishy business, this. Perhaps it would be advisable to go along to this quarry. Something may have happened." He turned to the house-keeper. "Was he out during the evening?"

"Don't know, sir. I leave each night dead on six."

"I see. Well, how do we reach the quarry from here?" asked Hawke.

"It's not far. I'll show you the way," said Jowitt.

He took them through a wood until the trees thinned out, and they could see the deeply-cut sides of an old, disused quarry.

Hawke began to walk round, with Tommy close behind. Suddenly the lad's keen eyes spotted something ahead.

"What's that?" he shouted, and ran on.

When the others came up, they saw he was looking down at a double-barrelled gun, lying close to the edge of the quarry.

Tommy, Hawke and the inspector gazed down at the mass of boulders and the shrubbery, mixed with tall weeds and grass.

"Tommy," said Hawke, "do you think you can get down there, and — "

The youth needed no second bidding. He found a place where he could scramble down. Reaching the bottom safely, he made across to the spot just below where the three men stood.

Suddenly he stopped dead.

The burly figure of a man lay face down, almost hidden in the growth.

Tommy's discovery brought the others down. Inspector Tindale took one quick look.

"That's Latimer all right — dead as a door-nail. Possibly suicide after killing Sir Fenton Jowitt."

He examined the dead man.

"Hmm! Yes, there are plenty of signs of a fight similar to those on Sir Fenton. See his hands — they're covered with blood. That would be from Sir Fenton — unless — "

Hawke, who had made a quick examination, too, anticipated him.

"No, it's not his own, although his face is cut and there's a gash on his head. They did not bleed sufficiently to get his hands covered." Tindale decided he would phone for more of his men from the Manor House. He and Jowitt made their way there while Hawke and Tommy went to go back to their car. Instead of going to the car, however, Hawke drew his assistant in another direction.

"Tommy, I'm not really satisfied with things. Let's go along to the archery alley again."

When they reached it, they found that Sir Fenton's body had been removed. Hawke surveyed the scene in silence, leaning against the tree where the dead baronet had lain. After a moment or two, he looked down, and, seeing how the roots formed a seat, he went to sit down. As he bent, he stiffened suddenly.

"Tommy," he called, "see this dark mark on the bark of this tree. What d'you think it is?"

"It's reddish, Guv'nor. D'you think it could be blood? What's that sticking in the wood — like a bit of steel?"

Hawke took a look, and then got out his penknife to prise the tiny object out. He stared at it in the palm of his hand.

"Tommy, do you know what this is? It's the broken-off tip of an arrowhead. D'you see how it's stained — stained with blood?"

Tommy gasped.

"My lad," Hawke went on, "all along I've been puzzled by the arrow in Sir Fenton's throat. As you will realise, the shaft of an arrow does not afford much grip. It puzzled me how anyone could drive such a slim weapon through a throat by hand.

"Another thing — only the tip of the arrowhead showed out through the back of Sir Fenton's neck. Yet the wound at the back was wide enough to allow the whole arrowhead to emerge. I'm convinced that an arrow was fired from a bow at Sir Fenton.

"Here's my theory. Sir Fenton was shot at from somewhere over there amongst those trees while he was sitting here. Whoever killed him tore the arrow loose and destroyed it. Then he placed Sir Fenton not as far as the first arrow. After that, he made things look as if a fight had taken place.

"Now, Tommy, I've a job for you. I want you to go down into the quarry once more. When we were there I noticed that Latimer's breast pocket handkerchief was hanging out. Like his hands, it had plenty of blood on it. Fetch me that handkerchief, lad."

They met a little later at Hawke's car, still standing outside Latimer's lodge. Tommy handed over the handkerchief. Hawke looked at it, and then, folding it, placed it in an envelope.

Giving this to his assistant, he said: "Now, Tommy, the car's yours. Go up to London and take this handkerchief to Max, the chemist at Scotland Yard. Wait for his report and phone it to me at the inn."

Tommy raced away in the car, and Hawke slowly walked back to Inspector Tindale's office. The inspector was very satisfied and considered the case closed.

Hawke went back to the inn where he and Tommy were staying. He had lunch, and then sat in the lounge, reading.

It was not until close on five that Tommy's excited voice barked into his ear.

"Guv'nor! What d'you think? Max says it's not human blood at all. It's the blood of a rabbit."

"Splendid, my lad," cried Hawke, feeling quite pleased. "Come down in your own time. There's no hurry."

He made his way to the police station, but found that Inspector Tindale had been called away.

"That decides it," he said to himself, and immediately set off for the manor, where Leslie Jowitt was surprised to see him.

"I've one or two points to settle," said Hawke.

Jowitt seemed worried.

"But I thought Tindale had — "

"Well, he has more or less, but I have one most vital question to put," Hawke broke in.

He looked hard at Jowitt, until suddenly the man dropped his eyes.

"Why, Jowitt, did you kill your uncle?" he asked sternly.

The man started violently.

Without halting, Hawke went on to explain his theory, although he did not describe it to Jowitt as that.

"You killed him. Perhaps you killed Latimer, too, or would it be too much of a guess to say that you found him dead at the quarry? He looked the sort who might pass out any time — bad heart. I do know, however, that you pushed him over into the quarry and took his pipe, breaking it to fit in with the fake fight you arranged."

"Ridiculous!"

"Oh! Is it?"

"Yes; can you account for the blood on Latimer's hands — my uncle's!"

"Unless your uncle was a freak, it is difficult to understand how your uncle came to have rabbit's blood in his veins."

That shook Jowitt. He sank into a chair.

"Why do you suspect me?"

"Your archery ability mainly. Another thing — this morning, when Tindale was about to introduce me, you turned away quickly. It was unfortunate for you that I caught a glimpse of your face in the mirror. Your face showed fear. Why? Why should any innocent man be afraid of my name and presence?"

There was a silence, then Jowitt, his face white, exclaimed, "Nonsense! Nonsense! You're crazy!" Hawke looked grim.

"You won't admit your guilt? Very well. I will let the police know my evidence. My reputation is a good one, and you can be sure that further investigation will be carried out."

Hawke left straightaway and at the station he met Tindale just returning. The inspector was amazed, but very much impressed at Hawke's news.

"I thought I might shock him into a confession and thus make a short cut," ended Hawke. "I've failed, but he's very shaky. My bet is that he will try to run for it. Have his place watched from now on!"

At two in the morning watching policemen saw Jowitt sneak from the house with a suitcase.

He was badly shaken and made a confession. In charge of his uncle's investments, he had indulged in reckless speculation on his own behalf, and had lost more than half. He could not cover up his losses and planned to kill his uncle. Chance gave him what he thought was an ideal opportunity.

Out walking he had seen Latimer collapse at the quarry — dead from a heart attack. Knowing that within an hour his uncle would be in the archery alley, he quickly conceived the murder of his uncle, just as Hawke had worked it out.

—o0o—

# THE CASE OF *The* LOOSE WINDOW-BAR

**Dixon Hawke and his assistant, Tommy Burke, were returning from a stroll after breakfast when the occupant of a black car leaned out and waved to them.**

"It's Inspector Baxter," said Hawke, "and, judging by the fact that he's got the divisional surgeon and the Yard photographer with him, he's on a murder case."

Detective-Inspector Baxter confirmed Hawke's surmise within the next minute.

"It happened right here on your doorstep in Dover Street, Hawke. He's a bookie named Clifton, and he seems to have got in the way of a burglar."

"H'm. Burglars don't go in for murder as a rule."

"This one did. Are you interested?"

"I'll give it the once-over. What's the address?"

Baxter pointed. "Right here. Planet Buildings. The shops and offices are on the ground floor, the flats are above. Clifton's is an office flat, number six. I can't give you a lift, I'm afraid."

"All right, we'll walk along."

An entrance between shops led on to a wide hall, where a big, black-haired man waited at the open door to flat number six.

"I'm Mr Clifton's clerk. My name's Torpey. You'll excuse me, but I'm quite upset."

The man looked hard-boiled, but there was little doubt that he had taken his employer's death badly. His face was pale and he looked thoroughly shaken.

"Inspector Baxter is here, sir. No doubt you will wish to join him."

Hawke and Tommy Burke went through a well-furnished office with a counter and glazed screens to find a couple of girls standing, as if uncertain whether to start work or not. One of them was crying quietly.

"He was a good employer," said Torpey. "One of the best."

He opened a door.

"He slept on the premises and his bedroom leads off from the office. This is his private office. The police are in there. I won't come with you, if you don't mind."

The detectives went in and the first thing they saw was an open safe. The next thing they noticed was a little dark-haired man in pyjamas stretched out on the floor. The front of his head had been smashed in, and the divisional surgeon was kneeling beside his body.

"He's been dead only a short time," he said. "Two or three hours at most." He flexed the dead man's fingers.

"Rigor mortis has not yet set in, as you can see. Death occurred, I imagine, at five or six this morning."

He scribbled in a notebook.

" ... fracture of occipital frontal... blunt instrument... death instantaneous... no sign of a struggle..." "That's the lot, I think." He got up.

"How are you, Hawke? Not your sort of case, I should say. Pretty obvious." He popped his notebook into a brief-case and turned to the police officer. "Do you mind if I take the car?"

When he had gone, and while the photographer was stringing out high-power lamps for Record exposures, Inspector Baxter took over.

"That's Clifton's bedroom door, just next the safe. He heard the burglar at work, came out, caught him red-handed and got — what you see."

Hawke shrugged his shoulders.

"Now what's the matter, Hawke? You're not going to say that this is not as simple as it looks?"

"N — no. I wonder why the body is on the other side of the room instead of against the bedroom door."

Baxter grinned.

"I don't know. Does it matter? Let's say he was making for his telephone on his desk there."

"That won't do either. He would have been struck on the back of the head then."

"All right. He was threatened and he backed away."

"That won't do either. He would have thrown up his arms to protect himself and his arms are uninjured."

"I never knew anybody like you for raising difficulties. What's your theory?"

"I haven't one. I just wondered — that's all. Let's go further. How do you know there was a burglary?"

"Well, there is an open safe, which was opened by an expert, and I know who the expert was."

"You do, eh?"

"So will you, Hawke, so will you. He has all but signed his name to it. See those bent drills on the floor? See those half-smoked cigarettes? See those dusters he's had to tie round his feet?"

Hawke was silent and his face showed his disappointment. The methods of leading cracksmen were as well known to him as they were to Baxter. This cracksman, who, as the police officer had said, had all but signed his name to the job, was one for whom Hawke felt a certain responsibility.

Hawke's mind went back to the day, two years before, when he could have put this man behind bars and had not done so. He heard again the man's pleading voice,

"I swear to you, Mr 'Awke, that I will go straight." He had believed this and had given the crook another chance. It might almost be said that he, Dixon Hawke, had been responsible for the murder.

Tommy Burke, who knew what had happened, was aware of what was passing through his employer's mind.

"Bossicks Oily is no killer," he said in a low voice.

Baxter jerked round in surprise.

"You know, then? I should have said you were right — but for this."

He pointed to the dead man.

Hawke played for time.

"How did Oily get in?"

"Easy. As you see, there are iron grilles over the windows, and one of them has a loose bar. Oily found it."

"H'm, there has been a burglary and there has been a killing, so you assume that the burglar is also the killer."

"Good heavens, Hawke, what other conclusion can you come to? Don't ask me to believe that one man cracked the safe, and, by a coincidence, for it could be nothing else, another man at the same time murdered Clifton. The common-sense, obvious explanation is that the man who cracked the safe killed Clifton, and what is common-sense and obvious is good enough for me."

Hawke turned to Tommy Burke.

"Inspector Baxter knows the answer to everything. He makes the whole thing sound so darned simple that I mistrust his conclusions, but probably I'm wrong. We'll just have a look round, then go back to the consulting room."

Mrs Benvie tapped on the door of the consulting room. "A person to see you, sir."

Dixon Hawke looked up with a smile.

"Is it a man or a woman?"

"It's a man," said Mrs Benvie.

"What is his name?"

"Oily, Bossicks Oily. He said you would know him."

Tommy Burke, who was busy at the filing cabinets, turned to exchange a surprised glance with his employer. Bossicks Oily, the man wanted for murder, had come to see Hawke of his own free will!

"Show Oily up, please, Mrs Benvie. I shall be interested to have a word with him."

Bossicks Oily, a thin, grey, quiet little man, slipped into the consulting room and stood twisting his cap in his hand, smiling apologetically at Dixon Hawke.

The detective looked at him coldly.

"Well, what is it?"

Oily soon told Hawke his story.

"Mr 'Awke, I told you as I wouldn't never do another job and I done another job; that's right, ain't it? And you're finished with me, ain't you? And they're after me for murder?"

"How do you know?"

"Seen it in the papers. Course, they don't say it's me what they're after, but as soon as I seen that you was on the job, to say nothing of Inspector Baxter, I knew me number was up. I knew it was me."

"Well?"

"Look, Mr 'Awke, you know my missus, don't you? She came and saw you when I was in trouble before. Well, she's 'ad a bit of an accident, 'ad her leg broke, and she's in the 'orspital, see? And me going and seeing 'er there, and them being so kind to 'er in every way, I says blow me if I wouldn't like to give them a donation."

"Oily, you're a scoundrel."

"Yes, Mr 'Awke, I am. Well, as I was saying — "

"And you talk too much."

"I got to explain, ain't I?"

"What is there to explain? You were at Clifton's place last night, he surprised you and — "

"Ain't I telling you," Oily almost shouted. "Ain't I telling you? I ain't never seen Clifton in my life. Look, Mr 'Awke, I'll cut it short. I was tipped off this was money for jam, and I went to do it, but I never got any money for I was disturbed and made a bolt for it. I suppose Clifton 'eard me, but I got away before 'e came out of 'is bed-room. I 'ad started on the job, but I was just about to open the safe when old Clifton 'eard me."

"Who tipped you off?" asked the detective.

"Well, it wasn't a tip-off really, it was a man in a pub talking. There's a lot of money, 'e says, in that there safe on a Sunday night. As for the bars outside the windows, 'e says, one of them's loose. It's a sin and a shame, 'e says, why people ain't more careful."

"How did you know what safe he was talking about?"

"Well, 'e says Clifton, then 'e says a well-known bookie, so I only 'ad to put two and two together. See what I mean?"

"Yes, I do see what you mean. What was the man like?"

"The bloke I 'eard talking? Well, I don't know. To tell you the truth, I never really saw him."

"H'm, rather unconvincing. What time did you do the job?"

"It might 'ave been 'alf-past eleven at night."

"Or it might have been five o'clock in the morning?"

"No, I was at the 'orspital from midnight on. My old woman — "

"Can you prove that?"

"Lor' love a duck, yes, the 'ouse surgeon was there most of the time. My old woman — "

"Listen, Oily, I've got an idea that what you've been telling me is true. No, don't interrupt! My advice to you is, give yourself up."

"What, me? Give meself up?

"That's my advice. What is more, I am about to phone the police that you have been here. Now go, and I'll do my best for you."

When Oily had gone, Hawke had a word with Inspector Baxter on the phone.

"Ah, Baxter, Oily has been to see me. Yes, Bossicks Oily, and I have advised him to give himself up. He will plead guilty."

"What!"

"To attempted burglary."

"Why only attempted burglary?"

"I'll answer that later."

"And what about the murder?"

"I don't think he did it."

"Well, if circumstantial evidence counts for anything — "

"In this case, I don't think it does."

When Hawke hung up after talking to Inspector Baxter, Tommy Burke asked a question.

"What makes you so sure, Guv'nor, that Bossicks Oily didn't murder Clifton?"

"The loose bar and the empty safe."

Tommy grinned and waited for more.

"One important fact is," Hawke went on, "that Oily knew there was a loose bar in the grille which protected the windows. How did he know?"

"He found it out when he looked the job over."

"That won't do. It was impossible to see, even in daylight, that the bar was loose, and, remember, with occupied flats all around it was impossible to use a file or a hacksaw. But for that loose bar, the job was out of the question. Do you see, my lad, what I am trying to establish? When Oily says he was informed of the loose bar, he is almost certainly telling the truth."

"If he is, Guv'nor, where does that get us?"

"It proves that someone wanted Clifton to be robbed, or, at any rate, wanted his safe broken open. Mind you, that somebody knew a lot about Clifton's flat — he even knew about the loose bar. Let me tell you something else; that bar had been made loose — not at the time of the burglary, the file marks were rusted over — but recently."

"But you said just now that nobody could use a file or a hacksaw on those bars without being detected."

"I should have qualified that statement; nobody outside the building, I should have said. Anybody inside the building could have done it, a little at a time, without causing the least suspicion.

"The open safe is another important factor," Hawke went on. "Bossicks Oily was disturbed. We can believe him there, for he left his trade-mark in the bent drills, half -smoked cigarettes and the dusters. Who opened the safe and took the large sum supposed to be in it? I say 'supposed,' for it could have been removed previous to the attempted burglary, or it is possible that it was never put in. Who is the person we could suspect of having done all these things?"

"You mean Torpey?"

"I haven't got that far, but I'm going to see Torpey now. I'm going to put my theory to him and watch his reaction. After that I shall know."

When Torpey arrived at Clifton's flat to keep his appointment with Dixon Hawke, he found the detective already there. Hawke explained that the hall porter had let him in, for he was alone in Clifton's office. Even the dead body of its late owner had been taken away, and only a chalk outline on the carpet remained to show where he had lain.

Hawke went straight to the point. "I asked you to see me, Torpey, because I want your opinion of a theory which I have as to the cause of your employer's murder."

Torpey looked surprised.

"I thought there was no doubt about that."

Hawke took a chair and motioned Torpey to another.

"At any rate," he said mildly, "there's no harm in theorising, is there?"

He lighted a pipe and puffed until it was going to his satisfaction.

"Let us suppose," he said, "and, mind you, this is sheer conjecture, that you yourself were responsible for putting the day's takings into Clifton's safe on a Saturday night. You thought to yourself — if one week-end I put Clifton's money into my pocket instead of putting it into the safe, and there was a burglary and the safe was opened, no one would suspect that I had the money. You could have thought that, don't you think?"

"I could have, but — "

"But, of course, before you could have a burglary, you had to make the burglary possible by filing away at one of those bars."

Torpey stood up. His face was deep red and he was choking with rage.

"If you think," he cried, "that I am going to listen to any more of these absurd accusations — "

Hawke shook his head with a smile. "I'm not accusing you, Mr Torpey, only theorising. You may as well hear the rest of it."

Torpey grunted something and relapsed into his chair, his hands gripping the arm.

"Well, let us say you have some knowledge of the underworld and you let it be known that there is easy money to be had by burgling this place on Sunday night. Sure enough, Bossicks Oily falls into your trap and at half-past eleven on Sunday night he breaks in here. Before he can get the safe open he is disturbed by Clifton, but he gets away in time."

Hawke took his pipe out of his mouth and leaned forward.

"That's where your plans went wrong, Torpey. As Clifton could see that the safe hadn't been opened he did not bother to check up on its contents. Meaning to report the attempted burglary in the morning, lie went back to sleep."

"How much more of this is there?" cried Torpey.

"Wait, Torpey! I'm almost finished. In the morning Clifton woke up between five and six and began to have misgivings about the burglary. Unfortunately, he got up to check the contents of the safe. When he found it was empty he knew you must have failed to put the money in the safe, because the burglar had never opened it and you are the only other one who knows the combination.

"He phoned you to come over on some pretext concerning the robbery. You arrived, quite unsuspecting, thinking that your plan had gone down well. Clifton, however, accused you of keeping the money and you snatched up the paper¬weight. You crashed it down on his head, wiped the fingerprints off and went back to your flat. Then you came in here at nine in the morning as if nothing had happened."

Torpey stood up.

"You're clever, Mr Hawke," he said, "but you've made one mistake — were alone here and I can kill you, the same as I killed Clifton."

He hurled himself forward and Hawke rose to meet him with a terrific right-hand punch which smacked home on the point of the big man's jaw.

Torpey collapsed in a heap. He was right out.

Hawke rubbed his knuckles.

"You can come in now," he said. The bedroom door had been partly open. Now it opened farther and Tommy Burke came in.

"You've taken down the confession, my lad?"

"Sure, Guv'nor."

"Help me to tie this fellow's hands. Then we'll phone Baxter and give him the solution to his murder."

—oOo—

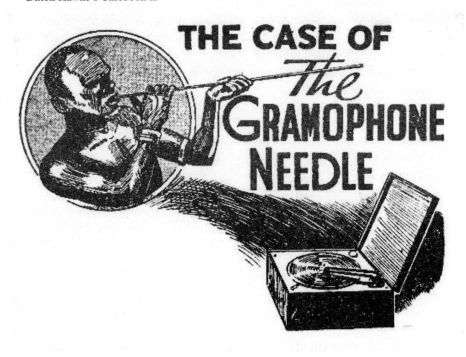

# THE CASE OF *The* GRAMOPHONE NEEDLE

"**Eleven o'clock,**" **said Dixon Hawke, glancing at his wrist watch.** "**It's time we were moving, Tommy. Dr Sykes needs his sleep, if we don't.**"

"Nonsense. Glad to have had you," laughed the doctor, as his visitors rose to go. "Well, good-night," said Hawke, as they reached the front door. "Hello, what's the matter with the bus?"

He nodded towards a double-decker corporation bus, which was approaching. The bus was being driven very slowly and close to the kerb. At the rear, the conductor, hanging on to the platform rail, was leaning well out and flashing a torch towards the name plates on the garden gates.

"Right, Bill, this is it," they heard him shout, and the bus came to a stop.

The conductor jumped out, opened the gate and ran up the short drive.

"Dr Sykes?" he inquired. "That's me," replied the doctor.

"A feller 'as collapsed on the top deck, Doctor. 'E seems to be in a bad way, an' knowing there was a doctor 'ereabouts, I didn't waste time trying to revive 'im myself. Would you look at 'im, please?"

The conductor led the way to the top deck of the bus, while Hawke and Tommy followed Dr Sykes. Slumped in a heap right at the front of the bus was the figure of a man, his attitude suggesting that he had slipped forward from the seat. Lifting the man up on to the seat, Hawke and the conductor held the helpless figure upright whilst Dr Sykes made his examination.

"Too late, he's gone," said the doctor, tapping the region of his heart significantly. "I wonder how he came by this?"

He indicated a wound at the angle of the left jawbone, and, from this, blood had flowed. The body was that of a middle-aged man of medium height, with a slim, yet well-built figure and deeply-tanned features. Wiping the blood from the cheek, Dr Sykes exposed a tiny puncture on the jaw.

"Only a scratch, probably cut himself as he fell, he said. "Well, we'll have to get the police on the job. I'd better phone now."

"I'll go," volunteered Tommy. "I'll get in touch with Lawton, Guv'nor. I know the number."

He was referring to Superintendent Lawton, of the Primborough City Police, with whom Hawke and his assistant had been engaged on a forgery case in the Midland town. The pair had called on Dr Sykes, an old friend, prior to returning to London next day.

Propping the victim in the corner of the seat beside the wide-open window, Hawke bent to pick up a briar pipe, which he had noticed lying on the floor. As he did so, his attention was attracted by a glittering object under the seat and, flashing his torch, Hawke saw that the thing was a gramophone needle. He was about to pick it up when he noticed that the point was stained a deep red, and, producing a pair of tweezers, he carefully lifted the needle, placing it on his handkerchief.

"This may explain the cut on his cheek," he said. "There's blood on it, as you can see and — " He stopped suddenly and felt in a waistcoat pocket. Pulling out a small magnifying glass, he examined the needle intently, then handed the glass to the doctor.

"What d'you make of it?" he asked.

"It's blood all right," agreed the doctor. "There's some other substance underneath, not unlike tar."

"It isn't tar," said Hawke. "Unless I'm wrong, this man did not succumb to a heart attack — he was murdered. If that substance under the blood is curare, as I strongly suspect, it explains the presence of the needle and the puncture on his jaw."

Dr Sykes looked startled, but his voice, when he spoke, expressed his complete agreement.

"I believe you're right, Hawke. At any rate, your theory would explain features in the case which had me puzzled. As it happens, I've had experience in curare poisoning, and the symptoms fit exactly. I must confess the idea never struck me, though."

Hawke knew that Dr Sykes had travelled extensively in his younger days.

"It's not the sort of thing you'd look for in this country," he replied. Then, turning to the conductor, whose name was Bert Hodge, he asked: "Do you know this man, and can you say what happened?"

Hodge shook his head to the first question, and explained that he had been standing on the platform at the foot of the stairs when he heard a thud up above. He did not quite know what made him go up, for noises were common enough, but he had gone up to find the man lying as they had seen him. "Then he is a perfect stranger?" asked Hawke.

"Well, not exactly, sir. I know 'im well by sight. One of our regulars, 'e is. Travels every day by bus, and lives in Linden Avenue, two stops farther on. Dunno 'is name, though."

At that moment a police car drew up, and the burly figure of Superintendent Lawton got out, and his heavy tread was heard on the stairs. The superintendent was surprised to see Hawke, but the detective explained matters, and Lawton's face showed his amazement when Hawke handed over the gramophone needle and outlined his theory.

"Gosh!" he exclaimed. "It's a good job you're still here, Mr Hawke. I'll be needing your help before I'm through, if what you think is right. Now, let's have a look at him." He moved towards the body.

"Why, that's Phil Grayson, of Grayson & Manders, the export people," he burst out. "He only came home from South America about six months ago. How did it happen?"

Bert repeated his story, and added that Grayson, with a companion had boarded the 10.20 bus at the City Hall. The two men had travelled with the same bus all week — it was now Thursday — and had sat in the same seat each night. The dead man appeared to have a liking for the top front seat, and usually contrived to get it.

"Where were you when you heard him fall?"

"We were just rounding the sharp bend at Thorpe Spinney when I 'eard the thud. 'Bout five minutes ago, it was."

"Huh!" growled Lawton, and explained to Hawke that Thorpe Spinney lay about a quarter of a mile away towards the town.

"How about the other man?" asked Hawke, and Hodge told that the man had got off at Tolford Corner, about half a mile back. He had heard the man shout, "Goodnight, Phil," as he descended the stairs, and had heard Grayson reply, "Cheerio, Frank." After Tolford Comer, there was only the victim on the top deck.

"I expect the chap with him would be Frank Foyle," said Lawton. "I know the two are friends and play snooker in the Rotarian Club several nights a week. As it happens, I'm a member myself. However, we can soon find out. Foyle lives in Morton Crescent, so I'll send Jackson round to let him know what's happened."

"If he doesn't know already," said Hawke, and the superintendent looked troubled.

"I see what you mean; he was the last person known to see Grayson alive," he replied slowly. "Still, I can't — "

He hesitated, and Hawke cut in. "You know Foyle well?"

"Not intimately, but he belongs to a well-known local family. He is a decent fellow, as far as I know, but, of course, you never can tell. We'll have this analysed right away, anyhow," he went on, placing the gramophone needle in an envelope.

He instructed the police driver to pick up Foyle and bring him along.

Leaving his sergeant to superintend the removal of the body to the waiting ambulance, he joined Hawke and Tommy in Dr Sykes' sitting-room.

"I say, Foyle couldn't have done it." Lawton broke a short silence. "Foyle got out at Tolford Corner, and according to the conductor, Grayson was alive then. No, Mr Hawke, it must have been someone hiding in the spinney."

"He must have climbed a tree, then," said Hawke drily. "The needle went in downwards, as Dr Sykes can testify." The doctor nodded, and Hawke went on. "In any case, it doesn't follow that Grayson was killed at the spinney. The body may have fallen when the bus rounded that sharp bend the conductor spoke of."

"True enough," agreed Lawton. "Ah, here's Foyle now, I think," he added as a car came to a halt outside.

A minute later, Frank Foyle entered the room. Foyle was a big, bluff man, of middle age, whose normally cheerful countenance now wore a look of concern.

"This is terrible news, Superintendent," he greeted Lawton.

"You can throw no light on the matter?" asked Lawton. "You saw no one acting suspiciously on the bus? But then, I understand there was no one else save yourself and Grayson on the top deck by the time you reached Tolford."

"That's right. It's a quiet bus — too late for the early birds, and not late enough for the young ones. That's why we like it — liked it," he amended with a shudder. "There was a courting couple in the back seat, but they got out a couple of stops before me, and after that, there was no one but Phil and I up top." He stopped as a sudden thought struck him, and his features paled as he faced the party. "Good God! I was the last to see him alive. You think I — "

He stopped again and shrugged his shoulders helplessly.

"It's an awkward position," said Hawke quietly. "Grayson was your best friend?"

"He was my best pal," replied the other simply.

"Can you think of anyone who might have a grudge against Grayson?" asked Hawke, "You'd better keep nothing back, however trivial it may seem, Mr Foyle. Remember, this is murder."

Foyle nodded. "I know, but I'd hate to create a false impression, and what I have to say may have no bearing on the case at all. It's simply that I know Phil has been pretty worried of late. He was in South America for twenty years as the firm's representative there, whilst Manders, his partner, ran the business here. Old Manders died two years ago and was succeeded by his son, George. Phil has told me that young Manders has let the business go to the dogs at this end, and that's what brought Phil home.

"He had a row with Manders last week, and had decided to split up the partnership as a result.

"That's not to say Manders had any hand in this," Foyle went on. "I don't like the fellow. He's a rank outsider to my mind. But murder, that's different. Anyhow, he couldn't have done it."

"Why not?" asked Lawton. "He's been going the pace of late, and we've had trouble with the man more than once. He drinks a lot, and he's a very bad drunk."

"That's just it," said Foyle. "Manders has been staying at the Blue Boar, at Tolford Corner, since he sold up his house some time ago, and my next-door neighbour was telling me, when I got home, that the man was dead drunk tonight. He had to be helped to his room about nine o'clock, so you can rule him out, Superintendent."

"Looks like it at that rate," said Lawton.

"What d'you make of his story, Mr Hawke?" the superintendent asked, when Foyle had gone, having undertaken the disagreeable task of breaking the news to Grayson's relatives. "He seemed straight enough."

"I think so, Lawton, and there seems to be no earthly reason why Foyle should want to murder his best friend. As to the story regarding Manders, that can easily be verified."

He nodded towards the telephone, and Lawton was quickly in touch with the Blue Boar Inn.

"True enough," he said, replacing the receiver. "Manders is in his bed, snoring like a hog right now. He's been in that state for a couple of hours, too."

"His story can wait till morning anyhow," continued Lawton, and a few minutes later the three took leave of Dr Sykes.

Hawke and Tommy accompanied Lawton to police headquarters before returning to their hotel, and learned that the gramophone needle had indeed been dipped in curare. Having arranged to meet Lawton next morning, the Dover Street pair made for bed.

Little after nine o'clock next morning, the three were shown into George Manders' office, and Hawke took an instant dislike to the man. Manders was a stout, flabby fellow though still in his early thirties. His face was flushed, and his breath smelt of alcohol even at that early hour. Through the open window of the office came the sound of an electric drill, and Manders closed the window with a bang.

"Deuced racket; I never could abide noise," he muttered thickly, then, turning to Lawton, he went on in contemptuous tones: "I suppose it's on account of my late lamented partner you've called, eh? They're saying he's been murdered, and maybe you think I did it? Well, think what you like."

"The death of your partner has not, apparently, overwhelmed you with grief," said Hawke icily.

"I'll say it hasn't," sneered the other. "I never did like him, and I don't care who knows it. I'm shedding no tears over Grayson, the slave-driver." He peered at Hawke and continued offensively: "And who the devil might you be? You're not one of the local flatfoots, I know that."

Lawton introduced the detective in brusque, angry tones, and asked the man to keep a civil tongue in his head. Manders laughed unpleasantly.

"I don't like your tone, and I'll ask you to mind your step, Mr Manders," snapped Lawton.

The other eyed him sneeringly, then, turning, he staggered to a cupboard, from which he produced a bottle and glass. Pouring himself a stiff glass of whisky, he downed this at a gulp before replying drunkenly: "You can threaten me, but you can't make me say anything. Get out of here!"

He flopped into his desk chair, and Lawton was about to reply angrily, when he caught Hawke's headshake and, shrugging his shoulders, led the way outside.

"He's a bad lot, but you'll agree he can have nothing to do with the killing. If he had, I reckon he'd have adopted a different line than trying to put our backs up from the start."

"You'd imagine so," agreed Hawke. "Yet the fellow may be playing a cunning game. He's certainly not nearly so drunk as he makes out to be. His hand, as he filled that glass of whisky, was as steady as a rock, when, by all accounts, he should be having a hefty hangover."

"The fellow riled me, and I didn't notice," confessed Lawton, "but, by Jove, if you think there's any purpose in investigating his alibi, let's get going. Nothing would give me greater pleasure than — " He stopped and shrugged his shoulders. "No use, though, Mr Hawke. There's no doubt that he was near the scene of the crime, but he wasn't on the bus, we're sure of that. However, we'll run out to Tolford Corner now. We've got to get a statement anyhow."

A ten-minute run in a fast police car brought them to that part of the straggling town known as Tolford Corner. The Blue Boar stood right on the corner of a busy cross-roads, and the roadway and pavement in front of the inn were very narrow.

Ben Yorke, the landlord, confirmed that Manders had stayed there for the past two months. A bad-tempered gent he was, too, with a nasty tongue when drunk, and he had seldom been completely sober since his arrival. Manders had sworn horribly when offered a front room, saying he could not stand the noise of the traffic, but he had taken the room and had said nothing further till that very morning, when he had asked for a change on account of the din.

"Though he couldn't have been bothered last night," said Ben. "Blotto, 'e was. 'E didn't get it in my bar, neither. 'E was soused when 'e came 'ome."

On the pretext that he might take the room himself, Dixon Hawke was shown up to a bedroom on the first floor, overlooking the street. The landlord was called below, and Hawke moved to the wide-open window and looked down on the stream of traffic. He was about to turn away when a double-decker bus drew up outside, and the detective gripped Lawton's arm.

"Look there!" he said.

Lawton looked through the window to see, within a few feet of him, the perspiring features of a stout lady who sat in the top left-hand seat on the upper deck.

"See what I mean?" asked Hawke, and, as the other shook his head: "Manders could have done it. As you see, there's little more than four feet separating us from that lady who is occupying the same seat as Grayson sat in last night. The conditions are similar, too. This window is open, the bus window is open. All he needed was a hollow pipe or an airgun. The needle could be shot — or even blown — that distance, and he could hardly miss. Remember, the least little prick with that deadly stuff would be fatal. Remember, also, it was pretty dark by eleven last night."

"It's possible, Mr Hawke. It's a plausible theory, but how was he to know the bus would stop here?"

"He knew Foyle got out here," retorted Hawke, "even apart from the traffic lights. And you may be sure he knows of Foyle's and Grayson's habits, and Grayson's fondness for that particular seat. No doubt the nearness of the traffic outside gave him the idea. He hates noise, yet he's kept this room for two months, and it must be the noisest room in the place."

"You've got something there, Mr Hawke. But how on earth are we going to prove it, assuming you are right?"

As Hawke looked across the street he noticed a sign opposite. "J. Fortescue, Photographer," he read, and suddenly he laughed aloud.

"I think I know of a way of proving or disproving my theory, Lawton," he said, and explained what he had in mind.

"It's a great idea, Guv'nor," said Tommy, and departed in the direction of the photographer's, while Hawke dialled Manders.

It was over an hour later that George Manders, after much swearing and blustering, was coaxed into a seat at the open window of the room he had lately occupied, and Hawke outlined his theory as to how the crime might have been accomplished.

"So you see, Mr Manders," Hawke ended, "it would be possible, even simple, for someone to sit here and shoot — or even blow — a gramophone needle that short distance."

"You shouldn't be a detective," sneered Manders. "You ought to take up novel writing. I never heard such a far-fetched yarn!" He laughed loudly, then continued in cunning tones: "But supposing you were right. How do you expect to prove it? You never thought of that, did you, Mr Smart Alec?"

"Oh, yes, I did!" snapped Hawke. "It looked pretty hopeless until I had an amazing stroke of luck."

He waved his arm across the street. "You see Mr Fortescue's premises? Perhaps you don't know Mr Fortescue, but I assure you, he's an excellent photographer. As luck would have it, Mr Fortescue was experimenting with a new type of night lens last night. The negative shows quite clearly a double-decker bus leaving the front of this inn, and a man leaning from this very window.

In his hand he — " He got no further. With a wild oath, Manders sprang to his feet. "It's a lie!" he yelled. "There's no such photograph!"

"Isn't there?" snapped Hawke. "The negative, Tommy, please," he added, turning to the youngster.

Tommy produced a strip of celluloid from his pocket and was handing it over when Manders jumped forward, snatched the negative from Tommy's hand and tore it in pieces.

"So much for your blasted proof," he began furiously, then stopped suddenly, as he realised he had given himself away completely.

"That won't help you," said Hawke icily. "The photographic experts can easily piece the thing together again, but it would be interesting to know why you found it necessary to do that!"

The man's truculence dropped from him. He subsided like a pricked balloon and, under Hawke's remorseless cross-examination, blurted out a confession. The open window and the sight of a bus so near had given him the idea, and he had simply waited for a favourable opportunity. Grayson had presented his father with a poison arrow on a previous visit home, and from this Manders had extracted the curare. Ever since his father's death, two years earlier, he had been living a fast life, and had already swindled his partner out of thousands of pounds. He dared not face the forthcoming audit.

"That was a lucky break," said Lawton, when the party were back in his office and Manders in a cell. "I'll soon have this negative put right." He spread out the pieces on his desk, then started in surprise as Hawke chimed in: "I shouldn't bother, Lawton. That's only an ordinary portrait study you've got there."

"Then you were bluffing? The story of the negative was pure invention?"

"Pure invention," smiled Hawke. "But it was necessary to find some way of trapping him into an admission, and necessity, as you know, is the mother of invention."

"Well, I'll be jiggered," said Lawton.

—o0o—

# THE CASE OF

## The THREE DOUBLES

Zachariah Cohen, the financier, turned in a startled manner from the open safe and his gaunt face suddenly became as white as the papers which he held. For a moment his free hand moved towards his pocket, then he recognised the intruder and gave a sigh of relief.

"Williams, I thought you had gone home at the usual time."

The man who had entered was far younger than Cohen, but about the same build. Justin Williams had been private secretary to Zachariah Cohen for the past seven years, during which time the financier had had countless brilliant successes on the stock exchanges of different countries. Now Williams looked grave and grim as he set a brief-case on the desk and took in the scene before him.

"I had a feeling that things were not right with you, sir, and that you might need my help."

Zachariah Cohen suddenly sank down into the nearest chair and covered his face with his hands. The papers which he dropped were bearer bonds. On the desk beside him were wads of bank-notes and an open bag. It was obvious that he had been clearing out the safe and putting everything readily negotiable in the bag.

He groaned aloud.

"It's no use deceiving you, Williams. You know the state of my affairs. You know that the day of reckoning has come and that I am ruined. You,

94

better than any man, know how I used the capital of one company to pay the dividends of the other, and how they were bound to catch up with me in the end. I'm beaten, Williams, and I was getting out. I won't pretend to you any longer. I stayed behind tonight to scrape together all I could, but I wasn't forgetting you, Williams, I swear it."

He fumbled amongst the papers on the desk and pushed across a sealed envelope with Williams' name upon it.

"You'll find £5000 in there, something to repay you for sticking by me all these years. Now you must let me take the rest and go."

"But how will you leave the country, sir? There may be a warrant out for your arrest even now. I heard that Dixon Hawke had been asked by Scotland Yard to make certain inquiries, and — "

"Yes, it was because I heard Hawke was on the trail that I decided to flee. There is a chartered aeroplane at Hendon. It will be ready for me at midnight and will fly me to Spain. From there I hope to make my way to South America."

The younger man moved round to the safe and glanced from the empty shelves to the desk. "You'll be taking about £100,000 with you, sir?"

"Yes, just about that — all I have left out of a one-time fortune of ten million."

"I wouldn't say no to it!" snapped the other in a changed voice, and an automatic appeared in his hand as he reached forward and tapped Zachariah Cohen's pocket. "I'll trouble you for that gun as well." Disarmed, the financier reeled back against the safe.

"What — what does this mean, Williams?"

"I'm not Williams, and it means that I'm taking this £100,000 as well as the £5000," said the younger man coolly. "I have been watching these offices for days, besides cultivating the acquaintance of Williams, and I guessed that tonight was the one you had chosen for your getaway."

"But — but you are Williams! Your face — clothes — voice! You are Williams, and you're — you're joking!"

"I'm not joking, Cohen. You've robbed the public for years and you were getting out with a decent nest-egg. Well, I'm having it instead, that's all. Ever heard of Zorn?"

"The Man with a Hundred Faces?"

"Yes, that's me. I flatter myself that even Williams would think I was his reflection.

"I thought I might have to talk to you in confidence before I got at this money; that's the only reason I made up as Williams. Now sit down where you are and I'll tie you up comfortably, otherwise I shall have to crack you on the head with this gun.

Zachariah Cohen subsided, staring incredulously at the man whose face now bore no resemblance to that of Justin Williams. He had heard much about Zorn, but had never expected to meet him under such circumstances as these.

"You'll never get away with it!" he said harshly. "You'll be caught before you've gone a hundred miles."

"Not me!" grinned the other. "You've got a plane waiting for you at Hendon. You told me yourself."

"Fool! They'll never allow you aboard that. The pilot is in my confidence and knows me intimately. He has orders to take only me aboard," said the financier, finding courage in his well-laid plan.

Zorn grinned again.

"Don't worry about that. It will be Zachariah Cohen who boards the plane — or so the pilot will think." He patted the brief-case. "Here I have all the make-up that I need, and the case will do nicely to carry all these notes and bearer bonds when I leave. Now sit perfectly still while I study your face from all angles. I like to make a good job when I start."

Half an hour later a man exactly resembling Zachariah Cohen let himself out of the side door of the office building into Haymarket, clutching a brief-case in his right hand. He closed the door behind him, glanced rapidly right and left, then stepped out swiftly.

Two figures emerged from a nearby shop entrance and gripped him by either arm.

"Not so fast, Mr Cohen. I have a warrant for your arrest on a charge of defrauding the public and falsifying accounts," came the deep voice of Chief Detective-Inspector McPhinney of Scotland Yard. "Hold on to him, Hawke, and take charge of that bag. Unless I'm very much mistaken, we shall find something of interest in there."

Their prisoner did not struggle, neither did he resist when they pushed him into a car which came at Hawke's signal.

"Bow Street Police Station," muttered McPhinney, as they sat on either side of the gaunt-faced man whose flight they had so unexpectedly checked.

That night a chartered plane waited in vain at Hendon aerodrome for the financier who had hired it.

There was a notice on the door of Zachariah Cohen's suite of offices the next morning declaring that they were closed by order of the Public Prosecutor, and that all communications were to be addressed to Henry Powys-Neil, solicitor.

Dixon Hawke and Tommy Burke ignored this when they arrived about 10.30, for they had a key which had been given them by the police. Cohen was to come up for a preliminary hearing at Bow Street that morning, but Hawke was not needed as a witness.

He wished to check on several matters connected with Cohen's complicated company accounts, and he also wanted to have a look at the books before the chartered accountants took them over.

They entered the long, well-furnished room, and Hawke paused when he saw the open safe and the scattered papers on the floor.

"He certainly left in a hurry. I don't suppose he's left much of value in there, Tommy, but fortunately my warning stirred the Yard at the last moment, and we were able to prevent him getting away with that £100,000. It will be little enough to go round amongst those he has cheated, but it will be better than nothing."

Circling the spilled documents, they looked into each of the other offices — one belonging to Williams, the private secretary, and the other where three or four typists had worked.

A startled exclamation behind him made Hawke turn. Tommy Burke had idly opened the door of the private washroom and was pointing as he stared. Queer grunting noises came from within.

Two strides carried Hawke to Tommy's side, for he had seen the bound figure in the chair, a middle- aged man with a gaunt face, bald head and staring eyes. The man was tied and heavily gagged. He appeared to be trying to say something.

Rapidly the two detectives tore away the ropes and gag. Dixon Hawke stared at the uncovered face.

"Zachariah Cohen, by all that's wonderful!" he gasped. "Then who in the world — Tommy, get some water!"

He held a glass of water to the exhausted financier's lips and Cohen finally spoke.

"Last night... attacked me here... Zorn."

"What?" Dixon Hawke almost shouted. "You say it was Zorn who did this? How do you know?"

"He told me so." Cohen seemed quite broken in spirit and made no attempt to rise. "He took some money that I had with me and — and made himself up to resemble me. It was uncanny. It was me —exactly! First of all he entered as Williams, my private secretary, then when he had found out all he wanted, he drew a gun and — "

Dixon Hawke waited for no more.

"Watch him, Tommy!" he gasped and leapt to the telephone, where he rapidly dialled Bow Street Police Station. "Get me Superintendent Palmer!"

There was a brief delay before he was put through.

"Oh, Palmer, this is Dixon Hawke speaking. I suppose McPhinney isn't there, by any chance?... No!

Well, I want to tell you a piece of good news. You've actually got Zorn in one of your cells!"

Gasps of amazement came from the other end before Hawke interrupted.

"I mean it! I helped to bring him in last night with McPhinney, though we thought it was Zachariah Cohen. I've just found the real Zachariah

Cohen here at his office, tied hand and foot. Zorn took his place and we arrested him… The joke's on him!"

"No, the joke's on us in that case, Mr Hawke," came the superintendent's dry reply. "Fifteen minutes ago that prisoner appeared before the magistrate and was identified as Zachariah Cohen. His solicitor bailed him out on a surety of £5000. They left together in a car."

Hawke stiffened and Tommy saw his face change.

"Bailed out! Solicitor arranged it! Who — what — who is the solicitor?… Powys-Neil of Lorimer

Terrace. Thanks! I suggest you send out the call at once for a search to be made for Zorn. Send some men over here for the real Zachariak Cohen. I want to get around to that solicitor's place as soon as possible."

"Tough luck, Guv'nor, but it wasn't your fault," Tommy Burke murmured.

"My fault or not, Zorn has fooled us. It's true he hasn't got away with that money, but he's fooled the law. I wish those police would hurry. I want to get around to Lorimer Terrace and see if Powys- Neil knows where his supposed client has gone. He'll have a shock when he hears what's happened."

It was only just past eleven o'clock when Dixon Hawke and Tommy Burke burst into the solicitor's office. Dixon Hawke asked for the solicitor and did not wait to be announced. He knocked on the door indicated by a clerk and walked in.

A grave, grey-haired man with a long nose and horn-rimmed spectacles was sitting behind a desk. He looked up over his glasses rather irritably.

"Yes, have you an appointment, sir?"

"No, but you are Mr Powys-Neil, the solicitor who acted for Zachariah Cohen?"

"I am, but — "

Hawke had noticed a door in the corner. There was no one else in the room.

"Where is he, this supposed Zachariah Cohen?" he demanded.

The solicitor rose to his feet, his eyes flashing angrily.

"I fail to see the reason for this intrusion, sir. Mr Zachariah Cohen left by my private entrance about ten minutes ago. Who are you?"

Dixon Hawke passed over one of his cards.

"Maybe it will surprise you to know that you bailed out the wrong man, Mr Powys-Neil," Hawke declared. "That was not Zachariah Cohen, but Zorn, the American criminal known as the 'Man with a Hundred Faces'. I only made the discovery about fifteen minutes after you had taken him away from Bow Street. Your real client is now in the police station after being found in his office, bound and gagged."

The elderly solicitor sat down heavily.

"But this — this is inconceivable!" he stammered.

"It is startling, yes, but the truth. Now please tell me where Zorn was supposed to be going."

"He said he was going back to his — to Zachariah Cohen's flat — in Park Lane, but if what you say is true, I doubt if he will have gone there."

"You're right — he will not. Having once slipped through our fingers he will make himself scarce. By now he will be turning himself into an entirely different person... I'm afraid you will not be able to help us at all, sir. You had better attend to your real client, who will need your services, though I doubt if they will grant bail after what has happened."

He smiled rather grimly as he said this. Powys-Neil did not smile in return.

"They will have to grant bail," he said, firmly. "The mere fact that they made a mistake in identity is nothing against my client. I shall insist upon his case being judged on its merits. Thank you for telling me, Mr Hawke."

As the detective and his assistant turned for the door to the outer office, they saw that the safe was open, and that the lid of a large cash-box was raised, revealing neatly-packed wads of notes. Powys-Neil was one of the old-fashioned solicitors who kept a large sum of ready money in hand against eventualities.

There was very little they could do except proceed to the Yard and have a conference with McPhinney. By that time he had heard what had happened and was as short-tempered as an angry bull.

"That fellow Zorn is like quick-silver," he complained, "forever running through our fingers. Where shall we hear of him next?"

"Well, he failed to get that cash from Cohen, so we may expect to hear of him making a grab for a consolation prize somewhere else. To think we actually had him in custody all one night, and didn't know it."

McPhinney nearly exploded at the thought, then calmed himself and asked if Hawke had completed the investigation at Cohen's office.

"No, I hadn't even started. When Tommy found Cohen tied up, we got out as quickly as possible with the hope of finding Zorn. If you like, I'll go back and sort things out as I'd intended."

"Ay, it would be a help when Cohen comes up for trial," admitted the inspector.

Hawke and Tommy motored back to Haymarket, and again let themselves into the financier's office. There Hawke worked until 12.30.

"It may be a dirty trick, but I'd like to question Zachariah Cohen about a few things before he's had a chance of getting over the shock of that attack. I believe he'd tell the truth about several things if

he was tackled at once. The police will know where I can find him."

"Maybe the police didn't grant him bail," suggested Tommy, as Dixon Hawke took up the receiver.

"They'll do that all right. Powys-Neil was certain of that, and he's no fool… Hullo, is that Bow Street?

Hawke speaking. Can I have a few words with Superintendent Palmer? Out? Oh, then perhaps you could help me. Where was Zachariah Cohen, the real Cohen, going when he left just now?"

"I don't understand, sir" came from the sergeant at the other end.

"Zachariah Cohen is in his cell."

"What?" cried Hawke. "Didn't you grant him bail?"

"Nobody has appeared to ask for it, sir."

"I see!" Dixon Hawke hung up and turned slowly. He was obviously startled by what he had heard, and thinking hard. Suddenly he grabbed for his hat. "Quickly, Tommy, a taxi!"

Due to the boy's fleetness of foot, they got a taxi-cab the moment they arrived outside, and Hawke gave the solicitor's address.

"I hope we're in time," he said.

"In time for what, Guv'nor? What's the excitement about? We know that Cohen hasn't escaped."

"No, he hasn't even been bailed out, and why, Tommy, why? When we left Powys-Neil more than an hour ago, he was about to dash off and arrange that bail, or so he said. Why has he not done so?"

Tommy shook his head.

"Because the chances are that he isn't the same Powys-Neil!" snapped the detective, jumping out, as the taxi slowed before the office building in Lorimer Terrace.

"Tommy, go upstairs and tell those clerks in the outer office that the man inside isn't their employer but an impostor!"

Tommy Burke went, and Hawke moved round to the side door.

He had not been there three minutes before loud voices were raised above and someone came leaping down the stairs inside the door. Hawke stood to one side, and, as the tall, grey-haired figure plunged out, holding a leather bag in one hand, the detective dived for his legs.

It was a magnificent tackle, and the runner went down with a crash. Before Dixon Hawke could take advantage of his surprise attack there was a horrified shout behind him. Two strong hands gripped him and hauled him back.

"What's the game, me lad, what's the game?" roared an outsize policemen, who had witnessed the whole affair.

In forceful fashion he restrained Dixon Hawke's sudden attempt to break free. The man on the pavement had risen and bolted, leaving his bag on the pavement.

As the policeman blew his whistle and Tommy came leaping down the stairway at the rear, the Dover Street detective snarled at the officer: "My name's Dixon Hawke, and you might be interested to know that the man you 'rescued' from me was not Mr Powys-Neil, but Zorn. You've enabled him to escape... Pick up that bag, Tommy, for that will be Zorn's consolation prize."

Hawke was proved right when they searched the office, for the real solicitor was found trussed and gagged in one of his own cupboards. He had been suddenly attacked after bringing the man he believed to be Zachariah Cohen back to his office.

Zorn had seen the necessity for getting rid of his "Cohen" disguise in a hurry, and had been quick to see the advantage of becoming Powys-Neil, who had the keys of the safe in his possession,

Zorn had spent the past hour going through the various strongboxes belonging to clients and taking out all cash and negotiable documents worth about £10,000.

They were all found in the bag which he had dropped.

—oOo—

# THE CASE OF
## *The* TELEPHONE KIOSK

The sound of angry voices came from the glade in the nearby wood, and the whine of a self-starter could be heard easily — all this made Joe Brack leave off trimming the hedge. He had seen the two- seater turn into the wood earlier on, and had also seen the excited-looking girl on a cycle who had followed a few minutes later. Now he saw the girl gesticulating fiercely at the couple in the car.

"I'll let Kitty know what you are, Jim Harland," Joe heard her shout. "She'll know before you get home." The car bumped slowly out into the roadway, and as it passed him Joe heard the driver speak to the woman by his side.

"Don't worry, I'll soon shut her up."

102

Joe turned once again at the sound of footsteps, to see a tall, prosperous-looking man come striding down the road — Joe knew it must be about two o'clock.

For the past fortnight Colonel Reave had come at that time to telephone from the kiosk at the cross-roads, ever since he had taken over The Lodge, which was not yet on the phone.

Joe touched his cap as the colonel passed, and watched Reave turn into the short-cut through the wood.

"Can you tell me where there is a telephone, please?"

Joe turned round again to find the girl with the cycle facing him.

"Yes, miss, there's one at the cross-roads, 'bout 'alf a mile away round the comer there. If you 'urry you'll get in before 'is nibs."

He pointed to the figure of the colonel striding through the woods, and the girl mounted and pedalled off furiously.

Colonel Reave exclaimed impatiently when he emerged from the wood to see a girl alight from her cycle, and hurry into the telephone kiosk. Turning his back, he leisurely proceeded to fill his pipe, and this duly completed, he turned again to glance towards the kiosk.

" What the — " he shouted, and crossed the roadway at a run.

The girl had slumped to the floor of the kiosk, the receiver clutched tightly in her hand. To the colonel's consternation, she appeared to be dead, and a faint smell of almonds came to his nostrils.

He stooped to disengage the receiver from the hand which gripped it, then noting that the instrument had been put out of commission by the wrench, he changed his mind. Mounting the girl's cycle, he rode rapidly towards the village.

When the telephone rang Dixon Hawke reached out and lifted the receiver. He grinned as he recognised the voice of Chief Detective-Inspector Duncan McPhinney.

"I just thought you'd be interested in a case which has cropped up," said the Scotland Yard man.

"It happened yesterday afternoon," went on McPhinney. "The locals, after letting the clues get cold, decided to ask the Yard for help this morning. A girl was found dead yesterday afternoon in a wayside telephone kiosk near Newfold, Bedford. She'd been poisoned — hydrocyanic acid!"

"Phew! Deadly stuff!" exclaimed Hawke. "The smallest drop is enough to kill."

McPhinney went on to tell how Colonel Reave had found the body and had gone at once for help. The doctor had certified death from hydrocyanic acid, and traces of the poison were found in the mouthpiece of the telephone receiver. Joe Brack's story and the quarrel in the wood were further evidence to be taken into consideration.

The victim had been identified as Miss Ethel Wood, of Mexwrell, the market town a few miles from the scene of the tragedy. The couple in the car were also from Mexwell, the man being Jim Harland, the victim's brother-in-law, and the woman, an actress from a touring company at present playing in the town.

Harland swore he had driven straight home after the quarrel, and in this he was supported by the woman. In spite of this, however, he had been arrested by the local police.

"That's about all," concluded McPhinney. "Harland is being held on suspicion. It seems he's the only person with any sort of a motive, as the girl was very popular in the town. Harland has been playing around with women lately, and the girl, his wife's sister, found out about his arrangements yesterday, and so followed the couple on her bike."

"How about suicide?" queried Hawke.

"The local police think it out of the question," was McPhinney's answer. "This chap Reave — he's the big steel magnate by the way — said the girl didn't look as if she contemplated taking her life. He saw her glance his way, and surmised that she was trying to beat him to the phone as, of course, she did."

"Lucky for Reave," said Hawke. "I'm very interested in the case — it sounds out of the usual."

"Very well, I'll get young Rennie to come round and pick you up," declared McPhinney.

"He'll be on the case, as I am due to go up to Manchester this afternoon. He's quite a good lad — newly promoted after great success in breaking up part of London's Black Market."

Half-an-hour later Hawke and Tommy got into the police car which had drawn up outside the house. Hawke liked the look of Detective-Inspector "Red" Rennie, with his red, curly hair.

The police car made short work of the journey, and it was only a couple of hours before the party were in the police station at Mexwell. Here they were greeted by Inspector Sparrow of the local constabulary.

When they had inspected the body, Hawke spent some time in examining the telephone receiver, which had been cut off and brought in as an exhibit. Under a microscope he could see the particles of a dull, wax-like substance which clung to the metal. He also noticed that gum or some other adhesive had been applied to one of the perforations.

Sparrow escorted them to the scene of the tragedy, and, while Rennie and the local men reconstructed the finding of the body, Hawke looked about him in interested fashion.

The kiosk stood on an island at the intersection of four roads in a rather isolated part of the county. The district was well wooded and thick plantations lined each of the four roads radiating from the island. There was no sign of any houses nearby, but Hawke's keen eye had noted smoke rising from behind the trees, some distance to the south-west.

"That will be The Lodge, sir, Colonel Reave's place," replied the constable on duty at the kiosk, in answer to Hawke's query.

The country to that side was flat, but to the north-east the ground rose sharply in a thickly-wooded ridge. Beyond this, amongst the trees, Hawke could see the roofs and chimneys of a substantial building.

"That's the Deneden Sanatorium, sir," volunteered the constable.

"Thank you, officer," replied Hawke, and he pointed to a small building on the crest of the rise. "Is that summer-house part of the sanatorium property?" he asked.

"Yes, sir."

When Rennie had heard the story all over again, and had taken note of the exact position of the body, Sparrow suggested that they might like to interview Colonel Reave, and Rennie readily agreed.

Colonel Reave received them pleasantly, but could help them little. He had taken over the house only a fortnight earlier, and the phone was not yet installed.

He told them he was chairman of Heave's Products, Ltd., among other things, and the firm had been worried lately by the leakage of trade secrets to a rival concern.

Although already in semi-retirement, he felt it his duty to keep in touch, which was his reason for his daily visit to the kiosk.

Sparrow had gone on to Mexwell, and Hawke, rather to Rennie's surprise, accepted the colonel's invitation to lunch for the party.

"We don't have time to listen to him rambling all day," Rennie objected, when Reave left the room to make the necessary arrangements.

Hawke, however, only smiled, and he encouraged the colonel to be talkative during the meal and after, as the ex-soldier rambled on about his business interests.

Hawke learned that the colonel intended retiring for good very soon in favour of his stepson, Harold Welling, who, until now, had been in charge of the firm's extensive laboratories. Welling had hinted that he was on the track of the culprit responsible for divulging the trade secrets.

"He's coming down tomorrow morning," the colonel concluded.

Rennie was silent when they got outside, and did not speak until Hawke expressed a wish to visit Deneden Sanatorium.

"Although Reave says he never even knew the victim, you spent a lot of time on him. I think I know what you are up to. You don't think Harland did it, Hawke."

"1 don't," replied Hawke shortly. "Harland didn't kill the girl. How could he? It doesn't make sense. You've agreed with me, Inspector, that the murder was premeditated, and the stage carefully set beforehand. How could Harland have done that?

"He didn't know the girl was following him, and he had no means of knowing that she would use that telephone. Why, the girl herself didn't know it was there until Brack told her. Now, Colonel Reave — "

He paused significantly and Rennie understood his implication.

"I get it, Hawke," he said. "You think the poison was meant for Reave. I believe you're right."

"I'm pretty sure of it," replied Hawke. "He used that kiosk regularly every day at the same time. Someone who knew that introduced the poison into the mouthpiece. How, I don't know, but it must have been by some highly-ingenious method, as hydrocyanic acid is tricky stuff with which to work. That blob of gum and those minute particles of wax suggest an idea."

As they talked, the car climbed steadily up a winding road, and soon they arrived at Deneden Sanatorium, where Rennie was quickly put in touch with the resident medical officer.

From the building itself it was quite impossible to see the cross-roads below, but from the outermost of a cluster of chalets, occupied by convalescing patients,

Hawke found himself looking down directly on the scene of the tragedy. He could see, inside the kiosk, the figure of a G.P.O. mechanic, busily repairing the phone. He could see the man's movements within the kiosk fairly clearly, but the distance was too great to distinguish his features.

Hawke chatted with the young man who occupied the chalet. The patient had no knowledge of the affair, and was wondering what all the fuss was about down below.

The detective's eyes gleamed when the man spoke of seeing the girl arrive and then, as he thought, have a fainting fit.

There was not a great deal of traffic, and he had not seen a car stop at the kiosk, but he had noticed a snappy sports car which had been parked inside the wood a couple of hundred yards away. The sunlight glinting on chromium plating had attracted his attention, and he had watched the car drive into the wood.

A man, in sports jacket and flannels, had walked to the kiosk, where he had remained for some time. The man seemed to be having trouble with the phone, and the patient thought he wore some sort of pad over his mouth.

The patient said the car had come shortly after one o'clock, perhaps at quarter past, and it had stayed there for at least half an hour.

As both Hawke and Rennie were ready, they all set out on the return trip.

Hawke and Tommy left Rennie at Dover Street, the inspector having undertaken to investigate the affairs of Howard Welling, the new managing director of Reave's Products, Ltd.

The inspector phoned next morning. He was able to tell Hawke that Welling had been living in luxury and spending money freely, although until recently he had been finding it hard to get along on his salary.

The man was spoken off as a brilliant chemist, and had already installed a small, but well-equipped, private laboratory next door to his own office in Clerkenwell. Hawke congratulated Rennie on finding out that Welling possessed a Bentley sports model, and had, moreover, been absent from business on the day of the tragedy.

Hawke repeated his information to Tommy.

"That's good enough for me," the famous detective decided. "We'll pay a visit to Mr Welling's office, lad. I'd like to see the inside of that laboratory of his. As you know, the gentleman has gone down to Newfold this morning to see the colonel, so we ought to have time to look around."

"OK, Guv'nor," grinned Tommy. "How are you going to get in though?"

Hawke achieved this by posing as an American business associate of Welling's, and declared positively that he had an appointment for eleven o'clock.

He was deaf to the plea of the clerk who admitted him, and he insisted on being shown to Welling's private office where he proposed to wait, in spite of the clerk's protestations.

"Phone him and tell him I'm here, and I don't like to be kept waiting," he boomed.

In vain the clerk protested that Welling could not be reached by phone.

"Then send a telegram!" snapped Hawke. "I'll give him an hour. Not a minute longer, and if he doesn't turn up, there are others who will be glad to take up my proposition."

He seated himself in a comfortable chair, and motioned Tommy to do the same. The clerk gave it up and went back to the office.

"I don't think we'll be troubled for a while," said Hawke after a few minutes.

"Let's get busy. This looks like the door."

He tried a door at the far side of the room. It was locked but a few minutes' manipulation of a handy little gadget which the detective carried soon overcame that difficulty. The pair found themselves in a small, but well-equipped laboratory. Hawke searched around for a time then turned his attention to a large steel cabinet which was locked, but it, like the door, soon yielded to Hawke's expert touch. The detective drew his breath in sharply.

"Aha, my hunch was right. This is where he's been practising!" he exclaimed pointing.

Inside the cabinet Tommy saw a telephone set of the type in general use. Amongst an array of bottles, Hawke pointed to two.

"Dilute sulphuric acid and potassium cyanide, the constituents of hydrocyanic acid," he explained. "It doesn't take an expert to know how he made it. What I'm interested in is how he got it on the receiver. Let's examine this."

He lifted out the telephone and laid it on a table. Like the one they had seen at Newfold, the receiver bore traces of dabs of gum and particles of the same dull waxy substance.

Hawke lifted out a black steel box. Unlocking this he disclosed a large tube of gum and a white cardboard container in which, set in sections and resting on cotton wool, were several tiny pellets. These were a dull black in colour, and Hawke showed Tommy how perfectly they matched the inside of the mouthpiece of the receiver.

With padded tongs which he found in the cabinet, Hawke very carefully lifted out one of the pellets. With great caution he inserted it inside one of the perforations of the receiver which Tommy held for him.

"That's how it was fixed," he said grimly. "A dab of gum and it will stick even when the receiver is upside down."

"Yes, I see that," replied Tommy, "but what happens afterwards?"

"Now you've got me," smiled Hawke, "but I suspect the wax of which the pellet is made is exceedingly delicate. Here, give me the receiver."

Taking the receiver, Hawke held it at arm's length and lowered it gently to the table before turning it over.

The pellet rolled out slowly and burst at once on contact. The pair were conscious of the smell of almonds.

"Gosh, it seemed to go off with a pop, giving a bit of a spray," said Tommy. "I didn't hear anything, of course."

"That's what happened," Hawke replied. "The wax, whatever it is, is highly susceptible to heat."

He held out the receiver.

"So there you are," he continued.

"When the victim spoke into this, her mouth was no more than an inch, at the most, away. She probably opened her mouth wide to say 'Hello'. The heat of her breath burst the pellet which gave out a spray. A small but deadly drop reached her lips. She would have sucked some of it in with her intake of breath.

"Now for Welling," went on Hawke, leading the way back into the office. "I expect him back soon. He'll have told the colonel a false story regarding the leakage of trade secrets and, being the culprit himself, he won't feel inclined to stay there long."

Hawke was right. Twenty minutes later they heard the voice of the clerk explaining their presence to someone, and presently the door was flung open. A tall, dark-featured young man looked at them in surprise. Then his glance went to the open door of the laboratory, and an ugly look appeared on his face.

"Who are you?" he demanded harshly, "and what the devil were you doing in there?"

He pointed towards the laboratory and Hawke rose to his feet.

"My name is Dixon Hawke," he said quietly. "I am investigating the mysterious death of a girl in a telephone kiosk in Wessex, and I thought your laboratory might help me. You'll be glad to know it did.

"The game is up, Mr Welling, you'd better come quietly," went on Hawke and the other swore loudly.

Then suddenly he sprang towards the laboratory door, and slammed it shut behind him. T

here was a click as the bolt was shot home. A minute later the pair heard the thud of something faffing, and, when the door was broken down, they found Howard Welling stretched lifeless on the floor. He had taken one of his own pellets.

It was later established that Welling had been swindling the firm for some time, and it was he who had sold the trade secrets to a rival concern.

—oOo—

# THE CASE OF *The Wicked Uncle*

"I find it everywhere," said the old man quietly. "In my food and drink. Even on the gummed flaps of the envelopes on my desk. Poison, Mr Hawke! Affairs have reached such a pitch that I dare eat nothing at home, but have to take all my meals here alone."

Strange words to hear in the smoking-room of a famous London club, and made still stranger by the man who spoke them. Sir David Magnoll, retired president of a big transport firm, was about as shrewd and level-headed as any business man to be found in the City of London.

"If somebody is trying to murder you, Sir David, why not go to the police?" asked Dixon Hawke.

Sir David looked doubtfully at the private detective, and hesitated for a moment.

110

"The trouble is," he admitted at last, "that the evidence of my own eyes and ears is forcing me to believe the last thing that I want to believe. The reason that I am seeking your help, Mr Hawke, instead of going to the police, is that the evidence points to my niece as the poisoner and I want you to prove that evidence to be all wrong."

Sir David sighed, passing a hand wearily across his eyes.

"And yet, Mr Hawke," he added, "I am afraid that in asking you to disprove the evidence I am asking you to perform a miracle.

"I had better begin at the beginning," he continued, "and tell you about Claire. My brother and his wife are both dead, and the poor girl had a terrible time for some months after their death, for her father died in poverty and in debt, having been too proud to turn to me for help in his time of need.

"He was my only brother, and his wife was my playmate in childhood, but they cut adrift from the family years ago, and I had completely lost touch with them.

"It was only when Claire was in hospital, after being rescued from an attempt to take her own life in the river that her relationship to me was discovered and the police communicated with me.

"I did not even know that I had a niece, but I took her into my home at once, and I can truthfully say that I have done all in my power to make her happy once more, and to win her confidence.

"I feel responsible for what her parents suffered. If only I had insisted in keeping in touch with them, I could have helped them. And I want to make up for that to their daughter.

"But the child — she is nineteen — has suffered so much that I fear nothing will wipe the bitterness from her mind. She seems to have made up her mind to hate me. She makes no bones about it. She tells people she hates me.

"Six weeks ago a chemist rang me up in the evening. My niece had called at his shop to buy poison to kill rats. He was suspicious and decided to phone the address she gave because of the extreme agitation of the young lady.

"Well, of course, I said it was all right, although I have never seen a rat in our house, and the servants would have dealt with them, anyway.

"When Claire returned I made a joke about it, but she flared up and abused me, making the most extraordinary accusations. Unfortunately some friends were there at the time and overheard what she said. They were horrified and suggested that a doctor ought to examine Claire, so I arranged for her to see Jewett, the brain specialist, but she refused to keep the appointment.

"Two days later I tasted something odd in my tea, and was taken violently ill directly after. To cut a long story short, the doctor's verdict was that I had narrowly escaped arsenical poisoning.

"Since then I have watched my niece's actions, and have had samples of food and drink analysed. Hawke, here is the analyst's report — almost every sample has contained poison!"

Sir David paused again, while Hawke studied the report; then the old man abruptly brought his fist down on the arm of his chair.

"And yet I refuse to believe it!" he insisted. "I cannot believe that Claire is guilty. Some enemy is at the back of this, and is trying to fasten his crime on her. That is what I want you to prove."

Hawke nodded slowly, folding the reports and putting them in his pocket.

"I had better come and stay at your house for a few days, Sir David," said the detective.

Dixon Hawke and his young assistant, Tommy Burke, arrived at the Magnoll home the following morning. There they found Claire Magnoll with her uncle.

She was small and delicate, with troubled, scared eyes that seemed too big for her pale face.

She looked like a child in a perpetual nightmare, frightened of everything around her, and in the days that followed, Tommy discovered that she spent most of her time in her own room, and often he heard her sobbing hysterically when he listened at the door.

And yet Sir David was kindness itself to her. He fussed over her like a hen over its only chick, always seeking some way of rousing her from this strange bitter sorrow of hers.

"It would be better if he dealt with her firmly in a good old-fashioned way, or sent her away to where they would know how to deal with her tantrums," snapped Sir David's doctor, having been called in on the night of the detective's arrival to cope with an attack of screaming hysterics that the girl suddenly developed.

"She is suffering from persecution mania.

"She has just been telling me that Sir David is cruel to her. Of all the rubbish! You must persuade him to send her away, Hawke, or I won't be responsible for the consequences."

"Could I have a word with you alone, doctor?" asked Hawke, and led him into another room.

When Hawke returned, there was a strange glint in his eyes that Tommy knew well. It told him that Hawke was on the trail.

Later that night, from a hiding-place near her room, Tommy saw Claire come out into the corridor and go down the stairs.

Inwardly hating this job of spying on an unhappy girl, he followed her. She went straight to the dining-room, where she mixed a whisky-and-soda and put it on a tray.

"Miss Magnoll!" exclaimed Tommy. "I thought you were all in bed," she admitted.

"My uncle sent me down to fetch this for him, as he is sitting up late with some work."

Tommy muttered an apology, but hurried to Hawke's room, and the detective immediately went to Sir David. He brought the whisky-and-soda back with him, and Tommy watched him make a careful analysis of it.

"Sir David says that he never sent her for it," said Hawke, "and see for yourself, Tommy — there is enough poison in this glass to kill off the three of us!"

"Then you mean that she's guilty?" asked Tommy. "It's hard to believe. I mean, she just seems an unhappy kid — "

"That is all she is," snapped Hawke. "She is being framed — framed with diabolical cunning.

"But the trail is too obvious, too blatant."

Hawke broke off abruptly and spun round. Both Tommy and he plainly heard the sound of the heavy front door closing.

"What's the meaning of that?" gasped Tommy, but found himself speaking to an empty room. He dashed out after Hawke and down the stairs, where they found a scared maid servant in the hall.

"What has happened? Pull yourself together, girl!" snapped Hawke, for she was obviously frightened almost out of her wits and on the verge of hysterics.

"Miss Claire —" she managed to gasp, calmed by Hawke's steady hand and voice — "she's gone out — without a coat — into the rain! She — she looked terrible — as — as though something dreadful — "

But Hawke waited for no more. He turned and raced up the stairs again, and along to Sir David's room. He knocked, but there was no answer, so he flung the door unceremoniously open.

Then he halted, his face a grim mask.

Sir David Magnoll lay on the floor by his desk, a broken cup in his hand. One glance was enough to show that he was dead. This time the poison used had been a corrosive, for his lips were burnt.

Less than an hour later, Claire Magnoll was found wandering dazedly in London and was taken to a police station. There she was formally charged with the murder of her uncle.

Tommy Burke went to see Claire in prison. In spite of the evidence, the young detective could not believe that this sad young girl had foully murdered her uncle.

"She's been framed, I tell you," he insisted to Detective-Inspector McPhinney of Scotland Yard, who was assigned to the case and whom he met at the police station.

"Ay, maybe she has," said McPhinney soberly. "After speaking with her, I'd almost think so myself, for — well, maybe I'm a sentimental old fool — but she's not the kind to do a thing like this.

"But the evidence, Tommy! You can't go against the evidence. I've never known it more conclusive."

"Circumstantial evidence has been faked before today," protested Tommy.

"Ay, but who by in this case? We've already checked up. Sir David seems to have had no enemies. Nor has the girl — except herself. Because of her strange behaviour, he cut himself adrift from everybody, devoting himself to her. We are checking up the servants, but I don't expect to find anything helpful there."

When Tommy left the police station he felt even worse than before. In the cell, where she was temporarily lodged, Claire had first seemed too dazed to speak. Then she had raved at him hysterically.

"She must be mad," Tommy reported glumly to Hawke. "All she can say for herself is that Sir David was cruel to her. She says he always hated and ill-treated her — not physically, for then you would have seen bruises on her — but with his tongue.

"She says that it was he who sent her to buy the arsenic on the night that the chemist was suspicious; that he made her prepare his food for him. She says he hated her because her mother preferred his brother to him; that he was the cause of his brother dying in poverty — he ruined her parents and made them suffer for what they did."

Tommy sighed.

"What jury is going to believe any of that in the face of people like us who saw them together, and know how well Sir David treated her, and how upset he was when she declared that she hated him?" he added bitterly; then realised that Hawke had moved quietly out of the room.

The detective was busy at his laboratory bench when Tommy came in, and now he was examining the chemical reaction in a test tube.

"I thought so," he snapped. "Like all his kind, Tommy, this killer has made a mistake. The poison that killed Sir David was argyros nitrate, so rare that nine people out of ten have never heard of it! And that's our first clue!

"This is the next!" Hawke turned to a big pile of newspaper clippings that had been rushed to him from an agency. "I have here just about every Press reference to Sir David Magnoll that has ever been made, and look at this one."

Tommy stared in bewilderment at a short notice in a clipping from an evening paper to the effect that Sir David Magnoll was found guilty of culpable negligence while in charge of a motor car, was fined £10 and forbidden to hold a driving licence for two years.

"That happened eighteen months ago," said Hawke briskly; "and Sir David had a seriously weak heart, as his doctor informed me this evening. There's a chance there. Now let me see."

He referred to more notes, and the glint in his eyes became more pronounced. "Sir David kept his car, but employed a chauffeur as he was not allowed to drive himself. Chauffeur's name is Alfred Henry Hawkins, a young man with an excellent record, who has been in Sir David's employment since the court case described in that cutting. He was in the habit of taking Sir David for a drive every day."

Hawke broke off abruptly.

"Tommy, I am going to take a long shot," he announced. "You go along and see McPhinney again. Ask him to arrange an appointment for me at the Yard with the Assistant Commissioner this evening. Tell him that I hope to have evidence that will completely alter the case against Claire Magnoll. Warn him that the police look like making a tragic blunder."

"Yes, sir!" said Tommy joyfully. "And, Tommy, when you've done that, go and cheer up that poor girl. Tell her I believe I can spring the trap into which she has fallen."

"I'm on my way!" said Tommy. "But what are you going to do?"

"Me?" said Hawke. "I am going to interview Mr Hawkins, chauffeur to Sir David Magnoll!"

Tommy was not sure what he expected to happen when Hawke set off to interview Mr Hawkins, but he certainly expected action. He arranged the appointment with McPhinney, and then obtained permission to visit Claire again.

He stayed with her for as long as he could, expecting every moment some word from Hawke. But the hours dragged by and nothing happened. The wave of optimism he had inspired in the girl began to ebb.

"Are you sure Mr Hawke said he could save me?" she pleaded anxiously.

"You bet! He's found the weak spot in some crook's rotten scheme against you and your uncle," insisted the young detective. "He'll put everything right soon."

But the day dragged to its close, and still there was no word from Hawke.

Tommy became anxious. He reasoned that his master was dealing with a particularly ruthless murderer. Could the detective have slipped up somewhere, and fallen into the clutches of the killer?

Grim now with anxiety, Tommy found Hawkins' address and went there, but all that Hawkins' wife could tell him was that her husband and the detective had driven away together in a car during the morning, and that she had heard nothing from them since.

Tommy went to Scotland Yard.

He communicated his fears to both McPhinney and the Assistant Commissioner, and the telephone wires began to hum with inquiries, joining the police wireless in broadcasting the description of Hawke, Hawkins, and the car, and ordering all police officers and patrols to keep a sharp lookout for them.

"I believe this man Hawkins was the murderer and he's done the governor in!" exclaimed Tommy at last; but, even as he spoke the door opened, and Hawke strode into the Commissioner's office.

"Confound you, Mac!" he said cheerfully to McPhinney. "A fine time I've had being held up by your patrols. Any time I want nursemaids I'll hire a couple of pretty ones at a registry office!"

"B-but — " began McPhinney.

Hawke, however, cut him short.

"This is Sir David Magnolia's chauffeur," he said, indicating his companion. "He and I have been out driving together."

He turned to the smart young chauffeur and addressed him. "Now, Hawkins, today I made you cast your mind back to recent drives with Sir David, did I not?" he asked. "I made you repeat those drives with me."

"You did, sir," said Hawkins. "I took you to the places that I used to take Sir David to, following exactly the same route, and stopping exactly where I put him down on various occasions."

"Just so,"snapped Hawke. "Some of those calls he made were normal enough, but Sir David never struck me as the sort of man to walk far. I base that statement on the fact that his doctor told me this evening that Sir David was suffering from acute heart disease. The doctor, in fact, had recently told Sir David that he could not live for more than a few months.

"But I'll return to that point later. When Hawkins put me down in certain streets, and then told me that Sir David walked away from the car and was absent for a considerable time, I became interested," went on Hawke. "I reasoned that he would not walk far, so I investigated around the nearest corner to each of those stopping places, and around each corner I found a small chemist's shop.

"Now," continued Hawke, unpacking the parcel that he carried under his arm, "look at these books. They are the poison registers of each of these chemists, and each records the sale of small quantities of poison — including argyros nitrate — to an elderly gentleman who signed a number of fancy names.

"As a handwriting expert, I can assure you that each of those signatures was written by Sir David Magnoll.

"Gentlemen!" declared Hawke. "Claire Magnoll speaks the truth. Her uncle hated her. It was he who was crazy. His brother took from him the woman he loved, and he never forgave him and her. He took their daughter into his home, not to save her, but to torment her, and he did it diabolically, never saying a harsh word to her in public and making her out to be the unreasonable one.

"Then — as Sir David's doctor will testify — he learned that he had not long to live, so he evolved the fiendish scheme of having the daughter of the pair he hated hanged for his death. He set to work to poison himself, while he spread further 'word poison' in the minds of witnesses to fasten the guilt on his niece.

"But two details wrecked his scheme — he became too interested in poisons, and finished himself off with argyros nitrate, which the girl would never have heard of; and, two years ago, he lost his driving licence and had to employ a chauffeur!"

"Then three details wrecked his scheme," supplemented the Commissioner abruptly.

"The third was that he tried to crown his scheme by reluctantly bringing you in as a witness against the unhappy girl."

Hawke shrugged, but he had his reward when Tommy and he went a few days later to take Claire Magnoll to friends in the country, for every detail of the detective's case was proved, and that, along with the happy smile he received from that pale face, was all the congratulations he asked.

—o0o—

# THE CASE OF The LORRY CHAIN

It was one of the hottest August days which Dixon Hawke and Tommy Burke had ever experienced in Scotland. As they sped along the coastal road towards Dundee, on their way to Edinburgh, they had the sliding roof of the car wide open.

The macadam road shimmered in the heat, while, in the cornfields, which they passed occasionally, perspiring men and women were gathering in the harvest.

"It's a real heat-wave!" muttered Tommy Burke. "I never knew it got so hot up here."

"Occasionally it does," grunted the Dover Street detective, as they came in sight of the silvery Tay and the smoke-stacks of Dundee.

"When he didna move, she went across tae him an' found him like this. The boss said I'd better get oot here. I took a short cut, comin' up the lane. I came on the motor bike."

Again he nodded, this time towards a motor cycle propped against the bank close to the cottage.

Dixon Hawke frowned at the lorry, walked round it and observed that it was neatly and correctly parked at the side of the road. It was an ordinary vehicle of the heavy type with six wheels and a chain hanging down at the back. There was fresh tar on the tyres, and Hawke looked back along the road to Dundee where the sprayed tar glistened in the sunlight.

Evidently the lorry had been the first to pass since the workmen had gone to their lunch. Hawke could distinctly see the two sharply-defined tracks made by the two sets of wheels when the lorry had slowed down and pulled into the side of the road.

It was obvious that he had been travelling more towards the centre before that. When it had left the newly-gravelled surface beyond and had come on to the warm tar, it had quite naturally swung over to the left. There was no sign of a wobble or a skid.

Hawke stood and stared at the tracks. For some reason he was doubtful, even though the whole thing looked simple enough. A driver with a weak heart had been affected by the heat and had collapsed while on duty. The exertion of climbing back into his cab had been too much for him.

That seemed to be the obvious and simple explanation, but Hawke had a vague feeling that there was some vital point which he had missed. Shrugging his shoulders, he again turned to the red- haired man.

"What did your wife say he was like when he called? Did she say if he mentioned anything about feeling ill?"

"She said he wis a' richt, but noo she's fair broken up aboot it, an' feels sick like. It wis a shock tae her, oot here alone."

"I'm not surprised," said Hawke sympathetically. "Have you phoned the police?"

"No. I wis tryin' tae dae somethin' for Jim when you came. I'll go noo an' — "

"Tommy can do that! Tommy, ring up Dundee Constabulary and say there's been an accident out here at — " He glanced at the man, who was mopping his face. "What do you call this cottage?"

"It hasna got a name. Say it's Louis Guthrie's cottage. They'll ken."

"Say there's been an accident near Louis Guthrie's cottage outside the town. Give my name and say we were passing, and that they had better bring a doctor with them."

Tommy Burke nodded and hurried away, keeping on the grass verge to avoid walking in the wet tar. Farther down the road he could see a group of workers returning.

something I've missed. Oh, let's forget it! It's nothing to do with us, and we're nearly an hour late for lunch. I wonder if we can get anything decent in Dundee?"

They lunched very well at one of the local hotels, and it was not until they were sitting over their coffee in the lounge that Dixon Hawke referred to the matter again. He had been stirring his cup slowly when a sudden exclamation escaped him.

"Got it, Tommy, got it! Now I know what was wrong back there on the road from Carnoustie. Phew, what a blind bat I've been!" He glanced at the clock. "I wonder where that detective-inspector is now? I must get in touch with him at once."

"You mean you still think there is something wrong about the business of the dead lorry driver,

Guv'nor?"

"Think! I don't think, Tommy. I know! I know it was deliberate murder. What's more, I feel sure I know who the murderer was!"

Leaving his assistant blinking in dazed fashion, Hawke dashed from the lounge and found his way to the hotel phone-box, where he hurriedly put through a call to the police station. Within a few moments he was in touch with McCubbin.

Ten minutes later they were driving out past the shipbuilding yard. Hawke was saying: "I noticed something at the time, but I didn't realise the significance of it until I was in the hotel."

McCubbin looked a little doubtful. "You are perfectly certain of your facts, Mr Hawke?"

"Certainly! I saw the chain dangling at the back of the lorry itself. It touched the ground, as it always does on steam lorries."

"But why, Guv'nor?" asked the puzzled Tommy.

"Because on a steam lorry the hot, dry steam passing through the valves into the cylinders causes a powerful electrical charge to be generated. The same thing happens on a locomotive, but in that case the engine is running with steel wheels on steel rails, and the electricity leaks away to earth as fast as it is generated.

"A steam lorry, however, runs on rubber tyres, and is therefore insulated, so the current packs itself into the vehicle, and the whole lorry becomes heavily charged with static electricity.

"Well, to eliminate the chance of anyone getting a shock by touching a lorry in that condition, a chain is usually left dangling to make contact with the road. That earths the current as fast as it is made."

"I often wondered why that chain was there," said Tommy.

They were now out of the town and heading for Broughty Ferry.

"You were with me, Tommy, when we looked at the tracks made by the lorry in that wet tar. How many tracks did you see?"

"Can you tell us if your husband and Jim Braddock were friends?"

"They were — mates. They had worked together ever since Jim Braddock came to Pollock & Pollock," she said.

"Yes, we know they were work-mates, but were they friends? Did they get on well?" persisted McCubbin.

"I wouldna know!" Her eyes were uncertain. "I never heard to the contrary."

"Did your husband not object to Braddock coming here so often?" put in Hawke casually.

The colour rose to Mrs Guthrie s cheeks.

"I don't know what you mean!" she flared, backing away, but her manner had told them all they wanted to know.

"Come, come, Mrs Guthrie, you must not think the police are blind," declared McCubbin. "We happen to know that Braddock often pulled up in the nearby lane when your husband was away."

"He only came to bring me a message from my husband, like he did today!" she gasped.

"What was the message your husband sent by him today?" queried Dixon Hawke.

"Some smokies for his tea."

"Were you surprised when they arrived?" McCubbin shot the question like a bullet from a gun.

"Yes — no !" She was almost shouting now. "Of course I wisna surprised. Why should I be? He likes smokies for his tea, and — "

"And I've no doubt you get him better ones from the Arbroath fishwives as they pass than he could buy in Dundee.

McCubbin could handle this local interrogation far better than Hawke could hope to do. "I put it to you, Mrs Guthrie, that it was the first time your husband had gone out of his way to ask Braddock to deliver a message here."

Mrs Guthrie burst into tears and buried her face in the apron.

"Ye-es," came muffled through the folds.

"In addition, your husband had found out that Braddock was paying far too many calls here when Guthrie himself was away with the other lorry, and was madly jealous about it?"

She was sobbing, but suddenly she put down the apron.

"But Louis did nothing to Jim. I swear it," she gasped. "He came here, gave me the package and went straight back to his lorry. When — when he calls on me he always parks the lorry in the lane, but today he stopped just outside and wisna here two minutes. I wis still at the gate when he — when he staggered back and fell."

The detective-inspector patted her on the shoulder.

"Hullo, more tar ahead, I wish they wouldn't leave these roads tarred without putting gravel over them."

"Twelve-twenty," said Tommy, with a glance at the clock on the dashboard. "I expect the workmen have knocked off for lunch. Hullo, there's someone waving from beside that steam lorry!"

Hawke had slowed to negotiate the stretch of newly-tarred road. On the right a cottage nestled among some trees, and alongside the road a heavy steam lorry, laden with sacks, had drawn up. A short, thick-set man with reddish hair showing round the edges of his greasy cap, had stepped out from the other side of the lorry and was signalling frantically to them.

The detective put on his brakes and came to a halt a short distance from the lorry.

The man came up and peered in at the open window. He was flushed and evidently agitated.

"Are you a doctor?" he asked abruptly.

"No, I'm afraid not. Is anything wrong?"

"Ay, my mate's ta'en ill. He's ower there on the grass."

Hawke was already opening the car door.

"I'll come and have a look. Perhaps he has been overcome by the heat. It must be even worse driving one of those lorries."

The man made no comment, but led the way round the lorry to the grass verge, where a younger man lay with upturned face, a rolled coat under his head for a pillow. His eyes were wide and staring; his hands were clenched by his sides. His face had a strange purple tinge. Dixon Hawke knelt down swiftly and felt for the man's heart. Tommy saw him bend still closer and watch the parted lips. The youth saw him lift one limp arm and let it fall, then sit back on his heels and shake his head.

"He's dead. How did it happen?" queried Hawke.

"Deid!" the local man gasped.

"He canna be! Jim Braddock deid, but — "

He gestured helplessly.

"How did it happen? Was he suddenly taken ill?" Hawke continued his questioning.

"I dinna ken. I wisna here. Jim an' me — we work for Pollock & Pollock, the Dundee hauliers. He left about forty minutes ago for Arbroath wi' that load. That's my cottage ower there in the trees. I asked him tae drop a message in tae the wife, an' he said he would. Aboot twenty minutes ago the wife phoned in fae yon phone-box."

He nodded towards a box about a hundred yards down the road. "She said there wis somethin' wrang wi' Jim. The lorry had pulled up an' he gied her the message, said he wis in a hurry, an' went back tae the lorry. Jist as he wis climbin' intae the lorry he fell back on tae the grass.

The police car had arrived promptly, and Detective-Inspector McCubbin himself had come, together with a sergeant and the police surgeon.

By that time, with the aid of the roadmen, the body had been carried into the shade of the cottage garden. The doctor's examination was quick but thorough.

"No injuries of any kind, not even a bruise. Apparently a case of heart failure, but we can tell better at the post-mortem. It looks perfectly clear to me that the heat had something to do with it. It's the hottest day we've had for three years," he informed the waiting group.

Detective-Inspector McCubbin looked at Hawke.

"You say you're not satisfied, Mr Hawke?"

"I'll not say that, but — "

The Dover Street detective shook his head. "Maybe I'm being foolish, Inspector. The man was out here alone; the woman at the cottage said he was perfectly normal when he delivered the parcel, and two minutes later he dropped dead. It's just one of these set-ups which get suspicious persons like me thinking.

"The chances are, however, that there is nothing in it, and that it was due to natural causes. I'm sorry I was not here soon enough to help the poor fellow, but I'm due in Edinburgh to-night for a conference, so I will have to be pushing on.

"Anyway, I'm glad to have met you, Inspector."

He held out his hand, and as they shook, Guthrie pushed forward.

"Will it be a' richt, Inspector, if I take the lorry on tae Arbroath? The boss says this load's urgent." Detective-Inspector McCubbin gave a glance at the sergeant.

"Have you looked it over, Wardlaw? Any sign of anything out of the ordinary? Do you think we need to hold it?"

"I don't think so, sir. Everything is in perfect order. The lorry's been repainted recently, and there's not a scratch on it, so there's no chance of him having been involved in a collision down the road. I've taken charge of his jacket which was in the cab. Otherwise I don't think it interests us, sir."

"Very well, you can take it on to Arbroath, Guthrie. But you'll be returning tonight?"

"Richt awa' !" Hawke heard the man reply, as Tommy and he got into their waiting car.

They drove off in silence, and they had gone some distance down the road before the youth spoke.

"You don't seem satisfied about that accident, Guv'nor."

Hawke shook himself as though coming out of a daydream.

"It's nothing. Perhaps I'm being foolish, but I've a feeling that there's

"Two lines of 'em," was Tommy's prompt reply.

"Yes. Two distinct tracks made by the wheels on either side, but where was the third one made by a dragging chain? In soft tar like that, on a smooth surface, the chain would have left a long, narrow scratch — and that scratch wasn't there. That's what I sensed was wrong, although I did not realise at the time what was actually missing. There should have been three tracks, not two."

"Then your theory is," broke in the inspector, "that someone tucked up the chain before Braddock left the garage, knowing what the effect would be.

"Then Braddock touched the metal part of the lorry, when climbing back into his seat after delivering that message, and got a severe shock."

"Yes, on a hot, dry day like this the conditions for generating a really strong charge would be ideal. In wet or damp weather there would be scarcely any. In leaving the lorry, Braddock would not be affected, for he would probably jump down.

When climbing back again, however, he would earth the vehicle and take the whole charge through him. If he had a weak heart, and I think you'll discover that he had, the effect could be fatal."

"But the chain was still hanging at the back when we were there, Guv'nor. I saw it."

"Precisely; and only one man had been there before us, according to his own confession — Louis Guthrie! It would not have taken him a moment to have unhitched the chain."

"But the motive — why should one lorry driver kill another?" growled McCubbin.

"That is what we have to find out. Maybe Mrs Guthrie can help us," said Hawke, pulling in at the scene of the tragedy. "I'm glad Guthrie is not at home at the moment."

"Wait a moment!" McCubbin seemed to have remembered something. "The constable who drove me out before lunch used to be on one of the mobile patrols. He told me that one of these steam lorries was often seen parked in that lane at the side of the cottage.

"They always took it for granted that Guthrie had used it to make a call at home in passing, but maybe — "

"Precisely!" said Dixon Hawke, as he led the way into the cottage garden.

Younger than her husband, Mrs Janet Guthrie proved to be a faded blonde of about thirty-five years, pretty in a tired sort of way.

She looked startled when she saw who her visitors were.

"My husband's no' back yet," she faltered.

"It's you we wish to see, Mrs Guthrie," said the inspector, quietly but firmly.

Reluctantly, she fell back and allowed them into her neat kitchen.

"Don't worry about it, Mrs Guthrie. Thanks for being so frank with us."

He nodded to Hawke, and they left. They climbed into the car, backed around and drove off in the direction of Dundee. Just round the bend of the road, Detective-Inspector M'Cubbin asked Dixon Hawke to stop. The man from Dover Street did so.

"Why?" he asked.

"Because I'm going back to watch that phone-box at the way-side. Unless I'm very much mistaken, she'll be out of the cottage in a few minutes and trying to phone her husband in Arbroath."

He hurried back the way they had come. Hawke sat in the car and puffed his pipe. Tommy Burke fidgeted until McCubbin returned. He nodded as he got in.

"She's in there now. Drive on as far as the next phone-box, please. I also have a call to put through to Arbroath."

Not until they were in Edinburgh that evening did Hawke receive a phone call from McCubbin.

The inspector reported that Louis Guthrie had tried to take the north road out of Arbroath instead of the one to the south when he had delivered his load. He had been stopped and questioned by two constables and had been taken into custody.

"Now he's confessed," concluded Detective-Inspector McCubbin. "It was just as you said, Mr Hawke. He tucked up the chain and made sure that Braddock would stop and leave the lorry by giving him that message for his wife.

"The motive for murder — jealousy. Thanks for your valuable help, Mr Hawke!"

—oOo—

# THE CASE OF THE CLOAKROOM TICKETS

**There was heavy midday traffic on London Bridge, and double-decker buses, taxis and commercial lorries were all packed bumper to bumper.**

Dixon Hawke and Tommy Burke, in their own car, came into the traffic queue from the Embankment.

Hawke was at the wheel and kept no more than six feet from a taxi directly in front of him.

This taxi had a solitary occupant whose head the two detectives could see through the small window at the rear.

About halfway across the bridge a man on the left-hand pavement darted between the taxi and a bus in an effort to cross the road. For a moment there had been a gap large enough to do so, but he suddenly found himself in the path of a lorry coming in the opposite direction, and he stepped back into the front off-side wheel of the taxi. The driver honked his horn and applied his brakes at the same time.

Dixon Hawke braked suddenly and managed to come to rest with his bumper a few inches from the vehicle in front.

The stricken man lay with one leg under the taxi wheel. He was conscious and blaming the taxi-driver for what had happened. A constable pushed his way through the growing crowd and asked for volunteers to lift the victim on to the pavement.

The jay-walker who had some form of leg injury continued to hurl abuse at the taxi-man.

" 'Strewth, 'ow could I avoid yer?" roared the angry driver. He looked around him, entreatingly, at those who had witnessed the incident, and saw Hawke getting down from the next car. "I asks you, sir. You saw it. Could I blinkin' well do anythin' but 'it im?"

"No. I don't think you could have avoided him," agreed Dixon Hawke.

"There y'are!" said the taximan triumphantly to the constable, who was examining his driving papers. "An' my passenger will bear that out."

Until that moment, everyone had forgotten about his passenger, who had neither opened the door of the cab, nor shown any interest in the matter. The driver now opened the door and put in his head.

"You must've seen what 'appened, sir. You're a witness! 'Strewth! Somethin' wrong 'ere ! 'E's ill, or somethin'!"

He stepped back with a look of sheer amazement on his face.

Hawke was nearest and looked inside the cab. The solitary passenger was lolling in a corner with his eyes wide open and no sign of any colour in his face.

Across one knee was a folded raincoat, which he gripped in one hand.

"What's wrong? Haven't we enough trouble already?" said the constable, reaching Hawke's side.

"He's dead, and he didn't die a natural death. Look!" growled the detective grimly.

He reached forward and pointed to something projecting under the ribs on the man's right side. It was the haft of a slender dagger, and the brown check suit which the man was wearing was almost black for a small area round the weapon.

"Stabbed!" whispered the constable in awe. "Stabbed in broad daylight!"

By this time the traffic-jam extended far beyond the edge of the bridge, and the noise was deafening.

During the next few minutes Hawke introduced himself to the policeman, and they were joined by the men from a patrol car, which had been obliged to stop some distance away.

The crowd were soon made to move, and traffic was diverted.

Anxious not to disturb anything, the police formed a protective cordon around the taxi, and made traffic by-pass it.

Detective-Inspector Baxter, chief of the Flying Squad, who had been called to the scene by the patrol car, arrived, and, with Hawke, was soon questioning the dazed driver.

"Blimey, but it ain't nacheral!" he was exclaiming. " 'E was in there alone. There wasn't anybody else with 'im. 'Ow did 'e get stabbed? 'E must've done it 'imself."

"That's hardly likely!" snapped Detective-Inspector Baxter, deftly going through the victim's pockets without changing the position of the body. "Where did you pick him up, and where was he bound for? "

"I picked 'im up in Dean Street, Soho. Signalled me from the pavement, after I'd dropped a fare at Sirelli's Cafe, 'e did. 'E told me to take 'im to 19 Porlock Street, Lambeth."

"And you haven't stopped since?"

"Only at the traffic lights; but if yer mean someone might 'ave jumped in then an' stabbed im, an' then jumped out again, you're crackers. It couldn't be done in broad daylight, mister. I've been in traffic all the time. 'E was alone when 'e got in, an' 'e's been alone ever since."

Dixon Hawke tapped him on the arm.

"What did he look like when he got in?" he asked.

"Look like? I 'ardly looked at 'im. I only saw 'is signal at the last moment. 'E was on the edge o' the kerb, an' 'ad is Mac across one arm. 'E looked sorter pale, but a lot o' those spivs around Soho look pale."

"What makes you think he's a spiv?" asked Baxter, looking up.

"Cor, I c'n tell 'em a mile off!"

"I don't think you're far wrong," said Baxter. "From his belongings, I gather his name is Tony Sawdon, and that that Lambeth address is his home one. He seems to have had some dealings in the black market recently, and he's got a wad of notes far too large for any honest man."

Dixon Hawke looked at the sprawling figure, that of a man of thirty, sallow, black-haired, wearing a bright green shirt, slashed across by a crimson tie.

There was little doubt that he was one of the post-war "spivs," one of the many who preferred to make an easy living conducting shady business deals and buying and selling goods in short supply on the black market.

An ambulance and a doctor were now on the scene, and the traffic was still being diverted. The doctor announced that death had been caused by a stab through the heart. The dagger was a long, narrow weapon with a circular blade, and had probably penetrated eight inches.

"If you had ever told me that a man could be stabbed to death when alone in a London cab, in broad daylight, I would never have believed it!" growled Detective-Inspector Baxter.

"I don't believe it now," said Hawke quietly.

"How do you mean?" asked the Yard man suspiciously.

"It stands to reason that it couldn't be done," drawled the Dover Street detective.

"As the driver pointed out, the cab has been in view of someone ever since the fare got in. It would be impossible for anyone to jump in, stab Sawdon and get out again, even at a traffic stop. Another point is that the dagger could not have been thrown through the window, for the blow was delivered upwards, from close beside the victim."

"But the fact remains that it did happen!" snapped Baxter.

"No, there must be some other explanation, and I think it is that Sawdon was stabbed before he got into the cab," Hawke went on. "The driver says he had his Mac over one arm, and doubtless that arm was pressed to his side. That would have hidden the head of the dagger. There are plenty of authenticated cases of men having walked a considerable distance after receiving a fatal wound through the heart."

Inspector Baxter looked at the doctor, who nodded in agreement.

"That is so. It is rare, but it has happened. An instrument of this kind would cause scarcely any loss of blood, so long as it was left in the wound. As the man seems to have a sufficiently powerful constitution, it is quite likely that he could have come a considerable distance after having been stabbed.

"Yes, I must agree with Mr Hawke it is definitely quite possible."

Baxter began to see what Hawke was getting at.

"His kind keep away from the police as much as possible," declared the inspector.

"If, as I suspect, he has been stabbed by one of his black market colleagues, he would make an effort to hide the fact. He would try to reach a spot where medical help of a discreet kind could be obtained. The chances are he didn't know the wound was fatal, although he had sense enough not to draw out the dagger."

The police had now taken charge of the cab with the body and were driving it away. The taximan had been left with the detectives, and was listening eagerly to their discussion.

"Can you show us the exact spot where you picked him up?" asked Dixon Hawke.

The man nodded. "Then I suggest, Baxter, that we go there at once, either in my car or yours."

"Right! I've given orders for a patrol car to proceed to that address in Lambeth to cover that end of it. We'll use my car, if you don't mind."

Leaving Tommy Burke to tail them in Hawke's own car, the famous detective got in beside the inspector. As they drove towards Soho, he had time to look at the various articles which had been removed from the dead man's pockets.

Over £600 in Bank of England notes, numerous scribbled memos of obvious black market dealings in cigarettes, a propelling pencil, a packet of a popular brand of cigarettes, a silk handkerchief with a prominent laundry-mark, and two stub ends of green-and-red cloak-room tickets made up the bulk of the inspector's discoveries.

Hawke was particularly interested in the cloakroom tickets.

He looked at the numbers and found them differing by only fifty or sixty. It seemed evident that Sawdon had deposited hat, coat, or both, in the same cloakroom on two successive days, or possibly twice in one day.

"May I keep these for a bit?" he asked, and Baxter nodded. They were nearing their destination. It would be better not to drive right up in a police car.

Round the corner from Dean Street they stopped, and Baxter, who was in plain clothes, with Hawke and the taxi-driver, walked into that narrow thoroughfare where there were many small eating-places.

"Over there, outside that green cafe," muttered the taximan. " 'E was standing on the kerb."

The three men crossed to the spot and stood there, looking about them.

"Well, he might have come from half a dozen different places near here," murmured Baxter. "Even if we accept the fact that he walked after being stabbed, he couldn't have come far."

"I agree with you," said Hawke.

" He may have stepped out from this cafe, or from the restaurant next door, or even from that narrow alley. What does that notice say? H'm, Chez Adolphe! There appears to be an entrance to a cafe of some description up that alley. I think we'll try there first."

The alley was so narrow that their shoulders rubbed on either side. Unasked, the taximan followed behind the two detectives. Not five steps from the pavement there was a narrow door in the right-hand wall, and over it a notice, "44 Chez Adolphe". It was one of the many discreet little restaurants tucked away in that labyrinth of passages and side streets within the area known as Soho.

A greasy-looking Cypriot came to meet them as they entered.

"The bar is straight ahead, gentlemen; or do you wish a table?" he asked.

Dixon Hawke gave the place one swift, comprehensive glance.

There were about twenty tables in the narrow room, each with a red-and-white checked cloth.

Nearly a dozen people were already eating lunch in the dim light from low-powered table-lamps.

At the back, partially screened by a curtain, was a bar running the width of the room, brilliantly lit with neon tubes. A number of men lounged on and about the tubular steel stools.

"We'll probably lunch when we've had a drink," said Hawke. "Can we leave our hats somewhere?"

The Cypriot waved towards a hatch in the wall, where a dark-haired girl received the hats and gave Hawke in exchange a red-and-green cloakroom ticket. He glanced at it as they walked the length of the room and nudged Baxter.

"This was the place," he muttered.

"The tickets are identical, and the numbers are only eighty or so different. I don't think Sawdon used the cloakroom today, but he certainly did yesterday."

There was a noticeable hush in the conversation at the bar when they passed through the opening in the curtain. About a dozen men were there, all of the spiv type.

Hawke ordered for the three of them, and leaned against the wall as he studied those around him.

Baxter plunged straight to the point with the barman, described Tony Sawdon, and asked if anyone answering this description had been frequenting the bar lately.

"No, sir!" came the prompt reply. "I think I know all our regulars, but not that gentleman."

Baxter went back through the curtain and spoke to the girl in the cloakroom. Hawke saw her shake her head, and he asked the taximan if he would have another drink. The man gladly accepted, and, as Dixon Hawke produced the money from his trouser-pocket, a half-crown rolled along the floor in the direction of two men.

Hawke at once dived after it, apologised for his clumsiness, and retrieved it from between their feet.

Two minutes later Baxter returned.

"They're hiding something here," he murmured. "They all flatly deny having seen anyone answering Sawdon's description, but these cloakroom tickets tell us differently."

At the other end of the bar the two spivs bade the barman a curt farewell and, as they turned, Hawke saw one of them give the barman a meaning wink. Slowly they made for the exit and were nearly there when Hawke let out a cry.

"Stop them! They've got my watch. I've been robbed."

The two turned and gasped, while everyone else in the bar stiffened and stared. Detective-Inspector Baxter looked as startled as the rest.

Hawke's companions jumped to his aid when he dived across the room, and grabbed both men by the arms.

They shook themselves free angrily. One snarled at Hawke.

"What sort of game is this? We've got no watch."

"I'm certain of it," replied Hawke. "I remember now that one pushed against me as he got down from his stool. Search him, Baxter!"

"Nobody's going to search me!" roared the man. "I know my rights. Even if you are cops — "

"Enough of that!" snapped the inspector, and he threw his arms around the speaker, locking his elbows to his side.

Dixon Hawke dived a hand into the man's nearest pocket and produced a gold watch. There was an incredulous gasp from the spiv, then he began to struggle violently, while his companion made a dash for the exit and was tripped by the taximan.

"It was planted there! I didn't know the watch was there! " roared the man whom Baxter held.

"Sam, call the boys. It's a frame-up."

Sam was finding himself fully occupied with the taximan, however, and the other occupants of the sinister little restaurant showed no eagerness to come to the rescue, so, between them, Hawke and his companions secured the two spivs.

"We'll see what this is all about when we get them to the police station," said Baxter gruffly.

At the mention of the police station, the two captives began to struggle even more violently, and one managed to produce a dangerous-looking knife, which Hawke promptly knocked from his grasp.

"We might as well see if they make a business of this sort of thing," drawled Hawke, as he went through their pockets with speed and skill.

From the side-pocket of the noisier of the pair he had taken a handkerchief smeared with blood. Hawke next examined the contents of the man's wallet, withdrew certain scribbled notes, and asked Baxter for the memos that they had found in the possession of Tony Sawdon. The writing was identical.

"H'm," grunted the detective, "so you did know Tony Sawdon and did business with him regarding a consignment of cigarettes!" As the spivs paled, Hawke turned on the man who had drawn the knife. "I've an idea you'll be charged with his wilful murder.

"You gave yourself away nicely."

The man's face paled with terror. His lips drew back from his teeth.

"It's a lie! I didn't — he did it," he screeched.

"It was Rinaldo who did it. I never touched him. I can prove it. I've still got my knife, haven't I?

"Rinaldo hasn't got his, because he left it sticking in Sawdon."

"Shut up, you fool!" snarled his companion, but it was too late.

After a little pressure the whole thing came out.

Sawdon, who had been mixed up with Rinaldo and Murren in several deals in the black market, had accused them that morning of double-crossing him. They had argued in the bar of the Chez Adolphe, when no one else had been there except the barman and the proprietor. Rinaldo had finally lost his temper, pulled out his skewer-like dagger and had driven it up under Sawdon's ribs.

Tony Sawdon had at once turned and walked swiftly from the place before anyone could stop him. He had hailed the first passing taxi.

The proprietor of the restaurant, threatened by Rinaldo and Murren, had arranged with his employees to say they had never seen the dead man in the establishment.

By deliberately accusing the wrong man after searching their pockets, Hawke had trapped Murren into blurting out the truth.

"But why the fools had to pick your pocket, Hawke, when they suspected we were cops, beats me!" exclaimed Detective-Inspector Baxter some hours later.

Dixon Hawke winked at Tommy Burke.

"I hate to tell you the truth, Inspector, but they didn't. I deliberately let that half-crown roll across the floor in order to have an excuse to get close to them. Then I planted the watch in Rinaldo's pocket. It gave us a chance to frisk them!

"A dirty trick, maybe, but one can't wear velvet gloves when dealing with these spivs."

—o0o—

# THE CASE OF
## The Bedpost-Top

**The incessant ringing of the telephone awakened Dixon Hawke from his deep sleep. Slowly he reached out and took the instrument from its rest.**

"Hawke here," he said, stifling a yawn.

"This is McPhinney," said a voice at the other end of the line. "Hawke, I've got a rather baffling case of murder on my hands. Sorry to bother you so early in the morning, but could you come down and give me some help?"

"I'll be there straight away, Mac. Where are you?"

"Number Ten Lansbury Grove."

In less than half an hour, Hawke and his assistant, Tommy Burke, turned into the quiet thoroughfare known as Lansbury Grove. No. 10 was a two-storied house of the Georgian period. Hawke and Tommy ran up the short flight of steps to the door, and Hawke pressed the bell. Almost immediately they were admitted by a uniformed constable.

"In there," he said, pointing to a door on their left. "The inspector's expecting you, sir."

As Chief Detective-Inspector Duncan McPhinney greeted Hawke, the detective noticed the puzzled frown on his friend's face.

"What's it this time, Mac?" asked Hawke.

"Murder, without any possible doubt, Hawke; but one of those seemingly senseless murders." He pointed to a sheet-covered object on a couch near the fire.

"That," he said, "is the body of Gilbert Merridew, Latin scholar and man of letters."

McPhinney lifted a corner of the sheet and revealed the face of Gilbert Merridew. The features were small, finely moulded, while the head was covered with a shock of silvery white hair. The man, Hawke judged, had been in the early sixties.

"Neck broken, cleanly and expertly," said McPhinney, "And death occurred about half-past two this morning. His body was found at the foot of the stairs in the hall."

He led the way to the hall and pointed out a chalk mark on the carpet.

"It looks as if he was jumped on when he reached the foot of the stairs," commented Hawke.

McPhinney nodded in agreement.

"But there's more to come," he said. "Just follow me."

They crossed the hall to another room, large and pleasant, with long windows on the outside wall of the house. From the numerous glass cases arrayed along the walls Hawke immediately gathered that it was some kind of a museum.

The room was an utter shambles. The doors of the cases were open, and the contents lay scattered over the floor. The articles were a varied lot. Hawke saw an old cracked teapot lying alongside an empty beer-bottle. A shattered coffee cup lay beside a dirty old tennis ball.

"Merridew was a souvenir-hunter," explained the Yard man. "He used to travel a lot and these were his souvenirs. Most of them are entirely valueless and had only a sentimental attraction for Merridew. However, as you see, someone has ruined the whole lot."

"Strange," murmured Hawke, "not the sort of stuff crooks go after."

"That's what's worrying me. Why should someone take the trouble to mess things up like this? Perhaps Howard Lane will be able to tell us something. He's Merridew's nephew, and I've yet to hear his story."

Howard Lane was a tall young man in his twenties. He had a pale, lean face with glaring eyes and he wore horn-rimmed spectacles.

"You discovered the body, I believe?"

"Er — yes. It was a really horrible experience, really!"

"Tell us exactly what happened."

"Well, I retired about ten-thirty, and so did Uncle Gilbert. At least he went up to his room about that time, but he may have read for a while. He did that, you know — read for hours at a time! Yesterday he received a volume of Tacitus and he had it under his arm when he went to his room.

"Well, I went to bed immediately and I suppose I fell asleep. I'm a pretty heavy sleeper and I don't remember anything until I woke up.

"I had the feeling that a noise had wakened me, but I listened and heard nothing. I was dropping off again when I heard a dull thud and the splintering of glass.

"I thought at first a window had been left open, but I waited five minutes before I got up to see to it.

"When I reached the hall it was quite dark and I — I tripped over something. I could feel it was a human being, and when I switched on the light, I saw it was Uncle Gilbert."

"You heard nothing else? No sounds of anyone moving?"

"Nothing. I phoned for a doctor and informed the police of what had happened."

"What time was this?"

"Half-past two. The hall clock chimed as I came down the stairs."

"Now, Mr Lane, what sort of a man was your Uncle Gilbert?" asked Hawke.

"Oh, splendid. I mean he was kind and courteous and a very clever scholar."

"He lived a quiet life?"

"Yes, very quiet. He hadn't many friends though he was a great traveller in his younger days. Latterly he spent his time here and at his club, with an occasional visit to the country."

"He wasn't the sort of man to have enemies?"

"Not at all. Everyone liked Uncle Gilbert."

"He had a passion for collecting things?"

"Yes. It was a sort of hobby with him. Wherever he went he would bring back some trifle as a souvenir."

McPhinney's men reported that they had found no fingerprints other than those of Merridew himself, his nephew' and the servants.

Hawke examined the catch on the window by which the murderer had gained entrance to the house.

"A neat job," he commented. "No bungling amateur did this. It is the work of an expert."

Hawke gazed at the littered room. "You said that nothing in the house had been touched?" he asked McPhinney.

"That's correct."

"The man who opened that window was an expert and had he come here hoping to get something valuable, one look at those cases would have told him that the articles in them were useless. Unless he came here to find one particular thing."

"But why pull everything else from the cases and scatter them on the floor? The cases aren't locked and he could have taken what he came for without so great a risk of discovery. As it was, he disturbed Merridew, who came down to see what was wrong."

Hawke walked down the room, pondering over the question. He noticed that at regular intervals along the glass shelves were small gummed labels bearing a number.

A possible solution of the question came to him.

"See here, Mac. It looks as if each article of the collection was numbered. Now, supposing the murderer came here for one particular thing and got it, too, but he noticed the numbers as well. If the murderer took that article it would leave an empty space on one of the shelves, and Merridew would know at once what was missing.

"Suppose that article could be easily linked to the crook and he realised that. He wouldn't want to give himself away so obviously, so he pulled everything from the shelves in the hope that Merridew wouldn't notice what was missing, but Merridew was probably reading in his room and heard the noise.

"He came to investigate. The crook heard him, and hid in the shadow of the staircase. He jumped on Merridew and murdered him before the old man could utter a sound."

"Feasible, but how can you prove it?"

"Find out if there's anything missing. If there is, then we have a clue to the whole business." Hawke called Howard Lane and asked him if his uncle had kept a record of his collection.

"Oh, yes, there's a book in the study. Uncle Gilbert was very methodical about it. He entered what each article was, where he'd got it, and the date."

"Bring it here at once, please."

The detectives set to work quickly. Merridew had given a pretty accurate description of everything.

Though it did not take them long to find each article to correspond with the entry in the book, the collection was a large one and took some time to wade through. Even so, in less than an hour the collection had been replaced.

McPhinney walked round the cases. "The only thing that's missing is the one numbered 2965."

"The carved top of a bed-post from the Fighting Cock Inn, Detling, Kent," read Hawke from the record book.

For a moment Hawke and McPhinney looked at each other. Then both of them grinned.

"I didn't expect that," admitted Hawke, " But as soon as we've had some breakfast, Tommy and I will drive down to Kent. I still think my hunch is right."

It was nearly lunch-time when they found Detling, a quiet little village surrounded by orchards, just off the main road to Maidstone. The Fighting Cock Inn, a rambling old structure, stood at the end of a dusty lane, and Hawke liked it as soon as he saw it.

He liked the atmosphere of the place and the cool parlour into which they were shown when he asked for lunch.

He also liked the large, jolly, shirt-sleeved host who came to see them when their meal was placed before them.

"Everything all right, sir?"

"Excellent, Mr — er?"

"Gunn. Benjamin Gunn, sir."

"Fine place you have here," said Hawke. "Old, I should say."

"Ay, that it is, sir. The Fighting Cock Inn was built by Jeremiah Gunn in 1689 and there's been a Gunn here ever since."

"It's seen quite a bit of history, at that rate," said Hawke, keeping the host in conversation.

"Yes, I believe the Fighting Cock Inn was quite famous at one time. You see the old road to the coast used to pass through Detling, and travellers from London used to change their horses here. The great Duke of Wellington spent the night here when he was on his way to France to fight Napoleon. The very bed he slept in is still in use upstairs."

"Then you must have a lot of visitors," went on Hawke.

"Yes, before the war we'd have visitors all the year round, and then the American soldiers came, and I think a whole division wanted to sleep in the Duke of Wellington's bed."

"I must try sleeping in it myself," said Hawke with a smile.

"Well, not for a bit, anyway," replied the landlord. "You see, about six weeks ago we had a gentleman — decent little man, but the missus said he was finicky. This gentleman took away the top of one of the bedposts when he went off and left a fiver to pay for the damage. Right annoyed I was when I found out, but I'm having the carpenter make another one.

"He's a good man, but a slow worker, and it might be some time before the bed can be used again."

Hawke smiled to himself. It was just the sort of souvenir-hunting in which Gilbert Merridew must have delighted. For the moment the detective did not reveal the real reason for his visit to the Fighting Cock Inn, as he hoped to gain all the information he needed without alarming the people at the inn.

"We had a peculiar incident about a fortnight ago," continued Benjamin Gunn.

"A friend of mine was sleeping in Wellington's bed — the night before I had it shifted to the carpenter's. He was awakened in the middle of the night by a man prowling in the room but the intruder escaped by the window. Nothing had been stolen, however.

"The day after, a gent came in and, as he had slept in the bed before, he wanted to do so again. He seemed quite upset when I told him the story of the missing bed-post, and how I had just had the bed sent down to the carpenter's. He asked all about the other old gentleman — the one who took the bedpost — his name and where he came from. Then off he went. Queer, don't you think sir?"

"Rather," agreed Hawke, who had been listening intently.

"Do you remember what this chap was like? Could you give me a description of him?"

"Well, he wasn't very tall, about the height of your lad there, but stocky-built. He had a peculiar pale face, not at all healthy like, and one of his eyes was pulled out of shape by a scar on his temple, crescent-shaped it was. Why are you wanting his description?"

"Never mind that just now," answered the detective, "But perhaps I may be able to find your property for you. Please don't say a word to anyone about this. Come on, Tommy."

Hawke threw a note on the table in payment for the meal and before the astonished host could say anything the detectives were speeding up the lane in Hawke's car.

Shortly afterwards he and Tommy were on their way back to London. They went straight to Scotland Yard and into McPhinney's office.

"Well, Hawke, what did you find in Kent?" asked Mac, as he looked up from his desk.

"Enough to satisfy me that I was on the right track. Listen."

He gave the Yard man an account of his conversation with the host of the Fighting Cock Inn.

" Now," he concluded, " it seems too much of a coincidence that a week or two after Merridew had taken the top of the bedpost someone else should come and break into the room at the inn, yet steal nothing. Then a man comes and asks all about Merridew.

"It's all too much of a coincidence, Mac."

"H'm, could be. But how can you be sure that the person who asked about the bed and the murderer of Merridew are the same person?"

"I'm not sure, for the present anyway, but I feel that if we find the man who asked about Merridew we will go a long way to solving the murder. For one thing we will find why he thought that post so important. Whoever broke into Merridew's house is a past-master in the art, and I wouldn't be surprised if he had passed through your hands.

"Gunn said the man had a crescent-shaped scar above his eye. If your records could identify a man answering to Gunn's description and who is an experienced burglar then we might be able to get further ahead."

"Right, Hawke, come along to Records with me. I'll look into this myself."

In the Records Office, known in the Yard as the Rogues' Gallery, they went rapidly through the dossiers of many noted criminals until at last they unearthed one which tallied with Gunn's description of his visitor.

"This is the one all right," said Hawke, waving the police photograph. "There's the scar and the corner of the right eye is pulled upwards by the stretching of the skin. There's a long list of convictions for burglary against him."

"Nick Charles," murmured McPhinney thoughtfully. "An old friend of mine, Hawke. I had him sent down for his last stretch of seven years. That was just before the war broke out. Do you want to read his history?"

"Yes," said Hawke, picking up the dossier. "You'd better phone the Governor of Parkhurst and find out whether Nick Charles has been set free or not."

Nick Charles was at liberty and had been released two months before, having done a year more than his sentence because of an affair in which a warder had received injuries. The difficulty now was to find Charles and to do this McPhinney set the machinery of the Yard in motion.

Hawke studied the criminal's dossier, and he and Tommy took a stroll down the back streets and alleys behind Covent Garden, a neighbourhood which Charles had haunted in the days of his freedom. At a corner near the famous market,

Hawke stopped to purchase a paper from a ragged youth, who was known by the name of Nosey.

"How's trade, Nosey?" asked Hawke, tendering a half-crown for his paper.

"Not so bad, Mr 'Awke," replied Nosey.

"Seen anything of a man with a small scar just here? Name of Nick Charles?"

"Don't fink so."

"Well, if you do, let me know and you can pass the word around."

Hawke slipped another half-crown into Nosey's eager palm. He knew that before many hours had passed every street urchin around Covent Garden would be keeping a sharp look-out for the scarred criminal.

The detectives continued their stroll and on two occasions they entered public-houses so that Hawke could run his eye over the customers. They had just come out of the second of these when Nosey and an even more ragged urchin came-up.

"Been looking for yer, Mister 'Awke. Joe 'ere says that Ma Briggs 'as a queer lodger. Tell 'im wot you told me, Joe."

"Well, Ma Briggs 'as got 'erself a lodger. Don't come out much 'e don't and Ma Briggs calls 'im Old Nick."

"Good. Anything else, Joe?"

"Ma Briggs goes down to the Bricklayers' Arms every night." Hawke gave Joe a couple of half- crowns for his information.

Hawke and Tommy turned in the direction of the Bricklayers' Arms. They found a corner of the bar vacant and here Hawke waited for the arrival of Ma Briggs.

He did not know the woman in question, but hoped that a stray remark might reveal her identity.

As it turned out he was quite lucky. Fifteen minutes after they arrived a large woman with a face like a full moon squeezed herself into the bar. She was immediately greeted by a chorus of " 'Ello, Ma!"

Mrs Briggs sailed up to the bar and pushed herself into the space which Hawke had adroitly made.

On to the bar she hoisted a string bag full of empty bottles and called raucously to the barman.

"Same again, 'Arry."

"Wot, again, Ma? Yer spend all yer time drinkin'!"

"Gorn, ain't me, it's 'im, the lodger, Old Nick 'imself I calls 'im."

While Ma Briggs exchanged a large wink with the barman Hawke saw at once the opportunity of discovering the identity of the lodger. As if about to call for another drink he pulled out a handful of loose silver and clumsily let most of it scatter over the floor.

Ma Briggs immediately bent down and began picking up the coins.

While her attention was so distracted, Hawke reached over and took one of the bottles from her bag and passed it to Tommy.

Ma Briggs handed over the coins to Hawke though he noticed that one half-crown which he had seen her pick up was missing.

He said nothing but dragged Tommy outside, making for the nearest place where they could hire a taxi for Scotland Yard.

"What the devil!" exclaimed McPhinney, when Hawke put the beer-bottle on his desk.

"This, Mac, may have the prints of Nick Charles on it. Have it checked at once. If it has, then I know where Charles can be found.

The report was soon handed to McPhinney. Amongst a multitude of prints there was one thumbprint which undoubtedly belonged to Nick Charles.

Thirty minutes later McPhinney and Hawke faced the crook in his own room.

"Where's that piece of carved wood you took from the house in Lansbury Grove?" asked McPhinney.

"Blimey, Guv'nor, I don't know what you're talking about!" protested the crook.

"You know quite well what I mean — the top of the bed-post from the Fighting Cock Inn at Detling."

"Strewth, Guv'nor. I don't know nofink about it. Honest, I don't."

" 'Ere, 'ere, what's agon' on 'ere?" said a voice from the door.

It was Ma Briggs back from her visit to the Bricklayers' Aims.

"I'm from Scotland Yard," announced McPhinney. "Mrs Briggs, I must warn you that you may be harbouring a murderer."

Ma Briggs did not need anyone to tell her what the implication meant.

"I don't know nofink," she said with an air of finality.

"Perhaps, but did you see this man with a large piece of wood carved like an acorn?"

"Yer don't mean wot 'e gave me fer me kitchen dresser? Big thing, like a bedpost."

"Yes, that's it," said Hawke.

Ma Briggs waddled down the stairs followed by one of McPhinney's men. A great puffing and blowing announced her return. In her hand was the missing acorn-shaped piece of wood.

Hawke took it from her. From the base protruded a wooden screw. He twisted this until it came out completely. Then he shook the acorn over his open hand. There was a flash of fire and a large diamond lay in his palm.

"The Rand Star," he said. "It was stolen by Nick Charles in 1939 when Van Ryn, the diamond merchant, was sending it to Britain.

"You remember the affair," Hawke continued.

"Van Ryn had a big business in Amsterdam but, with the threat of war coming, he transferred it to London. In his keeping was a famous diamond, the Rand Star, and it weighed over ninety carats. Van Ryn sent the diamond to England in the care of a special courier.

"On the way the courier disappeared. You, Mac, were in charge of investigations and discovered that O'Malley, the gang-leader, was on the boat from which the courier disappeared. You pulled the whole gang in, and though you never found the Rand Star, you managed to prove that the gang did have something to do with the theft.

"Just before the trial the body of Van Ryn's agent was washed up on the beach near Clacton.

"He had been stabbed and thrown overboard. Well, O'Malley was hanged, his lieutenants got life sentences, and the smaller fry got lesser terms of imprisonment.

"The point is that Nick Charles was, at the time, working for O'Malley, and you, Mac, arrested him as he was stepping on the Channel boat at Dover. The Fighting Cbck Inn is roughly half-way between London and Dover and I'm sure Charles will tell us how he got rid of the Rand Star."

The crook did not deny his guilt, and after a little persuasive questioning he told the whole story.

When the O'Malley gang had stolen the diamond, he had been entrusted with the delivering of it to an address in London.

By the time Charles had reached the city the hue and cry for the members of the O'Malley gang had started, and the man to whom he should have delivered the stone had bolted. Charles had bolted too, down to Kent where he had put up at the Fighting Cock.

He intended to cross to France but dared not take the stone with him so he had sought for a suitable hiding-place. He had hit upon the bedpost and spent the whole night hollowing out a cavity to contain the stone, intending to come back later and claim it.

As he was arrested he could not return for the stone until his release from prison. Then he found that the acorn-shaped piece of wood had been removed. That was the night of the burglary at the inn. He had traced Merridew to his house in London and the rest had happened almost as Hawke had reconstructed the crime.

"It was a million-to-one chance that Merridew should choose that particular acorn to add to his collection — but it came off," commented Hawke the day Charles was hanged for his crime.

—oOo—

# THE CASE OF THE SCARRED THUMB-PRINT

**"The old boy certainly does himself well if this is where he lives,"
muttered Tommy Burke, as Dixon Hawke turned his car in at the
great gates and they glimpsed the beautiful Tudor mansion at the
end of the drive.**

"Sir Stanstead Moorely is one of the richest men in England," the Dover
Street detective told him, "'and is one of the most famous of private art
collectors. Whatever losses Zorn has caused him, he can well afford them,
but that's not the point. I'm only too glad to have another chance of getting
on the trail of The Man with a Hundred Faces! "

A few minutes later they were being escorted across a lofty hall by a
dignified butler. Great canvases hung on the walls, while the carpets were
beautiful.

They were taken into a small, cosy room, where a dignified, grey-haired
man rose to greet them. In spite of his being seventy-two, Sir Stanstead
Moorely was as straight as a youth of eighteen, and his aquiline face was

144

bronzed by much hard riding over the neighbouring downs. He had two great passions in life — horses and pictures.

"Mr Hawke, it is good of you to come so quickly. This is your assistant, Mr Burke? Sit down, please, and I'll tell you my troubles. I hope you had a good journey. Would you like some refreshments?"

Hawke thanked him, and told him that they had had tea only a few miles back along the road, so that they did not need anything. Hawke asked him to get down to business as quickly as possible, as he was anxious to hear the full details.

"Well, Mr Hawke," began Sir Stanstead, "I told you the important facts on the phone. They are simple enough. I am a collector of pictures." He pursed his lips modestly. "I may say that I have one of the finest collections in the country, mostly Gainsboroughs and Van Goghs, with Monets and Orpens in the modern groups. My collection is — or was — valued at £500,000.

"My art agent, with whom I have had dealings for thirty years, is Humphrey Zither, of whom you will have heard."

Hawke nodded.

"We are great friends, and he visits me at least once a month, both as an adviser and because we like each other. He executes all purchases for me at sales, and attends to the general condition of my collection. He was down here last weekend, from Friday until Monday, and when he left he took with him a picture of Leonardo's. It needed renovation, and, as it is a favourite of mine, I wished it to be done straightaway. He promised to let me have it back again in a fortnight."

He frowned as he went on.

"You can guess my astonishment when, on telephoning to him yesterday about some other matter, and asking him how the picture was coming along, he not only denied all knowledge of receiving the picture, but declared he had not even visited me the previous weekend.

"Mr Hawke, I have known him for thirty years, and could have sworn I entertained him here, but he has proved to me that he did not leave London. Who is there who could impersonate Humphrey Zither so thoroughly that even I was fooled sufficiently to hand over to him a picture worth nearly £5000?"

"One man only," grunted Hawke, "an American ex-actor named Zorn, better known now as 'The Man with a Hundred Faces'. He has the most amazing gift for impersonation. Once he impersonated me at Scotland Yard, and got away with his own dossier."

"But the voice, the mannerisms, the very walk  — " exclaimed Sir Stanstead Moorely.

"They are always exact. Zorn takes the trouble to study the persons he intends to impersonate. I have no doubt that he visited Mr Zither several times on various pretexts in order to get all those points correct.

"It is not the first time he has done this. I am surprised he contented himself with a picture worth only £5000.

"Well, he could not very well walk away with the more valuable ones, for there was no pretext, and most of them are too large," explained the older man. "My faith in myself is shaken, Mr Hawke. Either I am getting old and unobservant, or this —this Zorn is a superman."

"A superman in his own line, yes. You need not blame yourself for being fooled. Everyone with whom he has ever come in contact has been fooled at some time or other."

"But is he likely to come back here again? How am I to know when the real Zither visits me? I shall never trust him again."

Dixon Hawke laughed.

"You had better arrange a code word with him, and get him to tell it to you on arrival. There is only one other way of telling. Zorn has a scar across the top of his right thumb, not clear enough to be seen normally, but it shows in his thumb-print. Now exactly what do you wish me to do, Sir Stanstead? I suppose you want your picture recovered?"

"Naturally, but it's far more important to lay the fellow by the heels. He's a positive menace to everyone."

"I agree with that," said Hawke, heartily, "but many of us have tried for a long time to catch him. He has a knack of slipping through our fingers. However, I'm doing my best, and I will tell you one thing. He never wastes an opportunity. He was in this house for three days.

"In that time he will have studied your servants, yourself, everything under your roof. I cannot imagine him neglecting such a chance. If he wants to pay you another visit he will choose another guise. He will become your butler, your chauffeur, your secretary, or maybe even you. There is no limit to his impudence.

"He has not been known actually to kill, but he is utterly ruthless when after his prey. You must keep a very close watch here for some time to come. If he is going to make another impersonation he will do it whilst the facts are fresh in his mind."

Sir Stanstead looked grave.

"We are nearly all old here, Mr Hawke. My servants have grown old in my service, and I fear some of them are not as alert as they might be. I want to invite you and your assistant to remain here with me until the danger period is past. You will be made very comfortable, and everything will be at your disposal."

Dixon Hawke thought of grimy London and its traffic-choked streets, of the jostling crowds and the fuel problems. He looked out at the magnificent grounds, the century-old lawns and the luxury about him, and he decided that a change would do them no harm.

"We shall be delighted to stay a while, Sir Stanstead," he replied.

Hawke and Tommy enjoyed themselves immensely. They went riding in the park and on the downs, and they swam in the private lake; they went for long walks and they lazed in the Italian garden. They enjoyed lots of sunshine and fresh air, and all the time they studied the servants, the visitors, and all who called at the great house, for Hawke felt sure that Zorn would try to strike again.

Sir Stanstead left them very much to themselves, and, when he was not out riding, he was in his art gallery or poring over art catalogues. He spoke of lending some of his finest pictures to an exhibition in Wales, and was making the necessary arrangements to do so.

Only now and then did he ask Hawke if he had anything to report.

Jenkins, the butler, helped Dixon Hawke take the fingerprints of all the staff. He was a grave, dignified man and a master of discretion. Hawke knew the butler never disclosed Hawke's real identity to the rest of the staff. He accepted them as friends of his master, and as such they could do as they wished.

There were a dozen indoor and outdoor servants upon whom to keep check, but when he had been there a full week Hawke felt sure that Zorn had not succeeded in taking the place of any of them.

One morning Jenkins, the butler, brought them their early morning tea rather earlier than usual. He put the tray down between the beds and drew the curtains.

He withdrew with his usual dignity, and Tommy grinned as he sat up and reached for the tray.

"I wonder if anything would ever shake old Jenkins? I bet he didn't even turn a hair when the bombs came down, and — Hm!" He bent and peered at the saucer, which Jenkins had pushed gently towards his side of the tray a moment before.

"Looks as though he doesn't wash first thing in the morning! I thought the perfect butler never left fingerprints on anything."

"It can't have been Jenkins," said Hawke, without much interest.

"But it was — a big dirty thumbprint! I saw him grip the saucer there to steady it. I'm surprised at him."

Half-chuckling to himself at the thought of finding some imperfection in so perfect a servant, Tommy picked up the clean table napkin with the idea of wiping the print off. Suddenly he gave another grunt, removed the cup from the saucer to hold the latter up to the light.

"What's the matter now?" demanded the detective, as he sipped his tea.

"Guv'nor, look!" The boy's voice was full of excitement. "Look at the print. Get your magnifying glass. It's a right thumb-print. Even with the naked eye it's possible to see a scar across it."

"What?" Dixon Hawke nearly upset his tea as he leapt out of bed. "Let me see!"

He pored over the dirty mark for a few moments, then drew his magnifying glass from his jacket pocket and made a closer inspection. The boy saw the colour rise to his cheeks.

"You're right, Tommy. It's the scar — the trade-mark of Zorn. The real Jenkins isn't here any more. That was Zorn who brought in our tea. Get dressed!"

Within five minutes, each with a loaded automatic in his pocket, they went downstairs in search of Jenkins. They found him in the passage leading to the kitchen quarters.

"I'm so sorry I'm late this morning, sir, but I seem to have overslept," he said. "I've got a frightful headache, and — "

"Nothing to the headache that you'll get when you hear your sentence, Zorn!" snapped Hawke, taking him firmly by one arm and prodding him gently with the end of the automatic.

The man's face paled.

"But I do not understand, Mr Hawke. I fail to appreciate what you are saying. What have I done?"

"Done? You left a thumb-print on Tommy's saucer when you served him with tea this morning," said the detective. "Sufficient to tell us you are not Jenkins."

"But I am Jenkins, sir, and I have not yet brought you your tea this morning."

Dixon Hawke dragged him to the window.

"You say you did not serve our tea this morning? Yet someone brought it in ten minutes ago, and left that thumb-print on the saucer. Press your right thumb against that window. That's the idea."

Hawke paused as he examined the print.

"He's not Zorn. There's no scar there. We've been fooled again, Tommy. There are two Jenkins in the house, or were a little while ago. You say you have a headache, Jenkins, and you overslept?"

"Yes, sir, I cannot understand it."

"Something was slipped into your supper drink, and this morning someone took your place to serve us with tea. Why?" demanded the man from Dover Street. "Was it drugged? You didn't touch yours, Tommy, and I feel no ill effects, but I only had a sip or two.

"There must have been some reason. Anyway, he's still in the house. Jenkins, I want every servant in the kitchen at once, everyone who has entered this house this morning. Hurry!"

Five minutes later he was walking along the line of puzzled servants, lifting and examining the hands of the men. He found no scarred thumb.

"Are you sure they're all here, Jenkins?"

"Yes, sir."

Having pressed all the men and boys into his service, Hawke organised a search from attics to cellars, but Zorn had utterly vanished.

Dixon Hawke was puzzled.

"Are there any secret chambers or hide-outs in the house, Jenkins?" he asked.

"I have heard of a monk's cell somewhere, sir, but Sir Stanstead would be able to tell you that. I heard him go down to the art gallery."

Dixon Hawke found Sir Stanstead Moorely in the art gallery. A dozen of the finest pictures had been marked with tickets for the exhibition in Wales. Men were coming that day to pack them. The grey-haired nobleman looked up with a welcoming smile when Hawke entered, but the smile died away when he saw Hawke's expression.

"Anything wrong, Mr Hawke?"

"I fear there is. I believe that Zorn was in the house a little while ago. Can you tell me where the secret room is — the monk's cell — or whatever it's called?"

Sir Stanstead stared at him blankly and shook his head.

"I've really never heard of such a place, Mr Hawke. It doesn't exist."

"But Jenkins said — "

"I'm afraid Jenkins is romancing. I have heard the legend, it is true, but no member of my family has ever found it, so I fail to see why your mysterious Zorn could have been more successful. No, there is no such place to my knowledge. If Zorn has gone, he has gone, and it's no use worrying. At least, he hasn't got another of my pictures. Which do you suggest I lend the exhibition, Mr Hawke — this study by Degas or this by Cezanne?"

Sir Stanstead pointed to two pictures in opposite corners. Hawke glanced at them casually.

His mind was not on pictures, but on the mystery of the vanishing butler who was Zorn. It was queer that Jenkins had distinctly said there was a secret room, and that Sir Stanstead had said there was not.

"Which do you suggest?" the old collector went on.

Hawke pulled his thoughts back to his present surroundings, and as he did so his expression changed almost imperceptibly.

"I think that Degas — " he said, pointing.

"Very well, Mr Hawke, thank you. I'll stick a ticket on that," murmured Sir Stanstead, and wetted one of his prepared labels on the moistened pad upon his desk.

The detective watched him affix this to the frame, then moved across and glanced keenly at the numbered slip. Thanks to the fact that he had stuck on more than one moistened label, Sir Stanstead's thumb had been damp and slightly grimy.

There on the white paper was a pale thumb- print. Dixon Hawke calmly produced his magnifying glass and focused on this.

Out of the comer of his eye he saw Sir Stanstead stiffen, then snatch at one of the drawers of the desk. In a moment Hawke was round, with automatic levelled.

"No, you don't, Zorn. Keep away from that drawer. We want no shooting if we can help it… Back against that wall, and raise your hands."

With blazing eyes the man did so, and Hawke shouted for Tommy Burke, who came running in great haste. When he saw his Guv'nor covering the man they knew as the owner of the house, the boy gaped.

"It's Zorn, Tommy. He gave himself away by trying to cover up a lie about a secret room by changing the subject to pictures. He called a Degas a Cezanne and vice versa.

"He did not know the difference when I deliberately misnamed them in the same way. I pointed to that as a Degas, whereas it's a Cezanne. Our friend here impersonated Jenkins for some reason or other, then changed back again into this other pose. Why, Zorn, why?"

The anger died from the American crook's eyes. He was leaning easily against the wall with raised hands. He grinned crookedly.

"In order to give you a run for your money, Hawke. I wanted to keep you guessing.

"I'd like to have seen Jenkins's face when you accused him of — "

"Grab him, Tommy !" shouted Hawke, but it was too late.

Under cover of talking, Zorn had pressed with his elbow at some spot on the panelling and a hidden door in the wall had opened. He was through it and had slammed the door in their faces before Hawke could fire. The detective reached the spot a moment later and thumped and pummelled the panel until he found the catch. Again the door opened, and they found themselves peering down steep stairs into a narrow passage in the thickness of the walls.

Tommy was never without a torch. He passed it to Hawke, who led the way to the bottom. On their right they found a door bolted on the outside, evidently the secret room. From it came the sound of banging and an angry voice.

"Let me out, you scoundrel! Let me out of here."

"The real Sir Stanstead Moorely," muttered Hawke. "Let him out, Tommy, whilst I follow this passage. I doubt if it will be of any use."

He was right. The passage led to a summer-house in the grounds, and there the door was open. Zorn had gone. Once again he had slipped away only just in time.

Hawke returned to find Sir Stanstead surrounded by his servants as he told his story. He had been down in the secret room more than a week, ever since the fake Humphrey Zither had come to spend the weekend.

That weekend he had shown the fake art dealer the secret room, and Zither, really Zorn, had imprisoned him there, afterwards taking his place before the entire household. Food had been taken to him each night.

It was obvious that Zorn had planned to take the pick of the art collection and to have them properly packed and dispatched to some rendezvous under pretext of sending them to an exhibition in Wales. In this way he would have got away with Old Masters worth hundreds of thousands of pounds.

"Yet he had to make that silly mistake about those two French painters!" marvelled Dixon Hawke, as they drove back to London later in the day with a handsome cheque from Sir Stanstead. "I would never have thought of looking at that label but for that."

"What I can't understand, Guv'nor," said the boy some ten minutes later, "is why he was fool enough to send for us in the first place. Why did he run the risk of getting us down there?"

"Because I am afraid he is getting to dislike us more and more, Tommy, and he wants to get even for all his coups we've spoilt.

"He thought he would do that by pulling off a great art robbery right under our noses. He thought to make a complete fool of me by having me there when it happened.

"He wanted to make me a laughing stock!"

—oOo—

# THE CASE OF *The* Eucalyptus Bottle

As Dixon Hawke and Tommy Burke entered the drive they saw two police cars standing at the front entrance to the big house in Hampstead. The first car they recognised by its number-plate as the one normally used by Chief Detective-Inspector Duncan McPhinney, of Scotland Yard.

A uniformed constable watched them park their own car and saluted respectfully as they hurried up the steps.

"You'll find the Chief Inspector on the first floor, in the library, Mr Hawke," he said.

Their feet sank into the deep pile of the costly carpets. The house was luxuriously furnished, but they had expected this, for Max Reardon, the cinema magnate, was one of the wealthiest men in Britain.

There was another constable at the foot of the wide staircase, and the mumble of voices guided them to the correct room on the first floor. The door was ajar, and, as they slipped quietly into the huge library, they heard McPhinney saying: "You two are willing to swear that nobody passed in or out of the grounds between midnight and dawn?"

"Yes, sir."

The reply was in firm tones and came from one of two sturdy men standing before the Louis XIV desk. McPhinney was seated behind the desk, while at one side a young constable took down rapid shorthand notes.

"Jones and I were on the watch all the time. The gates were locked, and we had the Alsatians with us. Nobody got in or out during the hours of darkness. The constable on the beat can verify that we spoke to him twice during the night."

It was obvious that the speaker and his companion were ex-policemen. McPhinney glared at them beneath his heavy eyebrows.

"You heard no unusual disturbance in the house — you saw no lights come on where they shouldn't have been?"

"No, sir. But if there had been lights on in the drawing-room we wouldn't have seen them because of the steel shutters over the windows. They're light-proof."

"Yes, and burglar-proof!" came from a far corner, where a short, stout man with a big nose sat on the edge of a chair, his podgy hands resting on his knees. "I had the finest system of burglar alarms that it is possible to buy. I had — "

"Yes, Mr Reardon, but please let me finish questioning these watch- men of yours," broke in McPhinney impatiently. "Isn't it unusual to employ permanent night-watchmen outside a private residence?"

The two men looked at their employer and he stood up.

"Unusual! What do I care if it is unusual? I make my living by being unusual. But what is there strange in employing someone to protect my property when there have been so many robberies in Hampstead, especially as the police have not been able to prevent them?

"If I like to pay two ex-policemen to watch over my house at night, what is there strange about that? Remember, I have art treasures worth over one hundred thousand pounds under this roof."

McPhinney wilted under this tirade, and for the first time glanced at Hawke and Tommy in the background.

"This missing picture was not worth one hundred thousand pounds?" he asked.

"No, no, I did not say that. Forty thousand was the valuation put on my Rembrandt, but there were other pictures, and my jades, my Chinese jades. In all they are insured for one hundred thousand pounds, and now you ask why I was anxious not to have a burglary!"

McPhinney rose and greeted the Dover Street detective.

"Mr Hawke, meet Mr Max Reardon, who insisted upon sending for you. I gave you some idea of the position over the phone.

"This house is better protected than any other house in London, with two watchmen in the grounds all night, not to mention a police dog, steel shutters on all the ground-floor windows, and a wonderful system of burglar alarms.

"Yet during the night someone got away with a picture from Mr Reardon's drawing-room, a Rembrandt worth forty thousand pounds."

Reardon nodded in agreement with McPhinney's statement. The two watchmen were ushered out by a sergeant. Dixon Hawke placed his felt hat on a chair.

"Clues?" he asked.

"None, except that one of the side doors was open, and there is evidence that the lock had been picked. No one heard any unusual sounds, and the watchmen saw nobody enter or leave, yet this morning it was discovered that the Rembrandt had been cut from its frame and had vanished. There are no fingerprints or any other clues."

Hawke looked thoughtful. His keen grey eyes lighted in anticipation of grappling with such a tricky problem.

"I would like to see the room from which the picture was taken," he said.

They led him to the door at the farther end of the library and across a wide corridor. Here another constable was standing and he was in conversation with a short, dark young man who looked round with quick interest. Max Reardon beckoned to him.

"Mr Hawke, this is Philip Lornesay, my confidential secretary," he introduced. "Philip, this is the famous Dixon Hawke from Dover Street. If anyone can recover my picture, he will."

"I've always wanted to meet you, Mr Hawke," murmured Lornesay, and opened the door of the drawing room opposite.

It was a magnificent apartment, about fifty feet long and twenty feet wide. Luxuriously furnished, it seemed larger than it was because of the light cream and gold wall-paper, and the paintwork and decorations to match. Two crystal chandeliers gave a perfect light, for the steel shutters over the windows were still in place.

There were no more than five paintings on the walls, but they were all old masters.

Over the fireplace was a vacant space, and on the floor nearby lay a heavy frame about five feet by four.

It held no canvas, for this was the frame from which the Rembrandt had been cut.

Hawke walked across to examine the frame. He at once noticed that a sharp knife had been used with skill and care. A brocaded chair in the fireplace drew his attention. Philip Lornesay noted the direction of his glance.

"Evidently the thief stood on that to reach the picture, Mr Hawke," he remarked. "Would it be possible to detect footprints?"

"Not on that corded surface; no — " Hawke was slowly taking in the details of the room. "The windows are still shuttered, I see. No sign of tampering there, McPhinney?"

"None. The thief walked in this door from the hall, just as we have done. The door is not locked at night, but I must admit that the outer doors are well protected with the finest locks and the very latest burglar alarms.

"Why the alarms did not go off when that side door was opened, I cannot imagine."

Again Hawke scrutinised the apartment, the gold and cream walls, the severely plain ceiling, the beautiful furniture and the remaining pictures. He shook his head slowly.

"Show me that side door where the thief entered," he said.

The side door opened into a porch which in turn led on to the lawns east of the house. In the light of day it was easy to see the scratches and streaks around the outside of the keyhole. As Hawke bent to examine these with a glass, the others stood back in silence.

"Hm!" grunted Dixon Hawke, straightening up. "That would not have been an easy lock to pick. You found the door unlocked this morning? — Tommy, get your screwdriver and let's have the lock off the door."

Whilst his assistant was engaged in removing the lock, the Dover Street detective walked out on to the lawn and looked at the house and the grounds. There were at least two acres of grounds and they were surrounded by a high wall with deadly spikes on top. The only gate was extremely high and again had elaborate locks.

Twice Hawke walked right round the house, examining doors and windows, then Tommy came to tell him that the lock was off. The detective carried it into a small ante-room off the hall, where he spread newspapers on the table and began to take the lock to pieces.

McPhinney fidgeted with impatience and said he would continue questioning the staff.

By then Hawke had the lock open and was focusing his magnifying glass on the wards inside.

"Just a minute, Mac," he said. "Don't be in too much of a hurry. This rather alters things — the lock has not been picked. There are no traces of the use of tools or instruments on the interior of the lock or on the wards. All the marks are on the outside. Someone has gone to considerable trouble to make it appear as if the lock was picked, whereas it was unlocked with a key in the normal way."

"But — but, why?" stammered McPhinney, peering through the glass which had been put into his hand.

"I see what you mean. But, why?"

"There can be only one reason. Someone wanted it to appear that the lock was picked from the outside, by an intruder, whereas it was actually opened in the ordinary manner from the inside."

He rose with a sigh. "No wonder the watchmen saw nobody come in or out. This was an inside job, I fear."

They looked at him in astonishment, and it was hard to say who seemed more surprised — McPhinney, Tommy Burke, Reardon or his secretary.

"Impossible!" snorted Max Reardon.

"I'm afraid not, Mr Reardon," replied Hawke.

"I thought at the time that no man clever enough to pick a lock of this description would leave-so many scratches. The fact that the burglar alarms did not go off was another puzzle.

"Of course, the explanation is that they were switched off by someone with a full knowledge of the system. The door was left open as a blind. The picture has not left the house. Some member of the household took it, and it is hidden under this roof at the moment."

"Then, by Jove, we'll find it!" roared the cinema magnate. "If one of my household has done such a thing — but, no, that can't be true, Mr Hawke. I've not a large staff, and I can trust them all."

Dixon Hawke shrugged his shoulders.

"I agree that it's an unpleasant prospect, but the facts speak for themselves. Who stayed in the house last night, besides yourself and Mr Lornesay?"

Reardon looked at his secretary, who went over the various people in turn.

"Besides ourselves, there were Mr Carrick, a business friend of Mr Reardon's, who had the best suite; the two footmen; the chef; two housemaids; the housekeeper and the chauffeur."

"No members of your family, Mr Reardon?" asked Hawke.

"Nonc. They are all away in Switzerland."

"And this Mr Carrick?"

"He is the owner of a string of cinemas in the North which I am anxious to acquire. He is so over-whelmed with the news of this robbery that he has remained in his room. He has a weak heart."

Hawke's expression was inscrutable.

"Who has been out of the house this morning?"

"Nobody as yet. Directly the discovery was made I forbade anyone to leave. Everything has been done by telephone."

"Good! As I surmise the picture must be still in the house. Even if rolled, as it will doubtless be by now, it would be four or five feet long. Nobody could walk out of here with a five-foot roll unnoticed.

I suggest that you have the house searched from top to bottom, McPhinney, for a roll about five feet long."

The Yard man nodded vigorously. "I'll get a squad of experts down from the Yard, and by the time they've finished we'll know if you're right or not."

"I am right," declared Hawke emphatically.

"Let nobody leave on any pretext! While your men are coming, and while they are busy, I'll interview every member of the staff in turn — and Mr Carrick."

For the purpose of these interviews Hawke chose the bare ante-room where he had examined the lock.

The interviews took quite a time and were not very satisfactory. Dixon Hawke, who was skilled at weighing up people, studied each person in turn. Tommy was present and noticed that he gave most attention to Ian Carrick, a sandy-haired, nervous little man who kept clutching his heart and declaring he felt faint.

Yet even Carrick seemed to satisfy the detective that he had not left his room during the night. Hawke had noticed several signs which indicated that the weak heart was not a fake. Carrick was undoubtedly a sick man, and he was finally dismissed.

The staff proved helpful, though indignant about being suspected. They were all a good type, intelligent, rather superior to the usual run of domestic staff.

Hawke knew from experience, however, that the more intelligent the person, the more likely they were to have done a job of this kind.

He grilled them all thoroughly, all the time hearing the searchers at work. The house was large, but they were going over it room by room. Even the carpets were being lifted to see if the painting could have been slipped flat underneath.

By the time he had finished his questioning, the top floor had been thoroughly gone over, and Hawke went up to examine the burglar alarm system and the switch which operated it. This was in Reardon's suite, which consisted of a bedroom for himself, one for his secretary and a small study.

On Philip Lornesay's insistence, his own room and those of Reardon had been searched as well as the others. McPhinney, when he met Hawke on the stairs, said they had found no trace of the picture.

"May I walk through the rooms myself?" asked Dixon Hawke, when he had checked the alarms, and he was readily given permission.

Tommy accompanied him from room to room. The detective did not disturb anything, but merely stood and scrutinised each apartment in a way which Tommy knew missed nothing.

In one corner of the secretary's room stood a long, canvas-covered roll about five feet in length. Hawke knew the detectives would not have missed that, but asked one of them what it contained.

"Apparently Mr Reardon has a portable cine-projector of his own. That is the portable screen, Mr Hawke. We've had it open, and the picture is not there."

By lunch-time, the house had not been completely searched. Reardon

157

managed to provide a very satisfactory cold luncheon for everyone, and directly afterwards the detectives got to work again.

Towards four in the afternoon the man in charge of the searchers came to McPhinney to make his report.

"There's nothing, sir! The picture is not in this house."

Before McPhinney could utter a word, Dixon Hawke was on his feet.

"It's here all right, it must be here!" he snapped. "I'm not presuming to teach you your business, but the fact remains that you've overlooked it. Nobody got in or out of this house, yet the picture has gone."

He walked into the hall and looked at the stairs. Then he turned and walked into the drawing-room. The shutters had been opened to let in light for the search, and the sunlight picked out the faint gold stripes in the wallpaper. The windows had not been opened, and Hawke sniffed.

"I noticed the smell of eucalyptus this morning when first I came in. How did it get here?"

"I'm afraid that was me last evening, Mr Hawke," said Lornesay. "I had a terrible cold coming on, and inhaled a good deal from my handkerchief."

Hawke glanced at Lornesay, then opened one of the windows. The smell of eucalyptus soon vanished, but the detective seemed to be sniffing.

"When was this room repapered?" he suddenly asked.

"Why, back in the spring, wasn't it, Phil?" asked the owner.

"Yes, in April." For some reason Philip Lornesay had paled.

The Dover Street detective snorted, and suddenly walked across the room to a far corner, where, in a wide recess, no picture hung. They watched him stick his finger-nail under the edge of the expensive wallpaper and, with a jerk, turn back a fair-sized flap of it. He pulled still further, but the paper tore away in his hand.

He turned the piece over, and sniffed.

"I thought so! Strip that length of paper off and you'll find your picture underneath.

"The paste is still moist. That is what I've been smelling the last few minutes, since the eucalyptus smell cleared from the room."

At a nod from Reardon the detectives stepped forward, and taking considerable care, they stripped back the top layer of paper, discovering that there was another underneath.

Between the two papers, flat to the wall, face outwards, was the missing Rembrandt, held in place by stamp paper.

Gasps of astonishment came from all present. The picture coiled up in a roll directly it was lifted down.

Dixon Hawke looked round the circle of faces, and his eyes stared at one.

"It seems that I was right about this being an inside job. Someone who knew about the burglar alarms switched them off before he came downstairs and opened the side door from the inside, making those marks on the lock to make it appear that the thief came from outside.

The same person had thoughtfully provided himself with a strip of paper to match this on the wall. Doubtless several spare rolls were left behind when the paperhangers did their work in the spring.

"During the night our friend removed the picture and hid it as you have seen. He was clever enough to know that fresh paste would smell in an enclosed room," continued Hawke remorselessly, "so the evening before, he took the trouble to develop a cold, so that he could use some eucalyptus. That smell killed the smell of paste."

Everyone turned to Philip Lornesay. He was deathly white, and his hands were clenched.

"It's a lie! I — I didn't. What good would a picture like that be to me? How could I ever get it out of the house unseen?"

"You could afford to be patient and wait," said Dixon Hawke. "Sometime in the future Mr Reardon would want to give a cine show at the house of a friend or in his office, and would ask you to take the apparatus and the portable screen there.

"That rolled screen in your room would be just the thing to hide the rolled picture when the time came…

"Yes, Mac, I think you'd better watch him in case he tries to make a dash for it."

—oOo—

# THE CASE OF
## The FRIGHTENED FINANCIER

**"Hello, what's this?" exclaimed Tommy Burke, who stood by the window looking down into Dover Street.**

"Some big shot, by the look of things. Gosh, that's a smashing Rolls in the middle, Guv'nor. Bet it cost a few thousand. Crikey! They're stopping here!"

Dixon Hawke laid aside his book, rose and joined his assistant at the window. In the street below, a glittering limousine had come to a halt opposite Hawke's doorway. A few yards in front, a powerful black tourer was drawn in to the kerb, and a little behind the limousine was yet another tourer. From each of these, two hefty men had alighted and were standing with studied nonchalance on the pavement.

As Hawke looked out a burly fellow stepped from the Rolls-Royce and held open the door. A short, flabby-looking man in morning clothes got out and was followed by yet another powerful fellow. The fat man made for the doorway and disappeared from view.

"Who is he?" queried Tommy. "A big shot, I'd say, judging by the bodyguard."

"He's a gentleman by the name of Samuel Levine," answered Hawke drily, "and I'd prefer to stay out of his company at any time. Not a decent man, Tommy, in spite of his great wealth."

Hawke stopped speaking as his housekeeper knocked on the door and presently Mr Samuel Levine was offering a podgy hand which the detective affected not to see as he indicated a chair.

"To what do I owe this visit, Mr Levine?" he asked coldly.

The other smiled, a sickly smile, as he sat down.

"You do not like me, Mr Hawke," wheezed Levine. "All on account of that unfortunate misunderstanding when I last engaged you, but  — "

"We will not discuss the matter," interrupted Hawke. "I shall be glad if you will kindly state your business. My time is valuable."

Samuel Levine was reputed to be worth several millions, but he cringed in his seat before the famous detective.

Some years earlier the man had engaged Hawke on a case which soon proved to be of a distinctly shady variety. The detective had dropped the case like a hot brick and had told Levine in no uncertain terms exactly what he thought of him.

"Very well," sighed the financier. "I will do so."

He faced the detective. "I'm a desperate man, Mr Hawke, or else I shouldn't have come. I am being hounded. My life is in danger. Look at these!"

He whipped out a pocket-book and passed over three plain envelopes, each containing a sheet of paper. On these, letters, obviously cut from a newspaper, had been pasted to form a message. The first read: "Your time is coming soon. All your hired thugs will not save you."

The second bore the words: "Nemesis is fast approaching," and the third ran: "You own five million sterling, but —you can't take it with you."

"I've had others, many others," said Levine, as Hawke returned the letters. "They come almost daily."

"You've been to the police?" asked Hawke, and Levine snorted angrily. "The police! Bah! I have no faith in the police. But I did go to Scotland Yard and all they could do was to advise me to take reasonable precautions. A fool called McPhinney."

"Chief Detective-Inspector McPhinney is a highly capable officer," put in Hawke coldly, and Levine quietened for a moment.

"All right, all right, perhaps he is," he began again, "but that doesn't help me. All he could promise was to instruct the constable on the beat to keep a special watch on my house, as if that would do any good. Talked of staff shortages."

"I happen to know that the police are dangerously short-staffed," said Hawke curtly, "and I really fail to see what more they could do. Is there anyone you suspect? How did you receive the notes, by the way? Bid they come by post?"

"At first they did, but now I find them in all sort of places. One I found under my pillow, another on the seat of the car when I got in, and once when I shook out my morning paper a letter fell to the floor. I tell you, it's getting on my nerves."

"H'm," mused Hawke. "Sounds like an inside job. How about the servants?"

"I thought of that and got rid of all of them except the cook, who's been with me for twenty years, and Rawlings, my butler, who's been even longer. Cook is almost seventy and half-blind, and Rawlings is a doddering old fool who'd give his right hand for me."

"And there is nobody else in the house?" queried Hawke.

"No. I've a dozen fellows who act as guards, and they patrol the grounds every hour of the day. But they were recommended by that fellow McPhinney, and they're all ex-members of the force."

"You certainly appear to have taken adequate precautions," said Hawke, and there was a hint, of irony in his tone. "I don't see that there is anything I can do except to advise you to ignore the cards."

Levine was about to reply when the sitting-room clock chimed the hour of ten. The financier glanced at his wrist-watch, then felt in his pocket and produced a small, cylindrical phial. From this he extracted a white tablet which he placed in his mouth.

"Got to take one every two hours," he explained. "I'm bothered with indigestion."

Hawke looked at the flabby figure and reflected that more exercise and a little less eating would serve a more useful purpose.

However, when he spoke it was to ask: "How about the tablets? Where do you get them?"

"I see what you mean," said the other, with a shudder, "but there's no chance of anyone tampering with those."

He explained that a supply of the tablets was kept in a safe to which he alone had the key. He was in the habit of replenishing his phial every morning himself, though, as it happened, he hadn't done so that particular morning. The man's voice shook as he told how, when he was about to open the safe, which was concealed behind a picture, one of these letters had dropped to the floor. This had so unnerved him that old Rawlings had had to fill the phial for him.

"Can you think of any enemy who might be doing this?" inquired Hawke.

"There was Bryan," Levine muttered. "It's the sort of fiendish thing he'd have delighted in, but, thank God, he's dead. He believed, quite wrongly, of course, that I cheated him that time."

The man did not have to explain, for Hawke remembered James Bryan very well. Bryan had been a partner of Levine's and had been abroad when the firm was involved in criminal proceedings in connection with certain shady deals. Levine had managed to wriggle out of the mess by throwing the blame on his absent partner, and Bryan had received a term of penal servitude. Yet Bryan's death in a drowning accident, shortly after his release from prison, had been reported only a few months earlier.

"What do you advise me to do?" Levine broke the short silence and Hawke faced the man squarely.

"I can't see that you are in any personal danger at the moment," he replied.

"The letters are no doubt annoying but they can do you no harm, and I advise you to ignore them. I fear there's nothing I can do, Mr Levine."

Levine had to be content with that, and a few minutes later the glittering limousine, with its formidable escort, had moved off.

The detective busied himself with other work and Samuel Levine was soon forgotten. Shortly after lunch, McPhinney of the Yard rang up to ask if Hawke was agreeable to repeating his usual generous subscription to the Police Orphanage.

The inspector profusely thanked the detective when Hawke promised an increased amount.

Hawke had barely replaced the receiver when the phone bell shrilled again. Tommy answered.

"It's Levine, Guv'nor," he said. "Wants us to go out to Hampstead right away. He's in a whale of a stew."

Hawke took the receiver. The financier was almost sobbing.

"Come at once, Hawke, for goodness sake come at once!" he almost shrieked, and the detective could not get him to say what was wrong. "Come, come at once," the man repeated. "I'll pay you anything, anything!"

"I'll be with you in half an hour," said Hawke.

Tommy Burke was about to swing the car into the drive leading to Samuel Levine's residence on the fringe of Hampstead Heath when a burly figure waved him to a halt.

The features of the man who had stopped the car underwent a change as Hawke stepped out and a somewhat sheepish grin took the place of the frown. "So you're on the job, Riley," said Hawke, recognising the man as a late member of the Metropolitan Police.

"Yes, sir. Sorry for holding you up, but we've orders to let no one pass."

The detective explained about the phone call, but Riley had no idea what might have caused his employer's fright. He was certain that no one had entered the grounds since morning either by the main entrance or any other way.

"H'm!" said Hawke. "Maybe two of you had better come up to the house with us just to be on the safe side.

"Something must have scared him badly."

Arriving at the house, Riley led the way inside, and, passing across the hall, tapped at the door of the butler's pantry. The door was slightly ajar and the bent figure of an aged butler was seen standing in front of a mirror, patting his few grey hairs into place.

"Excuse me butting in, Mr Raw-lings," said Riley, "but this is Mr Dixon Hawke, the famous detective, and I just brought him straight through to save you answering the door."

"That's all right, Mr Riley," replied the butler. "A privilege I'm sure, sir," he added, bowing to Hawke.

"Ah, yes, I expect it's that other letter which came this afternoon," he said, when the detective had explained Levine's urgent summons. Rawlings was as emphatic as Riley that no one had entered the house, but willingly agreed to escort Riley and the other guard on a tour of the building.

"You'll find the master in the library, sir," he said gravely. "He's in a state, poor gentleman."

Samuel Levine greeted Hawke with tears of joy in his eyes. A rapid change for the worse had taken place in the man and he was now a pitiable object as he shivered in his chair from sheer funk. An almost empty decanter of brandy stood by his elbow and it was clear that the man had been imbibing freely.

"Thank God you are here, Hawke," began Levine in a shaking voice. "It has come at last. Read that."

He nodded towards a small table and Hawke picked up the letter which lay there. The message in large letters, read: "You die today at four o'clock."

"You must do something, you must!" cried the wretch with a tremor of terror.

Feverishly he poured the remains of the brandy into a glass and drained this at a gulp.

"Bring another bottle," he roared, speaking to the ancient butler, who had appeared in the doorway.

"Very good, sir," said Rawlings.

"We found nothing, sir, and the men have returned to their duties," he added, addressing Hawke.

Levine appeared not to hear, and, as the old man left the room, he burst into a torrent of words, entreating the detective not to leave him alone.

This disgusted Hawke.

"Take a grip of yourself, man," he snapped.

"Now, when did this come and how did it come?"

"It came with the afternoon mail," quavered Levine.

At that moment Rawlings returned carrying a bottle of brandy from which he proceeded to replenish the decanter. Having done so, he produced a small wine-glass, poured a little of the fluid into this and gravely drained the glass. "The brandy is quite all right, sir," he said quietly and moved towards the door.

Levine glanced at his watch.

"It's five-past three now, but I feel better now that you are here. You will stay with me?"

"Now you are being silly," snapped Hawke. "Nothing can happen to you. I have work to do, and — "

The rest of his sentence was drowned in a torrent of entreaty from the terrified man.

"Don't go, don't leave me!" he shouted wildly. "I'll give you anything. Look, I'll write a cheque for a thousand if only you'll stay for another hour."

Hawke was about to decline when a thought struck him. The over-fed craven facing him had wealth — and plenty to spare. Here was a chance to help the Police Orphanage.

"I don't want your money myself," he said curtly. "Just make the cheque out in favour of the Police Orphans Home and we will stay here with you."

The millionaire wrote out the cheque with trembling fingers and Hawke placed it carefully in his wallet.

After a time the door opened and Rawlings appeared with a tea tray. "I thought the gentlemen might like a cup of tea," he said.

Levine waved him aside, but Dixon Hawke accepted a cup of tea as did Tommy Burke. The old man departed quietly.

"An excellent servant, Rawlings," said Hawke. "He's been with you for many years, you said?"

"About twenty-five," growled Levine. "He's getting too old for my liking now, though. I'll have to get rid of him. There are many butlers who will jump at the wages he's getting."

"I doubt if you'll get another to risk his life by sampling your food," retorted Hawke, disgusted at the other's complete selfishness. Levine looked uncomfortable.

"I don't really mean that. It's just that since he came back from Cornwall, he's been so confoundedly absent-minded."

"Rawlings has been away recently?" Hawke asked.

"His brother died in Cornwall a month ago, just before I moved out here. He was only gone for a few days, but it seems to have affected him. Keeps forgetting his proper duties."

The detective did not reply, but his face wore a thoughtful look. Levine leaned back in his chair and closed his eyes. The heat of the room and the drink he had consumed were beginning to take effect and presently loud snores filled the air.

Hawke picked up the letter from the table and reached for the envelope which, presumably, had held it. Suddenly he straightened up, and, bringing out his magnifying glass, studied the envelope carefully.

"Look here, lad," he said quietly, drawing Tommy over to the window.

He indicated the date stamp, which was badly smudged, and passed over the glass.

"Why, this is an old envelope," said Tommy, after a moment. "It's dated the 8th and this is the 17th."

"Exactly! Yet Levine said it came with the afternoon mail. Tut! Tut! We should have noticed this before. Remember Riley told us that no one had passed through the gates since morning."

"Then there was no afternoon mail," said Tommy.

"I believe I know the man behind all this. I think I know how he means to accomplish his end, despite our presence. No, Tommy, wait!" he smiled in answer to the youngster's eager questions.

"Another ten minutes will prove whether I'm right or wrong. Don't say anything to Levine."

A few minutes later Levine awoke and sat staring at the clock. The hands pointed to one minute to four when there was a tap on the door and Rawlings entered.

Hawke saw a look of alarm pass over the old butler's features as he looked at the figure of his master sitting staring at the clock. He glanced at the clock and spoke to Levine.

"It's almost four o'clock. Time for your pill."

"Let me alone. Go away," he growled, but Rawlings was persistent.

"Your tablet, time for your tablet," repeated the butler, leaning over his master.

"All right, all right, I'll get it myself!" snapped Levine, and fished in his waistcoat pocket. The old-butler stood aside and there was a peculiar glint in his eyes as the financier shook out the tablet.

Hawke glanced at Rawlings. Then, as Levine was in the act of placing the tablet in his mouth, the detective sprang forward and knocked the other's arm aside.

The tablet fell to the floor and rolled under the table. Tommy gazed in astonishment at Rawlings.

The butler's face was transformed into a mask of rage and hate. With a howl of fury, he flung himself at the detective, and for a minute the struggle was furious.

Then with startling suddenness the man went limp and slipped to the floor, his hands clawing at his side.

"He's dead," said Hawke after a brief examination. "A heart attack. Well, perhaps it is better this way."

A grey wig had slipped to the floor and the hair of the butler was seen to be glossy black beneath. Levine, who had risen to his feet and was swaying unsteadily, with wide-open eyes, gave a dreadful cry.

"Bryan. It's James Bryan!" he croaked, and fainted.

In the dead man's pocket was found a letter which led to the discovery of the real butler, Rawlings. The old man was being kept a close prisoner by an accomplice of Bryan's and was rescued none the worse for his imprisonment.

It was characteristic of Samuel Levine that, with the realisation that he was now perfectly safe, his miserly instincts came at once to the forefront. Later that night he telephoned Dixon Hawke.

"That cheque for a thousand I gave you," he said thickly, and it was evident to Hawke that the man had been drinking again. "Can't let you get away with that, y'know. A thousand pounds for an hour's work? Nonsense! Send it back or I'll have it stopped."

For once Hawke's iron control snapped and Samuel Levine, in the next minute, heard a few well-chosen home truths.

"The infernal blackguard"" said Hawke furiously. "I almost wish I'd let Bryan do his worst. The Orphanage, at least, would have benefited."

However, the Police Orphanage did benefit.

When Hawke picked up his paper next morning he read that Levine in his drunken stupor had fallen downstairs and broken his neck.

—oOo—

# THE CASE OF
## The Walking Pictures

**"You remember Dingo?" asked Chief Detective-Inspector McPhinney, helping himself to a pipeful of tobacco from Dixon Hawke's pouch.**

Hawke nodded.

"I remember him well," he replied.

"A cold-blooded rogue, if ever there was one. What about him?"

"Nothing much," answered McPhinney, "except that he's got his ticket. He came out ten days ago. Thanks, Hawke. Good stuff, that," he went on appreciatively, handing back the pouch before applying a match to his pipe.

"Yes, he was a tough nut, was Dingo," he declared, puffing contentedly. "It's a pity they didn't string him up alongside that brother of his. However, his ten years in jail may have taught him a lesson, though I doubt it."

The man under discussion was a notorious Australian crook, known to the police as Dingo, and he had been the ringleader of a dangerous gang, broken up about ten years earlier. The crook, whose real name was Joseph Denman, had heard his brother, Dan, sentenced to death, together with other members of the gang.

Dingo had only escaped hanging because there was insufficient evidence to convict him of an active part in the many murders for which the gang was responsible. Denman had created a sensational scene in court by hurling abuse at the judge, Mr Justice Hunnay, now Sir James Hunnay. Before being led away, Dingo had sworn to "get" the judge, if he had to wait a lifetime. Hawke alluded to this when he spoke up.

"Does Sir James know he's out?" he asked.

McPhinney nodded. "Oh, yes, I'm not forgetting what Dingo said when he was sentenced, even though it might only have been hot air. I rang up Sir James and told him to be on his guard, but I was laughed at for my pains. Hunnay reckons that, although he's turned sixty-five, he's good enough for half a dozen of Dingo's kind."

"I quite believe he is, too," laughed Hawke. "Sir James was one of the best wing three-quarters England ever had, and he's always kept in good physical shape. I've no doubt he'd still prove more than a match for Denman in a fair fight, but there's little chance of that.

"A bullet or a knife in the back is more in Dingo's line, and I think you'd be well advised to convince Hunnay of the necessity of having a guard, at least for the present."

"Haven't I tried?" snorted McPhinney indignantly. "I suggested sending a man round and had my head chewed off. Hunnay said he'd let me know when he was unable to take care of himself, and that, anyhow, he knew we were overworked and needing all the men we have."

"Still, Mac, it's better to be safe than sorry," insisted Hawke. "Dingo's threat may only have been bluster, as you say, but he's a killer who'll stick at nothing, even if we couldn't pin that on him last time. It would do no harm to take precautions, even if you do so without Sir James's knowledge."

"Perhaps you're right," admitted McPhinney. "As a matter of fact, the Assistant Commissioner himself suggested something of the kind. I'll put a man on the job this afternoon and say nothing to Hunnay."

Hawke changed the subject and, shortly afterwards, Duncan McPhinney, who had called in con¬nection with a case in which the detective was interested, took his departure.

Shortly after two o'clock the telephone rang.

"It's the Yard, Guv'nor," said Tommy Burke, handing over the instrument.

Hawke's face grew grave as he listened.

"We'll be ready for you, Mac," he said, concluding a short conversation and replacing the receiver.

"Sir James Hunnay has been shot — murdered!" he exclaimed, turning to Tommy.

The youngster started in surprise.

"Gosh!" he declared, "Dingo hasn't wasted much time, if it was Dingo. D'you think so, Guv'nor?"

"That remains to be proved," replied Hawke shortly. "Anyhow, Mac wants us to go out to Randwich with him, so we'd better get ready. He's picking us up in a few minutes. The quicker we get there, the quicker we'll get on with the case."

Sir James Hunnay had lived in the Hendon district, close to the big new housing estate known as Randwich, and on the run out in the police car, McPhinney told Hawke all he knew.

The baronet had occupied a big house standing amongst trees some distance from the main road. After lunch, at half-past one, Sir James had gone into his study, as was his custom. He was shot whilst seated at his desk by the large, wide-open window of the room.

Walters, the butler, had noticed a tradesman's delivery van come up the drive. The van halted on reaching the road round to the kitchen entrance, and the driver got out and stood, as if in some uncertainty.

Walters had then seen him run towards the study window, and a minute later the man had returned, jumped in the car and driven off at a fast pace. Rather mystified, the butler had stepped out from the dining-room window, and had walked along the gravel path to the study, where he had found his master dead. He had heard no sound of a shot.

"He used a silencer, no doubt," grunted McPhinney. "Anyhow we're almost there. The big house on the bend there amongst the trees, Brand," he instructed the driver.

Sergeant Brand swung the car into a short, curving driveway, and drew up before a substantial mansion. The house stood in a secluded avenue of similar dwellings, the nearest of which was two hundred yards away. There were two entrance gates about thirty yards apart, and the drive formed a half-circle between them.

Parking the car in front of the house, the party proceeded by way of the lawn towards a big window at which the butler was standing. A figure, bending over a chair beside a big, knee-hole desk, straightened up at their approach, and Walters, the butler, introduced the doctor, whom he had called. The latter shook his head.

"Killed instantaneously," he said, indicating a small hole between the victim's eyes.

Sir James Hunnay was huddled over the desk, his right hand still clutching the fountain-pen he had been using when he met his end, and there was a look of surprise in the wide-open eyes.

Hawke noted that, from where he now stood on the gravel drive, the distance to the chair in which the body rested was little more than ten feet. The window was separated from the drive by a foot-wide strip of grass and a narrow flower-bed, and the detective surmised that the killer had stood in the position he now occupied.

"Not a print on this gravel, not a clue, nothing," growled McPhinney, after a careful inspection of the scene.

"No, it was carried out very coolly indeed," responded Hawke. "Simple, yet dangerously effective. He simply drove up, got out of the car, shot Sir James, got back into the car, and was gone before anyone knew what was happening. Yes, a cool customer without a doubt."

"He had a nerve all right," McPhinney admitted. "It could be Dingo. Let's see what the butler can tell us."

The butler could add little to the statement he had made over the phone. Assisted by a maid, he had been clearing away in the dining-room, on the same side of the house as the study, and had noticed the delivery van come up the drive. He had noted the name of the firm, Harold and Warnock, Crombie Street, E.2.

The name of the firm was unknown to him, and when the driver stopped the van to get out at the bend of the drive, he assumed the man had made a mistake. The fellow had stood for a moment, then had walked swiftly towards the study window, and out of the butler's sight. A minute later he had reappeared, running, to jump in the van and drive off rapidly right past the front of the house and out of the other gate.

There was a considerable clatter of dishes as the maid cleared the table, and Walters had heard no sound of a shot. More out of curiosity than anything else, he had stepped out of the window and walked towards the study where, to his horror, he found his master dead.

The butler could only give a vague description of the man who, he said, wore a peaked driver's cap pulled well down over his eyes. The fellow was fairly tall, and slimly built, but the butler could give no details of his features.

"It could fit Dingo," growled McPhinney, as they walked towards their car, "or almost anyone else as well. Anyhow, I've had a man tailing Dingo ever since he came out, so I can soon check up on him. I forgot to tell you, Hawke, that he's in with another tough crowd down at Tony the Wop's place."

"It looks as if we can count him out, since your man hasn't turned up," said Hawke. "Of course, there may be others, not so loud-mouthed as Dingo, who have an equally strong grudge against Sir James for the same reason. Anyhow, we should be able to trace the van."

The van was quickly found where it had been abandoned half a mile farther on, where the avenue merged into the main road leading through the new housing scheme.

A policeman who stood by the van explained that he was waiting to book the driver for leaving the car unattended. He was decidedly surprised when the situation was explained to him.

The van was parked near a busy crossing, and on the farther side was the entrance to an underground station. Hawke, Tommy and McPhinney crossed the road and spoke to the constable on point duty, but he could not help them. His attention was fully occupied in dealing with the steady stream of traffic, so the party continued on their way past the entrance to the underground. As they were about to cross to their car again, something was thrust into McPhinney's hand.

"What the — " growled the inspector.

Hawke and Tommy laughed as they read the handbill which had been handed to McPhinney.

"You have just been photographed," ran the bill, and went on to give details of where the picture might be purchased, should the recipient so desire.

"Tcha!" exclaimed the inspector, crumpling up the bill and throwing it away before entering the car.

"Now for a trip to Tony the Wop's joint," he growled.

Half an hour later the party got out of the car at the entrance to a narrow cul-de-sac in which the frowsy dance-hall-cum-cafe, run by the Italian, was situated. As they left the car, a man came from a nearby doorway and saluted McPhinney.

"Have you been here all the time, Hammond?" barked the inspector.

"Yes, sir," came the quick reply. "I took over from Hill at twelve-thirty, and he told me Dingo came out about ten o'clock, went to a barber's and a pub, and came back about twelve. He's never come out again, sir, and there's no other way out."

"Good!" snapped McPhinney. "Stay where you are, meantime, and if he comes out when we've gone, stick to him wherever he goes."

Tony the Wop himself, a greasy-looking Italian, greeted them with a scowl as they entered the cafe. In answer to McPhinney's question, he said Dingo was playing pool upstairs. Pushing past him, the three of them mounted the stairway where, in a big room containing several billiard tables, they found about a dozen tough-looking rogues engaged in games of snooker. The crook, Dingo, was amongst them, and he greeted McPhinney surlily.

"What the heck d'you want with me? Done my stretch, ain't I?" he said truculently. "An' yuh can take your ruddy bloodhound away. 'E ain't got no call ter foller me around."

"You wouldn't have been out Hendon way a couple of hours ago, by any chance ? " inquired McPhinney, paying no attention to the other's protest.

"No business of yours even if I had!" snarled the crook, flushing angrily. "But yuh might as well know I ain't bin outa this place since twelve o'clock, an' that's fair dinkum. Ask your tail, he knows," he added with a sneer. "That 'tec's my alibi!"

The other crooks noisily corroborated his story, and McPhinney shrugged his shoulders as he turned towards the door.

"Let's take a look at the roof," suggested Hawke, when a tour of the building proved unavailing. The party mounted the stairs again and went out on the flat roof of the building by means of a storm window. From here they could see the plain-clothes man on duty at the end of the alley, and behind them was the blank wall of a tall factory building, built right up against the rear of the cafe.

"Huh, no way out from here," growled McPhinney. Looks as if he's got a stonewall alibi."

Hawke walked round the roof. Suddenly he stiffened and called to McPhinney.

"Look there," he said, nodding towards another tall building adjoining the factory.

A window in this structure enabled them to look inside the building, which was a large storehouse. They were able to look downwards through another window at the far side to the yard beyond.

"What is it?" growled the Yard man. "You're not suggesting he might have gone through that window, are you? You can see that it hasn't been opened for years."

"Yes, I can see that," replied Hawke quietly. "But look beyond, through that other window down there."

McPhinney looked and saw that the yard contained a number of lorries and delivery vans bearing the name of the firm on their sides, and a light of understanding came into his eyes.

"Harold and Warnock's yard!" he exclaimed.

"Yes. Rather too much of a coincidence, don't you think? I've a notion that a visit to that yard might repay us, Mac."

"You're right!" snapped McPhinney. "Though how anyone could get from here without wings beats me. Let's give it the onceover, at any rate."

The party clattered downstairs again, ignoring the ribald remarks of the toughs crowding the doorway to the pool-room, and the sneering smile of Tony the Wop, as he watched them leave. Entering the car, they drove round several narrow streets before arriving in the narrow lane in which Harold and Warnock's yard was situated. The heavy door leading to the yard was slightly ajar, and farther up the otherwise deserted lane a man, engaged in painting a doorway, watched them curiously.

Hawke went up the lane and engaged the man in conversation. He learned that this was the firm's half-day, and all the vans in the yard had been garaged at twelve o'clock. The man had not seen a van leave, but he had knocked off for dinner just after twelve. He had noticed a man in dungarees enter the yard about two-thirty, but had paid little attention, A mechanic, he reckoned, and said the man must be there still, as he had never seen him leave.

"Well, we'll soon see if he's still here," said Hawke, after reporting the conversation to McPhinney. "It looks like that van at Hendon was stolen and abandoned, Mac, and I'll be surprised if our mechanic friend is in the yard."

Hawke was not surprised. Except for a dozen vans and lorries, the yard was empty. Half the area was roofed over, and, in the back of the shed so formed, stood a dilapidated heavy lorry, obviously long out of use. The tyres were fiat and the ironwork rusted, but it was this vehicle which attracted Hawke's attention.

"This has been moved — and quite recently," he said, indicating marks on the dusty concrete. "Let's move it again!"

It took the united efforts of the three detectives to move the cumbersome vehicle, but when they had shifted it a few feet, Hawke pointed.

"I thought as much," he said grimly.

The others followed his glance and saw the cover of a manhole which had been concealed by the heavy vehicle. Hawke removed the cover without difficulty and revealed an iron ladder leading downwards. Descending, the party found themselves in a tunnel. The walls and sides were quite dry, as was the floor, but covered in dust and cobwebs, and it was clear that they had stumbled on a long-disused sewer.

By the light of Hawke's torch they moved forward in the direction of Tony the Wop's cafe, and, after a journey of fifty yards or so, they came to another iron ladder. Tommy quickly shinned up this and tried unsuccessfully to raise the manhole cover. Leaving it alone, the lad pressed his ear against the cover and listened intently.

"That's Tony's place all right," he said excitedly, as he came down, "I could hear Tony talking."

Hawke, who had been flashing his torch on the floor of the tunnel, interrupted with an exclamation of satisfaction. The detective had picked up a crumpled piece of paper, and this he smoothed out and handed to McPhinney.

"Why didn't I think of that earlier?" he snapped. "This might hang him, Mac."

The inspector looked at the pamphlet, and for a second time that afternoon found himself staring at the headline: "You have just been photographed."

"What's on your mind, Hawke?" he growled, but the detective was already making his way along the tunnel.

"Let's get back to Randwich as quick as we can," he snapped. "It seems we weren't the only ones to be photographed today, at least I hope this is also today's, but we can soon make sure. I want that cameraman."

The photographer was still plying his trade opposite the tube station when they arrived at Randwich after a record journey. The man protested vehemently when McPhinney brusquely ordered him to step in the car, but Hawke soothed him by promising to purchase the whole of his negatives for that day if necessary.

At Scotland Yard the man was given the run of the photographic department, and in remarkably short time he was displaying the results of his labours in McPhinney's office. Hawke and Tommy grinned as they looked at the picture of themselves and McPhinney in the pile of roughly-finished snapshots. Then the detective, with a whoop of triumph, pounced on a photograph.

"We've got him!" Hawke cried, and the others craned forward.

There was no mistaking the features of the tall, slimly-built man who was pictured striding along the pavement. The man was hatless, and the face that stared out at them from the picture was the face of Dingo. A clock in the background showed the time to be two o'clock.

"He ditched the car, took the tube back, and, wearing dungarees, dodged into the yard, where his pals were waiting to help him," went on Hawke.

An hour later, McPhinney, Hawke and Tommy faced a dozen protesting, but cocksure, crooks, including Dingo and Tony the Wop. It was clear that the gang, while putting on a show of indignation, were very sure of themselves. Their expressions underwent a sudden transformation when Dixon Hawke held out the photograph for all to see, and McPhinney stepped towards Dingo.

"Joseph Denman, I arrest you for the murder of Sir James Hunnay at Randwich this afternoon.

"The camera doesn't lie, Dingo," went on McPhinney, after delivering his caution, "and you really should have destroyed that pamphlet instead of leaving it for us to find in the sewer."

Dingo duly paid the penalty, and Tony the Wop's place is now occupied by a more respectable concern. The proceeds of many burglaries were found on the premises, and Tony, with all his gang, are now behind bars. The photograph of Dingo, together with that of Tommy, McPhinney and himself, are recent additions to Dixon Hawke's scrapbook.

—oOo—

# THE CASE OF The Worthless Masterpiece

"Thieves broken into my gallery. Please come at once. Frantic about stupendous irreplaceable loss. Crazy with worry. You are my only hope. Counting on you. Will meet all trains. Don't fail me. Roger Aylward."

Dixon Hawke looked up from the telegram which Tommy Burke had handed to him. Tommy was grinning, for the frantic message was typical of the huge, bearded, eccentric Roger Aylward, artist and collector, who was an old friend of the two detectives.

"Poor old Roger!" chuckled Tommy. "I can just see him charging around in circles, squawking like a hen that has been shut out of the coop, and tearing handfuls out of his beard. Probably all that has happened is that he has moved one of his pictures and forgotten where he put it! Considering the litter he gets that cottage of his into, I'm surprised he doesn't lose himself and send us a telegram to come and find him!"

Hawke smiled slightly, for the tempestuous Roger was capable of doing anything crazy, but to his assistant's amazement, the detective reached for the railway timetable.

"You don't mean to say that we are going to answer this by dashing down to Cornwall?" Tommy de-manded.

"We are — for three reasons," replied Hawke. "One, because neither of us would be alive if Roger Aylward hadn't come blundering in and rescued us from a very tight corner during the 'Body on the Beach' Case.

"Two, though his pictures are horrible, the sort of crazy daubs that only a lunatic would buy, he has, in that gallery of his in the cottage, several most valuable paintings inherited from his father. They include a Tonnetti that any collector would give his soul to possess, so one of the big art thieves may have made a haul down there.

"Three, we can do with a break in Cornwall — just what the doctor ordered. So pack a couple of bags and get your hat. We'll catch the Cornish Riviera if we hurry."

On their arrival in Polgelly Station the detectives found the artist pacing the platform like a caged lion. He was so excited that he could only slap them violently on the back in turn and bellow, "Rescuers! Saviours! I knew you wouldn't fail me. If you had I'd have shot myself — jumped over the cliffs — taken poison — only thing left to do! I've been robbed — ruined!"

They managed to get him into the back of the battered jeep which he had waiting in the station yard. He sat there — an astonishing sight, in an old green jersey and paint-stained corduroy trousers, with long red beard and hair streaming in the wind, still waving his arms wildly and roaring about "vandals! robbers!" while Hawke took the wheel and drove to the quaint cottage on the cliffs.

Roger Aylward's home had been designed by himself and was an odd-shaped building, with long windows running from floor to ceiling in each room. It seemed to stand like some fantastic lighthouse high on a promontory, with magnificent views out to sea, along the coast and up the wide estuary of the river.

The first thing which Hawke observed when he stepped out of the jeep was a broken window.

"That's how the vandals got in!" bellowed Roger. "They broke that pane, slipped the catch, entered my gallery and took it from the wall."

"It?" exclaimed Hawke. "You mean that they got away with the Tonnetti?"

He climbed through the open window into the gallery as he spoke, and his exclamation ended abruptly, for the first thing he saw, in all its splendour, was the Italian masterpiece.

"The Tonnetti?" boomed Roger, also climbing in. "No, they didn't take that. I tell you, they took my best."

"You mean to say you had something better than that?"

"Of course, my dear fellow," snorted Roger. "The vandals stole my latest — my masterpiece — the best thing I've ever done!"

"You — you mean — " Tommy Burke goggled at several paintings of green, odd-shaped cows in purple fields and nightmare ships on vivid blue oceans, which were hung among the old masters on the walls. "You mean that the thieves went to all this trouble to break in and only took one of these — these awful daubs of yours — that they ignored the priceless Tonnetti and went off with a worthless splodge?"

Hawke restrained the outraged artist, while Tommy apologised for his tactless words.

"I didn't mean to hurt you, old chap," protested the young detective. "After all, the Tonnetti is worth hundreds of pounds — and some of these other pictures you've got here are worth almost as much — so it does seem strange that thieves should take the risk and the trouble of breaking in, then take only your picture."

"My picture is priceless," snorted Roger huffily.

"Quite so, old chap, but I mean in hard cash," ventured Tommy. "Thieves are usually after either cash or what they can turn into cash — "

"These thieves were evidently men with good taste, with artistic appreciation, who recognised the best thing in the gallery," stormed the artist.

"Now, Roger, tell me, what exactly happened?" cut in Hawke, realising that the present argument could go on for ever.

"I was in the other room, old boy," declared the artist, "and I heard the sound of breaking glass. I'd only just hung my masterpiece, so my mind flashed to it at once. I dashed in here. It was dark, so I flicked the light switch, but nothing happened. I realised in a flash that some sneaking hound had cut the burglar alarm, putting the lights out of action as well.

"I headed straight for where I'd hung my picture," he went on, pointing to a bare space on the wall alongside the Tonnetti masterpiece. "I was reaching for matches, to look and see if it was all right, when, biff-oh, some slug walloped me on the skull and felled me like a log. I don't know how long I was out to the world — not long, for we Aylwards have concrete nappers — but when I recovered enough to find the matches I was alone in the gallery. The first thing I saw was that it had gone — my masterpiece, my magnum opus — the best thing I shall ever do!"

Hawke allowed him to rave for a few moments, while he considered the problem of this extraordinary robbery. Although he had managed to avoid being as tactless as Tommy, he was just as puzzled that anybody should break the law to steal one of Roger Aylward's pictures.

Roger was a staunch and amusing friend, but Hawke's private opinion was that the average youngster could paint better pictures, and the detective was recognised as a sound judge of art. Yet thieves had come to this gallery, knocked out the owner, ignored paintings of great value and gone off with a piece of rubbish!

Any feeling of annoyance at being brought from London, which Hawke might have experienced, soon disappeared. He decided that this promised to be a most intriguing problem.

He examined the gallery and its surroundings and found traces showing that several men had entered by the window. They had left tracks which led to the steep, winding path to the beach far below, but the tide had washed away all traces at the base of the cliff, so it was impossible to form any idea where they went from there.

"What time did this happen, Roger?" asked Hawke.

"Eleven-thirty last night, old boy," was the artist's reply. "I know the time exactly because I have ten clocks, and they were all striking at once. They always do. It helps to make the passage of time more interesting."

Hawke was not listening, however. He was looking out of the window at the magnificent seascape.

"The tide must have been up then," he remarked.

"Pretty well," agreed Roger.

Hawke noted this for reference. It told him that the thieves had come in a boat, for there was no other way of reaching the path at the bottom of the cliff at high tide.

He next made Roger go through the gallery and the rest of the house, to see if anything else was missing, but the result was negative. The entire place was in the untidy chaos in which the artist habitually lived — boots and shoes on tables, dishes on the floor, easels and canvases mixed up with hats and coats, empty beer bottles and heaps of books spread everywhere, but Roger insisted that nothing was missing — except his picture. Hawke did discover a quantity of money lying around, also valuable ornaments and silverware, so it began to look as though the thieves had actually only been after one object — Roger's latest painting!

Who but a lunatic would commit such a crime — and the attack on Roger made the crime doubly serious — to secure a piece of trash?

"Tell me something about this new picture of yours," said Hawke at last, glancing at the weird daubs on the gallery wall, among the superb paintings which Roger's father had bequeathed to him.

"My dear old boy, it is magnificent," boasted the artist. "Even better than my 'Storm Off the Lizard.'"

He pointed to a large canvas depicting a lop-sided ship apparently wrapped in dirty cotton wool.

"Another seascape?" queried Hawke.

"Of course, of course — the sea is my metier. That is why I live on the Cornish coast," declared Roger. "This time I caught the spirit of the sea even better than before, but I can't describe it. My dear man, one can't describe a painting in words!"

Hawke sighed. He had come up against artistic temperament before.

"Could you do me a rough sketch of it?" he suggested. "After all we must know what we are looking for."

The artist raised his hands in horror. The painting, he declared, was the result of a flash of inspiration, a glimpse of the beauties of the sea and coast and sky. One could not turn on a tap and repeat such a flash of inspiration.

"Of course not," agreed Hawke smoothly, collecting a blank canvas and a piece of charcoal, "but you could give me an idea what it was all about. Where did you paint it — in here?"

The artist tore at his beard again, for to him only a soulless clod would think it possible to catch the wind-tossed spirit of the sea when seated in a room. No, he had painted his picture from a spot on the cliffs.

Protesting furiously and vowing that he wished he had never asked the detectives to come down, but had shut himself up alone to grieve over his loss, he was steered out of the cottage and on to the cliffs. With firm patience, Hawke found the spot where the painting had been done. He persuaded the artist to sit where he had worked before and put the canvas on an easel before him.

"Now, Roger," he urged, "If you really want me to find you the missing picture, you must co-operate. Forget all about inspiration. Simply give me some idea of the picture I've got to find."

The artist grumbled; he tugged at his beard and swore like a bargee; but Hawke and Tommy stood over him until he obeyed. The result was a messy sketch of the estuary, with a solitary sailing vessel in one comer.

"Ghastly," commented the artist.

"All the fire and fury missing. How do you expect me to reproduce a flash of genius on a dead calm evening, when the original was painted at night, with clouds scudding across the moon, and a tempestuous sea lashing great waves around the one little ship, lit for an instant in a flicker of moonlight, as it scurried for shelter?"

The artist's angry bellowing was suddenly stilled, for he discovered that Dixon Hawke was not attending to him. The detective had turned and was striding away along the cliffs.

"I am going for a walk," called Hawke over his shoulder. "Try and come down to earth sufficiently to get some food for your guests when I return, Roger!"

"But my picture!" wailed the artist. "Aren't you going to get it back for me?"

"I hope so," replied Hawke. "In fact, I begin to suspect that I shall find considerably more than your picture."

Darkness had fallen when Hawke returned to the cottage. He looked tired and muddy, but, although he had been away for several hours and had not eaten since lunch on the train, he ignored the bread, cheese and beer which was all Tommy had managed to find in the house for supper. He went straight to his baggage and took out an automatic. "Get yours!" he said to Tommy.

"Hey, what's all this about?" demanded Roger. "You came down here to find my picture, not to go shooting."

"We are going after your picture now," retorted Hawke. "We may have to do some shooting in the process."

"You mean that the blighters will fight to the death rather than give it up!" exclaimed the artist. "Gad, I'm coming with you. I must meet these chaps. They evidently think highly of my work."

Hawke led the way along the cliffs and down to the river estuary. There a number of men crouched in the bushes, and nearby were several rowing boats. Hawke offered no explanation as he issued orders to embark; his only words were to order complete silence.

When Tommy clambered into a boat he discovered that the rowlocks were padded with cloth.

Swiftly, but almost noiselessly, with strong, accustomed hands on the muffled oars, the small fleet of boats crept out across the dark water of the estuary.

Tommy was in the leading boat with Hawke, and he observed that the men with him were all armed.

The boats were linked by a line of cord, running back from the leader, and almost noiselessly they followed Hawke as he steered up the estuary. Suddenly he signalled for them to halt, then he clambered into the bows of his craft and felt into the thick darkness ahead.

The night was pitch black with no moon, and thick clouds obscured the sky, so that Tommy found he could not see his hand before his face, but Hawke located what he was seeking. There was a faint swishing, splashing sound, and Tommy heard a grunt of surprise from the man beside him.

The boats were moved forward, bumping slightly against obstacles, and Tommy realised that what had seemed to be solid land ahead was no longer there. They were creeping along a narrow channel.

Suddenly Hawke jerked at the cord again and there was another halt. A faint light showed ahead, and, gradually, peering eyes made out the shape of a small, rakish, auxiliary schooner, a magnificent little craft, built for speed.

Muffled sounds came from her — movements and the murmur of voices — and the faint reflected glow of light showed men moving along a plank to and from the shore.

"There are your liquor smugglers, Coastguard," said Hawke abruptly to the man beside him. "We've caught them red-handed, bringing a cargo ashore!"

As he spoke, he jerked the cord, and lights blazed through the night. From every boat streamed the beam of a powerful lamp, disclosing plainly the startled men, carrying boxes and bundles from the schooner.

"Look out — we're copped!" shouted a frightened voice.

"Keep away there — or we shoot!" cried another.

But the coastguards and police had leapt out into the shallow water of the narrow channel and were scattering, working to Hawke's carefully-prepared plan of action.

A shot rang out, answered by one of the police, then a pitched battle started.

The smugglers fought with the desperation of cornered rats, but Hawke's shrewd generalship was too good for them. They were surrounded and overpowered without the loss of a single man on either side.

"Got you, you rogues!" exclaimed the leader of the coastguards, as he surveyed the crestfallen smugglers and the heap of valuable goods intended for the black market. "Thank you, Mr Hawke."

His words were cut short by a wild shout. Out from the cabin of the schooner appeared Roger Aylward, prancing like a maniac and waving his picture in the air.

"Your thanks are really due to Mr Aylward and his painting," said Hawke to the leader of the coastguards.

"You see, he was inspired to paint the estuary on a stormy night. When he made a rough copy of the picture for me, it included a ship where no ship could be, for, looking across in daylight, I saw that where he had put his ship was dry land.

"But he was very confident about having glimpsed the ship there, so I went to investigate," continued the detective. "In the village I learnt that there used to be a channel through this way, but that it had been closed for years. When I walked around here, however, I found traces that the channel had been opened.

"That is why I planned this attack, for I jumped to the conclusion that the only explanation why thieves should steal Mr Aylwards painting in preference to the Tonnetti beside it was that the painting must have some peculiar value to them.

"I suppose one always thinks of smuggling when considering a Cornish mystery," added the detective, "and, when Mr Aylward talked of seeing a ship where a ship shouldn't be, that fitted in with my guess. So I came looking for smugglers, and found them! I can only guess that they discovered in some way that Aylward's picture showed their ship slipping into hiding. This endangered their secret, so they raided his cottage and stole the picture."

Hawke proved quite correct in his reasoning. Roger had boasted in the local inn about his painting, telling of the beauty of that sudden glimpse of the little ship.

He had been overheard by one of the smugglers and a party of them had taken a boat round to the base of the cliff.

They had climbed up to the cottage that night and had knocked the artist out. They had then examined the painting and when they had seen that it did indeed show their ship, they had removed it.

Hawke was congratulated by the authorities for his good work. They were pleased, for they had despaired of catching the gang. Hawke was satisfied too, because he had enjoyed solving an intriguing problem.

Roger was another happy man, because he sold his picture — the first one for which he ever found a buyer. Hawke bought it with part of his reward for catching the smugglers.

It hangs in his Dover Street flat — much to the amazement of those of his friends who know anything about painting.

—o0o—

# THE CASE OF THE BLACK MARKETEERS

**In the Coach and Horses the afternoon gossip was unusually excited. In the corner two passing travellers listened to the group of locals by the bar.**

"Black market, that be one thing, I says. But when it comes to coldblooded shootin' and murder, it be too much."

"Ay, all day growing the stuff and up all night seein' as no devils in cars come out of the town to pinch it, an' maybe get shot into the bargain like George Stone! These black-marketeers come from the towns, don't 'em? Well, then, the police to deal with 'em ought to come from the same place!"

"I been sayin' it for weeks, ain't I? I said it when old Firby had his two Guernseys took. I said it when old Mrs Hallett got cleared out of 'er pullets, didn't I?"

"Poor George Stone — he was in 'ere only two nights ago, he was," said the barmaid morbidly. "Cruel hard luck, I reckon — just when he'd got something behind him."

One of the older men sniffed.

"Well, I says it's a judgment. All this gambling and easy money, I don't hold with it. People's mad! George Stone wins a hundred quid or summat on these 'ere football pools, then a few months later he gets killed. Well, I looks on it as a judgment."

One of the strangers in the corner moved towards the bar.

"Excuse me butting in, but gather there's been a murder here?"

An iron curtain of suspicion dropped abruptly in the Coach and Horses.

"It's all right," smiled the stranger "I'm not one of the black market rustlers from the big bad city, though I must admit I have a close connection with crime. My name is Hawke, Dixon Hawke, and this young fellow here is my assistant."

The buzz of conversation broke out again. Several rural voices all spoke simultaneously, and Hawke gathered that a man named George Stone had been shot dead during the night while trying to prevent a "black market" raid on a poultry farm.

"We're actually on our way back to London, but if there's any help we could offer to the local police — "

"Oh, there's carloads of 'em come down from Marshampton by now — when it's too late. You'll have a job to get near for police, you will, sir."

"Well, we'll try anyway."

"Good for you, Mr Hawke."

Obtaining directions to the scene of the crime — about a mile and a half from the village — Hawke and Tommy drove off.

Inspector Deakin from Marshampton was in charge of the investigation.

"Well, it's very good of you, Mr Hawke, but I don't see that it's your sort of case. I mean, it's not a complicated case. Smash-and-grab raid on some poultry and one of the two used a gun, then they bolted. They could have knocked the chap out and got away — no need to shoot him!"

"Was he killed at once?"

Deakin nodded.

"Through the heart. I suppose he heard the fowls being disturbed, went up there out of decency — "

"Not his own birds, then?"

"No, he was just a casual farm labourer. He lived in a cottage nearby. Actually the poultry belong to people with a hundred pounds for every penny this chap's got — the Sholtos, local bigwigs. Young Sholto was the first to get there after the shot. It was moonlight, so we've got a fair description of the men from him."

"I'd like to look at the scene myself," said Hawke.

"By all means, if you'd care to," agreed Deakin willingly. "I don't mind admitting this is only the third murder case I've had to handle, and the other two were open-and-shut jobs anyway."

The dead man's body had been moved to the Sholto house, a fine Elizabethan farmhouse, expensively renovated and modernised.

Hawke was introduced to William Sholto, the owner, and his son, Jeremy. The old man walked with two sticks, his back bent with rheumatoid arthritis; his face was lined and tired-looking. The son, about thirty-five, seemed to be smug and self-satisfied.

"Mr Hawke, eh?" said old Sholto. "We are honoured indeed. Well, if it catches the killers any quicker, all the better. Dreadful business. I heard the shot. I couldn't do a thing, though, crippled like this. By the time I got to the bedroom window Jeremy was halfway up the hill. It's a wicked business, almost as bad as Chicago gangsters! It's a good thing you were home, Jeremy, eh?"

Jeremy smiled diffidently.

"I didn't make all that difference, I'm afraid. I heard the chickens kicking up a shindy — I was on the way there when the shot was fired. My father's account suggests I'm a super-sprinter. I never saw Stone till they shot him — he'd come up the other side of the hill from his place, of course. The two blokes dashed off immediately after the shot. I only had to look at Stone to see he'd had it, poor devil! By then the two of them were breaking through the hedge to the main road. I was just in time to look over the hedge myself when they jumped into a van and dashed off.

"There was enough moonlight to show one chap in a light mac, army sort of cut. He was hefty, round about six feet. The other bloke was short and wiry, spidery-looking. All I saw of his get-up was a soft felt trilby."

Deakin nodded.

"It's the same lot as did the other jobs all right. The same chaps were seen when Firby lost his cows — and when they lost the fowls at Mrs Hallett's."

"At what time did all this happen?" asked Hawke.

"I never looked at the clock," said young Sholto. "I just grabbed some clothes and dashed out — "

"I know the time," the father broke in. " I looked at my watch just after I heard the shot. Ten to one. It was ten past when you got back, Jeremy, and by then I'd phoned the police."

"Then I phoned again," Jeremy went on, "to give the description of the men and say what had happened, but by that time the constable was on his way."

Hawke examined the body. Death certainly had been instantaneous. The bullet had cut through the man's clothes just above the heart.

"Stone must have kept late hours," said Hawke casually.

"How do you mean?" asked the inspector.

"His clothes. He's wearing coat and waistcoat, collar and tie. Young Sholto, remember, said he heard the chickens squawking, and grabbed some clothes and rushed out. Stone, however, arrived fully dressed — in fact, quite neatly dressed. He must have been out, on his way home, perhaps, when he heard the noise. It might be worth checking. Stone has also had a good deal more cash to spend lately."

Deakin stared at the detective incredulously.

Hawke smiled back.

"No, that's not a brilliant deduction. I heard a good deal of local gossip at the Coach and Horses before I came up here. The story goes that he'd won something on the pools."

The Dover Street man bent down and began to examine the contents of George Stone's pockets. The cash amounted to six pounds and a few shillings. Cigarettes, an expensive new cigarette lighter, handkerchiefs and an ugly-looking knife made up the contents. A fairly new wrist watch gave another sign of recent wealth.

A torn half of a postcard, however, interested Hawke most. Scribbled rather crudely in pencil were the figures 1245, and below these figures the odd word, "Wens."

"An illiterate hand — pretty certainly his own," said Deakin.

Hawke nodded.

"I'd like to see the actual scene of the murder," he said. "If young Sholto could come with us and repeat the details again — "

From the rather small garden of the Sholto house a wicket gate led to a six-acre meadow running gently uphill. At the top of this hill a few large chicken houses could be clearly seen. Hawke, Deakin and young Sholto trudged up the meadow towards them.

The bodies of six dead chickens still lay by the houses.

"They'd got that far when Stone disturbed them," said Jeremy Sholto. He pointed to a vague track running up from the other side of the hill. "Stone would have come up this way — his cottage is about three hundred yards down the road. Immediately they'd shot him they dashed off towards that hedge — the main road's just the other side. They burst through the hedge just to the side of that tree."

He pointed to the left, where a thick hedge grew about two hundred yards away.

"Not the slightest chance of foot-prints," Hawke said to Deakin.

"No. There's been no rain this week — the ground's quite dry."

"There might be something left behind where they got through the hedge," said Hawke.

The hedge was about five feet high and two feet wide. It had not been cut back for many years, so that the thorny branches were formidably interlaced. It grew across a deep and wide drainage ditch, so that it was not difficult to penetrate the hedge by pushing between the lowest stems of the branches and getting right into the ditch.

"You're certain it was just here they broke through?" Hawke asked Sholto.

The younger man nodded.

Hawke lay flat on his stomach and pushed his head into the hedge so that he could peer into the ditch. He repeated this procedure several times until he had covered a distance of fifteen yards from the tree.

Then he similarly examined five or six yards to the other side of the tree.

He finally stood up and brushed his clothes with his hands. His face showed that he was puzzled. He shrugged his shoulders.

"Has Stone got a family?" he asked Deakin.

"There's his wife. She was told first thing, of course, by the local constable."

"Perhaps we might see her now, then."

On the way to the cottage the local constable explained that the Stones had not got on particularly happily together.

"When your husband went out last night had he been to bed?" was Hawke's first question.

"He was sitting up late, sir," was Mrs Stone's reply.

"Did he usually sit up after mid-night?"

"Sometimes. He never told me anything, sir. He just did as he wanted."

"You don't know why he was sitting up last night, then?"

"No, sir."

"Filling up his football coupons, perhaps?"

Mrs Stone stared dumbly back at them.

"He did win some money recently from football pools, didn't he?"

"He never told me nothing, sir.

"We — we didn't speak much. Unless he'd been on the drink — then it was shoutin' like, not what you'd call talk. I know he'd had more money lately — to spend on 'isself."

"Did a telegram ever come here? Within the last few months, I mean?"

Mrs Stone shook her head.

"Did you ever see him filling up football pool coupons? They'd be — well, forms of a kind?"

"He was never a writing man, sir."

"Is there anywhere in the house where he kept his papers — letters and so on, things like that?"

"There's his drawer, sir, what he always kept locked."

She led the way into the front parlour and she pointed to one of the two drawers in a sideboard. "I don't know where he kept the key hid. I've never seen that drawer opened, not since we come here."

"We'll open it by force," said Hawke. "We'll see that any damage to the drawer is made up to you."

The dead man's widow watched blankly while they forced the drawer.

There were old photographs, yellowed newspaper cuttings, referring to the deaths of Stone's parents, and a meaningless assortment of souvenirs.

There were also some items of more recent significance. There were three cuttings from the Marshampton Gazette, each dealing with the death by drowning of a girl of twenty named Anne Haywell. The latest cutting gave an account of the inquest at which a verdict of suicide was brought in. The other cuttings dealt with her disappearance and the subsequent finding of her body in the river.

There was also an exercise book in which Stone had recently kept a record of his heavier expenditures. Twelve pounds for a wristwatch, nine pounds for a suit, seven pounds for an overcoat — altogether he had spent over £70 on himself in the past nine weeks! But a Post Office savings book, issued at the main post office in Marshampton, showed he had paid in over £100 without drawing out more than an odd pound or two. The payments had been made on three occasions at intervals of two to three weeks — £40, £37 and £33. There were also eight pound notes loose in the savings book.

"The writing's the same as on the piece of card in his pocket," said Hawke. "But no records of football pool entries," he added.

They left the Stone cottage.

"What do you think, Hawke?" asked Deakin.

Hawke delayed answering for a full minute.

"You had better press on with the obvious methods of attack, Inspector. Put out your descriptions of the men, such as they are. It may be all there is to this affair — and Stone's private life may be just a coincidence. But remember, despite the dry weather, the bottom of that ditch was still moist — "

"But it told us nothing!"

"Exactly." Hawke's tone changed. "I'd like to look through the papers at your headquarters dealing with Anne Haywell — "

Three hours later Hawke made an urgent contact with Deakin.

"I want you to get a statement from young Sholto."

"How do you mean? Just what he's told us — "

"Make him come to Marshampton for it! Tell him you need it in detail and signed, something like that. No progress with news of the two men, I suppose?"

"None."

"All right. Can I rely on you to have Sholto in Marshampton by eight and keep him for half an hour?" "All right, I will," said Deakin.

Unpleasant Visitors.

A few minutes after eight two men knocked at the door of the Sholto house. The taller man wore a light mackintosh of army cut, the shorter man a soft felt hat which had long lost any pretence of shape.

"I want to see Mr Sholto," said the taller visitor in a sharp Cockney accent.

The maid dashed into the house, leaving the door open. After some delay, William Sholto appeared, slowly hobbling to the door on his sticks. He gave a violent start at the sight of the two visitors standing in his hall.

"Who are you? What do you want with me?"

"A quiet, private chat, Mr Sholto."

The old man motioned them into a small room off the hall.

"Very well. What is it you have to say?"

"Just this, Mr Sholto. That we might know something abaht other farm jobs lately in these parts, but we wasn't on a job last night — although we was 'seen' by you and your son! What's the game, eh?"

William Sholto remained silent.

"Why exactly have you come to me?" he asked.

"If we're going to be the stooges in this job, we might as well be paid for it, that's the rough idea, guv'nor."

"Paid? Paid for what?"

"Oh, we're safe enough. If they nabs us, I got an alibi, and Nobby 'ere, 'e was only out on 'is own doin' a look round the country like. Two of us wasn't out, so the facts won't square with what you and your son saw. But Nobby weren't so far off, was you, son?"

"I saw it all right," said Nobby.

William Sholto caught his breath.

"Saw what?"

"You 'eard! He knows who got up there first, the man what was shot or the 'ero who's supposed to have chased a couple of armed bird-fanciers. Mind, it's a risk for us to go to the police because of the other jobs, but it might be riskier to get nabbed for murder 'avin' said nothin'. My alibi might not be so convincing dug up in a month's time, so we felt a little compensation in 'ard cash — "

"How much do you want? To get right away from here, miles away, and never come back?"

"Now you're talking. Five 'undred?"

"Five hundred ! Don't be ridiculous — "

"Murder's expensive."

" So is blackmail — as — "

Sholto stopped suddenly.

"As George Stone found out last night, is that what you were going to

190

say, Mr Sholto?" asked the visitor in a completely different voice and tone. It was Hawke! He turned to "Nobby." "All right, Tommy! Get to the phone and tell Deakin to detain Jeremy Sholto for murder!"

"No — no, not — not my boy!"

"The girl was somebody else's child," said Hawke grimly.

"Stone's fully-dressed appearance at that time of night was one pointer," Hawke explained to Inspector Deakin later. "Then there was the card in his pocket—'1245 Wens.' It could have meant an appointment on Wednesday night at 12.45 with the day spelt illiterately. If so, it agreed with the time of the crime, and the place could have been a rendezvous. Then there was that ditch — not a footmark in its damp bottom, the one place where we ought to have found evidence.

"There was also Stone's recent wealth — with nothing to substantiate the rumour he had put round that it came from the pools. The payments into the savings bank suggested blackmail — the cuttings about that girl's suicide seemed to tie up with it. Well, my inquiries into that affair showed that an unknown man had been responsible for the girl's trouble.

"Very well. If the Sholtos were lying, then young Sholto was the unknown man. Stone knew it and had been blackmailing them. His demands were getting too regular and insistent. The appointment was made for 12.45 and, instead of cash, he got a bullet. The Sholtos, father and son, covered it up with their evidence. They even killed half a dozen chickens to lend reality to their story.

"The father was the weak spot. He must have been an accessory, for his evidence, remember, stated that he saw his son running across the meadow after the shot. That is why I asked you to get the son out of the way, while I bluffed the old man into an admission. As you know from the old man's confession since, the son hadn't merely got the girl into trouble, he'd disposed of her in the river, and Stone had seen them together just before it happened.

"You'd have got it in the end. You had one clue yourself, Deakin. You said they could have knocked Stone out, not shot him. Well, why hadn't they?

"It was that remark of yours that started me wondering."

—oOo—

# THE CASE OF The Chinese Cord

**"So Aylmer is being arrested today!" Chief Detective-Inspector Duncan McPhinney of Scotland Yard frowned at Dixon Hawke's remark, as the famous private detective joined him at a table in the MacMahon Square of Lourenco Marques, the capital of Portuguese East Africa.**

McPhinney was enjoying the strangeness of the scene around him, the dapper Portuguese and the odd mixture of African natives thronging the wide square and the busy streets around it. He was also enjoying the contents of a long glass in which ice tinkled. He did not want to be reminded that this short trip abroad was almost over. He had been flown out from England only a few days before, to arrest a crook whom Hawke and he had been after for many months.

Frederick Aylmer was a mean type of swindler. He had specialised in tricking ex-servicemen and robbing them of their gratuities and savings. He had finally bolted with the best part of a hundred thousand pounds, leaving many ruined men behind him. Hawke had kept relentlessly on his trail, however, tracking him halfway across the world to Portuguese East Africa. Now McPhinney had arrived to settle formalities with the Portuguese police and take the crook into custody.

Hawke was not entirely satisfied, however, and McPhinney knew it.

"I wish you wouldn't do it, Mac," protested Hawke. "In fact, I am beginning to regret letting Scotland Yard know that I had located Aylmer."

"But we've got to pull him in and take him back to answer the charges!" snapped McPhinney.

"And how is that going to help the men he swindled?" retorted Hawke grimly. "Aylmer will get so many years in prison, but will they get any of their money back? No! They won't see a penny of it, for Aylmer is much too cunning to have anything more than small change found on him. He will have the rest invested somewhere, and, when he has done his stretch, he'll collect his loot and live in luxury for the rest of his life."

"We'll make him say what he has done with it!" snapped McPhinney, looking about him nervously, for the crowded little cafe in the square was not the place to discuss police business.

"How will you make him tell you where his loot is?" Hawke insisted, raising his voice earnestly. "You can't third-degree a man in England, and it will take something more even than ordinary third-degree methods to make a crook like Aylmer disclose where he has hidden a hundred thousand pounds.

"He will be sitting calmly in his room in Rua Nova, realising that he has been tracked and waiting to be arrested, because he has decided that a few years in jail is not too high a price to pay for the hundred thousand pounds that will be waiting for him when he comes out."

McPhinney shifted uncomfortably in his seat, for he knew that Hawke was right. He thought of the unhappy folk in England, whose hopes of a new start in life had been wrecked by Aylmer, and whose lives would stay wrecked unless by some miracle the loot could be discovered. The Scotland Yard detective could only do his duty, however, which was to get the Portuguese to arrest Aylmer and hand him over for extradition.

"I wish you wouldn't keep talking about that hundred thousand pounds," warned McPhinney, again looking about him, for he suspected that the men at the next table were listening.

Actually they were, and one of them spoke to the other out of the side of his mouth.

"A hundred thousand quid, Colonel! We could do with that. I lost more than I could afford at the Casino last night."

"Shut up, Doc!" The man addressed as Colonel was a neat, grey-haired, soldierly man, with a square, handsome face, and he was very popular among the British people in that corner of Africa, being looked on as a typical old soldier of the best type.

Doc, another popular British resident in Portuguese East Africa, turned his attention sulkily to his drink. The Colonel was losing his touch, he decided. It was months since the two crooks had last pulled off a coup, and here was a hundred thousand pounds going begging.

"Here comes Hawke's assistant, Tommy Burke. This place is crawling with 'tecs," muttered the Colonel abruptly, and again lowered his face nervously over his glass.

Doc watched him and grinned. "So that's it?" he jeered. "You're scared they'll recognise you."

"Of course I am! Hawke's pulled me in three times in the past, and he's got eyes that match his name," admitted the Colonel.

But, my dear friend, that was before I went to work on you," boasted Doc. "Your own mother wouldn't recognise you now. Facial surgery is my speciality, and you haven't a single feature left of the ugly mug you had when the British police knew you as Slink Waters. Nobody's recognised you yet, and nobody ever will."

Tommy Burke had evidently brought a message, for he whispered to Hawke and McPhinney, and the three left their table.

"Where now?" asked Doc a moment later, when his companion also rose.

"To get that hundred thousand, of course!" snapped the Colonel curtly.

Hawke and Tommy left McPhinney in the Rua Arajo, where the Scotland Yard detective got into a police car which was waiting for him.

"They are going to arrest Aylmer this afternoon," Hawke said to Tommy, "and the moment they do those poor chaps in Britain can say good-bye to any chance of getting back the money that means so much to them. We've got to do something about it, Tommy, and we've got to do it quickly. We've only got a few hours in which to make Aylmer talk."

He turned abruptly and began to stride towards the railway station.

"Where are we going?" asked Tommy.

"To Aylmer's hide-out. I am going to tackle him about this message."

The detectives took some time to reach the quiet side road known as the Rua Nova. They separated and Hawke waited for a while at the corner, while Tommy took the lane that ran along the back of the dilapidated old houses. Their timing was so exact that they reached the front and back doors of No. 14 simultaneously.

A startled native servant tried to bar Tommy's passage through the kitchen, but Tommy pushed him aside as Hawke dealt just as unceremoniously with the fat Portuguese woman he met in the hall. Both detectives showed warrants which the Portuguese police had given them, and converged on a door on the first floor. Hawke flung it open without knocking.

Aylmer was seated at a table with an opened bottle of wine, and he eyed them calmly.

"I have been expecting you, Mr Hawke," said the dark, thin-faced crook whose glib tongue had deceived so many unfortunates.

"I guessed you would get tired of running, Aylmer," retorted the detective.

"Quite! If you are so determined to get me that you follow me round the world, it gets monotonous and is bad for my nerves," declared the crook. "Have you got a warrant and arranged extradition?"

"Both," replied Hawke, "and Chief Detective-Inspector McPhinney of the Yard is here to take you back, Aylmer."

"Decent of him to come all this way! When do we start?" asked the crook, holding out his wrists, as Hawke produced his handcuffs.

"After I have finished with you," said Hawke, laying the handcuffs on the table.

"What do you mean?"

"That not only are you going back to England, but your loot is going with you, to be returned to the men you swindled," declared Hawke.

"My dear sir," protested the glib crook. "Now you are suggesting the impossible. My loot, as you call it, cannot go with me unless you can persuade the Casino authorities to hand back their winnings. I always was a gambler, Mr Hawke, and I have been most unlucky. I have lost the lot."

"That's a lie, Aylmer!"

"Really?" retorted the swindler. "Well, it is as good a way as any of telling you that there will be no money for you to take back to England with me."

"You have salted it away, so that you can collect it after you have served your sentence," accused Hawke.

Hawke broke off, for he realised that Aylmer was not listening to him. The crook was staring past the detective towards the door. His face paled and his jaw sagged.

Hawke and Tommy Burke, who had been watching Aylmer, both swung round and found, standing in the doorway, two masked men, each with a gun in his hand.

"Who are you?" demanded the detective.

"You can call me the Colonel," was the cool retort of the shorter of the two men. "It doesn't much matter what you call me, really, for Doc and I are going to do the job you are making such a mess of. Then we'll put you and your assistant and Aylmer together, where you won't be able to give evidence against anybody in this world. The sharks in the bay are hungry and we have a boat waiting."

"What do you want here?" asked Hawke.

"A hundred thousand pounds," replied the Colonel.

"You mean that you are going to make Aylmer tell you what he has done with his loot?"

"Precisely."

"Go ahead! I am going to enjoy this," said Hawke calmly.

All three crooks stared at Hawke, suspecting something behind the calm way in which he spoke. They guessed right, for he moved with sudden lightning speed, snatching a chair and hurling it at the Colonel.

At the same moment Tommy Burke came to life and flung himself at Doc. Both closed with their opponents before they could use their guns, and the four crashed to the floor together in a struggling mass.

Aylmer saw his chance and sprang forward, intending to leap over the heap in the doorway and get away. Hawke, however, saw him out of the corner of his eye and swung round to snatch at his ankle.

With an angry curse, Aylmer crashed to the floor, but Hawke's speedy move had given the Colonel the chance he wanted. The detective had had to concentrate on Aylmer for the moment, and the Colonel was able to twist an arm free. He smashed his fist home behind Hawke's ear, momentarily dazing him. Then he found his gun and smashed it down on the detective's head, and Hawke became limp and still.

When he recovered he found himself roped to a heavy chair. Across the room from him was Tommy Burke, also a prisoner, but Hawke no more than glanced at his assistant. The strange scene taking place in the room caught and held his attention.

The heavy table had been dragged into the middle of the room, and Aylmer was bound to it. He lay spread-eagled on his back, with wrists and ankles roped to the corners, and with his head sticking out beyond the table. Almost the first thing that Hawke heard was the swindler whimpering with fright, for he was neither tough nor brave — just a mean swindler who dared to take advantage only of defenceless people.

The Colonel stood with his back to the door. In each hand he held an automatic pistol.

"Get busy, Doc! Make the rat talk!" he ordered.

Doc approached Aylmer. In his hand he carried a length of rawhide and a short, thick stick.

"What's that for? What do you want with me?" protested Aylmer, his eyes wide with terror.

"We want a hundred thousand pounds," said Doc softly.

"I haven't got anything like that. I'm a poor man — otherwise do you think I'd live in a dump like this?" argued Aylmer desperately.

"Try that on someone else," retorted Doc. "We heard Dixon Hawke say that you have salted away a hundred thousand pounds and he always speaks the truth. So, do we get it without trouble, or do I have to work on you?"

"What do you mean, work on me?" snarled Aylmer.

"I have made a speciality of making people talk," retorted Doc. "I spent many years in China, where I picked up a thing or two, and I have learnt some more since I have been in Africa."

"You mean you are going to torture me?"

"Aylmer! We are going to do to you what you are banking on the British police not being able to do," warned Doc. "They can't use force to make even a rat like you talk, but we can. So, come on! Where is your loot?"

"I tell you — " began the swindler, but broke off, staring in fascinated horror at Doc, who now bent over him and slipped the noose of rawhide over his head so that it drew tight over the temples.

"What are you doing?" bleated Aylmer.

"You'll soon know," was Doc's grim retort. "This little trick is known in China as the Helmet of Truth, and is believed to have been invented by the great Emperor Ghengis Khan himself. It is quite simple. I insert this stick into the noose and twist slowly. At first it won't worry you much, but as the noose tightens the rawhide bites into your flesh, and presses on the nerves until you suffer agony in every nerve in your body.

"If I keep twisting, the top of your skull will come off like the top of an egg, but you will talk long before that. How about starting now — where is the loot, Aylmer?"

Aylmer made no reply, so Doc began to twist. Slowly he twisted and gradually Aylmer's face turned livid till the sweat of pain began to bead his brow.

"Talk, Aylmer!" urged the Colonel from the doorway. "Where is your loot?"

"I — it's all spent!"

"Hawke doesn't think so and I believe him in preference to you! Keep twisting, Doc!"

The watching Hawke and Tommy Burke had to pity the swindler as he began to writhe with agony.

"Steady! You're killing him! This is murder," warned Hawke; but still Doc twisted ruthlessly on and the hide bit in deep, raising purple ridges in Aylmer's livid flesh.

"Talk, Aylmer — where is your loot?"

Time after time the question was asked, only to be answered by moans of pain. The atmosphere in the room became tense, even the Colonel and Doc losing some of their confidence, as they realised that the swindler was tougher than they had expected.

"Hurry, Doc! Hawke said that Aylmer was to be arrested this afternoon. He's got to talk before the cops come," urged the Colonel.

Doc obediently took two savage twists with the stick.

Aylmer screamed, then began to babble.

"I'll tell you!" he whimpered, all the cowardice in him coming to the surface.

The watching detectives forgot their pity as they thought of this yellow scoundrel swindling good men of the money that meant so much to them.

"I'll tell you!" cried Aylmer. "It's here — in Lourenco Marques!"

He stopped short, for Doc had relaxed the rawhide, and the evil, cunning eyes betrayed that the swindler was still trying to evade losing his loot.

"Where?" demanded the Colonel.

"Hidden in a — a cave on the Polona Peach," panted Aylmer.

Doc drew back, but Hawke cut in abruptly.

"There aren't any caves on the Polona Beach," declared the detective. "He's lying!"

"Twist again, Doc!" snarled the Colonel.

Aylmer screamed again as the thong cut in and his tortured nerves responded, pain searing through his body.

"I'll tell! I'll tell! I bought jewellery with the money, as being the best way of carrying it around the world."

"And where is the jewellery?"

"In a safe deposit box with the Mozambique Security Company — Box 2837 — the key is hidden in a crack in the pedestal of the Vasco da Gama statue in MacMahon Square!" moaned Aylmer.

"Okay, Doc! That sounds like the truth to me," decided the Colonel. "I guess we've got what we want!"

"You mean, I have!" interposed Hawke coolly and raised his voice to shout, " All right, Mac — pick them all up!"

The Colonel and Doc both swung round, but could do nothing as the room rapidly filled with Portuguese policemen led by Chief Detective-Inspector McPhinney of Scotland Yard.

"Phew! That was a gamble, Hawke," protested McPhinney, when the crooks had been rounded up.

"It was worth taking," retorted Hawke. " Almost every penny of the money Aylmer got from those unfortunate chaps in Britain will now be returned to them. It was simple ready, after I had spotted Slink Waters. He always was a ruthless thug, just the man to use the rough methods on Aylmer to make him talk!"

" So that was why you told me to sit at that particular table in the Band Square, next to that pair, and why you talked so loudly about Aylmer's loot!" exclaimed McPhinney.

"Exactly! That was also why I told you to bring the local police to this house, but not to raid until I shouted," declared Hawke. "I was determined not to return to Britain without Aylmer's loot."

"And now we've got it, as well as Aylmer, Slink Waters and Doc — what a haul!" exclaimed McPhinney, then frowned. "But, tell me one thing, how on earth did you recognise Slink Waters when Doc had altered him beyond recognition?"

Hawke smiled.

"Doc had altered every main feature for him," he agreed, "but he missed the most important detail. The first day I was in Lourenco Marques I met a man in the Casino, who turned quickly at the sight of me. That made me suspicious, for only crooks do that. Also the man was rattled so much that he automatically dropped into a most distinctive way of walking — the swift, gliding gait that earned Slink Waters his nickname 1

"I found that he was known here as the Colonel, but in every detail except his face he fitted Slink Waters, so, needing a ruthless crook for my plan, I tried a daring gamble. I got you to sit next to him, and by talking loudly to you, I told him that there was a hundred thousand pounds waiting to be picked up.

"Then Tommy and I dawdled to give Slink plenty of time to follow and catch us with Aylmer. We had to put up a fake fight to bluff the crooks, then sat by while Slink and his friend, Doc, did our dirty work for us. Although, mind you, I did have to butt in when Aylmer almost got away with a bluff! But my gamble came off!"

When cars arrived to take the crooks to the police station, Hawke, Tommy, and McPhinney went in the same vehicle as Aylmer. They drove to MacMahon Square, and there the swindler showed Hawke the exact spot where the key was hidden in the statue.

"Now we'll visit the Mozambique Security Company," said the detective, pocketing the key. "We'll soon find out if the money is all there."

A quarter of an hour later they all knew that Aylmer had not been lying. The deposit box had been opened, and it contained jewellery and securities totalling £100,000.

"Well, Mac, now I'm quite willing to let you lock Alymer up," chuckled Dixon Hawke. "His victims will get their money back, and it will be a lesson to them for the future."

—oOo—

**THE CASE OF** *The Posted Key*

Dixon Hawke, the famous detective, was thumbing through the pile of letters on his desk. Those from personal friends he set aside for perusal later, then he began to weed out the others. He came to one, rather bulky and enclosed in a cheap Manilla envelope. To his practised eyes it was obvious that an attempt had been made to disguise the writing that constructed the printed capitals of the address.

He slit it open and shook out the contents.

A decent-sized key fell out, bearing the number 56493 and the printed name of the London Merchants' Bank. There was nothing else in the envelope.

"The key to a safe-deposit box," murmured Hawke.

"Now I wonder whose it is?"

He looked at post-mark "W.1., so it could have been posted within a stone's throw of Dover Street."

He toyed with the key for a few moments then replaced it in the envelope and laid it on his desk. Hardly had he done so when Tommy Burke announced that Chief Detective-Inspector McPhinney of Scotland Yard had called.

"Good morning, Mac," greeted Hawke, as McPhinney entered and lowered himself wearily into one of Hawke's comfortable chairs.

"You look all in, Mac," Hawke observed. "What'll it be? Coffee or a drink?"

"Coffee, Hawke, if you don't mind."

"Coming up, Mac. Now what's on your mind?"

"An accident which turns out to be a murder. I've been up all night on it. The chap is called John Burford, and he was run over by a car in Rose Street. You know the place — quiet, graveyard on one side, the back of St Luke's Hospital on the other.

"Burford was crossing the road when a car came up behind him, hit him, then went on.

"We thought it was an accident and a scared driver at first, then a nurse from St Luke's tells us she saw the whole thing from an upstairs window of the hospital.

"She said the car was about thirty yards away and moving quite slowly, when Burford started to cross the road. Then the car accelerated and was nearly up to Burford when he noticed it.

"He skipped to the kerb, but the car swerved to hit him — and did it deliberately!

"We found the car this morning in Cheapside with plenty of evidence on it to show that it was the one which had hit Burford. It belongs to a man called Harley and he reported that it was stolen from outside his club around five last night.

"Burford was killed a few minutes after seven.

"There was a rather poor print on the windscreen, but Records are trying to identify it now."

"Do you know anything about Burford?" asked Hawke.

"He's an ex-Army Commando, who used to be a bookseller's assistant. He's had no regular employment since his demob, but always had plenty of cash.

"We've been keeping an eye on him, but we've managed to get nothing definite against him although he has been sailing pretty close to the wind recently.

"He palled about with Jake Masters and you'll agree that that's no recommendation."

"You're certain that it was murder?"

"I'm pretty sure about it.

"There was no other traffic on the street at the time and the street itself is pretty wide. The sudden acceleration of the car when Burford crossed the road is definitely suspicious."

"H'm! By the way, what's happened to the Kingsmead case? Have you dropped that?"

Hawke was referring to the theft a few weeks previously of the famous Kingsmead necklace.

McPhinney sighed wearily.

"I've still got men on it. There's no sign of the necklace yet, but I've made sure that it won't get out of the country. I've also put the fear of death into all the fences who might be asked to handle it. I guess we'll just have to wait and see.

"Well, I must be going now and thanks for the coffee, Hawke."

"By the way, Mac," said Hawke, picking up the envelope which had been in his mail that morning, "This arrived by the post. There's nothing in it but the key to a safe-deposit box.

"I think it would be worth while investigating it. You wouldn't like to come with me when I call at the bank, would you? I'd need your authority to have the box opened."

McPhinney glanced at the key.

"Well, Hawke, one good turn deserves another and you've done me many a good turn. We can go now, if you like, for the bank's on the way to the Yard.

"Be quick, though, for I've got to make out a report for the A.C."

The manager of the Merchants' Bank did not seem very keen to carry out Hawke's request, until McPhinney pointed out that he was a police officer.

The manager then spoke through an inter-office telephone and a few minutes later a clerk came into the room carrying the safe-deposit box. Hawke opened the box with the key and brought out the two items which the box contained.

One was a bundle of notes, two hundred pounds in all, while the other was an oblong parcel, wrapped in brown paper, securely tied and sealed with wax.

Hawke cut the string and, with a rustle, the paper fell away. Hawke was left with a long jewel-case in his hands, the sight of which made McPhinney sit forward attentively.

Hawke pressed the clasp, the lid flew open and a million points of light flashed out at him. On the black velvet lining lay a necklace of magnificent diamonds.

McPhinney gasped, and Hawke had never seen him so surprised.

"The Kingsmead necklace!" he exclaimed. "But how did it come here, Hawke?"

"I couldn't have thought of a better hiding-place, Mac," replied Hawke, as he turned to the manager. "Could I have the name and address of the gentleman who rented this box?"

"Of course, Mr Hawke, at once," and he hurried away to find the appropriate ledger.

"Well, I'll be blowed, Hawke!" gasped McPhinney. "I've been scouring the country for three weeks for that thing and here it is in a London bank."

The manager returned with a ledger and thumbed over a few pages.

"Ah! Here it is. Box 56493 was rented by Mr John Burford on the eighteenth of last month."

"Burford! Hawke, this gets more complicated every minute."

"Something wrong, gentlemen?" asked the manager. "Is my client in trouble?"

"Your late client, Burford, was killed last night," Dixon Hawke answered. "Could you give me a description of him?"

"Er-no, but Rogers may be able to — he looks after the boxes." Rogers was summoned, and he was asked for a description of Burford.

"Mr Burford? Ah, yes, of medium height, dark, stockily-built, and he spoke with a slight American accent."

Hawke looked at McPhinney.

He had not known Burford, but he knew that the description fitted Jake Masters exactly.

McPhinney got to his feet.

"You will not say a word of this to anyone," he told the manager and his clerk. "Of course, I shall have to take the necklace with me, but I will give you a receipt for it."

"A fine little puzzle!" exclaimed Hawke when they were back in McPhinney's office.

"Masters, in the guise of Burford, rents a safe-deposit box. The necklace is stolen, Burford is run down and the key of the box sent anonymously to me.

"Now, Mac, did Masters, aided by Burford, steal the necklace?"

"I wouldn't put it past him. He's one of the best cracksmen in the business," replied the Yard man.

"Very well, something happens between the confederates, a quarrel perhaps, and Jake Masters sends me the key in a fit of anger.

"You and I know, however, that once having the necklace, Masters would never have sent me the key, for he would surely have thrown it into the river first."

"Couldn't Burford have sent you the key?"

"Impossible. The letter was posted in my own postal district."

"I happen to know there are two evening collections, at seven-forty and ten forty-five. Burford was killed a few moments after seven.

"The letter bears the post-mark at ten forty-five."

"Therefore someone else is involved?"

A telephone on McPhinney's desk rang, and he picked up the receiver.

"More information about Burford's killing," he said, as he replaced the instrument after a short conversation. "Brand thinks I should see this man Edwards. He's bringing him up now."

Edwards was a man in the late fifties, and he looked after the graveyard in Rose Street, so he told McPhinney.

"You say you have evidence about the accident, Mr Edwards?"

"I didn't see that there accident, sir, as I was in the graveyard, but I saw the car passing."

"And what do you have to tell us?"

"Well, sir, reading of the accident I saw no one mentioned the young lady."

"Young lady?"

"Yes, sir. She passed by where I was cutting the grass, right in front of the car she was. She must have seen the accident. I thought you might like to know about her, sir."

"It is possible that she may be of some assistance. Could you give us a description of her?"

"Well, I didn't notice particularly, but I'd say she was dark and pretty, a bit on the thinnish side."

"Would you know her again if you saw her?"

"That I would, sir."

"Very well, you can go now. We might need you again later. Leave your address with the sergeant."

"That's queer," said McPhinney, when the door had closed on Edwards. "There was no mention of a woman witness in the report."

"Mac, if I remember correctly, Rose Street is quite long, without any side turnings, and only walls on either side. Where exactly did the accident occur?"

"Almost opposite the back entrance gates of St Luke's."

"Then, if the woman was just in front of the car, it was impossible for her to get out of Rose Street before Burford was run down.

"I wonder why she disappeared so quickly."

A detective-sergeant looked round the door of the office.

"Report from Records, Inspector. That fingerprint on the windscreen of the stolen car belongs to Jake Masters."

"Masters, by Jove! Now we can get to grips with this business, and I think I know how to get at him!" snapped Hawke.

"Through his girl," added McPhinney.

"He's pretty fond of her, and it was on her evidence that he established an alibi when I brought him in for questioning in connection with the Kingsmead affair."

"Is that so, Mac? Look at this envelope then tell me which sex you would say the writer was," asked Hawke, showing the Yard man the envelope which had contained the key.

"A woman, of course, Hawke. A blind man could see that."

"Exactly! Masters had a girl, and Masters had also the key to the safe-deposit box."

"I'll have her picked up at once        — "

"No, wait until I have a word with her, Mac — and besides, she might be more useful to us at liberty. Have you her address?"

When Hawke and Tommy found Glebe Street they saw it was a dingy thoroughfare of tenements.

The entrance to No. 14 was dirty and drab. Hawke went to the end of the hall and stood on the threshold of an open door, through which he could see a stout woman bending over a stove.

"I'm looking for a Miss Jenkins," said Hawke, "Kitty Jenkins, I believe."

"Yer do, do yer?" asked the woman, giving the detective a cautious glance.

Hawke's hand went to his pocket. "1 would be willing to pay for the information," he began, taking out a handful of silver.

"Second floor on the right!" she snapped, snatching the money from Hawke's hand.

Hawke went upstairs, found the door, and knocked several times before a sleepy voice answered, asking him what he wanted.

"I want to speak with you. My name is Dixon Hawke."

There was dead silence for a couple of minutes before the key turned in the lock. Kitty Jenkins had pretty features and, thought Hawke, with the aid of make-up she might even become more than pretty.

So early in the day, however, her prettiness did not show to best advantage. Her dark hair was screwed tightly into curlers, her face was deathly pale, while there were dark patches under her eyes and her thin lips still retained a smear of last night's lipstick.

Above all she sported a beautiful black eye.

She stood facing Hawke, one hand clutching the bed-post, the other holding a thin negligee which she had drawn over her pyjamas.

"Wot yer want?" she repeated. "A little friendly talk," Hawke answered, "about a friend of yours, Jake Masters."

Kitty's lips twitched.

"I don't know nothin' a baht 'im."

"Come, Miss Jenkins," smiled Hawke. "Would it be too much to presume that Masters gave you that lovely black eye?"

Kitty's hand went to her eye.

" 'Ow do yer know?" she blurted out.

441 was right then, and, looking at that eye, I shouldn't say you received it earlier than last night. What time last night?"

" Nine — 'ere wot yer try in' to do. I ain't done nothin'."

"Nine o'clock, eh? You quarrelled and you sent me the key to the safe-deposit box."

Hawke's random shot had struck home. Kitty quailed visibly and stark fear showed in her eyes.

"I — I don't know wot yer talkin' abaht."

"All right, Kitty, but can you tell me where you were at seven last night?"

Kitty swayed and the hand clutching the bed-post went limp.

"Yer 'ave no right ter question — "

"Would you rather let Scotland Yard do it, Kitty?"

The woman gave a low moan, then she collapsed on the bed and began to weep violently.

"I told 'im not to do it," she gasped between sobs. "I told 'im not to."

Hawke saw it was useless to question Kitty further. He left her still weeping and went down to the hall. Once more he visited the woman in the kitchen.

"Do you know a man called Masters, Jake Masters?"

"Wot's it ter you?"

"A pound maybe."

"Well, now yer mention it, yus."

"He was here last night?"

"Around nine, yus. 'Orrible row he kicked up, 'nough ter wake the dead."

"You didn't happen to hear what it was about?"

Hawke waited for her answer.

"Yus now, I did. It was abaht 'er leadin' 'im a dance wiv anuvver man and abaht some key 'e didn't want the coppers ter get old of."

Hawke paid over the pound. His suspicions were beginning to form into definite clues.

At the corner of Glebe Street he drew Tommy into a shop doorway.

"Unless I'm much mistaken, Tommy, Kitty is going to come out of that house shortly and we are going to follow her."

"Where's she going, Guv'nor?"

"To Masters, I hope. I think she knows much more than she let on she did, and, in the state she was in, I really couldn't trap her into any more admissions."

They waited thirty minutes before Kitty appeared. She looked up and down the street, then started in the opposite direction to that which Hawke and Tommy had gone.

Unobtrusively, using the natural cover of the street, the detectives shadowed her.

In Whitechapel Road she entered the tube and went to King's Cross. She rode twice round the Inner Circle before getting out at Edgware Road. Then she set off, Hawke and Tommy quietly following.

She halted before a dingy house in a side street and the detectives ducked into a convenient doorway. Kitty looked up and down before running into the house.

"Tommy, there's a call-box down the street. Phone McPhinney and ask him to come here!"

McPhinney's police car arrived in under ten minutes.

"Kitty Jenkins is in that house, Mac. We followed her here from Glebe Street. She may have gone to tell Masters of my visit."

"Come along and we'll find out."

They discovered that it was a boarding-house and Kitty had gone up to No. 10. McPhinney knocked on the door, and, when it was opened, he promptly stuck his foot in the opening.

"Jake Masters, I have a warrant — Hawke, this isn't Masters, it's Tommy Farrow."

Inside the room Kitty stood by the window, and in the centre stood Farrow, a crook well known to both Hawke and McPhinney. Farrow took one look at McPhinney and turned on the woman.

"You little nark!" he shouted in anger. "I thought you told me the cops weren't tailing you.

"You brought them here — you double-crossed me like you did Burford and Jake. You — "

Before he could be restrained he advanced and struck Kitty across the face. He was beside himself with rage.

"You dirty double-crosser," he shouted. "You told them about the box, about the job we did. I'll get you — "

The threat was left unfinished for Farrow was taken away, and, behind him, Kitty.

Half-an-hour later a much calmer Farrow faced McPhinney and Hawke across the charge room at Scotland Yard.

"Are you ready to talk, Farrow? We know from your own admission that you were in the Kingsmead affair with Masters and Burford. Do you want to tell us anything more?"

"Yes, I'll talk if it'll make it any easier for me."

"You're very wise and I'll do all I can for you," replied McPhinney.

The tale which Farrow told was, Hawke thought, a masterpiece of feminine cunning.

A week after the necklace had been deposited in the box, Kitty had begun to make up to Farrow.

She told Farrow that she had evolved a plan whereby she and Farrow could have the necklace to themselves.

She said to Farrow that Burford had fallen for her charms, and, as he had a deal of influence over Masters, he could easily persuade him to get the necklace from the box.

When Burford had done this he would hand it over to Kitty, as she had promised to leave with him. Instead she would leave with Farrow as soon as she had received the necklace.

Two days previously Burford had reported to Kitty that Masters would not agree to open the box.

Burford, however, stole the key and gave it to Kitty.

The next day Masters became suspicious that Kitty was not being true to him and threatened her, so she phoned Farrow and arranged to see him that evening.

She did not know that as she went to the appointment Masters was following in a car. She was passing down Rose Street when, purely by chance, Burford had hailed her from the other side of the road and had crossed to meet her.

"Masters must have thought that it was Burford she was going to meet," Farrow concluded.

"You know what happened — Kitty saw it all. She got out of sight as quick as she could and came to me. We decided to do nothing for a bit, but when she got back to her flat Masters was waiting for her.

"He beat her up and left her. Kitty was mad, for her pride had been hurt. Masters would watch her carefully so that she wouldn't be able to slip off with me.

She had the key and she wasn't going to let him get the necklace.

She didn't want to go to the police herself, so she sent the key to Dixon Hawke."

"It is amazing that a woman will go to such lengths just to avenge her wounded pride," declared Dixon Hawke.

"What we want to know now is where Masters is hiding."

Tommy Farrow gave them an address in Soho and McPhinney's men soon picked the killer up. Masters was sentenced to death for the murder of Burford, while Farrow received two years for his complicity in the jewel robbery.

As Kitty's sentence of six months was passed, Hawke turned to McPhinney.

"To think that this case was solved for us — because a man gave his girl a black eye!" he chuckled.

"Anyway, Kitty helped us to sort out a real tangle of evidence."

—oOo—

# THE CASE OF
## The Pearl Stud

**The dead man sprawled across the pavement, his head against the base of the lamp-post. In the dusk three constables were dispersing a crowd of morbid sightseers. Usually, Perkin Street in North Kennington was one of those mean and narrow London byways which few people bother to use.**

Detective-Sergeant Maggs, of the Kennington Division, stepped forward briskly as the police car approached and drew up with a squeal of brakes. Inspector Baxter, Chief of the Flying Squad, got out first, followed by Dixon Hawke and Tommy Burke.

" 'Evening, Sergeant. Mr Hawke happened to be with me when the call came through — so we're well staffed tonight. What is it?"

Maggs cleared his throat. "Well, Inspector, there's been an assault, and a man's dead. Whether murder was meant, or the bloke passed out, I reckon that will be for the coroner to decide. It seems as if the chap cracked his head on the lamp-post, and then on the kerb."

The doctor, in somewhat more technical terms, confirmed Maggs' version of the cause of death —severe main fracture of the skull, and a rather less severe subsidiary fracture.

"There are some bruises on his chest and legs, suggesting that another man fell heavily on top of him," went on the doctor.

"Who is he?" asked Baxter.

"According to his pockets, Inspector," said Maggs, "he's Frank Snelgrove of 23 Wilder Road — that's about five minutes' walk from here. Also one of the passers-by has recognised him. I sent a constable to his home address, but it seems that his wife's visiting her sister on the other side of the river, somewhere in Holloway. However, the neighbours said he'd gone off as usual to the Mucky Duck round about nine. The same constable's gone round there to check at what time he left."

"Good. What sort of pub is the Mucky Duck? Do you get any trouble there — hooliganism or rough- house stuff?"

"It seems well enough run always. Regular lot of locals use it."

"Any witnesses to the fight?" asked Baxter.

"Not so far as we know. A man and a girl passing the end of the street heard shouting, but it was too dark to see far. That was dead on ten-fifteen — the witness says he'd only just looked at his watch. Then they heard a man groan, and running footsteps, so the witness, after a bit of hesitation, went up Perkin Street to investigate. He was the first to find the body.

"A watchman from a chemical factory in Perkin Street had heard the same noises, and he arrived on the scene a few minutes later. It was the watchman who phoned the station."

Baxter turned to Dixon Hawke. "It seems to be a fairly primitive job — just a street brawl, with worse results than were intended. It's more in our line than yours, I'm afraid."

"There is one unusual factor, though," said the Dover Street detective. "Snelgrove looks a poverty-stricken chap. Nobody within ten yards of him, even in the dusk, could fail to see dearly that he was almost down and out. Why should anybody think he was worth attacking? An ordinary motive of robbery seems hardly likely. If that's the case, then there must be some private motive tied up with Snelgrove as a person — or, alternatively, Snelgrove had something valuable on him which doesn't fit in with his appearance or circumstances."

Dixon Hawke bent down beside the body.

"As the attacker bolted immediately after the fall, he probably had no time to go through Snelgrove's pockets. Let's see what there is."

There was very little. Six shillings and a few coppers, a pipe whose stem had snapped in the fall, an almost-empty tobacco-pouch, and some crumpled scraps of paper recording each-way bets on various races.

At that moment the constable who had been making inquiries at the Mucky Duck returned.

"That's where he was, all right, sir. Got there soon after nine. They say he left there sharp on ten."

"Did he leave there alone?" asked Baxter.

"No. He went off with a chap named Harris. I've got his address."

"Sober? I suppose they'll swear black and blue he was sober as well as leaving sharp on time."

"They said he'd only had a couple of pints. He took a quart away with him as he always did on Saturday nights."

Hawke gave Baxter a significant glance.

"Did he? A quart bottle — and there's no broken glass or spilt beer, despite the fight! We'd better check on that with this chap Harris."

"He doesn't live far away," said the constable. "Hallet Buildings — L.C.C. flat."

"Hop off and fetch him here!" ordered Baxter.

Darkness had fallen, and rain clouds were gathering. A wet night would wash away any clues which might have been left at the actual scene, or in the street. So they started to examine the area with hand torches.

At the farther corner of Perkin Street, about sixty yards from the scene of the tragedy, Tommy found a long wet patch on the pavement. It smelt like beer. He called Hawke and Baxter.

"Beer it certainly is," said Hawke "Yet there's still no broken glass. The attacker must have run off in this direction, or he'd have passed the fellow who followed up the shouting from the other end of the street."

Hawke scanned the surrounding area rapidly. A quart beer-bottle was not to be seen.

"If it is the beer from Snelgrove's Saturday-night quart, the man must have undone the stopper as he ran and emptied some or all of the contents."

The man named Harris arrived and was soon answering Hawke's questions.

"Yus, I left Frank on the corner of Perkin Street. Then 'e went off 'is way, and I went mine."

"He had a bottle of beer with him when you left him?" said Hawke.

"Yus, that's right, Guv'nor. Same as me."

"He was quite sober when you left him?"

"Yus, he had only had a couple of pints. Very slow drinker was Frank — make a pint last near the whole evening, he would. He had to, poor devil! What with 'is missus keeping 'im short, and 'im being on the dole more often than 'e wasn't. Anyway, what's 'appened to 'im — run over?"

"Somebody seems to have attacked him here on the way home. Did he have any personal enemies, do you know?"

"Blimey! Who in the world 'ud want to go for old Frank?"

"So far as you know, Harris, would he have had much money on him tonight when he left?"

Harris shook his head emphatically.

"Not him. A few bob most likely, no more. Whatever 'e gets 'e 'ands over most of it to 'is missus."

"So if I tell you," said Hawke, "that he had a little over six shillings on him when he was found, you wouldn't think he'd been robbed?"

"I wouldn't," snapped Harris. " 'E was all right when I left him, and several others from the pub was about at the corner at the time, and they'll say the same."

"Snelgrove never carried anything valuable about with him, I suppose — gold watch or anything of that kind?"

Harris shook his head.

" If 'e'd 'ad anything like that, it 'ud 'ave been pawned years ago. All 'e'd got was 'is weekend drop of draught bitter, an' 'e was carrying it like a baby in case 'e would drop it."

"Exactly," said Hawke. "All right, Harris, we can contact you again if we need more information."

All this time Tommy had been searching around, and his persistence was at last rewarded. In the gutter, about a yard from the body, he found a small imitation pearl stud, the kind used instead of a button for clipping the front of a dress shirt.

The stud had been lying in the gutter, and it was clean, which suggested it had not been in Perkin Street for long.

"If it has any connection with the job," said Hawke, "it's very significant. At any rate, it's just the kind of thing which might break loose from a man's clothes during a struggle."

Baxter frowned.

"A man in evening dress in Perkin Street? He would be pretty noticeable — both before and afterwards. Besides, why on earth should a man of that type attack a chap like this poor devil?"

"It's not as improbable as it sounds," Hawke replied. "Anyway, it will be worth checking — whether a man in dress clothes of some kind was seen running away from Perkin Street soon after ten-fifteen. Also, I think we might see if there's any connection between dress clothes and the Mucky Duck. After all, the significant fact in the case is the bottle of beer, and that came from the public house."

Horace Slater, the licensee of the Mucky Duck, had not gone to bed.

"I thought you'd be round," he said. "Though it don't seem to be anything that happened on my premises. As I told the constable, the bloke was as sober as a judge when he left."

"You said he left at ten?"

"Well, soon after. He never had a drop after time, if that's what you're getting at."

Baxter interrupted.

"Look here, we're not worried about closing time at the moment. We're more concerned with a dead man."

"Now, Mr Slater, what time do you think Snelgrove actually left," went on Baxter. "Ten, five past, ten past, or what?"

Slater hesitated sullenly.

"Well, maybe it was about ten past. We was a bit held up behind the counter tonight. My best barmaid — she's usually reliable, mind — she didn't get the weekend bottles put up early like she does any other Saturday. As a matter of fact, I had to butt in meself. About a dozen of me regulars all takes a bottle or two home for the weekend, and there they was ready to go, but waiting.

"Yes, we were a bit late for once. You know how it is with women today — if you says anything, off they goes to another job, and maybe for better money. Her boyfriend turned up during the evening and upset her or something. Blame him, not me! There's one thing, though — he won't come in this house again. I'm not having no Italian upsetting me staff during working hours!"

Hawke looked interested.

"A foreigner, is he? Italian! Not by any chance a waiter?"

"He's in thc hotel game all right, somewhere up the West End. Mabel reckons he's going to marry her, and they'll set up in a place of their own. He came in here proper agitated tonight. He kept on talking in whispers to her across the counter. In the end, I told her to take him round the back and settle whatever it was, then come back and do her work proper."

"What does round the back mean?"

"In the cellar-room right behind the saloon. It's above the cellars."

"Is that where the bottles which your customers take home are put up?"

"That's it. Mind, customers ain't allowed in there. I — "

"When you closed — I mean, when Snelgrove and the others left — was this waiter boyfriend still here?"

"Yes, he was. That's how Mabel was so behind."

"Where can we find your barmaid?"

"Mabel? Oh, she lives with her mother down Camberwell way. Wait a tick. I've got the address on her cards."

Twenty minutes later they were knocking on the door of a small house in Old Camberwell Road.

Eventually the barmaid of the Mucky Duck appeared.

"Who are you — what on earth do you want at this time of night? Can't a girl — "

Inspector Baxter apologised and explained tactfully.

"We have to ask you some urgent questions about your visitor at the Mucky Duck this evening — your boyfriend, according to Mr Slater."

"What sort of questions?"

Dixon Hawke moved forward.

"He's a waiter, I believe — "

"Well, is that a crime? 'Ere, what's the game?"

"Never mind that, my girl. What's the name of this friend of yours, and where does he work in the West End? You need not answer if you don't want to, but we shall draw our own conclusions."

Mabel sniffed.

"He works at a hotel. Assistant head waiter, he is. Albert Peloni. What — what's he done?"

"He seems to have upset your work tonight at the Mucky Duck. What did he come to see you about?"

"Upset my work! So old Slater's been gassing, has he? We — we 'ad a quarrel the night before — 'e came to make it up."

"You didn't put up the weekend bottles of beer."

The barmaid's face went white.

"I — I forgot. I did in the end, though — when Slater came rushing in at the last minute."

"You didn't tell me the name of Albert's hotel, did you?" said Hawke quietly.

She hesitated for a few seconds. Then she said unwillingly: "The St Clair, it is — in Milford Street."

"The St Clair, eh?" Hawke whistled.

Mabel stared and backed nervously.

"What about it? What's different in that to any other 'otel? What are you getting' at?

"You've no right asking me all these questions."

"I told you, you need not answer. A valuable necklace was stolen this morning at a West End hotel." Hawke drew a paper from his inside pocket.

"Yes, I thought I had remembered the name correctly. The St Clair Hotel — necklace — the property of Lady Mary Pultney — valued at £3000. Did your friend Albert mention the matter to you?"

"What if 'e did? If you see an accident in the street you talk about it after, don't you?"

"True enough. There has been an accident, too. Mr Snelgrove, one of the customers of the Mucky Duck, taking home his bottle of bitter, was killed. "

Panic showed in her face.

"Killed? 'Ow? Run over?"

"No — "

"Not — not killed by — not murder?"

Mabel swayed and steadied herself against the half-open door.

Hawke nodded gravely.

"You haven't seen the boyfriend since he dashed out of the Mucky Duck tonight?"

"No."

"All you know is that he hurried away to get that bottle of draught beer back from Snelgrove, eh?"

"I never said it — you're putting the words into my mouth — "

"But it's true, isn't it?"

Again Mabel swayed, but this time she fainted. Hawke sighed.

"It's a pity we had to put her through it, but we had to find out. Still, she'll get over it — and get over Mr Peloni."


In the small hours of the morning, in Baxter's room at Scotland Yard, they conferred with Detective-Inspector Williams, who was handling the necklace robbery case.

Lady Pultney had come back to the hotel at three in the morning after a dinner and dance. She had had too many drinks for an elderly woman, and forgot to hand over her necklace to the hotel night clerk for putting in the safe. She awakened very late in the morning, and the necklace had gone.

" While she was sleeping, almost every member of the staff could have walked in and pinched the necklace," said Williams.

"Including Albert Peloni, a waiter!" said Hawke.

"Yes, I questioned him. He didn't look guilty, though. The manager gave him a good name. We had him shadowed when he went off duty at lunch time. Nothing suspicious was reported. He was due back on duty at eight last night. We had plain clothes men dining there."

"He must have cut his duty short. He visited a Kennington pub soon after nine."

Williams looked annoyed. "The devil he did! Why wasn't that reported to me, I'd like to know!"

"Peloni must have been r*rattled by your plain-clothes men," said Hawke. "He dashed down to Kennington to his girlfriend at a pub. He got her to draw him out a quart bottle of beer, and he dropped the necklace into it. He reckoned it would be a safe hiding place if he was searched.

"But the girl got behind with bottles for the weekend trade of the regulars. The boss came in later and grabbed the bottle with the necklace and handed it over to a customer.

"Peloni saw what had happened, but couldn't stop it in time. He darted out after the customer. Later, there was a struggle in Perkin Street for the bottle, and the customer was accidentally killed. Peloni got away with the bottle."

"It's a pretty good build-up, Hawke," said Baxter.

"What else can explain the significance of Snelgrove's humble quart of draught beer? Why did Mabel faint when I guessed about her knowing he'd dashed out after Snelgrove?

"Who else would the stud from a dress shirt tie up with better than a waiter? A waiter with a coat over his outfit would not be so very unusual in Kennington late at night.

"It also explains the beer at the end of Perkin Street. Peloni wanted to make sure he'd got the right bottle. By emptying some of the beer, he could shake it better and hear the necklace inside."

On Sunday afternoon Albert Peloni was run to earth — hiding at his sister's roadside cafe in Surrey. Stunned by the stop-press item in the Sunday papers, he had bolted from London.

He confessed to the theft of the necklace, but denied any intention of real violence.

"The fool — I offered him four shillings for the bottle — four shillings! He refused it. But I say then I must take it, and he starts to struggle — we fall. Kill him? It was his own stupid fault."

Albert Peloni was convicted of robbery and manslaughter and sentenced to ten years.

The £500 reward offered by Lady Pultney was claimed by Hawke, and he handed it on to the unfortunate Snelgrove's widow.

—o0o—

THE CASE OF *The Star-Gazer's Twin*

**"Maybe it is unfair to ask you to help us after this lapse of time, Mr Hawke, and after the police have had no success. I shall fully understand if you refuse to handle the case."**

The tall, dignified, grey-haired man, who was the only surviving partner in Messrs Norton & Perrish,

the famous Oxford Street jewellers, fiddled nervously with a jade fob on his gold watch-chain. He gazed anxiously at Dixon Hawke and his young assistant, Tommy Burke, whom he had invited into his private office.

"I would not have come here, Mr Perrish, if I had not been somewhat interested," said the detective. "Of course I read about the affair in the newspapers, but as I was not asked to help, I had nothing to do with the investigations. Perhaps it would be better if you told all the facts to Tommy and me."

Alexander Perrish moved across to his chair and sat down.

"The facts are very simple. A month ago, on the third of last month to be precise, we received a visit from the aide-de-camp of the Rajah of Ranpuna, who was staying at the Carlton Hotel. His Highness was desirous of purchasing some large diamonds to complete a necklace. None of the stones was to be less than ten carats, and only flawless, perfect stones were wanted. We were asked to send a selection to the hotel for him to inspect."

"You often do that for clients?" asked Dixon Hawke.

"Yes, frequently, but naturally we take every precaution against fraud and make careful inquiries about the client. In this case we knew the Rajah was a man of fabulous wealth and we did not hesitate.

"Roger Jefferson, our oldest and most trusted assistant, was sent to the hotel with a selection of twenty superb stones. A taxicab was summoned to the door of this shop and took him away to the hotel. Normally, he would have been back within an hour, but when one and a half hours had elapsed we telephoned the hotel, only to learn that he had never visited the Rajah with the stones.

"His Highness was very annoyed at what he considered our rudeness and refused to do business with us again. From the moment he left this shop with diamonds worth £50,000 Jefferson has not been seen."

"The taximan who drove him to the hotel was questioned?"

"Yes, and he remembers putting Jefferson down at the entrance to the Carlton. Whether Jefferson went inside or not, the man did not notice. It was a busy hour and the foyer was filled with people. No one remembers having seen Jefferson. He was not the type to attract attention."

Perrish passed across a photo which showed a man of medium height with a lean, uninteresting face, dark hair swept well back from his forehead, a high, stiff collar and horn-rimmed spectacles.

"You informed the police immediately?"

"Naturally. A nationwide search was made for more than a fortnight, every ship and plane was watched, but no trace of Jefferson or the diamonds has ever been found. He has vanished into thin air, a thing which Scotland Yard declares to be a very rare occurrence."

"Very! And the diamonds have not been offered for sale in this country?"

"No, they could not be sold in Britain without attracting attention, for they are exceptional stones. We do not even know if Jefferson stole them and decamped, or whether he was kidnapped and murdered. He was with us 22 years and I find it hard to believe that he betrayed the firm in the end. Yet it seems impossible that he could have been kidnapped and murdered. It was the middle of a bright afternoon when he left here."

Dixon Hawke glanced at Tommy Burke and saw that the youth was keenly interested. "And so, Mr Perrish," he continued, "you want me to find Jefferson, or at least to discover what has happened to the diamonds. What about his background? How did he live?"

"He was unmarried, and had a small flat in Ealing. The woman who owned the house cooked and cleaned for him when necessary. He was interested in juvenile welfare, and was one of the leaders at the local boys' club. His way of life was regular, and completely respectable. He neither drank nor smoked."

"Any relatives?"

"Only one that I knew about, and the police failed to find any others. He has a twin brother living down in Sussex at a village called Porthington. He is a rather eccentric recluse who dabbles in astrology. I believe he is writing a book about it. He came here once to see his brother, but Roger Jefferson was away for a few days at the time. He struck me as being a complete crank, and I was very glad when he left.

"The brothers used to see each other only about once a month I believe. But Jacob, as this twin is called, says he has neither heard from nor seen Roger since his disappearance. He says his brother's horoscope shows that he is dead, and that this was pre-ordained. Of course, the police have thoroughly investigated this man, and are convinced he knows nothing about Roger's movements."

"I'll look into the matter for you, Mr Perrish," declared Hawke. "I'd like to keep this photo for the time being. I also want the police description of the missing man, and a sample of his handwriting. I will go over to Ealing and try to find out what I can about him."

Three days later Dixon Hawke had to admit that his efforts had failed. In Ealing he had interviewed the woman who had looked after Roger Jefferson, and everyone who was in any remote way connected with the man. All that he learned was that Jefferson was a man of unimpeachable integrity and respectability.

"In fact he seems too good to be true," murmured Hawke on the third day.

"You think he must have been decoyed away and murdered, Guv'nor?" asked Tommy Burke.

"No, I do not. It was broad daylight, he actually reached the Carlton, and he was not the sort of man to be decoyed away when he had a fortune in diamonds on his person."

"But he doesn't seem the type to have absconded!" objected his assistant.

"There is no such thing as a type," Tommy. For all we know, Jefferson may have been planning this for years.

"One thing is certain, he did not merely walk out that day on impulse. This was cunningly planned and premeditated, and so well done that all the police in the country have been unable to find him."

"It looks hopeless, Guv'nor."

"It doesn't look promising. I don't think there is any need for us to hunt up the taxi-man and those who last saw Jefferson. I've had all their statements from the police. No, I think we'll go down and see this brother of his."

Hawke and Tommy motored down into Sussex the following morning, and after some trouble located the village of Porthington, tucked away in a hollow of the Downs. In the village their inquiries for Jacob Jefferson caused sly grins.

"You mean the old star-gazer who lives out at Rose Cottage," said someone. "He won't see you. He won't see no one. He's crazy and lives alone with a cat. Only comes in here to the shop once a week."

Hawke got directions for finding the cottage, and discovered that it was necessary to leave his car at the bottom of a lane, which was very narrow. Tommy and he walked about 50 yards before they saw the cottage, a tumbledown place under the lee of a high bank, with a wilderness which had once been a garden around it. Had it had not been for the smoke curling up from one of the chimneys, the two detectives would have believed the cottage unoccupied.

On the gate was a notice scrawled in untidy handwriting: "No callers wanted. No hawkers. No agents. No time to answer the door. The stars in their courses are more important to me than anything you may have to say. Leave me alone. Jacob Jefferson."

After his name were some signs of the Zodiac.

Hawke glanced at Tommy, shrugged his shoulders, then strode up the weed-grown path. There was neither knocker nor bell, and the detectives noticed that there were shutters on the lower windows. Hawke banged on the door with his knuckles.

There was no reply. He knocked again and again. He shouted. He walked round to the back and banged on the rear door, but without any effect. They could hear slight movements inside, but nobody responded.

Baffled, the detectives returned to their car and drove to the village police station. The constable grinned when Hawke introduced himself and described his reception at Rose Cottage.

"He's always the same, sir. It doesn't matter who knocks at the door, Jefferson won't open it when he's working. He says he's making out a horoscope for the whole world, so as to find out the fate in store for humanity. He's quite crazy, sir, but harmless. He was terribly upset when he heard about his brother, but he says he's not surprised as it's all in his horoscope. He wears a black band for him now. Says his brother is dead."

"How long has he been here, constable?"

"About three years, I think. I don't think I've set eyes on him more than five times in all that while. Sometimes he takes a walk over the Downs after dark, but only on starlit nights. Once a week he comes down to the village shop and buys his groceries.

"He always pays cash. The locals say he's a miser and that his house is packed with money, but when we searched it we found only a few pounds."

"Then it has been searched?"

"Oh, yes, sir. Soon after the disappearance of Roger Jefferson some Scotland Yard men arrived to interview the brother. They had a search warrant. It was thought that the missing man might be hidden there, but he wasn't. Old Jacob made a rare fuss about it."

"You call him 'Old ' Jacob, but he can't be older than his brother if he's a twin."

Hawke held out the photo he had been given by the jeweller.

"Yes, maybe they are the same age," admitted the constable, "but Jacob's hair is grey, he looks older and more wrinkled, and he wears ancient clothes. He doesn't wear glasses, but he's got a long white beard that's always stained with tobacco juice from his pipe. He never stops smoking."

The detective next visited the village shop, and learned that it was always on Fridays that Jacob Jefferson came to get his supply of groceries. As it was Friday on the morrow, Hawke drove to the inn in the next village, and booked a room for the night. He was determined to see Jacob Jefferson about his brother.

The following afternoon Hawke and Tommy Burke were waiting near the general shop in the village when they saw a strange figure approaching, a bent man with greying hair and white beard, hatless, wearing a long-tailed frock-coat, velvet trousers and elastic-sided boots. He carried a carpet-bag, and sucked at a foul-smelling pipe. People sniggered as he passed, but he paid no attention, and went straight into the shop.

"That's our man," muttered Hawke. "We'll waylay him near his cottage."

They hurried off, and hid behind a hedge near his gateway. It was nearly an hour before Jacob Jefferson returned, the bag heavy with flour, bacon, sugar and other foodstuffs. Hawke and Tommy kept out of sight until the last moment, then the detective stepped forward.

"Good afternoon, Mr Jefferson, can I speak with you for a few minutes? I want to ask you about your brother, Roger."

The man turned dreamy eyes towards them.

"My brother is dead. What can be said about him?" he asked in a deep voice. "Saturn and Mars in conjunction brought about his downfall. It was pre-ordained."

"Yes, sir, exactly," agreed Hawke, "but I would like to ask you a few questions, and I might mention that I am a private detective."

He handed over his card, which the hermit did not attempt to read.

"A detective!" he snorted. "Am I never to be left in peace, just because my brother fell under malign influences? I suppose you are one of the disturbances mentioned as due to me under the present moon ... You had better come in."

They followed him up the pathway. He inserted a large key in the lock and opened the door, whereupon a large black cat rushed towards him and leapt on to his shoulder.

Since the shutters were closed, the room was in darkness. They heard him fumbling with a box of matches, and finally an oil lamp was lit, revealing a large table piled with books on astrology, charts, star tables and horoscopes.

There was a writing-desk in one corner of the room, and in another was a large bookcase packed with more books on astrology. Star charts and horoscopes hung on the walls, and in one corner there was a revolving globe showing all the stars in the heavens.

A Strange Horoscope

Jefferson offered them broken-backed chairs and pushed the cat off his shoulder.

"Now?" he prompted. "Perhaps you would kindly state your business quickly, for I am in the middle of a very difficult calculation."

"Yes, Mr Jefferson, I will be brief. When did you last see your brother?"

"The police asked me that. On the 21st of the month before last, about twelve days before he disappeared. I warned him at the time that the planets were massing to cause his downfall. He refused to listen to me, and — "

His hair was long and looked dull in the lamplight. He kept pushing it back from his forehead.

"And do you believe your brother is dead, Mr Jefferson?" asked Hawke.

"Believe? I know he is dead, and here is the reason." He rose and moved to one of the horoscopes on the wall, one of which was entitled — "Horoscope of Roger Jefferson, born January 29, 1896."

"You will see that Mars was in the ascendant at the time."

"Yes, Mr Jefferson. I am afraid I do not understand all those things, but could you please tell me where you get your hair cut?"

"Hair!" The man whirled round and gaped at Hawke. "What has my hair got to do with it?"

"I understand that you do not leave the village, and I happen to know there is no hairdresser in the place, yet your hair is very neatly trimmed."

"Very observant of you," snapped Jacob. "I cut it myself, of course. After living more than half a century, I hope I am capable of cutting my own hair. What a footling question! You were asking me about my brother's horoscope."

"If you wish to continue about horoscopes, yes — " agreed Dixon Hawke, stroking the cat which had leapt on to his lap. "I know very little about astrology, but I do know that twins should have more or less the same horoscope, being born about the same time and definitely at the same place.

"How do you account for the fact that your life has been so entirely different from your brother's? Do the stars show a great calamity or

223

upheaval for you also? If the stars and planets affect our lives, why did not those same stars bring death to you last month as well as your brother?"

Jacob Jefferson licked his lips nervously with the tip of his tongue.

"You choose to mock at our science," he exclaimed.

"I do nothing of the kind," said Hawke, turning the cat round so that it was perched with his back to him. "I merely ask for information. I should have thought that two people, born at the same time and in the same place, should have had similar fates."

Jacob Jefferson glared, drew a deep breath and leaned forward until his face was no more than four feet from Hawke's. He extended a finger.

"I say you are mocking! You came here to mock me. You did not come to ask about my brother. You are a scoffer!"

Hawke's expression did not change, but he gave the tail of the unsuspecting cat a vicious pinch, and the startled creature screeched as it leaped wildly from him, straight on to the greying head of its owner.

For a fraction of a second it clawed a hold there, then rolled to the floor, taking with it a wig which had covered a head of jaggedly cropped dark hair in which no single strand of grey showed.

Jefferson let out a yell of rage and leapt towards the writing-desk on which was lying an ornamental knife which he normally used as a paper knife. Snatching it up, he turned and hurled it at Dixon Hawke. Fortunately his aim was bad and the weapon whistled past the detective's head. It stuck quivering in the table in front of the now thoroughly-enraged cat which had taken refuge up there.

When Jefferson saw that he had missed, he made a dash towards the door. Tommy Burke put out his foot and tripped the fugitive, causing him to crash down on the floor. Before he could recover, Hawke was sitting on his back and pulling his arms behind him. There was a click of handcuffs and the Dover Street detective said: "I have no power to arrest you, Roger Jefferson, but I can send for the village constable to do it. You might go and fetch him, Tommy."

The snarling, struggling jeweller's assistant suddenly became limp.

"How did you know?" he gasped.

"Firstly by a process of elimination. I felt sure you had absconded with those diamonds, and that you had not been kidnapped. You were unable to get out of the country, therefore you must have gone to earth, intending to lie low until such time as you could get the diamonds to the Continent or South America. To hide from the entire police force was no easy feat, therefore you must have had a clever hide-out already prepared, and have gone there immediately.

"When I learned of a twin brother who was a hermit, I became suspicious, even after people said he had been here three years and was unlike you. His very objection to having contact with people backed up my suspicions. At last we got to see you, and you put over this act about being a keen astrologer. I brought up the question of twin-ship, and when you did not have an immediate answer to my query I knew you did not know as much about astrology aa you pretended."

Tommy Burke paused in the doorway to listen.

"But your hair was the thing that clinched my doubts, Jefferson. You were supposed to be a hermit, who never left the village, where there is no barber. That meant you would have to cut your own hair. No man living could trim his hair as beautifully as yours was at the back, therefore I knew you were wearing a wig ... Now where are the diamonds?"

"Find them yourself!" snarled the prisoner.

The arrest was duly made, and before long the newspapers carried the story of how Roger Jefferson had for three years built up a background and an identity into which he could slip when he brought off his big coup. It was proved that the jeweller's assistant had waited patiently for some such chance as that which the Rajah's visit had given him.

For years he had managed to get down to Porthington on Friday afternoons, which was his one afternoon free from the shop. He had travelled in a simple disguise, had approached the cottage over the Downs, and had made it his business to visit the village shop and show himself. For the rest of the week some very slow-burning peat piled in an extra-large stove had sent some smoke up the chimney during the winter periods. Jacob Jefferson's reputation as a hermit had kept away all callers. He had carefully cultivated the reputation of being cranky.

Once, when Roger Jefferson had been on holiday, Jacob had even visited the Bond Street shop to prove to the manager that there was a twin brother. When he had made his getaway with the diamonds, it had been Jefferson's intention to remain in Porthington for about a year. Once he was sure he was not being watched, he intended to head for South America.

The diamonds were not so easily found. Not until the cottage was almost dismantled were they discovered embedded in knot-holes in some panelling and skilfully varnished over.

—o)o —

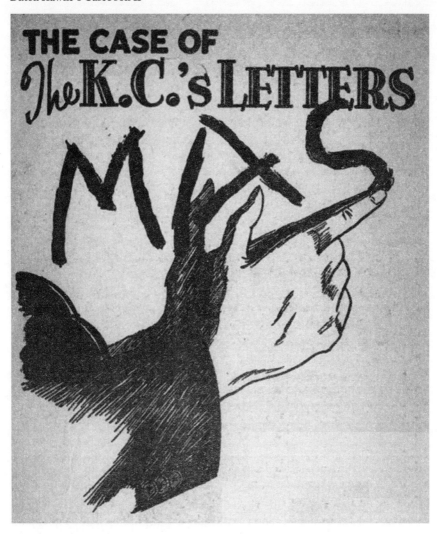

THE CASE OF
The K.C.'s LETTERS

"Montague Marsh to see you, sir." Chief Detective-Inspector McPhinney looked up testily as the tall figure of the famous K.C. pushed past the sergeant and entered the office. "I'm sorry to butt in, Inspector. Don't blame the sergeant. He told me you were engaged, but I have an urgent appointment, and I won't keep you a minute.

"No, don't go, Hawke," added the barrister. He saw Dixon Hawke, who, with Tommy Burke, had been in conference with McPhinney, rise as if to leave the room. "This may interest you as well."

226

"What's the trouble, Mr Marsh?" asked McPhinney.

"Just this, Inspector." The K.C. pulled an envelope from his pocket and flung it on the desk.

"Actually, the best place for a thing like that is the fire. Had it come to me, that's where it would have gone, and I shouldn't have troubled you. As you see, however, it's addressed to my wife, and, of course, she opened it herself.

"Go ahead and read it!" he added, as McPhinney fingered the envelope uncertainly. "Read it out!"

McPhinney picked up the envelope, took out a half- sheet of notepaper, and read: "Lady, if you value your life and that of your husband, you'll get him to go easy with my brother, Jean Mascal.

"If Jean is sentenced to death as a result of your husband's prosecution, it will be just too bad for you — and for your husband! If Jean dies, you die. Don't say I didn't warn you!"

"Pierre Mascal."

"Huh!" grunted McPhinney, and held the notepaper up to the light. "Cheap stuff, no watermark," he went on, passing the paper over to Hawke. He picked up the envelope again.

"Posted at Croydon at 5.30 p.m. on the 12th — that was yesterday. Address typewritten, same as the note. It was typed on a new machine, I'd say. H'm! There's nothing to go on there, Mr Marsh. What would you like us to do about it?"

"Nothing at all!" snapped the K.C. "I promised Mrs Marsh I'd give it to you, and, having done so, I wash my hands of it."

His voice softened slightly as he went on: "My wife is rather easily upset, Inspector, and I wish she'd never seen the thing. She's not very strong, and she seems to think there's some danger to me.

"That's all rot, of course, and I think she'll be content with the knowledge that I've notified Scotland Yard. Put it in the wastepaper basket and forget it!"

"Just as you like, Mr Marsh. This Pierre Mascal is a bad lot, though. He has been giving the authorities in Canada no end of trouble, I know, but I didn't think he was over here. He's a nasty piece of work, like his brother."

He faced the K.C.

"I'll tell you what. It's better to be safe than sorry. I'll put a man at your front door, and another at the back for a few days. You have a lane there, don't you?"

"Yes, but I didn't intend to put you to all this trouble, Inspector. However, I'm much obliged, and I know Mrs Marsh will be relieved. There's nothing like the sight of a blue-coated bobby to inspire confidence.

"Now, I'll be off, and once again, I'm sorry for bothering you."

The K.C. moved to the door and was gone. McPhinney pressed a button and issued instructions to the clerk who appeared.

"That's that," he said to Hawke, when the man had departed. "What d'you think of that Marsh bloke, Hawke? He's a pretty cool customer, I reckon."

"He's right at the top of his profession, anyway," replied Hawke. "There is no more able counsel in the country. I don't expect he'll let this threat interfere with his conduct of the prosecution either, though, as a matter of fact, the case should be an easy one for him.

"The case against Mascal is overwhelming, I'd say. It's Mellish-Jones, for the defence, who has a really tough job."

"You're right there. We've got Mascal where we want him — and not before time. It looks as though we'll have to get after this brother of his. However, let's get on."

The three returned to the business in which they had been engaged, prior to the interruption, and Montague Marsh was soon forgotten.

Hawke and Tommy were seated at a late tea that night when the phone bell rang. It was McPhinney, and he angrily demanded to know whether either of them had given any information to the Press regarding the K.C.'s visit.

"Sorry, Hawke, I shouldn't have even suspected you," apologised McPhinney, when the detective had curtly repudiated the charge. "Some blighter has talked, and Marsh is in the devil of a temper about it. Probably some of his own servants did it. Anyhow, it's splashed all over the afternoon papers."

Dixon Hawke had already seen the big headlines in his evening paper: "Threat to Famous K.C.," and, with a shrug of annoyance, he sat down again.

He was silent for a few minutes as he scanned the headlines in the "Evening Comet".

"They seem to have the whole story," he remarked at length. "I think I'll ask Somerville where he got it."

Hawke dialled a number and was soon in touch with the news editor of the "Evening Comet", to whom he was very well known. The detective followed this short conversation with similar inquiries to "The Meteor" and "News Planet". There was a thoughtful look on his face as he laid down the phone.

"What's it all about, Guv'nor?" asked Tommy, and Hawke laughed. "There's no great mystery as to how these three papers got their stories. In each case the news room was rung up by phone and given the information. They all say it was a man's voice.

"In each case, the paper got on to Marsh for confirmation, and it seems his language was more forcible than polite.

"He actually dared them to print the stuff, but his very rage, however, led them to suspect that the story was indeed true and, of course, they printed it like a shot."

A few days later Hawke and Tommy sat in the crowded courtroom at the Old Bailey listening to Mr Montague Marsh as the famous K.C. presented the case for the prosecution in the case of Rex v. Mascal.

Marsh had the reputation of being a real terror to witnesses, and, on this occasion, he excelled himself.

The few witnesses for the defence wilted under Marsh's inexorable cross-examination, and only succeeded in discrediting the accused more thoroughly than ever. Mr

Mellish-Jones did his best for the defence, but long before the judge had concluded his summing-up it was clear to most people that there could be but one verdict, that of guilty.

The prisoner himself obviously shared this belief. Jean Mascal, a hairy, vicious-looking French-Canadian, charged with the brutal murder of a shopkeeper, shrugged his shoulders resignedly as counsel for the prosecution addressed the jury.

Mascal was found guilty and duly sentenced to be hanged by the neck until he was dead.

Shortly after dusk that evening, Tommy Burke answered the telephone to hear the excited and enraged voice of Chief Inspector McPhinney.

"Tell Hawke that Mrs Marsh has been murdered!" exclaimed the inspector. "I'm going out now. I'll pick you up in ten minutes."

Shortly afterwards, Hawke and Tommy were in a police car racing towards Putney.

"Don't ask me how it happened!" groaned McPhinney, as Hawke put the question. "I've had a man in front of the house, and another at the back for the past week. This will get me into a mess with the A.C.

"All I know is that when Marsh got home he found his wife shot dead. Not only that — the cook and the butler have also been murdered."

"Good lord!" exclaimed Hawke. "That's terrible!"

"You're telling me!" growled McPhinney.

He was silent till the car swung into the drive of the big house standing in its own grounds near Putney Common.

Montague Marsh received them in his study, and the man appeared to be badly shaken. A brandy decanter stood by his elbow, and he helped himself liberally from this when his visitors declined his offer of a drink. Waving them wearily to seats, the K.C. told his story.

He had been delayed at his chambers, and dusk was already falling when he reached home.

He had stopped for a brief word with the constable at the front gate, and the man's assertion that he had neither seen nor heard anything out of the ordinary reassured him. His chauffeur was off sick, and he was attending to the car himself. As a result, he had remained in the garage for ten minutes or so, refilling the petrol tank and making the car ready for next morning.

The man's voice broke as he described what he had found on entering the house.

At the door of the lounge lay the butler, in a pool of blood. Inside the lounge, seated in her favourite chair, was his wife, shot dead. Rushing, half-demented, to the kitchen, he had found the cook dead by the kitchen stove, shot through the head.

His cries had brought the constable who was on duty at the gate, and the man had summoned his partner from the lane behind the house. The two had quickly taken charge and had phoned Scotland Yard.

His story ended, Marsh sank back in his chair, passing his hand wearily over his eyes.

"We'll do what we can, sir — you may be sure of that," said the inspector, but the other did not reply and, moving quietly to the door, the three left the room.

They turned towards the kitchen where the buxom cook lay beside her shining grate.

There was a neat, round hole in her forehead, and an expression of astonishment on her face. Mrs Marsh's features, as she eat in the armchair in the lounge, were as peaceful as if she had been asleep.

The butler lay half in and half out of the door of the lounge.

He had been shot twice through the body. A pool of blood had formed on the polished surround where the dead man lay, and the detective at once noticed that the butler had tried to write something there.

The fingers of the right hand had now stiffened in death, but, before this had happened, he had managed to trace the letters "M-A-S " in his own blood.

"Mascal!" exclaimed McPhinney excitedly. "That's the message he tried to leave. We must get after him at once, the callous murderer."

Dixon Hawke said nothing, but he listened carefully when the police surgeon expressed the opinion that all three deaths had occurred within the hour. Mrs Marsh and the cook had died instantly, but the butler had lived for perhaps a minute or two.

The only other members of the household were two frightened maids, who had been upstairs when their master made the discovery. They had heard no shots, and could shed no light on the matter.

"He used a silencer, of course," observed McPhinney.

The two constables were questioned, but both were emphatic that no one had entered or left the grounds by the front or back gates.

The grounds were not extensive, but were surrounded by a high wall.

A lawn separated the front of the house from the main road, from which a short, curving drive led to the front door.

At the back, and a yard or two from the rear of the building, a door in the wall gave access to the lane in which the second constable had been posted. The ground sloped upwards from the back of the house, and there was a tangle of bushes in the hundred yards or so between the house and the boundary wall at that side.

Beyond the wall stretched the common.

The constables had made a discovery. The bushes and long grass beyond the kitchen garden were trampled and broken.

McPhinney, Hawke and Tommy followed the men as they crashed their way upwards to the wall marking the extremity of the estate. The wall was ten feet high at this point, but a rusty lawn-mower stood against it, and from marks on this and on the wall, it seemed obvious that the intruder had made his getaway by this means.

"Humph!" growled McPhinney.

"Well, we can do no more here till daylight. I'll have a word with Mr Marsh before we go. Come on, Hawke."

"I'll wait outside for you, Mac," replied the detective, rather to Tommy's surprise.

When McPhinney had gone indoors, Hawke made for the garage, which stood beside the house. Using his torch, Hawke proceeded to examine the K.C.'s small car.

Tommy looked on wonderingly as his guv'nor poked about the place, spending a few minutes in examining a heavy wooden cupboard which stood against the wall nearest the house. Hawke did not satisfy the youngster's curiosity, and presently he led the way out.

McPhinney was taking his leave of Marsh at the front door, and Hawke walked towards their car.

Tommy was left to his own devices the next day. Hawke spent most of the day in the city interviewing various business associates, and dusk was falling before he finally returned home. He was scarcely seated when McPhinney's arrival was announced.

"So you're back," he greeted Hawke.

"I've been trying to get you all day. I wanted to tell you we're on the wrong track as far as Pierre Mascal is concerned.

"He spent last night in Liverpool Prison, for he was caught red-handed breaking into a store.

"Dash it, say you're surprised," he went on impatiently, when Hawke received the news in silence. "This knocks our case sideways and we've got to start all over again."

Hawke continued to smile maddeningly, and McPhinney puffed furiously at his pipe.

"Aha!" he burst out again. "I get it. You've got a theory, eh? O.K. Out with it!"

"Very well," said Hawke quietly. "What I'm about to say may seem wildly fantastic, but I'm convinced I'm right. Let me first tell you the result of certain inquiries I've been making today."

Hawke spoke for some time and McPhinney's face was a study as he listened.

Tommy Burke's eyes were almost popping out of his head when Hawke ended by saying quietly, "There you are then, Mac. That's my theory and I'm willing to test it myself, and at once. If I'm wrong, you will suffer no loss of prestige by agreeing to my scheme. I'll take the risk."

"It sounds crazy to me," growled McPhinney.

"But I'll take a chance. It's quite dark now. Let's go!" Half an hour later the police car came to a halt a hundred yards from Montague Marsh's house and Hawke got out.

"If I'm not back in twenty minutes, come in!" he said as he moved off, and McPhinney nodded.

The inspector and Tommy saw Hawke's tall figure pass across the lawn in the light of an uncurtained window a few minutes later.

The garage door was locked when Hawke reached it, but an implement which he took from his pocket made short work of the lock.

Using his torch, Hawke made for the cupboard against the left-hand wall. Grasping the woodwork, he pulled, and exclaimed in satisfaction, as the apparently heavy cupboard moved easily outwards, disclosing a door in the wall behind. The handle yielded to his touch and Hawke found himself in a short passage. A few feet away was a second door and this was also unlocked.

Hawke passed through into the darkness beyond and was about to use his torch again when, suddenly, a light came on, and Hawke saw that he was in a small, bare room.

Facing him from a doorway on the far side was Montague Marsh. The K.C.'s features wore a sardonic smile and, in his right hand, firmly held, and pointed straight at the detective, was a wicked-looking automatic, on the barrel of which was a bulbous attachment.

"I rather fancied you would come, Hawke," said the barrister, in conversational tones.

"The inspector didn't worry me in the slightest, he'd never have suspected, but when I saw you'd been in the garage last night, I began to prepare for your arrival. You're right, of course. I killed my wife, for we hated each other anyhow and I gain a cool fifty thousand by her death. I need the money."

"So I've found out," retorted Hawke. "Yes, Mr Marsh, I was fairly certain you were the guilty party.

"One thing I can't understand, though, is why you killed your cook. The butler, I imagine, came on the scene at the wrong moment and had to be silenced, but why kill the cook?"

"I'm sorry about that," said Marsh, and there was genuine regret in his voice, "but you see, this door," he inclined his head backwards, "leads into the passage directly opposite the kitchen and, as bad luck would have it, cook saw me come out.

"I'm sorry about Jenkins, too. As you surmise, he came on the scene at the wrong moment and there was nothing else for it.

"Tell me!" he went on curiously. "Where did I slip up? The idea looked foolproof to me."

"The threatening letter and the subsequent publicity given to it were rather overdone," said Hawke. "You picked a bad case, too. Mascal didn't have a dog's chance of getting off anyway.

"Then I suspected the bushes and grass, which the constables found trampled, might have been done earlier and, of course, the men obligingly crashed their way up to the wall, completely ruining any evidence to this effect.

"I was definitely sure, however, when I inspected the petrol tank, which you claimed to have filled and I found it nearly empty."

"Yes, yes, that was careless," conceded Marsh coolly. "Though, mind you, the inspector never even gave it a thought.

"Well, there's no harm in admitting you've been completely right, since you won't be able to do anything about it. I'm going to kill you, Hawke — now. I regret the necessity, but you leave me no option."

He raised the weapon slightly and Hawke knew that his life hung on a thread. The detective tried an age-old trick.

"O.K., Tommy," he said, looking beyond the lawyer.

It worked, and for a split second the barrister turned his head, ever so slightly, but it was enough.

Hawke flung himself sideways and forward in a lightning move Marsh pressed the trigger and there was a sound like the cork being removed from a bottle.

Marsh fought with the strength of a madman to free his gun arm from the vice-like grip of Dixon Hawke, and the detective had to exert all his strength to prevent him using the gun.

The pair were rolling over and over on the floor when the door to the house burst open and McPhinney and Tommy hurled themselves on the K.C.

"All right, I give up," said the barrister at length, panting for breath, and McPhinney quickly snapped a pair of handcuffs on his wrists.

"Give me a cigarette," requested the prisoner, sitting up on the floor. "They're in my left-hand pocket."

McPhinney took a case from the man's pocket, extracted a cigarette, placed it in Marsh's mouth and snapped on his lighter.

"Thanks," said Marsh. "You don't know how kind you are."

He took a long puff at the cigarette then suddenly his body shook convulsively and he slid to the ground to lie still.

"Dash it!" yelled McPhinney. "He's beaten us after all."

"It's probably the best way out of a bad case," said Hawke.

"Well, thanks a lot, Hawke," said McPhinney later.

"I'd never have looked further than Mascal at first. Not after that message the butler tried to leave."

"That made me more suspicious than ever, Mac. Why should Jenkins try to write the name of a man he almost certainly never saw in his life.

"What he really tried to write was 'Master'. "

# Dixon Hawke
## will return

www.dcthomsonshop.co.uk